Secrets of the Lost Caves

ALSO BY CHERYL POTTER

Handpaint Country: A Knitter's Journey

Lavish Lace: Knitting With Hand-Painted Yarns
with Carol Noble

Rainbow Knits For Kids

Ribbon Style: Knitted Fashions And Accessories

Skein For Skein: 16 Knitted Projects

Special Little Knits from Just One Skein

The Broken Circle
Book One of the *Potluck Yarn* Trilogy

Secrets of the Lost Caves

CHERYL POTTER

POTTER PRESS

Vermont

COPYRIGHT © 2015 CHERYL POTTER

Published in 2015 by Potter Press

Potter Press / 100 Cherry Tree Hill Lane / Barton VT 05822

All rights reserved. No part of this publication may be reproduced, distributed or transmitted in any form or by any electronic or mechanical means including information storage and retrieval systems, without the prior written permission of the author, except in the case of brief quotations embodied in critical reviews and certain other noncommercial uses permitted by copyright law.

All of the characters in this book are fictitious, and any resemblance to actual persons, living or dead, is purely coincidental.

ISBN: 978-0-9856350-9-1

First edition

Printed in the United States of America by Versa Press

All illustrations except where noted by Frank Riccio
Map by Joe Wilkins
Icons and graphic design by Mary Joy Gumayagay

www.potluckyarn.com

For Knitting Witches Everywhere

May you always believe in your yarns!

CONTENTS

Acknowledgments   *ix*
Cast of Characters   *xi*
Map of Bordertown and Glacierland   *xii*

	INTRODUCTION	1
1	Disaster in Plain Sight	5
2	Close Calls	19
3	A Fine Yarn	33
4	Burning Questions	51
5	Secret Counsel	61
6	Stones and Skells	73
7	River Walk Ruse	91
8	Cuts Like a Knife	99
9	In the Cards	115
10	Tavern Tales	135
11	Three and Three	157
12	Six of One	165
13	The Bad, Bad Man	179

14	Done	189
15	Picking Battles	199
16	The Fossicker's Creed	213
17	The Magic of Men	227
18	Circle of Stones	243
19	Ancient Unrest	253
20	The Kindling	265
21	Blindsided	279
22	Waking to a World Without Magic	293
23	The Restless City	305
24	The Road More Traveled	315
25	The Guardian's Watch	331
26	Winterhaven	339
27	Witches and Warren	359
28	The Out Crops	375
29	Walkers and Wolverines	393
30	A Show of Hands	405
31	Speaking Their Minds	419
32	Consent of the Clan	433
33	Visions of the Lost Caves	443
	WORKBOOK: Discussion Prompts and Where to Download	*457*

ACKNOWLEDGMENTS

Welcome to *Secrets of the Lost Caves*, the second book of the *Potluck Yarn* Trilogy, a fiber fantasy filled with Yarns of the Knitting Witches. Its been two years since the first book of the series, *The Broken Circle* was published. Thanks to everyone for waiting!

You may recall that I began writing the first book of the *Potluck Yarn* Trilogy years ago and abandoned it in discouragement, convinced that my desire to combine a fantasy novel about knitting witches with a pattern book featuring magical garments was foolish. Such combination books are labeled "cross genre" which is jargon for "not desirable" by commercial publishers. In addition, I thought kids would like the storyline as well as adults. Now my novels would be classified as YA for Young Adult. How terrible!

Flash forward to present day. Now the second book is complete and available at yarn shops and book stores nationwide thanks to the undying support of *Potluck Yarn* fans. I can't thank you enough! As a special addition, *Secrets of the Lost Caves* is available with discussion group prompts at the back of the book and a free print on demand Student Workbook at www.potluckyarn.com. Teachers, parents, librarians, and educators of all kind, I hope you find the workbook helpful!

I owe a special thanks to my publicist, Jared Kuritz who broke new ground for me and I believe indie authors everywhere with the distribution of *The Broken Circle* and now the second book in the series, *Secrets of the Lost Caves*. Without him, *Secrets of the Lost Caves* would not be in your hands or on your E Reader. He is the reason you can access independent publications like the *Potluck Yarn* Trilogy everywhere, from small independent shops to large bookstore chains.

Thanks as well to my savvy new editor Mary Altbaum for treating this novel as seriously as she would a mainstream book at Harcourt, and to Deb Robson, who provided me with sound advice long after her work with me was done. Many words and phrases used in the book do not appear in Webster's and I have Deb to thank for the Potluck style guide.

Special appreciation goes to artist Frank Riccio for his beautiful cover art and illustrations that appear in this book as well as the last one. He even brought the knitting witches to life for their biographies on our website, Potluck Yarn. Kudos also to Mary Joy Gumayagay for the beautiful book design, and careful attention to detail.

Once again, I have to thank our resident cartographer Joe Wilkins, for his detailed design of Bordertown and the legendary Northlands beyond. No, he does not really illustrate maps for a living, though it's difficult to tell.

Finally, thanks to my family, especially my husband Tim who has heard various drafts of this book read aloud far too many times, and mother-in-law Judy Marschke, a former educator who spent most of a vacation helping me write the Student Workbook.

CAST OF CHARACTERS

THE BLUE FAMILY
Kendrick
Warren
Skye
Garth

THE FOSSICKERS
Trader
Clayton
Ross

PEOPLE OF WINTERGARTEN
Niles of the North
Steadfast Lars
Goodmother Gabriella
Minister Mason
Goodwife Alyssa
Able Ian
Marshall Warden of the North
Honorable Devon
Deliberate Rye
Jayden
Jeffryn

FIRST FOLK, WANDERERS
Cyrus

HED CLANSMEN, OUT CROPS
Maddig Hoar
Lewellyn
Healer Borac
Healer Horehound
Lorn
Gretchell

OTHER CHARACTERS
Miles from Nowhere
Ozzie
Nellie
Fish-Eye Annie
Periwinkle
Gideon
Hairy Bear
Raven
The Bad, Bad Man
Mamie Reborn

THE FOURTEEN
Following pages; for complete bios see
http://potluckyarn.com/character-bios/

Aubergine

Potluck Yarn's founder and dye mistress, she is able to conduct magical simmers around the dye pot.

Smokey Joe

Mistress of the dye shed, she alone is entrusted with the great pot, keeping the dye pot bubbling all day.

Esmeralde

Wielding crystals as a doctor would medicine, Esmeralde concocts magical potions from dried roots and herbs.

Indigo Rose

She tends to quarrel with Esmeralde over supposed properties of the mixtures of herbs and ground crystal tinctures.

Lavender Mae

She has a hidden treasure trove of dyestuffs and crystals that she has scavenged from the First Folk tombs and beyond.

Lilac Lily

Lily found she could glean anyone's inner thoughts. Soon she could read the mind of any she encountered.

Sierra Blue

Calm and patient, she lies in wait watching those around her... Nothing escapes her all-knowing eyes.

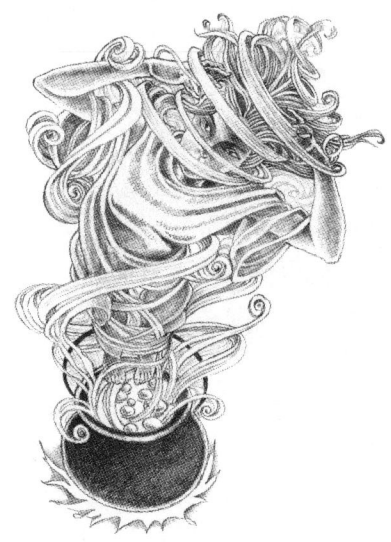

Tracery Teal

Before she was destroyed, Teal had developed an ability to disappear and travel—sometimes through time.

Little Teal / Trader / Traitor / Trickle T

Unaware of her legacy or that the Dark Queen seeks her, Teal roams the docks and watches the fossick boys steal.

Mamie Verde

Keeper of the Tales of Old, she alone knows all of the stories of the Ancient's Folly.

Ratta

Having never practiced the ancient ways, Ratta does not realize the power of the lost tale.

Winter Wheat

Known as a sheep whisperer, one who kens all creatures by touch and communicates with fiber animals of any kind.

Tasman: The Dark Queen

Tasman became Aubergine's protégé, and slowly began
to bend all will to herself including natural law.

Skye

Naturally impetuous and brave, she is less easily fooled
and more skeptical than [her mother] Sierra was at her age.

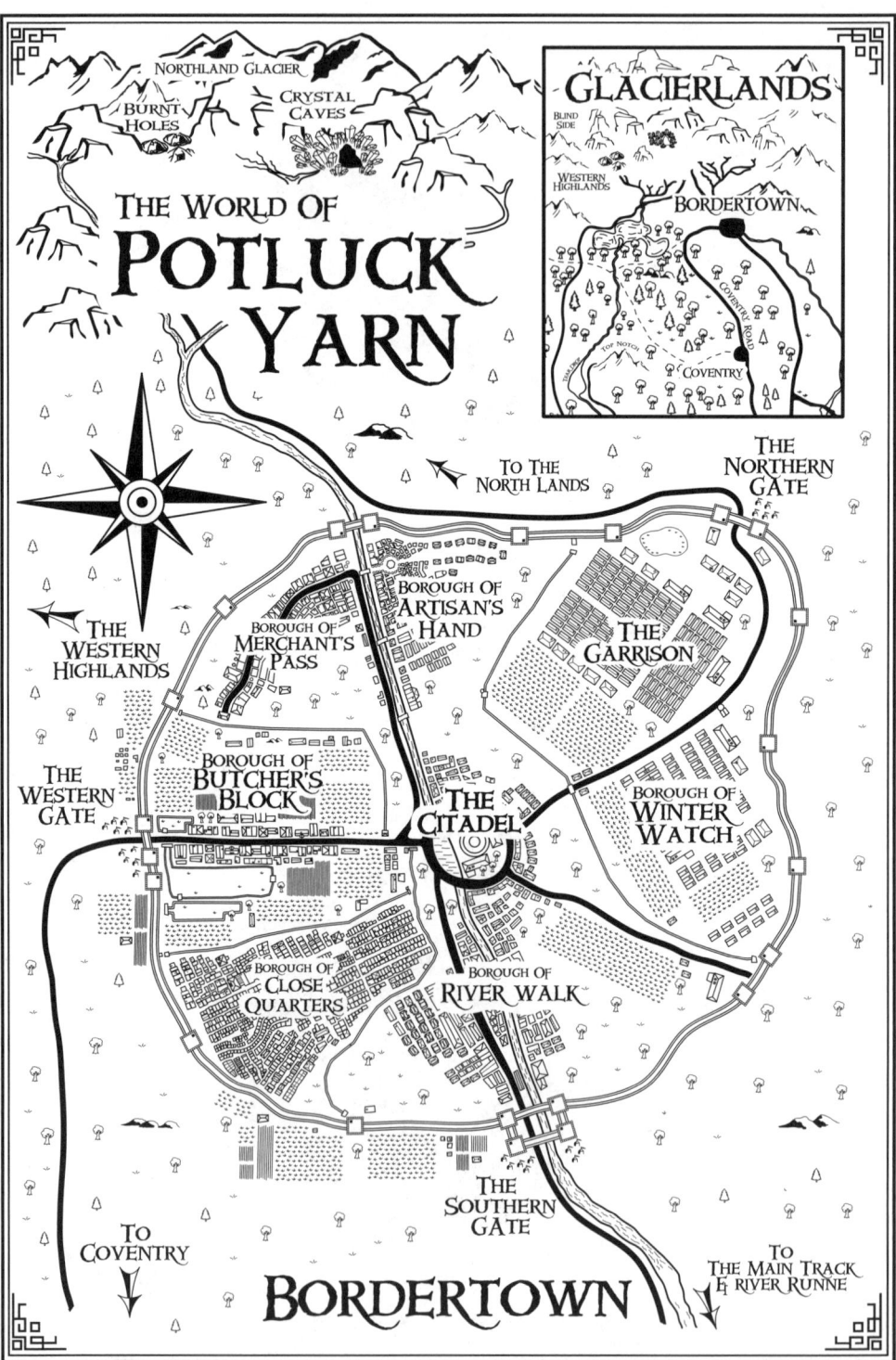

INTRODUCTION

Welcome to the legend of the potluck knitting witches, a trilogy of tales told over and again by traveling bards who regale patrons in the pubs and public squares of the Middlelands with a cycle of stories the knitting witches commonly refer to as their yarns.

In Book One of the *Potluck Yarn* Trilogy, we witnessed Potluck Queen, Aubergine, summon the Circle of Twelve for a simmer around the dye pot as she had not done since it sundered more than twenty years before. By now the other witches are scattered throughout the lands. Not all can heed the call and of those who do, few can find their places around the pot as they once did. Much like Aubergine's amethyst necklace, almost as soon the Circle completes, it is broken again.

Or is it? Like the Potluck witches, some folk are not who they seem, and what appears truly lost is merely hiding in plain sight, if you know how to look. Finding a certain lost stone, a damaged playing card, and quelling a kindled ember may be all that stands between the witches and a world otherwise destroyed by fire or ice.

Continuing the adventure begun in *The Broken Circle*, in this second book of the *Potluck Yarn* Trilogy, *Secrets of the Lost Caves*, the knitting witches and Fossickers unite and the desperate race to find the Crystal Caves and unlock the secrets of old begins.

Who will discover the Lost Caves first? The Dark Queen and her Kindred Spirit? The party of Six plus One with addled Lavender Mae as their guide? Or Aubergine, the Potluck Queen, with the help of Second Sight Sierra and Trader turned Teal?

We soon learn that Mamie Verde has not drifted peacefully to the Land of Dreams, but is reborn high above the lost city of old Tigeria, deep within the Northland Glacier to assume guardianship of the ancients, twenty years too late.

And in the war-torn Middlelands, nothing is certain but the power of the Fire and Ice Shawl, the need to make the amethyst necklace whole, and the necessity of possessing the Skell of House Crystal Keep.

Follow the continuing adventures of the Fossick boys and knitting witches as they journey north to the windswept Out Crops to ally with Hed Clansmen and lift the curse of the Glacier Born in an attempt to reawaken the Magic of Men.

Quick as a cat, Tasman moved around the pot toward the girl.

CHAPTER 1

Disaster in Plain Sight

AS THEY CIRCLED THE GREAT POT in the dye shed behind the Potluck Yarn shop, the knitting witches could barely believe what they had just witnessed. Scarcely a week ago, their former teacher and dye mistress, Aubergine, had finally summoned them back to herself to conjure a simmer. Her call of cold-fire crystal bursting over the horizon was the signal they had hoped for these past twenty years. It meant they would gather to use their outlawed magic in an attempt to save their world, now being ravaged by war and greed. Just tonight, for the first time since the Potluck disbanded so long ago, they had stoked the fire under the great pot, seeking a shared vision. But would the simmer reveal a true revelation? That required all twelve witches and they could only come up with eleven … they thought.

Fearing to wait any longer, Aubergine had begun the simmer anyway. First billowing steam clouded above the dye pot, to transport their dear elder Mamie Verde to forgotten caves known as Guardian's Watch deep within the Northland Glacier. There she could assume her role as the next custodian of the First Folk, whose ancient secrets threatened to destroy them all if they should fall within the Dark Queen's grasp. Then the witches encountered the image of Mamie, when young, in the heavy hourglass filled with shards of crystal—the hourglass that in some circumstances made time stand still. Finally, red-haired Ratta recited a legend none had heard before. It was the Lost Tale, imparted to her through Mind Speak by Mamie, who had been Keeper of the Tales before she slipped into her half-dead state. Now it looked as if the simmer had finally released her to take up her new responsibilities, many years overdue.

For the forbidden crystals to release their magic into the dye pot, a Potluck simmer required a full quorum of witches, known as the Twelve. Nonetheless, this simmer looked like it was working, which puzzled Sierra Blue, who had been the last witch to arrive tonight. Mamie was safe, the Suri Alpaca they had plunged into the pot was dyeing nicely, and as Mamie's successor, Sierra had been named the new Keeper of the Tales. Yet she counted only eleven witches including herself. Her lion eyes scanned the broken circle, trying to determine how it could have become whole.

Their Potluck Queen, Aubergine, stood with her back to the broken dye cupboard, the mantle of her black and violet Simmer Shawl draped over her aged shoulders, urging them to continue. Next to her, on a stool because she was so short, was Smokey Jo, the gnome who loved to play with fire. Then came Esmeralde and Indigo Rose, skilled with remedies and plants. Mamie's former place in the circle came next, the one Sierra herself had just inherited. Two odd witches filled the next spaces: Ratta, tender caretaker to Mamie who had inadvertently become the keeper of one last tale, and Lavender Mae, driven near mad by her quest for the amethyst missing from the powerful crystal necklace, stolen all those years ago. Sierra paused to consider her own daughter Skye Blue, in the place formerly held by herself, and Little Teal, whom all knew as Trader, the youngest and most recent addition to the group. A gap stood between the two girls' spaces, made more noticeable now that Trader held the hourglass high for all to see. That gap was where Tasman had stood among them before she destroyed Trader's aunt Tracery Teal, who had been one of their own. Tasman betrayed them all and fled south to become the Dark Queen and was the cause behind the present war. Finally Sierra's eyes rested on the Highland shepherdess Winter Wheat, the one among them who wandered farthest, and housemother Lilac Lily, who traveled least. Sierra looked around the room carefully. If Teal was really just a ghost and Mamie no longer counted among the Twelve, there were just eleven witches here.

Suddenly the raven-haired servant girl, whom Smokey Jo had fetched from the kitchen to help carry a final load of firewood, stepped from the shadows where she had been hiding and fully occupied the open place in the circle beside Skye. As the maid joined the group, the young Mamie, still visible in the hourglass, turned and stared in her direction. Gazing back at the shadowy figure, the serving girl laughed loudly, a sound out of keeping with her submissive appearance. Mamie's shape began to blur. The hourglass went dark. After waiting a few seconds, Trader set it slowly down on the table.

"Mamie disappeared." Trader raised her eyes toward the girl who stood before her. "Why would she do that?"

"Only with twelve in the circle can the simmer succeed," the kitchen maid said. She eyed Trader intently. "But more than one of us is not who she seems."

"No!" Aubergine's eyes raged violet. In one swift move, she jerked Trader away to keep her from rejoining the circle. The frightened girl stumbled to her side, knocking the dye table. The hourglass tumbled to the floor and broke into bits, scattering the purple shards. Glaring at the infiltrator, Aubergine shielded Trader with a protective arm.

"What in cracked crystal . . . ?" Wheat began. The words that followed died in her throat as the kitchen maid shifted shape before their eyes, maturing from a servant girl into a regal woman. The air around her rippled as she outgrew her guise like a snake shedding skin. The serving girl's body split and fell to her feet as she grew taller and more imposing. Her gaze turned from reserved hazel to cold green, while her hair darkened to the intensity of coal.

Smokey Jo plucked at Aubergine's sleeve. "Who is she?"

"You!" Ratta stared in disbelief. In the dark-haired woman's features Ratta recognized the probing eyes of the man at the stagecoach inn, the one who had flipped a piece of Lowland gold to a wandering bard for tales of the Twelve.

The stranger's mouth twisted into a cruel smile. Then Esmeralde, too, saw something familiar. Wasn't this woman's profile stamped on the magic coin she'd traded Ozzie for at the Banebridge Trading Post?

"Who?" Smokey pestered again.

Sierra looked at Aubergine. "Hiding in plain sight," was all Sierra said.

Without answering, Aubergine crossed possessive arms around Trader's shoulders. The dark woman spoke defiantly: "Mamie may be safe within the Crystal Caves at last, but the path you seek is more impossible than you can imagine."

Impertinent was the word that came to Aubergine's mind as she locked eyes with the trespasser across the still-simmering pot.

The uninvited woman pulled off her apron, revealing an intricate waistcoat knit from kettle-dyed merino. Gathered at the bodice, the bottom fell in swinging folds of shaded black, shot with white where the dye had failed to take properly. The top was striped with alternating bands of semisolid bronze and an eerie green that matched her eyes. Stiff ruffles of ruched fabric fanned the inside of the deep V-neck collar held together beneath her breastbone by a single button encrusted with shards of cracked crystal.

No one needed to ask if the garment harbored magic. The crystal bits glittered wickedly in the light of the fire under the pot. Aubergine feigned indifference and tightened her hold around Trader's shoulders.

Esmeralde nudged Indigo Rose and lifted her chin toward the stranger. "There's our intruder," she whispered.

"Interloper," Indigo murmured back.

"Imposter," Aubergine declared firmly. "Imperious imposter."

Smokey Jo offered Lilac Lily a fearful look. "Do we know her?"

Lily nodded, but seemed afraid to answer.

Smokey gave Sierra a pleading look. "Tasman," replied the new Keeper of the Tales. "Hiding in plain sight, as is her wont."

"Sierra Blue," the Dark Queen acknowledged with a nod. "Aubergine." Her haughty eyes shifted. "Lily." She tossed her soup-stained apron past Wheat to where Lily, the housemistress, stood. The garment crumpled to the floor, where it threatened to catch on fire from the flames licking the dye pot. "I'll take no more instructions from you."

Lily grabbed the smock away from the embers and said to the rest of the group, angrily, "I hired her in the marketplace. She was posing as a char girl from Coventry, seeking employ."

Ratta gave Tasman a smoldering stare. "She is not from my homeland of Coventry, nor is she one of us."

"Her willingness to start work that day was too convenient," Lily said. "I should have known."

"That's why the vision worked when we returned with the firewood," Smokey said. "There really were twelve of us, after all." She peered up at Aubergine anxiously. "The Dark Queen heard the Lost Tale. She heard everything."

A storm brewed in Aubergine's eyes. "It could not be helped."

"You have fooled me twice now," Lily admitted to Tasman. "You will not fool me again."

Tasman laughed. "You are all fools."

"Now that you know the tale," Sierra said, trying to keep a hint of pleasantry in her voice, "leave this place, for we have much to do."

"Always the little peacemaker, weren't you?" Tasman replied. She smiled at Ratta. "I didn't come here for the Lost Yarn, although that was a nice addition." Glittering, her green eyes shifted to Aubergine. "Where is it?"

Aubergine's eyes flashed violet. "I shall have the necklace whole."

Tasman shook her head. "No, old woman. You shall forfeit the missing crystal."

"I do not harbor such a stone." Aubergine loosened her hold on Trader only far enough to open her empty palms.

Tasman's eyes flicked over Trader. "Little Teal, I've been searching for you," she said in a singsong voice.

Wresting herself free from Aubergine's grasp, Trader snatched up her walking stick to bar Tasman's path. "I know," she said bravely.

Quick as a cat, Tasman moved around the pot toward the girl. With a flick of a finger, she batted the stick from Trader's grasp. It spun in the air and snapped in half and both pieces clattered to the floor. The invader arced her hand, letting her fingers spiral toward the girl. Her long lacquered nails clicked together. A swirl of energy transfixed Trader and jerked her from the floor. The power that radiated from Tasman's talons lifted Trader roughly by the neck of her leather jerkin, dangled her a few inches from the floor, and drew her closer to the Dark Queen.

"I would have found you eventually," Tasman purred. "You're too comely for that silly boy's disguise you were using."

Aubergine raised her veined hands and stretched out her arms in an attempt to summon a surge of electricity that might break Tasman's power. As Trader began to shrug out of her jerkin in her own attempt to escape, Tasman's thumb and forefinger met and retracted, pulling the leather laces of the jacket taut, choking the young girl.

"Trader!" Lily shouted, running to aid the captive as she kicked and sputtered.

Aubergine's arthritic hands shook with the effort to muster enough force to free Trader. Over the dye pot the air hissed and crackled between the opposed fingers of the two witches. Wheat unhooded her staff, preparing to muster the magic of its crystals to help.

Tasman held up an unlined palm. "Interfere and this young Teal will share the fate of the last one," she warned.

Wheat caught the glowing scarabs in her fist to still their sparking. Lily stopped short and shot a warning glance at Aubergine, who let her hands drop to her skirts.

"Wise choice," Tasman observed with a smug smile. "Not only fools, but paltry fools, can sometimes make wise choices." She drew the struggling girl close and held her fast. "This Teal you call Trader is coming with me. I may give her back—after she shows me the missing stone."

Tasman lifted the edge of her waistcoat and turned. In a swirl of smoke she and Trader disappeared, leaving behind only sooty traces and a choking cloud.

Wheat and Lily began to cough.

"Trader!" Skye screamed, reaching toward where her friend had been but grasping only air.

As the black fog dissipated, Smokey wiped its acrid sting from her eyes. "I would like to know what just happened," she sputtered.

"Tasman made off with our Trader," Aubergine said, mildly. "She has been trying to find the girl for years. For some reason, Tasman believes that our fossicker possesses the lost amethyst that was once her aunt Tracery Teal's."

"My guess is that the original Teal really has it," Smokey grumbled. "One day you'll open a cupboard in the root cellar or a wardrobe in the attic, and from a high, high shelf the crystal will fall on your head."

Skye's eyes had filled with tears. "Where did they go?"

"My guess is that Tasman will hasten to the glacier." With a glance toward Lily, Aubergine rephrased her statement, turning it into a question that Lily, who knew all of their minds, would then be required to answer. "Am I correct in surmising that she will waste no time seeking the Lost Caves ahead of us?"

"Tasman knows that Mamie Verde now wards the ancient burial grounds," Lily said. "Mamie was never any threat to her."

"That was before Mamie assumed her watch," Ratta said. "As Guardian, she won't let Tasman pass. Even if the Dark Queen could force her way into the graveyard, the ancient voices would drive her back."

"She may first return to the South to gather reinforcements." Wheat recalled the band of Lowlanders she had met at the Crossed Tracks.

"Perhaps she knows an alternate entrance to the Caves," Sierra suggested, seeing again in her mind's eye the Dervish who had disappeared around the Blind Side of the glacier.

Aubergine nodded wearily. "This simmer is over." She turned to Smokey Jo. "Douse the fire."

With a satisfaction bordering on delight, the gnome tipped waiting buckets of water into the flames, causing billows of damp steam to rush to the ceiling. As the embers hissed, Esmeralde hefted the wooden paddle and dipped it into the pot. With Indigo Rose's help, she lifted the steaming fiber out of the now-clear water. All the colors in the dye bath had been absorbed by the soft tendrils.

Wheat examined the brightly shaded Suri Alpaca. "It really does look like Fire and Ice," she breathed. She smiled at Skye. "You will turn this into a fine yarn."

"Dry it overnight, so it will be ready to spin tomorrow," Aubergine directed. "Even now, the task of safeguarding all that is good and true appears unachievable. For there is one—the one we saw among us tonight—who would usurp the magic crystals and attempt to conquer nature much as the First Folk did."

"I'll go, if that will help," Smokey volunteered, raising her hand. "Though I must admit I hate the cold."

Aubergine smiled, and shook her head. "No, little one, you shall remain here by my side." She turned to Lily. "And you."

Lily nodded her consent, unsurprised.

Aubergine paused to consider the talents of the others. Her eyes came to rest upon Skye. "You shall stay, too. Even if our quest to rediscover the entrance to the Lost Caves proves successful, unlocking the secrets of the ancient crystals from the tombs beyond is uncertain." She studied the three she had chosen. "After the others leave, we have much to do."

"I wanted to go help find Trader," Skye protested in a small voice.

Sierra's face was serene. "That is not your fate."

"Do you forget there is war going on?" Wheat argued, unconvinced. "Those of us you send out on this impossible errand could be killed along the track. By either side!"

"Yours is not a fool's journey." Aubergine shot the shepherdess a hard glance. "Forget about the war between the North and the South. The foolish North believes that the Lowlanders seek nothing more than water rights, which is a lie. Under the guise of wresting water from the glacier, Tasman secretly searches for the magic crystals. She doesn't care who wins the war, or who lives or dies, as long as in the end she alone harbors the secrets of the Crystal Caves."

"Then we all may wish we had died in fire or ice," Ratta grumbled.

Lavender Mae uttered a plaintive "Mae," and buried her face in Sierra's shawl.

"Heed her, for she is not mindless," Aubergine advised, as Sierra began to pry Mae gently but firmly from her shoulder. "Much is sane within Mae's addled brain. The First Folk murmur to her so often that she can do naught but cry out."

"Mae always looked to the stones for answers." Wheat gave Lily a questioning glance. "Why?"

"It's simple." Lily watched Sierra brush Mae's wispy white hair back from her jittering eyes. "She understands that rejoining the necklace can restore power to the Circle of Twelve once more."

"And it will." Aubergine said. "We need to find that amethyst."

"The necklace Tasman took had a string of eleven stones," Indigo pointed out. "Our time might be better spent looking for that."

"A string is not a circle!" Aubergine said angrily.

With a sidelong glance at Aubergine, Mae scuttled away in alarm.

Aubergine sighed. "If Tasman had the necklace in her possession, she would certainly not have left here without it." The old woman yawned. "Get some rest, everyone. Tomorrow will be a busy day. We will need to prepare those who are going for the journey into the Northlands."

Without a word, Wheat took up her shepherd's crook and stomped upstairs to tend the Jacob ram she was keeping in her room. Ratta turned to follow, but paused in the parlor doorway at the foot of the stairs. The front of the room, where the viewing table holding Mamie's body had been, was empty. The vases of lilies to either side were wilted and the candles burned to nubs. Making sure no one could see her, Ratta stepped inside and softly closed the pocket doors behind her.

With her back against the wall, she slumped to the floor in the soothing darkness, welcoming the tears that washed down her cheeks.

Skye hurried up the hall to the kitchen to catch up with her brother Warren, for she knew he'd have plenty of tales for her and their younger brother Garth. In spite of all the turmoil, her step was light at the thought that she, her mother, and her two brothers had all been reunited, at least for a short while. A prickle at the back of her brain reached out to wonder where her father was, but she simply had to assume he was alright and to focus on the work she'd been given here.

Just beyond the scorched doorway to the dye shed, Sierra and Lily stepped into an alcove to talk in earnest, pausing only when Aubergine swept past to retire to her private chambers. Alone but for Lavender Mae, who seemed preoccupied with the shards of amethyst crystal that had spilled across the floor from the broken hourglass, Esmeralde and Indigo spread the damp alpaca fleece carefully over the drying rack.

When they had finished, the two slipped out the dye shed's secret entrance to revisit their childhood haunt in the back alley. "Too bad about that Trader," Indigo said. She lit a smoke. "That little fossick boy was starting to grow on me."

Esmeralde unstoppered her flask of Crystal Cordial. "Trader was a girl," she reminded Indigo, taking a nip.

Indigo reached for the flask. "Yes, I liked him."

Mae stayed behind in the shed, scuffing through the shards of crystal on the floor. She paused to turn over the splintered pieces of Trader's walking stick with the toe of her boot. The dull purple stone that had decorated the top interested her. It had come loose from its bindings. Mae picked at the strips of leather that had lashed the crystal into place. The stone dropped into her hand.

"Mae?" She ran practiced fingers across the rough underside of the stone, which had been tied jagged side down, to buffer its sharp edges. She plopped cross-legged on the floor to further examine the broken crystal.

She studied the rock from all angles. Then she lifted the heavy pouch of stones from her neck. She pried the drawstring open.

Carefully she raised a long length of amethyst gems set in tarnished silver from the pouch and fit the one from Trader's walking stick into the bit of ragged stone still left in the twisted silver setting. The pointed edge of the cracked crystal matched the sunken nub seamlessly.

"Ohhhhhh . . ." Mae's mouth dropped open.

In the shadows cast by the candlelight, she blinked at the circlet of twelve amethyst stones. "Oh yes!" She began to shriek. "Yes! Yes Mae! Yes Mamie! Yes Aubergine!"

Suddenly, she clamped a hand tight over her mouth. Sitting stark still, she peered warily toward the open doorway, watching and listening. The hallway was empty. The only voices she heard beside those murmuring in her head came from the kitchen.

Quickly and quietly, Mae pulled one stone after another out of her pouch, placing each silently on the floor as she removed it. When she had emptied the bag, she surveyed her collection. Several crystals were about the same shape or color as the lost gem, but none was its twin. Mae did what she always did in such cases: she chose a near-matching rock at random. Hunched over Trader's broken walking stick, she stole furtive glances toward the door as she nimbly lashed the replacement amethyst in place and laid the walking stick back where it had fallen. Mae began to sift the loose crystals back into her pouch, but changed her mind and dumped them onto the floor, secreting within the bag only the silver string with its now-twelve amethysts. She slung the pouch back around her neck, surprised at how light it had become. Standing, she gazed wistfully at the small pile of stones on the floor.

"Mae," she waved in farewell. But that didn't seem right. Stepping over the stones to the great pot, she looked within. The water was clear and still steaming. Over it hung a thick veil of green haze. Did she dare?

Mae scooped up the loose amethyst crystals with both hands and dropped them into the dye pot. They disappeared into its depths.

With a shrug, Mae left the dye shed and tripped down the empty hall toward the staircase, unmindful of the fog that followed her up the stairs.

In a small courtyard, a pair of draft horses stood harnessed to a rolling cage.

CHAPTER 2

Close Calls

"YOU LITTLE WITCH!" RATTA SCOLDED MAE. "You're not supposed to take things without paying for them!"

Lily sighed. This morning she had led her small group of witches into the shops along the well-healed streets of Artisan's Hand, hoping to find all the provisions and sundries they needed for their journey to the glacier before day's end. But nothing had happened as planned. As they stood in the bakery, the flour-dusty baker glared at them across a counter filled with baskets of fresh-smelling sweet rolls and crusty bread. Mae was glancing around the shop, seemingly oblivious to the others' reactions.

"I swear I only left her alone long enough to collect our parcel next door," Warren apologized. Lily rummaged in her change purse and then dropped a few coppers into the baker's outstretched hand.

"Keep her out of my shop." He pointed at Mae.

The scrawny crone didn't notice his gesture as she crammed the other blackberry scone she had stolen into her mouth. Closing her eyes, she chewed loudly and with pleasure.

Lily looked at Warren. "Someone needs to take her back to Potluck Yarn before she calls more attention to us."

"I will," he volunteered. "I'm getting tired of this costume anyway." Earlier he had put on the garb of a Western Highlands shepherd, hoping the foreign outfit would keep him from being noticed by guardsmen searching for army deserters. The shapeless trekkers he had traded his nailed glacier boots for lacked support. His feet hurt. He shouldered the pantry sack of supplies the small group had already purchased for their quest north, and took Mae's elbow. "Come along."

Lips smacking, she paused just long enough to lick her fingers and then followed obediently.

Their departure left Lily and Ratta with only Garth to help them procure the rest of their rations. Sierra had slipped away without a word on a private mission early this morning. With little interest in traveling gear or trail food, Esmeralde had joined them just long enough to purchase a few odd tinctures at an apothecary in Merchant's Pass. Soon after, she disappeared into the doorway of a wine merchant advertising Crystal Cordial varietals. Not long after, the group crossed into the borough of Artisan's Hand, where Indigo Rose discovered an herbalist offering pouches of hand-cured glacier weed in a back alley.

"I've been searching for this very shop," she announced, scurrying down the side street. At the sign above the shop, she turned. "I'll be just a minute or two."

"Or three?" Lily asked with a tired edge to her otherwise pleasant voice.

Indigo considered whom she was talking to. "You know better than to wait," she admitted. "Go ahead. I'll catch up."

"Like moth-eaten yarn she will." Ratta eyed Lily sourly.

They had not seen any of the others since.

"Where do we go now?" Ratta asked as they stood outside the bread shop.

Lily pulled the shopping list from her market bag. Only half of the items were ticked off. She sighed. "We need preserves still—smoked meat, dried jerky, aged cheese, salted nuts. I thought to find most of it in Butcher's Block."

"That's a long carry back," Ratta said.

"I can help," Garth offered the witches, guessing that his young years would disallow him from both the wine sinks and the smoke shops. Indeed, he had stuck close to the remaining witches hoping to accompany them to the bawdy borough of Butcher's Block, even if it meant he had to act as their kitchen boy.

Before Ratta could protest, Lily held up her hand. "Let him come. He's likely to be caught otherwise."

Fuming, Ratta closed her lips. Lily was right. Alone, Garth risked capture by the zealous soldiers who roamed the outer districts in groups of two and three searching for conscripts. Though Garth was too young to serve, few wearing a uniform emblazoned with the white crest of the Northland Glacier would hesitate to grab him. The Guard had raised the finder's fee to a newly minted piece of Northland silver for each fresh recruit surrendered to the Winter Watch Garrison. Seemingly overnight, notices to this effect had appeared chalked across slates in the marketplaces and papered onto the signposts.

"You look sharp, boy, while we're on the streets," Ratta advised. "Don't wander off while we're in the Block. They'll sell the likes of you for a sliver of silver."

"I know," he answered, trying to suppress an eager grin. "I saw the signs."

The largest of Bordertown's seven boroughs, Butcher's Block housed the city stockyards, slaughterhouses, rendering sheds, and, Garth had heard, Shambles. He had never seen a Shamble or encountered one of the nightwalkers who were said to frequent them, but he wanted to be able to boast to other boys that he had.

"I'm not talking about the army!" Ratta pushed frizzy hair from her face. "There are other dangers, worse."

Garth nodded absently, thinking only of what he had heard about the rough borough that the locals he'd met these last few days called Fresh Meat.

"I mean it!" Ratta turned to Lily. "Can you tell him what I mean?"

"Butcher's Block is no Merchant's Pass," Lily explained to Garth. "Keep close always. Don't let us out of your sight."

"Give the lawless Closes a wide berth." Ratta growled. "We have neither the time nor the coinage to fool with the folk who frequent such places. Neither do you."

Outside the city walls, the Western Highlands trails met the Coventry Road some miles south of Bordertown to form a broad thoroughfare that led to the busy Western Gate, the only entrance to Butcher's Block unless you dwelt within the city. Beneath the wide stone arch rumbled the turbulent traffic of farm wagons crowded with crates of geese and chicken, carts loaded with fresh catch such as rabbit, ruffled grouse, and river fish, and flatbeds laden with gutted boar and hart. Cattlemen drove beef animals directly down the middle of the thoroughfare, while through the postern gates herding dogs worked smaller groups of sheep and swine. They nipped at the heels of stray lambs and stubborn sows, all the while trailed by watchful shepherds and swineherds, who prodded the laggard livestock with the butts of their walking staffs.

"Did you bring the boy's Potluck Hat?" Ratta asked.

Lily shook her head without bothering to look in her market bag.

"That's a shame." Ratta said. "I hope he doesn't need it."

As they entered Butcher's Block over a pedestrian causeway that separated it from the manicured cobbles of Merchant's Pass, Garth's senses were assaulted by smoke and noise. He found himself on a dual carriageway of hard-packed earth lined on both sides with storefronts and stalls filled with raw meat, fish, and fowl.

Garth fell in step behind the witches as they made their way through the crowd of slow-moving shoppers that milled through the marketplace. Trams clattered by and street vendors hawked their wares. At one open-air window, heavy strings of garlic and onions hung over wild ducks stuffed with what looked like ground greens and wild rice covered with sticky orange glaze. In the next shop, he watched a butcher boy cut small diagonal slashes into a huge spitted roast encrusted all over with cracked peppercorns and sea salt. With the tip of his sharp blade, the youth deftly inserted cloves of peeled garlic into the pockets he had slit in the meat.

Some stalls held only ribs—beef, sheep, pork, venison, and bigger ones Garth didn't recognize—trussed for grilling. They passed larger meat markets where whole haunches of lamb, hart, and boar sprinkled with fresh mint hung from rafter hooks. One booth was filled with trays of tiny yard birds stuffed with chopped cinnamon apples and roasted chestnuts.

As they walked on, smokehouses appeared, crowding the side streets with enticing displays of giant eels and fantastical fish, whole turkeys and suckling pigs. In the alleys, grills sputtered with herbed sausages heaped with onions and peppers, and stands of street fare such as cooked faggots, pork cracklings, and black pudding overflowed into neighboring courtyards.

Garth wrinkled his nose. However heavily the aromas of roasted meat and cherrywood-smoked sausage spiced the air, they could not mask the underlying coppery odor of the blood and offal that trickled through the open gutters on both sides of the thoroughfare.

Pausing before a smoker fashioned from barrel halves that stood sentry in a narrow passage, Garth reached toward what looked like a bloated wine skin fitted with fins and horns hanging in the entrance. "What's that?"

Ratta slapped his hand away. "Poison Puffish."

"Poison?" Garth gave Lily a questioning look. "Fish?"

"Far East Puffish harbor venom in their spikes," Lily explained. "They protect themselves by puffing up to loom larger than their enemies and defend by attacking with needles packed with paralyzing serum."

Garth reached out his fingers. "I guess that didn't work for this blowfish. He's dead."

"Leave the horns be." Ratta warned. "Unless you want Esmeralde digging through the deepest parts of her Possibles Bag for something to leech out the poison." She eyed Garth. "You might rather wish you were dead."

Frowning, Lily gazed at the peculiar array of preserved oddities that hung on the wall behind the smoker. The stand was empty except for a gypsy child perched on a stool picking bits of smoked eel from a stick. The girl popped the cured meat into her mouth and chewed slowly, watching them all the while.

"Few know what to do with snake venom and spider ichor, especially when it has never been properly extracted," Lily said.

"Esmeralde would," Garth replied.

Lily eyed Ratta. "Why would anyone try to sell such creatures in a public alley?"

The other witch pointed above the walled entrance. "Because it's not public. Lily, look."

Crudely etched in stone above the Puffish at the alley's opening was a name.

"Madame Marry's Close," Garth read. He peered into the twisted passage. "Does that mean there's a Shambles down there?"

Without answer, Lily took his arm. "Let's go buy the rest of our provisions."

"What's the big deal?" Garth craned his neck back toward the dark alley as Ratta took his other arm and the witches marched him away. "So it's a Close. So what?"

"Closes are unsavory," Ratta said, releasing her hold only when they stood safely on the side of the crowded carriageway once more. Her eyes flickered toward the maw of the narrow passage. "There are no rules in there."

Garth sighed and said nothing.

As was custom in Bordertown, abandoned alleys, vacant courtyards, and constricted shortcuts connecting busy boulevards were claimed by folk with squatters' rights, whose families had settled in these unwanted areas long before. Because they were unrecognized, the Closes were not regulated or maintained by the city.

Within such spaces, hole-in-the-wall shops advertised cure-alls laced with mind-numbing flowers and fungi, while unlicensed wine sinks crowded with scarred tables sold cheap spirits and ales fermented from dandelion weed and rotted fruit. Shantytowns frequented by runaways, immigrants, and other unfortunates snaked through larger Closes that spilled into vacant lots. Twisted alleys catered to games of dice and Skells. Closes no wider than footpaths harbored private staircases to city streets above or below, where swift passage might cost a penny round-trip.

Garth had heard that some Closes dead-ended in courtyards called Shambles, recognizable by narrow doors painted bright red flanking all three sides. Shambles were secret places meant for private encounters, Garth surmised. Why else would each door open to a solitary room that it was rumored you could only rent if you were in the company of a nightwalker, and then only for a few hours?

Garth looked longingly at Madame Marry's Close. "What's the big deal?" He asked again.

In answer, Lily and Ratta took his arms once more and propelled him across the dusty boulevard to the other side of Butcher Block's main thoroughfare, avoiding the gutters filled with bloody water and bits of gore.

To Garth's dismay, the witches paused to peer into the front windows of almost every shop along the street, pointing out dressed yard birds, cured hams, oven roasts, and pork chops. They also sought stores of salted beef, bacon ends, and dried jerky. Of special interest to them was a disgusting mixture of rendered fat and sprouted grain, pounded into rounds called Peasant Meal. The stuff could, they told him, be eaten hot or cold, fresh or old, plain or spread with sweet mustard, ground nuts, or fruit preserves, and it never went bad. To him, it looked rancid enough already.

After a few forays into butcheries reeking of entrails, Garth grew bored. He decided to wait just outside the open door of a smokehouse where Lily haggled with the butcher's wife and Ratta waited at the meat counter for the sliced ham and bacon they had purchased. As she collected the various parcels tied with twine, Ratta motioned for him to join her.

Gath shook his head. "I'm keeping close! I can see both of you just fine."

Outside the butcher shop, he loitered, pretending disinterest in the lively street scene, as he had seen city boys do. He jammed his hands into his pockets and rested one booted foot squarely on the packed earth, bracing the other against the stone storefront. It wasn't long before a sandy-haired youth about his own age sauntered by, showing a pair of bone dice cupped in his palm.

Garth grinned and held up a finger. A swift glance into the storefront told him that Lily and Ratta would be there a while longer. Jingling a few Northland coppers in his pocket, he trailed the other boy around the corner. If he turned his head, he could still glimpse the back door of the butcher shop. In the alley, the other boy stood before the opening of a narrow Close from which hung a piece of planking scrawled with the words Fish Eye.

"Is that what you call it in the Block?" Garth asked the youth. "Where I come from, when you dice double ones you say snake eyes."

"Snake eyes, fish eyes," the other boy laughed easily. "Just where are you from?"

"Banebridge way," Garth said, feeling a little nervous. He peered back at the butcher shop. "Let's dice out here."

"The tumbling stones are better inside," the other boy said, disappearing into the mouth of the Close.

Garth followed him into the darkness. Further down the alley, he could see smooth flagstones pushed up against the stone wall, fit for dicing. A lantern balanced nearby on a bit of broken crockery cast a dim light on the scene.

The dice had just come out and the other boy was matching his coppers when a large woman approached them from the gloom. Her rouged cheeks and painted lips were framed by hennaed hair. Most disconcerting were her eyes. Beneath heavy lashes, they stared out sideways, seemingly at odds with her face.

"Who are you?" Garth gaped at her. "A nightwalker?"

The walleyed woman laughed. "Is that what you want, boy?"

"This here is Fish-Eye Annie." The other boy picked up the money and pocketed his dice. "She runs this Close."

"If it's nightwalkers you're looking for, just pay the tariff and come along to the Shambles," Annie leered.

"Tariff?" Garth glanced back toward the entrance to the Close, hoping to see Lily or Ratta walking by. He looked helplessly at the other boy. "I thought we were decided on a game of dice."

"Snake eyes," the other youth scoffed, ignoring him. "This Banebridge bumpkin thought fish eyes was snake eyes."

From the murk behind Annie, a fat man wearing a tunic belted by a length of rope emerged from the depths of the Close. From one hand swung a set of fetters. As Garth turned to flee, the sandy-haired boy tripped him and Garth went down hard in the dirt. No matter how he struggled, he couldn't rise because the other boy sat on his back and held his arms.

"Hey!" Garth shouted, as the fat man bound his hands behind him. "I don't need to dice or see any Shambles. Let me go!"

"No worries," the fat man soothed. "You won't be dicing or visiting Shambles. At least not today."

As the fat man hauled Garth to his feet, the city boy gave the money to Annie. "All he had was a few coppers." She pocketed the change. The man took Garth roughly by the arm. The youth lingered in the alley. "Go find us another," Annie told him, sharply.

"Lily!" Garth screamed as the fat man pulled him deeper into the twisted Close. "Ratta!"

In the darkness, he stumbled and fell to his knees. A sour rag filled his mouth. Annie tied the gag tight. "You shush."

The fat man pulled him up, and they hauled him along the narrow alleyway in silence. Moments later, they emerged from the dark Close into small courtyard where a pair of draft horses stood harnessed to a rolling cage.

A soldier lazing on a bench rose to unlock the cell door. "Stand back," he told the boys jailed inside. Garth blinked, letting his eyes adjust to the brightness. He could barely believe what he saw.

"In you go," the soldier grunted, boosting Garth up and shoving him inside the wagon.

"That a full load, then?" the fat man asked.

The soldier shrugged, locking the door. "There might be room for one more."

Annie nodded. "That's what I thought." She and the fat man turned and trudged back into the Close. Garth glanced at the dirty fossickers sitting on the benches and sprawled on the floor.

"I know you, mate," a voice said softly. Small hands reached up to loosen the gag from his mouth. "'Member me?"

Unable to speak, Garth nodded. "Ross," he tried to say.

The small boy turned to his skinny companion. "Look, Clayton, it's that farm boy we found in the river." He picked at the knotted cloth in Garth's mouth. "What was your name again?"

Garth spit out the foul rag. "Garth."

"That's right, Garth!" Ross tugged at Clayton's sleeve. "He had the sister with them strange ponies. 'Member them ponies? They were fat and liked to chase people."

"I remember." Clayton eyed Garth curiously. "So we meet again."

Garth nodded. "I wish I could say well met, but that would be a lie." He gazed at another boy sound asleep on the floor.

"Don't know him," Ross said. "He was here when we got pinched."

Clayton slid over to make room for Garth. "The last time we saw you was under the Banebridge trestle when the Guard found us. Sorry we left you there."

Garth shrugged. "We outran the Guard on the ponies, easy enough." He sat. "We lost them in the Copse and rode until dawn."

"You know where Trader is?" Clayton asked.

Garth shook his head.

"That's the reason we came up here, to find him," Ross said. "Something bad is happened." He eyed Clayton briefly and gave small nod. "Trader's in trouble, pro'bly."

"I don't doubt it," Garth replied, trying to decide if he should say more.

"We're all of us in trouble," Clayton said glumly, as the fat man and Annie emerged from the Close leading another boy in fetters.

The soldier loaded the frightened youth into the cage and slammed the door. The boy fell to his knees and began to cry.

"Five pieces of Northland silver." Annie smiled. "Now there's a good day's pay." The fat man held the horses' heads while the soldier mounted the wagon, using the front wheel as a step to the high bench seat. "That's three for us." She offered up a dirty palm. "We'll have ours now."

The soldier reached down for the double set of reins. "Now you know I can't do that. Paid you last time, didn't I?"

"That was an awful long wait," the fat man said.

Annie nodded. "P'raps you'll go with him this time," she suggested.

"P'raps I will," the fat man agreed, attempting to climb up onto the bench seat while still holding the reins. "Move over."

Garth never did figure out exactly what happened next. Maybe the front wheel turned, for the fat man fell as he tried to mount the wagon. Possibly the horses got scared, because all at once the rolling cage began to clatter toward the dark alley, picking up speed. Behind them Annie screeched and the fat man moaned, and then rocks began to hit the back of the cage. From his vantage point behind the front wheels, Garth could at first witness the soldier, still perched unsteadily atop the driver's seat, trying to bend down to catch the dragging reins, but once they got inside the Close, it was too dark to see. Finally the reins must have fouled the wheel spokes, because the wagon jerked to a stop as suddenly as it had started, just after they broke into daylight once more.

"Shards!" The soldier shouted, rubbing his brow where the sign swinging in the archway had hit him in the head.

"What did I tell you?" a familiar voice growled.

Garth had never been so happy to see witches in all his life. "Lily!" he called. "Ratta!"

Lily glared at the soldier. Without a word, she pulled out her change purse once more.

There could be no doubt the sky-blue ribbon was hers.

CHAPTER 3

A Fine Yarn

WINTER WHEAT HEFTED THE HEAVY PAIR of hand carders from the cluttered table in the front room of the yarn shop and drew the fine metal teeth of one across its mate to clear the embedded fiber, a clean start to her next job. Then she set to work with long regular strokes, teasing strands of the fine alpaca loose from the dried mass of multicolored fiber. After last night's simmer, Indigo had pulled the Suri Alpaca fleece from the great dye pot with the wooden paddle. Then Esmeralde had helped her spread the clumps of curly locks across the wooden rack before the fire. Overnight, the crystal-dyed alpaca had stiffened to tight spirals as it had dried. The morning light revealed curls of scarlet and sunflower, fuchsia and goldenrod. Now, as Wheat expertly flicked the curly locks from one card to the other, the silky fiber began to loft as the staples opened out into fluffy clouds.

"Oooh!" The gnome Smokey Jo lifted her face to admire the magical fiber as it seemed to come alive through the fluid motion of Wheat's practiced hands.

Lavender Mae had coaxed vibrant hues from the powdered dye, ground from crystals of ruby and topaz, garnet and jet. In the morning light, and under the heavy drag of Wheat's carders, it blended into soft ribbons of roving alive with the colors of flickering fire.

The rhythmic thump of the carders reminded Smokey Jo of the informal bands she searched out at street fairs and on market days. These merry groups of kitchen musicians seemed to assemble randomly. They made music with whatever was handy: they blew across the tops of earthenware jugs, stroked thimbles over washboards strapped to their chests, and even clanged together pot covers like cymbals. The most normal instruments they had were mouth harps.

Next to the gnome, Skye Blue sat perched on a three-legged stool behind a sturdy beginner's spinning wheel once used by her mother, Sierra.

Smokey confessed to the girl, "No matter how many times I worked my own set of tiny hand carders as a child, my fleece and roving matted into snarls fraught with guard hairs and plant bits, leaves and twigs, and the like."

Skye nodded numbly, waiting with red-rimmed eyes for Wheat to lift the first batt of prepared fiber from the carders. Her job was to spin the alpaca into fine lace-weight yarn Aubergine would then pattern into a knitted shawl they would call Fire and Ice. The magical motifs would safeguard her mother and the small band of witches chosen to travel to the Northland Glacier in search of an entrance to the Lost Caves.

Now that she was Keeper of the Tales, Sierra needed additional protection. All the witches hoped that the magic trapped within the shawl's design would ward her from the insistent voices of the ancients as she passed through the First Folk tombs, if the travelers were fortunate enough to locate the Crystal Caves at all. Without the shawl's protection, the unrelenting murmurings of the ancients might possess Sierra as they had Lavender Mae. If that happened, the stories of old could be lost forever. Those at the Potluck also feared that if the First Folk or their Watchers found a way to detain Sierra, they might captivate her into remaining and release Mamie prematurely. A Guardian serving out tenure could only be relieved of duty when a newly named Guardian was presented. But how would the ancients know that Sierra had arrived only for a visit? She was destined one day to leave them all and liberate Mamie, according to some yarns. There were, however, questions of timing, and of course the entire undertaking they were embarking on was riddled with unknowns.

This morning at breakfast, the remaining ten of the Potluck Twelve had agreed that there was no time to linger and they must knit the multicolored shawl Aubergine had designed in shifts, quickly and carefully. The ancient mosaic Aubergine had outlined on crosshatched parchment was extremely difficult to knit. The pattern stitch had no true repeat, and had never been replicated. To make matters worse, a missed row or dropped stitch could jeopardize the garment's integrity and diminish, or entirely negate, the shawl's power.

Aubergine's intricate lace design depicted random licks of candlelight against a backdrop of cavern walls glistening with ice crystals. She promised to cast on the initial set of stitches, establish the pattern, and place ring markers between motifs. As her arthritic fingers began to falter, she planned to hand off the knitting to Esmeralde, who pledged to work until her eyes grew bleary and then relinquish the project to Indigo Rose. Skye gazed at the waves of color filling Wheat's carders.

35

Even unspun, the sunstruck shades shimmered. The shifting shapes reminded Skye of the hand-blown carnival glass that traveling gypsies sold at the Middlemarch Fair.

Just thinking about the fair made Skye blink and turn her reddened eyes away. She pulled the frayed bit of bloodied silk from her dress sleeve and looked at it once more. After last night's simmer, she had tarried in the kitchen with Warren over a cup of hot tea, after Garth had fallen asleep. It had just been the two of them, their chairs pulled close to the cookstove. First Warren had told her funny anecdotes from his training days at the Garrison, and she had made him laugh with her description of meeting his friend Niles of the North and of their pony ride across the Middlemarch bridge.

After they both fell silent, Warren related the sadder story that accompanied the hair ribbon he had found in the frozen hand of the dead boy, Averill. Although his quiet voice was full of sorrow, his sister's face filled with tears of denial. Before she could protest aloud, he produced the length of bloodstained silk he still kept hidden in his moose mitts. He held it out to her and, hesitating, she took it gently and spread it on the palm of her hand.

There could be no doubt the sky-blue ribbon was hers. She had dyed it two years ago, in anticipation of the Spring Fling at last year's Middlemarch Fair. There, the fiddle music had been lively. Small children cavorted through the new grass, while their parents danced in the clearing under the stars. Skye joined the other unwed maidens who frolicked around the Maypole. Ribbons streamed from their hair as they skipped breathlessly in the circle to welcome spring, as was customary in the Middlelands. Suddenly, Averill grabbed her hand and pulled her from the pole into the main dance, where adults were paired as couples. Hooting with delight, her brothers clapped to the music on the sidelines. At the night's end, Skye relinquished one of her hair ribbons as a promise to Averill while she kept the other, a tradition among Middlefolk. He was her beau. That had been more than a year ago.

Averill was gone: Skye's sweetheart, Warren's friend, and also one of their closest neighbors in the Lower Valley. The baker's son from the Mill on the Rill. One of the reliable and constant presences in her life. His lightness was now an empty space in her heart, one she dared not feel the pain of yet. The rusty-tinged ribbon she held had once been bluer than a summer sky, as blue as her eyes. It seemed those innocent days were lost forever, gone with the laughing and kind boy whose loss she could not fully accept.

Here in Bordertown, the sky was pale pink haze, suffocating under a ceiling of gray smoke that settled into the foothills below the glacier and crept over the Seven Boroughs. None could escape the sooty sky or acrid breeze. The air irritated the nose and eyes, causing tears to well as if crying were normal. Maybe now it was.

Silently Skye smoothed the frayed silk and tucked it into her cuff. Her mouth trembled and tears threatened to track down her face anew for the boy: the boy she thought she would wed one day, and the brother her friend Katerina waited for but who would never return to Lavender Rill. How could this have happened to Averill? He had not been a soldier. He was just a humble baker's boy, younger than Warren yet skilled in the ways of wheat and stone-ground corn. Averill had left with the Glacier Guard mere weeks ago. Now Warren had handed her a sign that he was dead. She still resisted accepting that it was so, although she certainly feared it was.

With a practiced swipe of the carders, Wheat loosened the first batt from the metal teeth. Smokey caught the cloud of lofty fiber and presented it to Skye, who slipped off her boots and set her stocking feet on the wooden treadles, then, depressing them alternately, set the spinning wheel in motion.

The drive wheel revolved slowly as she held the first few fibers spread in a V formation and allowed the twist to enter them, cinching them into a strand of yarn that followed a spiral path onto the turning bobbin. She picked up speed as her fingers adapted to the rhythm of the twist. Her feet took up a steady cadence that created a counterpoint to the strokes of Wheat's carders, already preparing the second batt. To Smokey Jo, the sounds of the treadle wheel and the teeth of the metal carders sounded like a merry song. All she felt she needed was a flute or lute or some such instrument to join in.

Instead, the bell over the front entrance rang, announcing visitors. The heavy carved oak door swung inward. Lavender Mae lurched unceremoniously into the shop, followed by Warren, who carried a bulging pantry sack. He had abandoned his gray Northland Guard tunic and wore instead an oilskin poncho and shoulder bag, such as shepherds from the Western Highlands favored. To complete his disguise, he had traded his army-issue boots for a worn pair of sheepskin trekkers and a sun-bleached hat from the mercantile. He kept the hat's wide brim pulled low over his brow to shield his eyes from notice. Skye noticed he was also letting his beard grow.

In contrast, Lavender Mae was just Mae, clad today in an out-of-date blue schoolgirl's uniform she had filched from an upstairs armoire. Although meant for a graded student, the moth-eaten wool coat fit her just fine. One oddity was a smear of purple jam across her face. Another was a heavy pouch that swung from her skinny neck, pulling her slight form forward as she walked.

Warren noticed Skye's tearful face, but said nothing.

"Where's Lily?" Wheat asked over the swish of the carders.

"Still shopping. She was going to Butcher's Block to see about salted meat for your journey." Warren settled his sack on the worktable. "I had to bring Miss Mae back. She was calling too much attention to herself."

"How so?" Wheat asked, with a glance at Mae's face.

"She made a scene at the confectionary."

"Mae likes her sweets." Smiling, Smokey wet her index finger and swiped it across the jam on Mae's cheek. "Is that blackberry, perchance?"

"Mmmmmm." The scrawny crone licked her lips and rubbed her belly as she watched Skye spin the bright alpaca into fine yarn.

"Watch her," Warren warned the others. "Don't let her run off." He hefted his sack and disappeared down the hall to the kitchen.

"Fetch the broom," Wheat called after him, eyeing the bits of fiber and plant stems with bits of broken leaves that had wafted to the floor.

"Those were pretty dye crystals you chose." Smokey reached up to Mae's chin and wiped the rest of the jam away with a cloth. "I just love the fiery colors—anything to do with flames, really—the licks of yellow and orange, and the singe of burning wood." She raised her brows at Mae. "The sizzle of green branches."

Mae touched a hand to the bottom of her precious pouch. "Mae," she agreed.

"Do you have any other gemstones in there?" Smokey asked. "I like to dabble in the dye crystals myself, if the truth be told. But every time I do, Teal comes in and stirs up my projects."

As Smokey climbed a chair in an attempt to peer into the bulging pouch strung around Mae's neck, the crone twisted away. Wheat loosened the second Suri batt from her carders, and Smokey caught the gossamer cloud and laid it on the table with a flourish.

"That ought to be plenty." Finished, Wheat began to clear stray guard hairs and other trash from the tines.

Skye nodded, her head bent in concentration as the bright yarn filled the first bobbin. "You don't need much fiber for singles this fine."

Warren returned with the kitchen broom. Wheat took it and began to sweep up the debris that had dropped from her combs.

"I had a whole batch of marigold heads drying in the sun, along with some indigo and madder, and you wouldn't believe what Teal did," Smokey said. "She strewed the flowers all through the pet cemetery and threw the madder into the soup pot. Everyone knows you can't substitute madder for celery and onions!"

The dye shed door opened and Aubergine glided up the hall, carrying the splintered pieces of Trader's walking stick. "Who has been playing in the dye pot?" she demanded, entering the yarn shop.

At the worktable, Smokey shrugged and Mae looked away.

Skye paused her wheel to change bobbins. "What do you mean?"

"The water was clear after last night's simmer," Aubergine said. "Now it's purple from half-dissolved dye crystals." She looked from Smokey Jo to Lavender Mae. "Did either of you throw any of the amethyst shards from the hourglass into the pot?"

"Not me," Smokey said.

Mae shook her head in denial. "Maaaaaeee," she swore.

"Maybe Teal did it," Smokey suggested.

"Oh, how I wish Lily was here." Aubergine sounded exasperated.

"Who's Teal?" Warren asked.

"She used to be one of us, but now she's a ghost," Smokey explained. "She steals things for attention and gets us into trouble. Just the other day she got mad that I took her cardigan and she left me locked in the dye shed."

"For borrowing a sweater?" Warren asked.

"Well, it was a magic knit," Smokey admitted. "But why does she need it now anyway? She's just a green fog ghost."

"I saw sage-colored haze in the stairwell when I went to bed last night." Skye paused. "Could that have been her?"

"Well, it couldn't have been anyone else," Smokey said. "If you saw her, she was up to no good. It's apples to oranges that something of yours comes up missing."

"Tracery Teal lingers because the lost stone is close," Aubergine said, with a glance toward the stairway. She fingered the crystal lashed to the top half of the broken walking stick. "At first I thought the missing amethyst might have been this purple rock bound atop Little Teal's hiking pole."

"Let me hazard a guess," Wheat murmured. Aubergine handed the splintered length of wood across the worktable. Wheat picked the stone free of its bindings.

"It's not the one," Wheat said with barely a glance.

Aubergine shook her head. "No, it isn't."

"Honestly, how can you tell?" Warren asked. "It looks like any crystal to me."

Wheat dropped the stone into his palm. "It's too smooth and regular to be the lost gem. See how round it is? That comes from tumbling through freshet after freshet, year after year." She looked at Aubergine. "This amethyst was in the water a long time before anyone found it."

"The lost stone was broken from its setting and jagged on the underside." Aubergine remembered. She gave Mae a curious look. "This is mere river rock."

"It's better than river rock." Skye rose to examine the crystal. "Trader used it to light our path through the roving branches of the Copse." Skye took the smooth stone from her brother. "I thought this rock might be enchanted glass, like the pieces of glowing quartz that travelers use to light their way." Skye peered at the crystal more closely before raising her eyes to Aubergine. "This isn't the jewel that was atop Trader's walking stick," she whispered.

For no apparent reason, Mae dropped to her hands and knees and scuttled underneath the worktable. She wrapped her arms around her chest, protecting the heavy bag that swung between her breasts.

"No, it isn't," Aubergine said, directing her gaze to the small form under the table. "This low-grade rock harbors little magic. It's about as useful as beach glass."

Mae rocked back and forth on her haunches, hugging herself. "Maeeeee," she groaned.

"What's she doing down there?" Warren asked.

"Trying to hide," Wheat answered with an exasperated sigh. "We call it hiding in plain sight."

"It isn't working," Smokey added.

Skye set the river stone on the worktable and resumed her place on the stool behind the spinning wheel. "Trader's amethyst was deep violet with rough edges."

"I remember," Aubergine nodded. "I was the one who put it there."

"You lashed the lost stone to a child's walking stick?" Warren asked. "Whatever for?"

"Safekeeping," Smokey guessed. "Not many folk would think twice about a bit of crystal decorating a hiking pole."

Aubergine smiled.

"Was it the lost stone?" Wheat wanted to know. "Truly?"

"I thought so at the time," Aubergine replied, watching as wisps of green fog filtered down the staircase and into the front hall. "Sometimes I still do."

"To be absolutely certain, we might have to try the broken stone in its original setting," Wheat observed. "Who knows where the necklace is now?"

"I wonder," Aubergine said. She prodded the skinny witch hiding under the table with the toe of her felted house slipper. "Who knows?"

"Mae!" Mae yelped, scuttling away. She clamped her hands over her ears. "Mae, Mae, Mae!"

Warren reached down and pulled her to a standing position.

"Could the Dark Queen have stolen the lost gem when she kidnapped Trader?" Skye asked. The cloud that had crept into the hall collected and settled outside the door.

Aubergine shook her head. "If Tasman had found the stone, she would have left here with it, and without Little Teal. If she has the amethyst already, she has slight use for our fossick girl."

"Well, where would it be?" Warren asked, as green fog seeped into the shop.

Aubergine gazed at the haze that hugged the ceiling. "Close," she murmured. Her eyes dropped to Mae, who cowered beneath the murky cloud. "Very close."

"Mae," the crone whimpered and wrapped her skinny arms around her head. She peeked out and gave Aubergine a pleading look. "Maaaee?"

Smokey stole a brief glance at the hovering vapor. "That's Teal up there," she announced.

Aubergine eyed Mae steadily. "Lavender Mae, did you replace Little Teal's jewel with this imposter?"

Without answer, Mae clutched her pouch of crystals to her chest. "Mmm," she growled, wrestling with herself. "Mmm."

"What's she doing?" Warren asked.

"Fighting avarice," Wheat observed. "There is only the one lost stone."

"Mine!" shouted Mae.

"No," Aubergine's eyes grew violet. "Not yours, ever. And neither is the rest of the necklace."

"You have crystals aplenty." Wheat held out her hand. "Let us see."

"No," Mae spit, crouching over her pouch. "No, no, no!"

"That necklace stone was Teal's before it became Trader's," Smokey warned, as the mist hovering over Mae condensed into a cloud the size of a hornet's nest. "If you took it unchallenged, Teal's going to be mad!"

Without warning, the miasma began to buzz like a swarm of bees, engulfing Mae's head and upper torso. In no time, wispy stingers began to pry open the drawstrings of Mae's pouch.

"Mae," she cried in pain as small green barbs stabbed her knuckles. Suddenly she scurried out of the room, and fled down the hall, trailed by the angry swarm.

Warren started to follow.

"Let her go," Aubergine said. "There is only one place I know of where the bees cannot reach her."

Smokey began to snicker. Taking up her staff, Wheat laughed out loud. Together, they hurried down the hall. When the rest of the group reached the dye shed, Mae was in the cauldron, submerged under the cold purple water. The green swarm had dissipated into the gloom. The threat of danger was gone.

When Warren pulled the crone from the pot, she cried "Mae" weakly. Her jewel pouch was open and her swollen fists were clenched tight. Dye water dripped from her clothing and puddled on the floor.

"I told you," Smokey chastised. "When Teal made it rain on me in the dye closet the other day, it was not fun." She glanced around at the others. "Did I mention that all I had to eat all afternoon was an apple?"

"Fetch a blanket from the linen closet," Aubergine said to Warren. Mae shivered and moaned. After he left, Aubergine nodded to Wheat, who once again held out her palm to Mae.

With the fingers of one hand, Mae began to pry the digits of her other hand away from the object clenched in her fist.

"Ooooh, Teal stung you good!" Smokey said at the sight of Mae's red and swollen knuckles.

Returning to the dye shed, Warren wrapped a threadbare blanket around the shivering crone. After much effort, Mae's one hand began to loosen the jagged amethyst from the grip of her other hand. Finally, it dropped into Wheat's palm.

Skye's breath caught in her throat. "That's Trader's gem."

"I believe it is." Aubergine said. She asked "Can you tell for certain?" as Wheat ran practiced fingers over the sharp edges of the wet stone.

"Not as well as I ken animals and fiber," the shepherdess said. "Mae knows her crystals better than I."

Warren regarded the wet witch huddled in the blanket. "Well, she's not talking."

Holding the amethyst loosely in her cupped palm, Wheat closed her eyes. Unsatisfied, she unhooded her staff and touched the crook to the crystal. The amber cabochons encasing the crystalized insects within began to swirl, clicking and sparking.

"The beetles know." Smokey smiled in delight. "It is the lost stone!"

From the front of the room a door squeaked and Sierra passed through the hidden alley entrance into the dye shed. She threw back the hood of her traveling cloak, surprised to find the gathered group.

"Mother, we found the lost stone!" Skye's eyes danced with excitement as Sierra approached the group around the cold dye pot. "The whole time it was pretending to be a bit of glass decorating Trader's walking stick."

"So it was the one?" Sierra asked Aubergine.

"It was," the dye mistress confirmed. She eyed the small witch wrapped in the blanket. "For some reason, Mae switched it for a fake after last night's simmer."

Wheat held out the crystal. "Here is the real stone. See the jagged edges? Mae had it hidden in her pouch."

Sierra took the stone, and turned it over to examine the damage on the underside.

"It was hiding in plain sight, just as you thought," Aubergine noted.

Sierra nodded. "Good, then. I've just come from the silversmith." She looked at Aubergine. "No amount of pleading will sway him. He will not see us at his shop."

"Too risky," Aubergine surmised. "There's no telling where Tasman is now or what lengths she'll take to get this stone."

"Periwinkle says he might meet us tomorrow evening at a tavern called Cask and Barrel."

"How I dislike pubs," Aubergine said. "Anything to do with sticky counters and bar stools, really."

Sierra gazed at each member of the small group. Flecks of gold stood out in her irises. Instinctively Warren and Skye shrank back, for as children they had learned to fear that look, the gaze they called her lion eyes. Upon whom was she about to inflict her stare, they wondered?

"Would you care to wait for the others?" she asked.

"No," Aubergine answered quickly. "We have the stone. Nothing else matters."

Sierra's unblinking stare moved around the group and came to rest on the small witch who shivered and cowered next to Warren. "Mae, the time has come to decide your fate," she said quietly.

Aubergine nodded grimly. As she seemed to grow taller and more imposing, the rest became increasingly aware that she was the Potluck Queen. The storm that brewed in her violet eyes matched the multi-colored shawl she wore across her shoulders. Her long swirls of gray-white hair cascaded across the wrap of purple, plum, and black, held at her throat by a silver pin inset with amethyst.

"I regret it has come to this," Aubergine told the crone, a hint of ice in her voice. "The necklace was always mine."

Mae cringed.

"There's no turning back now," Sierra warned the small witch. "Tell her," she urged Aubergine. "Say the words."

Aubergine's stare grew darker. "I challenge you," she told Mae coldly.

Whimpering, Mae fell to the floor, flailing in her blanket, as if an arrow had pierced her heart.

"Mae has the necklace?" Wheat asked in disbelief. "How can it be that Mae has the necklace?"

"She does not harbor the necklace, just a broken string of eleven stones." Aubergine's eyes never left the witch who twitched on the floor.

Sierra addressed the small form writhing in the blanket. "You are challenged. You know what happens next."

"What?" Skye wanted to know.

"Mae must prove the broken necklace is hers or offer it up," Wheat said as Mae began to cry softly. "If she is unwilling to do either, Aubergine can summon anything in her power to possess it once more. She can strip Mae of her witchery or even destroy her."

"If that is as Wheat says, give the stones back," Warren urged Mae, pulling her to a sitting position. He crouched before her on the floor and pulled the tangled blanket away from her face. "You have a whole cave full of crystals. I brought some with me in my rucksack. I'll go get them for you," he promised.

"Decide," Sierra told Mae. "Pick your fate before you no longer have a choice."

Slowly and tearfully Mae lifted the pouch from between her breasts and pulled the cord over her head. The sturdy strand of boiled leather that had circled her neck for so many years had worn a dark groove into her skin, like a tattoo. She worked the opening of the pouch wide enough to release the string of silver-set gems and upended the bag over Aubergine's veined hands. The necklace dropped into them with a gentle rattling sound.

"Maeeeeeee," she sobbed, clutching her naked neck. "Oh Mae," she shrieked, scratching at the dark line that encircled it. "Oh Mae, Mae, Mae!"

"What you're feeling now I've borne for the last twenty years," Aubergine said, not unkindly, as she fingered the string of stones.

She handed the linked crystals to Wheat, who laid the circlet on the dye table and clipped the lobster-claw clasp into the ring that awaited it. Then she took the damaged stone and fit it into the broken setting. All the witches caught their breath as the circle sparkled in the light. It was complete.

"It is the one," Smokey Jo said, her eyes shining.

Aubergine let out a deep breath, tears welling in the corners of her eyes. "I was beginning to think I would not live to see this day."

Sierra's nod was solemn. "We shall have the necklace whole."

"That was a wise choice," Warren said, patting Mae's shoulder. "And brave. That was very brave of you."

The distraught witch tore the worn fabric of her empty pouch into pieces, which she let drop to the floor.

Sierra came over to comfort her. "Mae, do you know what you've done? What you've done for us all?"

Tears streamed down Mae's face, and all she could do was nod. Even uttering *Mae* once more required effort beyond what she could muster now.

A FINE YARN

The air around Garth rippled and he dissolved into the darkness.

CHAPTER 4

Burning Questions

GARTH LED THE OTHER BOYS THROUGH the alley to the stables behind the Potluck dye shed. "Here they are," he said softly, unlatching the pony stall door. Clayton reached in to pat Shep's thick neck. Ross smiled with delight as Chuffer bent to nuzzle his small hand. "He wants treats," Garth said. "We can go into the summer kitchen and get them lumps of sugar. Lily won't mind."

"You ain't wary of them witches?" Ross asked. "Not one bit?"

Garth shrugged. "My mother is one of them. Turns out Skye is, too."

Clayton turned from the ponies to offer him a curious look. "Your sister?"

"She will be one day," Garth replied. "Witchery is a mother-daughter kind of thing."

Ross gestured toward the two-story timber frame dwelling that towered over the long dye shed across the alley. "You live with all them witches. In the same house?"

Garth nodded. "Want to see something hard to believe? That fence over there has a secret door."

"No!" Ross said.

Clayton peered at the solid wood enclosure. "Let's see."

Shutting the stable door behind them, Garth crossed the alley. His practiced hand released a hidden latch and two pieces of the plank fence swung inward, revealing a narrow opening. Wriggling through the dark passage sideways, Garth led the boys into the back of the dye shed. They stood among the sacks of fleece and roving, letting their eyes adjust to the gloom.

"Whoa," Ross whispered in awe as they made their way toward the dormant dye pot. "Is this where the witches cast their spells?"

Garth laughed. "No, it's just a pot where they dye yarn." Spying something on a bale of carded fiber, he went over to retrieve it. "I've been looking for this."

"A hat?" Clayton asked.

"My Potluck Hat," Garth said. "Wish I'd had it with me." He settled the watch cap on his head and turned up the brim. "Then I wouldn't have been rounded up into a rolling cage with the likes of you."

As he finished speaking, the air around him rippled and he dissolved into the darkness.

"Garth?" Clayton reached for him in the darkness.

"He's gone." An edge of fear crept into Ross's voice. "Clay, it's like what happened to Micah. What do we do now?"

Footfalls behind them made Clayton whirl around. "If you're a shape-shifter show yourself," he hissed, drawing his knife and pulling Ross close.

Before them, the dye shed door opened, casting a swath of light from the hallway, and Lilac Lily stuck her head into the room.

"I thought I heard noises in there," she said, opening the door wide. Beside her stood a large woman holding a shepherd's crook. Tucked under one arm, she carried a small spotted sheep.

"Boys, the dye shed is no place to fool around," the housemother cautioned. "Come wash up for supper."

The shepherdess nodded. "Garth get that hat off your head."

The air rippled and Garth materialized beside the other boys, his cap in his hand.

"That's a magic knit!" Ross pointed to the hat. "Does it work for everyone?"

Garth nodded. "They come in different colors dyed with different crystals depending on what they can do."

Clayton examined it. "What's this color called, pink?"

Garth shook his head. "Pass Unseen, 'cause that's what it lets you do."

"Except in front of witches, apparently," Clayton grunted.

"Well, that one," Garth admitted, heading into the hallway. "Winter Wheat is a shepherdess from the Western Highlands. Kenning fiber and animals is her talent."

"Was that big Wheat witch carrying a sheep?" Ross asked, hurrying to catch up as Garth let the savory scent of beef stew lead him by his nose toward the kitchen. "I never seen one with so many horns."

"His name is Tracks. He's lame." Garth explained. "You'll get used to him."

From the kitchen doorway, he spied the small round table near the cookstove, set with stew bowls and soupspoons. To one side, Smokey

Jo perched on a step stool, her knitted cowl bunched around her neck. She had pried an iron disc from the cooktop to feed bits of dried moss and pinecones into the flames.

Garth stepped to the sink to wash his hands in the basin. "We eating in here?" he asked the gnome.

"Just you boys." Smokey looked up, eyes dancing in her merry face wreathed in pink light. "Your brother, too."

Garth turned to his companions who stood frozen in the doorway. "Come wash up mates," he urged. "Lily won't allow you at table with grimy hands."

Ross elbowed Clayton in the side. "Look, she's so tiny," he whispered, his eyes trained on Smokey Jo. "No larger than me."

"Hush," the big boy said, watching Jo warily.

Oblivious, Smokey Jo donned a giant oven mitt to replace the hot circle of iron into the cooktop and hopped down from her stool. "We women are supping in the dining room," she announced, dragging the stool out of the way. "We've much to discuss." She marched past Garth to the fossick boys. "Introduce me to your friends."

"Excuse me, but are you a full-grown witch?" Ross blurted out.

"I am," the gnome said. "Are you a full-grown boy?"

Ross shook his head.

"I guessed as much," she said. "My name is Josephine, but you can call me Smokey Jo."

"This is Ross," Garth introduced. Pulling off her felted mitt, Smokey Jo shook the small boy's hand politely. "And Clayton. They're fossickers from Banebridge."

"A pleasure," Smokey beamed. "We love fossickers."

"I never met a witch smaller'n me." Ross muttered, standing on his toes to wash at the basin.

"You never met any witch before," Clayton said, watching Smokey Jo hustle out of the kitchen and down the hall.

Garth lifted the lid of the stew pot and sniffed the fragrant steam. "That's not true." He replaced the cover. "They're all around, you just don't notice them."

Before the others could protest, Lilac Lily swept in through the pantry that connected the kitchen to the dining hall. She handed Garth a soup ladle.

"Help yourselves," she invited, setting a crock of freshly churned butter and a breadboard of warm sourdough on the table. The boys didn't need to be asked twice.

"What do you mean I don't see witches all around me?" Ross said stubbornly, when the three of them sat before steaming bowls of stew. Rail-thin Clayton slurped his so quickly that Garth wondered how long it had been since he'd had a meal. "I would have noticed that big one with the pet sheep or that little one that plays with fire."

Garth slathered butter over a slice of bread and rolled his eyes toward the pantry. "Lily and Ratta, who bribed the guard to free us from the rolling cage, are witches."

"They don't just work here?" Ross questioned.

"They do work here and they're witches, too." Garth said.

"They look like kitchen help." Already finished with his first bowl, Clayton got up for more stew.

"'Cause that's what they want you to believe." Garth gave him an annoyed look. "Around here, they call it hiding in plain sight. And you don't need a hat for that."

Clayton sat and scraped his chair closer. "So what else can they do?"

"All different things." Garth bit into his bread. "Ratta speaks the tongue of the First Folk. Lily's special talent is she knows what you're thinking. Why do you suppose they were waiting for me at Fish-Eye Close?" He snorted. "Lily knew I went in there."

From his seat at the table, Ross had a good view of the hall beyond the kitchen doorway. Lifting his head from his soup bowl, he watched Lavender Mae trip down the passage toward the dye shed in an outlandish assortment of cast-off clothing, singing to herself. "Everyone here is witches!" He exclaimed.

"That remedy woman you sell fossicks to?" Garth eyed Clayton over his soup bowl. "Remember her?"

"She gave me powder for a toothache one time," Ross interrupted. "Trader liked her."

"Esmeralde is a witch?" Clayton asked.

Garth smiled. "The lady that has the greenhouse up above Banebridge? Indigo Rose? Her, too."

Chewing more slowly, Clayton frowned. "Prove it."

"I don't have to prove it," Garth set down his spoon and tipped his soup bowl to his lips. He wiped his mouth on his sleeve. "She's here right now, working on some kind of magical shawl for my mother. Both of them are."

Ross looked at Clayton. "Well that explains a lot, don't it?"

Clayton bent over his soup bowl once more, saying nothing.

From outside, a door opened and Warren appeared in his Highlander outfit. He paused in the vestibule of the summer kitchen to kick mud from his boots.

Garth turned his head. "There's my brother. Warren, come eat!"

"He's a shepherd?" Clayton's eyes narrowed as he watched the young man in sheepskin trekkers shed his oiled mantle. "You said he was a soldier."

"He was a scout for the Northland Guard," Garth countered. "The best sledder in all the lands. But now he's a deserter with a price on his head."

"More wanted than witches?" Ross asked.

"Mayhap." Garth pointed his soupspoon at his brother's faded brimmed hat. "That's not his garb. It's just a disguise."

"Something smells good." Warren entered the kitchen and bent over the basin to wash up. Wiping his hands on a dishcloth, he regarded the ragtag boys. "You must be Garth's fossick friends. I heard you escaped the rolling cage."

Ross nodded eagerly. "We came here lookin' for Trader. But then a walleyed woman caught us. Your Lily witch paid our way out."

"Would I have been so lucky," Warren said ruefully, helping himself to a bowl of beef stew. He sat beside his brother, sizing up Clayton. "Well met."

"The same," the other boy replied quietly.

Warren tasted his stew before peppering it. "Whatever brings you to Bordertown, I'd leave," he advised, stirring and then tasting again. "A boy your age and size is ripe for Lowland fodder." He lifted a hearty spoonful to his lips. "There might not be any Lily next time."

"We came cuz of Trader and Micah," Ross piped up.

"You'll find no trace of Trader here." Warren said. "The fossicker's gone." He turned to his brother. "Who's Micah?"

"Just another fossick boy," Garth said. "He was with them that rescued me from the Rill after the Teardrop spilled."

"Micah's gone, too," Ross gave them an anxious look. "He unsuppeared, just like when you put on your unseen hat."

"Don't you mean disappeared?" Warren asked the little boy, hiding a smile.

Clayton let his spoon clatter into his empty bowl. "No he means unsuppeared." His voice had a hard edge. "It's what happens when a shape-shifter takes you over. When it's done with your body, you're gone and all traces of you are gone, like you were never born."

"A shape-shifter inhabited your friend? " Warren stopped eating. "How long had you known this Micah?"

"Not long," Clayton admitted. "Boys come and go."

Ross nodded vigorously. "For Micah, it was all of a sudden. His bedroll, his grub, his fossicks—poof, unsuppeared. And in his place was the Bad, Bad Man."

"The Bad Man?" Garth questioned, recalling the kitchen girl who had turned into the Dark Queen just a few nights before. He caught his brother's eye. "What kind of bad man?"

"A crazy man," Ross remembered. "A burning man.

"We were camped the Dell in our usual spot when all of a sudden Micah started turning into someone else." Clayton glanced at Warren. "A big man with watery-blue eyes. 'Bout as tall as you. He kept asking about a lost stone and a walking stick and a girl. We thought maybe he meant your sister."

Garth nudged Warren. "Sounds like Trader."

"We didn't know who he meant," Ross broke in. "Fire started coming from his fingers. He burnt up our camp, lookin' for this stone. We couldn't stop him. All the boys 'cept for me 'n' Clay ran for the High Rocks."

"We figured Trader was in trouble," Clayton admitted. "So we came here."

Ross's chin began to tremble. "Trader's not unsuppeared, is he?"

"No," Garth looked at Warren. "At least I don't think so."

The two frightened boys sat in silence. "Trader's been kidnapped." Warren said at last. "Trader's not who you think."

"Nobody is!" Ross pushed his soup bowl away. Twin tears tracked down his cheeks and he poked Clayton in the arm. "You better tell them everything," he cried.

"Trader always knew that evil folk sought him," Clayton told the brothers. "Southerners. Folk with fire. That's why he kept us moving from hideout to hideout, fossicking the riverbeds."

"Lots of Middleland boys disappear into fossick camps to wait out the war." Warren shrugged. "We're farmers, not soldiers. Peaceful folk, who don't like to fight. Lowlanders are different. They're brought up to be trueborn raiders. When they invade from the South, they wield fire as a weapon—burn out as part of battle." He eyed Clayton closely. "Tell me something I don't know."

"These folk aren't Lowlanders. They look like Middlefolk, except they're pure evil." Clayton said. "And Trader wasn't fossicking for truck to sell so we could put beef and carrots in the stew pot. We did all that. He was looking for something. Something First Folk fierce."

"What?" Warren interrupted. "Magic crystals? A relic, perhaps?"

Clayton shook his head. "I don't know. He just said that these evil ones would do anything they could to capture him." He leveled his eyes at Warren. "And if they came with fire, we should go to the ice."

"We figured he meant Bordertown." Ross gave Warren an anxious look. "It's the closest city to the glacier, ain't it?"

Warren started to get up. "Lily should hear this."

"Sit back down," Lily said from the shadows, startling him. From the pantry, the remnants of the Twelve had somehow filed into the kitchen unnoticed. They stood around the dim edges of the room.

Clayton's breath caught in his throat as he recognized Esmeralde and Indigo and Skye, who somehow looked older than her years.

"We heard everything." Ratta said.

"Skells." Ross wiped his runny nose on his shirt. "Trader said to find the sundered Skell."

"Skells is just a card game," Garth countered.

But as soon as he'd said it, he wished he'd kept silent; for he saw his mother suppressing an ironic smile and Aubergine's eyes grow dark and thoughtful.

In Aubergine's private chambers,
the tapers burned long into the night.

CHAPTER 5

Secret Counsel

IN AUBERGINE'S PRIVATE CHAMBERS, THE TAPERS burned long into the night. Melted wax trickled down the candlesticks to drip on the floor. Unmindful, the three witches sat around the low tambourine table in quiet conversation.

"Personally, I believe those fossick boys know more than they're willing to tell," Sierra said. Flecks of gold gleamed in her irises as she turned her tawny gaze inward. "When I search the horizon, I can pick out their path to Bordertown in my mind's eye. The route meanders."

"They were frightened," Lily offered. She took a sip of the headache medicine Esmeralde had prepared for her earlier and swallowed with a grimace before setting the goblet on the round table top. "And now homeless. They witnessed one of their own destroyed."

Aubergine rose to softly close the door that adjoined her counsel room to the bedroom suite beyond. In a small alcove near the foot of her carved oak bedstead, Smokey Jo lay on the same threadbare settee she had slept on as a child, snoring softly beneath a knitted throw.

"I originally supposed that after Tasman left the simmer, she would waste no time journeying to the Northland Glacier, intending to find the Lost Caves well ahead of us," she mused, returning to her old velvet rocker before the highly wrought table. She picked up her knitting.

Sierra gazed at the pair of beaded wristlets, complete but for sewing the seams. According to ancient legend, a circle of crystals worked into wrister designs warded the wearer from unseen danger. Aubergine had knit a ring of raw garnets into her set of wrist guards. The plum-colored stones shone dully in the light.

"I had hoped that Tasman might fool herself into thinking she could locate the secret entrance to the Crystal Caves and catch Mamie unaware, which would allow her enough time to set a trap for the rest of us." Over the top of her half-moon spectacles, Aubergine eyed Lily expectantly. "Now I believe otherwise."

Lilac Lily sighed. "Ask any question you wish. Just remember that during my last encounter with Tasman, I was unable to recognize her masquerading as a scullery maid." Lily paused to add a measure of cordial to her medicine in hopes of masking the bitter taste. "She has deluded me many times. I may be able to perceive her intentions no better than you."

Aubergine laid her needlework beside an hourglass partially filled with amethyst shards, a miniature of the one that had smashed to the dye-shed floor just nights before.

Sierra glanced at the dark vessel on the table between them. "Have you been able to coax aught from within?"

"The glass remains dormant. Since Mamie assumed the Guardianship, it has been impossible to discern whether Lowlanders have overrun the caves or Tasman lays hidden in wait." Aubergine removed her glasses. "I find it maddening."

"What about Ratta?" Lily persisted. "Has she heard anything?"

"According to her, there's been no Mind Speak, no visions, nothing." Aubergine paused. "I would ask this—and either of you feel free to answer. Given a preference, would Tasman travel south to the safety of the Lowlands to muster her forces? Or would she circle the Northland Glacier with Little Teal in tow and just a handful of invaders, planning to enter the Crystal Caves through the Blind Side to surprise Mamie before we arrive?"

"Tasman has little power to thwart us without the lost stone, and by now she must realize that Trader doesn't have it. She might choose neither option," Sierra said simply.

"Or maybe she'd pick both." Lily sipped the tincture she had laced with cordial and eyed Sierra thoughtfully. "We may have been wrong regarding Tasman. To be everywhere and nowhere she must have an ally, perhaps this so-called Bad, Bad Man the fossick boys mentioned. While her armies regroup, it could very well be that the Dark Queen is in the Middlelands, preparing to rout us one by one, beginning with burning down Trader's fossick camps."

"Out of spite?" Aubergine prodded gently. "For revenge? Or merely to acquire the stone?"

"For those reasons and possibly more we aren't privy to," Lily answered. "Sierra, you misunderstand the fossickers. They are not unwilling to talk. Those two just don't know how to describe what they can't understand. Unlike us, they were born into a world bereft of magic."

"The smaller boy Ross did mention the Skells," Sierra recalled.

"Are we to assume he meant the cards from the yarns of old?" Aubergine asked.

"Perhaps," Sierra murmured, turning her vision inward. She gave the other witches a quick glance. "That is one story I recollect clearly."

"Enlighten us," Lily urged her.

"The original set of Skells weren't playing cards at all," Sierra began. "They were ballots carved from thin layers of horn, accompanied by a set of bone dice. Each ruling class First Folk family possessed a card, which was a symbol of the power and wealth their district held. One card depicted the twined rivers, another the lidded eye, there was fire and of course, ice—perhaps a dozen or more cards in all—depending upon how many families were politically active at the time and which districts they controlled. Each card cast an equal vote. Ties between issues especially important to the popular vote were broken by an additional measure of casting dice during private counsel. The higher the number, the more credence a card possessed, thus the more compelling that family's argument."

The ancients gambled to make law," Lily observed. "Interesting."

"They did not perceive it that way," Sierra countered. "Casting Skells was not the game of chance we see in the cards these days. In First Folk times, it was how men wielded magic."

"The Magic of Men," Aubergine mused. "How I dread the day that magic awakens once more."

"The time is upon us," Sierra murmured. "The Snowflake Watch Cap Mae knit for Warren will not quell the Kindle of First Folk Fire. I'll not watch my son die."

"I know you believe your yarns, truly. But how can this rumor of Skells be true?" Lily asked Sierra. "It is said that the few cards not destroyed when the world fell to ice were confiscated long ago."

"By whom?" Aubergine ruminated. "More men?"

"The Glacier Born." Sierra nodded. "Supposedly the North holds the cards now."

"Clansmen of the North may have recovered some of the sacred relics." Aubergine groped under the tambourine table for the sewing basket of knitting notions she kept there. Beneath a set of carved ring markers lay a felted change purse. Gently, she shook it out onto the tabletop. "Over the past twenty years, I've collected one or two of my own."

As Sierra leaned over to examine the ballots, her breath caught in her throat. With reverence, she smoothed her hand over a fragile rectangle of thin horn engraved with faded ink. "The lidded eye of the first sun."

The second card had been cut on the diagonal long ago, but Sierra could make out the symbol of a crystal incised on the triangular piece that remained. "The Crystal Caves." She gazed at Aubergine in wonder. "Where did you get these?"

"The whole Skell I bought from a fossicker wading the Trickle," Aubergine explained.

"It belonged to the family governing the ancient city's oldest district," Sierra said. "Called House of the First Sun."

"The other fragment is a half Skell in my possession since I was a girl." Aubergine rested her eyes on Sierra. "I believe it is the one all seek."

"Part of it anyway." Sierra held the etched triangle aloft. "This Skell belonged to the most powerful family of all, House Crystal Keep, whose First Folk warded the magical crystals." She fingered the edge of the splintered card. "The city elders halved it after warring members of House Keep disagreed so vehemently over who should wield the crystals that the family divided into two opposing groups. The split ballot caused a powerful rift, for neither side was able to cast a full vote in the city council without consent of the other. Unable to see eye to eye, Crystal Keep entered a long, slow decline, which eventually led to the death of the first sun." Sierra's face flushed with excitement. "The

First Folk of House Keep alone held the keys to unlock the secrets of old."

"If the voices Mamie hears in her head ring true, the ancients may still harbor such mysteries," Aubergine murmured.

"Are you saying that this sliver of horn may possibly gain us access to the Crystal Caves?" Lily asked.

Aubergine nodded. "Exactly."

"But part of it is missing," she protested.

"A problem," Sierra admitted, handing the whole Skell back to Aubergine. Holding the half horn in the candlelight, she turned the card over to scan the other side for clues. Finding nothing, she passed it back. "Is it likely that Trader possessed a Skell, a companion to this one, perchance?"

"Perhaps." Aubergine returned the cards to her felted purse, which she stored beneath the notions in her sewing basket once more. "What do you think, Lily?"

"Trader may not have owned a card, but she probably saw one somewhere in her travels through this city." Lily answered. "It might be the real reason the fossick boys came to Bordertown."

"I see another cause for their journey," Sierra said with faraway eyes. "When I survey the landscape of the lower valleys I glimpse a haze of gray smoke hovering over the Middlelands." She focused her gaze on Lily. "What's happening down there?"

Lily pursed her lips and gave Sierra a troubled look.

"I would know," Sierra said.

Aubergine nodded. "As would I."

Lily put a hand to her pounding head and heaved a sigh. "When the fossickers fled to Esmeralde's hoping to find some magical remedy or medicinal spell to save their friend, they witnessed her cottage burned to the ground with the blackened timbers still smoking." She paused. "In terror, they trekked through the dark Copse, in search of what they thought would be the safe shelter of Indigo's stone cottage and the healing herbs of her garden above Banebridge. When they reached her farmstead in the foothills, Indigo's plants were swarming with locusts. In what seemed like minutes, everything was eaten and only flats of dirt remained under the empty glass shell of her greenhouse."

Aubergine offered them a grim look. "Tasman will seek us out one by one to destroy any safe haven we have in search of the stone."

"She will neither burn me out, nor infest me with pests," Sierra said bitterly. "My Lavender Rill Farm washed away during the rains this spring thaw."

"Surely you know otherwise." Aubergine's eyes grew violet. "When the Teardrop spilled, the flood was no natural disaster. Tasman plagued you first."

"I discerned an aura of dark magic rolling off the water as the prison wagon took me up the military road," Sierra whispered.

Lily's eyes glistened. "We'll all be bereft of hearth and home before long. My sister's boardinghouse in Middlemarch has hosted guests for three generations. How will Lorna forgive me when it's gone?"

"Your dread is distant and perhaps unfounded." Aubergine reached behind her for the silver tinderbox she had shelved among leather-bound books and odd balls of yarn. Until last week the small tin had housed cold-fire crystals that she and Smokey Jo released into the sky. Her arthritic fingers found the hidden spring inside the metal container and its lid came off whole. "Do not forget we harbor all twelve jewels."

Sierra and Lily gazed at the string of eleven sparkling amethysts set in silver, nestled around the one jagged stone. Even damaged, the ring of deep-violet crystals was splendid to behold.

"Even if the silversmith Periwinkle meets us at the Cask and Barrel as agreed, and consents to remake the necklace into the unbroken circle it once was, something may easily go awry." Sierra cautioned.

"Venturing outside the Potluck with all twelve stones is risky," Lily agreed, her eyes on the raw gems. "There will be countless opportunities for foul play."

"As usual, we shall be hiding in plain sight." Aubergine replaced the lid on the silver box. It locked into place with an audible click. "Only this time, we will be concealing the most powerful jewels in all the lands, but unable to draw upon their strength until the necklace is complete. That is an irony I do not relish."

"If we do relinquish the crystals to Periwinkle, how can we be certain he possesses the skill to repair the broken one?" Sierra asked her consorts. "What if his offer is false, a mere ruse to allow Tasman to possess the necklace once more?" She frowned at Lily. "Has anyone said anything?"

Lily rubbed her temples. Esmeralde's medicine had hardly helped. It seemed nothing could quell her headache. "Bribes have changed hands over promises whispered in the dark," she said finally. "Plans have been made, a trap laid and mercenaries on both sides wait in ambush. Tasman's eyes and ears are everywhere."

"Your prediction is no less than I expected," Aubergine said, brushing aside Lily's warning with a wave of her hand. "Once we have the necklace, I propose we split our forces, in order to catch Tasman unaware. Some of us shall journey to the glacier, for that is what the Dark Queen anticipates. We others join forces with the North." She fixed her gaze on Sierra. "I believe you know why."

"The Bad, Bad Man," Sierra murmured, unable to meet her violet eyes.

As Lily opened her mouth to speak, Sierra held up a hand to shield herself from the words.

"Lily you don't have to say anything," Aubergine said quietly. "She knows."

"I can't bear to hear it," Sierra gave Lily a bitter look. "You lament that Tasman has tricked you time and again. Considering what has come to pass, I am the bigger fool. My married life was nothing but a lie!"

"How long have you suspected?" Lily asked gently.

Sierra's voice dropped to a barely audible whisper. "I've known in my heart since I left the Potluck. My children, do they realize . . . ?"

Lily nodded. Sierra's face filled with tears.

"Now is no time for regret," Aubergine declared. "Recall that it was I whom Tasman duped first. I willingly let her don the necklace."

"And I sacrificed Teal by placing her in Tasman's path, little good that did," Lily added. "I allowed that traitor to destroy one of our own."

"I would have done the same to Lavender Mae yesterday to possess Teal's lost stone once more." Aubergine placed a veined hand on Sierra's arm. "No regrets."

Sierra lifted her reddened eyes. "It may be time for my eldest son to test his fate."

"It may be time for us all," Aubergine said with finality. "The Fire and Ice shawl is nearly finished, but you shall not wear it. As Tasman was present at the simmer, we can assume she is well aware of our plans."

"The Dark Queen expects to confront Sierra at the glacier," Lily reminded Aubergine. "She will do anything within her power to force her to assume the Guardianship prematurely and send Mamie to the Land of Dreams."

"An efficient way to rid herself of Mamie and imprison Sierra within the glacier, affording her two less witches to contend with." Aubergine gave Sierra a judicious nod. "Skye must go in your stead so that we can remain behind to see what can be done to stop the Bad, Bad Man."

"My pleasure," Sierra said with resolve. "Lest we forget, there is one other small advantage. Warren returned this evening to report that the Northland Guard is massing its armies to march to the Out Crops, as you predicted," she told Aubergine. "With a war to be won, they need not bother with knitting witches."

"What makes you believe that Tasman will be lying in wait within the glacier? She will risk no such thing unless she has the upper hand," Lily warned.

"She will think she possesses the necklace whole, which shall afford her false power enough," Aubergine said mildly. "We witches shall blithely continue our expedition to the Crystal Caves as if we know nothing."

"Periwinkle won't meet us until tomorrow night, and even that may be a trap," Sierra said gravely.

"This time we shall set the trap," Aubergine promised. Her eyes darkened to deepest violet. "And the fool will be Tasman."

SECRET COUNSEL

One of the guards thrust the bedraggled girl forward.

CHAPTER 6

Stones and Skells

SMUDGE FIRES SMOLDERED IN THE LOWLAND encampment hidden in a frozen river valley far to the northwest of Middlemarch. Foot soldiers clad in the crimson and burnished-gold raiment of the Dark Queen's Color Guard moved noiselessly among the quiet clusters of army tents and cook fires as the temperatures began to drop moderately on this cool spring evening.

From the privacy of her well-guarded pavilion in the center of the Lowland stronghold, Tasman lounged on a few of her favorite knitted pillows clustered among those scattered across the rich carpet woven of crystal-dyed fibers, whose magical colors sparkled in the light. Propping her elbow on a garter-stitch bolster, she regarded her brother by lamplight. "I must have the lost stone," she said, not for the first time.

Leaning toward her from cushions piled on the lavish rug, Kendrick shook his head regretfully. "Your fossick girl does not harbor the amethyst, that is clear."

"No," she agreed, her green eyes glittering in the ambient glow. Behind her hung elaborate tapestries obscuring four men at arms, poised to defend each corner of the tent, should intruders infiltrate the camp. "Nor does it appear that she knows where to find it."

"As do none of the Twelve?" He sipped from his goblet before settling back comfortably. "Not even the Keeper of the Stones, your own trusted Lavender Mae?"

"Ancient voices have reduced her from my willing servant to a crazy crone," Tasman said in disgust. "I've looked through the portals of the enchanted gold and silver you planted in the Middlelands and they show me plenty, but nothing of the amethyst's whereabouts."

"How could that be?" Her brother protested. "I scattered your spy coins throughout Banebridge, Coventry, Middlemarch, and even Woolen Woods."

"The only one of the Twelve tempted to deal for one sliver of my newly minted money was Esmeralde at the Trading Post in Banebridge," Tasman said. "She traded the shop keep for a piece some weeks ago, leaving him with naught but a set of spectacles."

"I tried to get your red-haired wench to accept a dark coin at a stagecoach inn near Coventry," Kendrick remembered. "When I paid for her meal and left your crystal-clad change, she threw it in my face."

"As she would." Tasman gave the slightest of nods. "A murky haze floats over the likeness stamped into each piece of precious metal."

"It can't be helped." Kendrick smiled at his sister. "It is your own visage after all."

"Not all of them recognize my silhouette," she murmured. "But a witch of Ratta's talent would be able to sense the aura of dark magic that smolders there."

"Like smoke," Kendrick said with pride. "My sister the Dark Queen burns."

Tasman hid a smile. To some, Kendrick was known as the Lord of the Lowlands, to others Northland's Bane. To her, he was a Kindred Spirit, but her brother had not always treated her with such deference.

As children they had scarcely known each other. Although birthed hours apart, she and Kendrick bore no resemblance, for they were half siblings with different mothers. Like her matriarchal ancestors, Tasman stood tall and slim, her skin a light sheen of olive. Her folk had fought their way across the windswept seas by ship from the craggy isles far beyond the Fisheries of the Far East. Tasman's silky dark hair framed clear green eyes fringed with black lashes, her irises like icebergs floating at sea and just as cold. Once a thin gawky girl, she had grown into a wickedly regal woman with an arresting appearance of startling beauty. In contrast, Kendrick had inherited the fair complexion of the Northlands combined with the easygoing mien of the Middleland folk who plied their trade along the border. His pale coloring and blue eyes bespoke his heritage.

The inexplicable bond between them was the unsullied blood of their wayfaring father, Maddig Hoar, Hed Clansman of the Glacier Born who dwelt in the Out Crops at the northern most tip of the glacier. Like other Men of Ice who dared claim direct lineage from the First Folk, Hed Maddig ranged far from the icy caverns of his homeland, intent on spreading his seed, hoping to rekindle male magic once more.

According to ancient legend, the ability to control the natural world passed from father to son like a smoking ember waiting to catch. Some Clans assumed their boys were born with the spark, while others conjectured that the coal blazed when youths came of age. In truth no one knew what force fueled the fire.

All agreed that Glacier Born carried within vestiges of the Magic of Men, remnants of mystical forces now dormant. The trueborn boasted that such magic would be awakened by a male child known as The One who bore the spark of First Folk Fire. When it burst to flame in a ceremony known as the Kindling held in the sacred Caves of Blue Ice, he would brave fire within the walls of ice, gifted with the power to rule nature as the ancients had. For generations, Clansmen who dwelt within the glacier had been trying to produce such progeny, but no Glacier Born youth had survived his Kindle.

Ignored, a Glacier Born girl child had to discover what trace amount of dormant magic she might inherit on her own. Why else would Tasman have apprenticed at Potluck Yarn so long ago? She hardly thought of her half-brother Kendrick until the last year of her training. One night, high in her attic room, her almost-twin visited her in a dream.

Until that time, Tasman had proven a quick student who easily mastered the simple witchery taught at school. She could mix her crystals into dyes fit for animal fiber whose magical shades permitted the wearer to be serene or pass unseen. Her knitted garments grew or shrunk to fit as needed; her bags and packs were no heavier full than empty. She possessed no physical signs of magic like Winter Wheat's cabochon beetles encased in jeweled amber coffins, or Esmeralde's Possibles Bag filled with poxes, plagues, and poisons, for her budding talents smoldered within. Even as young girl, she mastered small acts of shape-shifting, and succeeded in eluding all by disappearing into the twirl of her cloak to vanish from the room, transported outside.

The only other novice as clever was Second Sight Sierra as she was called—everyone's friend and Aubergine's favorite. The tall Northland maid was gifted with fateful eyes, fearless in the face of the unknown. Casting her far-flung gaze over the horizon, she recognized the landscape of the future, although she dared not tempt destiny. Sierra was as dangerous as an unseen lioness on a bluff overlooking fair game, calmly awaiting her time to strike. Her serenity in the face of such rare knowledge infuriated Tasman.

On that night long ago when Tasman felt Kendrick seeking her, she was lying abed restlessly dreaming, scheming how to usurp Sierra's place in the Circle of Twelve, so that she could assume Aubergine's mantle one day.

She felt her brother's charmed touch before she woke. In her reverie he suddenly appeared, not the half-blood boy she had left behind but an enchanted youth lit from within. In her dream he hunted her like lost treasure, for he sought something she unknowingly possessed. His glow was the bright flare of unrealized power, the Magic of Men. The innocent spark inside had Kindled into first fire at last but far too late, for now he was a full-grown man. The Hed Clansmen had already forsaken him to move on to other boys, younger and more promising.

Entranced, Tasman watched smoke seep from her brother's nostrils as he lay abandoned on an altar in the Caves of Blue Ice. With nothing to nourish it, the magical spark in his chest began to falter. Kendrick gasped for breath, to no avail. Fire consumed what air he inhaled, leaving him to suffocate on the dying flames that fumed within. This is what must have befallen the other boys who failed to survive, Tasman realized. They choked on their own smoke, and died.

As her almost-twin reached out in a final desperate attempt to breathe, Tasman took his hand. The jolt threw them both to the ground. Freed at last, fire bolts burst from her brother's fingers, electrifying them both. Within the raging inferno, Tasman clung to Kendrick, unsure if he lived or died while flames danced around them. The fantastical fire subsided as quickly as it had started. Soon it was spent. Tasman disengaged herself from her brother's blackened body, curled against the flames. She watched him slowly stir, gazing at her with grateful eyes. Wordlessly, he rose to step safely from the ashes, reborn, his face ruddy and bright, and his blue eyes blazing with eternal flame. Tasman smiled at the man who now stood before her. Her half brother and almost-twin had become the first of his name to harbor the Magic of Men. He was The One.

Tasman woke with a start in her cold attic room, the dream dissipated along with the vision of Kendrick. Alone in the dark, she rubbed her blistered hand and coughed, bringing up the taste of ashes in the back of her throat. She touched her hand to her breastbone, where something smoldered. The constant burn was rekindled magic, which her brother's touch had roused unbidden. The mystical magic dead these thousand years was awakened within her now, the same as him. How would they feed such forces, she wondered? How could they keep the living flames from consuming them both? For Kendrick was no longer her sibling, but her Kindred Spirit now. They were bound to each other, two halves to a whole.

What she felt was no practical magic or simple trick taught at Potluck Yarn but the blaze of First Folk Fire once wielded by men. The fact that she sensed it made Tasman wonder if their women possessed something key to unlocking the crystal power. If so, learning how to channel such potential would be tricky and time consuming. She and her Kindred Spirit might have to wrest the secrets of old from the crystals hidden within the legendary Lost Caves, the tale a dusty yarn her aged instructor, Mamie Verde had retold until she could speak no more.

As dawn crept through the attic, Tasman developed her plan. First she must prevent Sierra's rise to power, then she must steal Aubergine's necklace and flee to the southern wastelands, where no one would dare to follow. Although it was probable that Aubergine's circle of linked amethysts possessed weaker magic than the twined forces she and Kendrick fostered, the circle of stones symbolized the Twelve's united strength. She would break them apart, stone by stone. Questing to master First Folk Fire himself, Kendrick was certain to come to her aid.

   Soon after the revelation of their shared dream, Tasman coaxed Kendrick to Potluck Yarn to sway Sierra from her destiny. She introduced her Kindred Spirit as Kendrick Blue, for his captivating eyes were the color of summer sky. Blazing with the cold flame that burned within, Kendrick mesmerized Sierra. Under his spell she abandoned her second sight for a moment, but it was all he needed. Sierra was blinded. By love, she thought.

The Dark Queen gazed over her wine glass at her handsome brother, reclining on the cushions opposite. It had been twenty years. As promised, he had taken Sierra far from Potluck Yarn and distracted her with farm and family. In return, Tasman had broken the necklace and stolen its pieces save one lost stone and gone south to practice her lore in the Lowlands. Reunited at last, she and her Kindred Spirit would conquer all. As she had never borne children, the fire within her was pure and strong. Not so for Kendrick, who had spilt his seed carelessly.

Tasman had little concern for his two sons, or whether they harbored the ember. The boys were pawns destined to die in the war or choke on their smoke. What disquieted her was his daughter, who perchance inherited a heady combination of ancient magic from her father as well as Sierra's fateful eyes. Tasman smiled, showing teeth in a way that made Kendrick chuckle. She would dispatch the girl, leaving him to decide the boys' fate. Her Kindred Spirit had not failed her yet.

From without, the tent flap opened and a crimson-clad soldier parted the privacy curtains surrounding their carpeted enclosure. A series of eye movements between the queen and her guardsman ensued. After watching their exchange for a few moments, Kendrick closed his eyes in boredom. Not long after, the burnished Lowlander withdrew with a silent bow.

"I have never understood how you learned their language." He rubbed his brow. "All that squinting and flinching gives me a headache."

"Southern speech is one without words." Tasman sighed. "But not the one I had wished to master."

The curtains parted again and kitchen maids entered bearing covered dishes from which the scent of curried potatoes and spiced meat wafted.

"Ahhh," Kendrick breathed deeply as the copper tureens were arranged on a tablecloth between them.

"One of the reasons I fled south, was that I hoped Lowland folk understood the unheard voices of the ancients as Ratta and Mamie Verde did." Tasman lifted the lids of the steaming bowls. "They do not."

"You had other reasons?" Kendrick asked. "From what I've witnessed, the South is naught but an arid waste of shifting sand."

"It was a land leached to dust even then," Tasman admitted. "I had to see it." Satisfied with the food, she passed him an empty plate. "After I arrived, I found I couldn't leave." She put a palm to his breastbone. "It was the burn inside, tethering me to a sun-scorched land fraught with wildfire and heat lightning. Don't you feel it?"

"No I don't." Ignoring her touch, Kendrick helped himself to hot curry and mild yogurt seasoned with cracked peppercorns.

"Liar." Tasman withdrew her hand. "It was you who Kindled the fire inside me."

"I try not to ponder it," Kendrick said brusquely. Offering her the serving spoon, he changed the subject. "I meant to ask, what happened to your spy coin I tossed into the hat of that Middlemarch minstrel? Did it yield nothing?"

"That smoky silver has shown me plenty." Tasman conceded. "Your Miles from Nowhere will be at the Cask and Barrel this week entertaining all with his Woolgathering Tales." She ladled a few dollops of potato and yogurt from the serving dishes onto her plate. "How the Twelve became Twelve. Where did he learn such stories, I wonder?"

"You do not care to know," Kendrick muttered with averted eyes.

"My informants report that Aubergine and Sierra plan to attend." Taking a bite of curry, Tasman licked the yogurt from her spoon. "Apparently they have arranged a private meeting with a certain jeweler from Artisan's Hand in hopes of having their necklace made whole."

Kendrick chewed steadily, his eyes watering from the hot southern spice. "Perhaps they found the lost crystal."

Tasman laid aside her plate. "Anything's possible, I suppose."

Kendrick let out a satisfied belch. "Whatever the case, we can't allow them to have their string of stones joined with another jewel just yet."

"Just so," Tasman agreed. "For then they would learn their necklace is fake."

From the shadows, a servant appeared to refill their goblets with watered wine.

"Where is the real necklace now?"

She glanced at him with cool green eyes. "Safe."

"Do not dodge me if it is the ancient crystals you protect," Kendrick warned. "Whenever we shape-shift, our worldly possessions are vulnerable. Any one of the Twelve could have snatched the string of stones unchallenged whilst you masqueraded as a kitchen wench. It's foolhardy to put such powerful gems in needless danger."

Tasman eyed him steadily over the rim of her goblet. "I said the stones are safe."

Her brother glared at her but said nothing. Instead he took a round of bread from the basket and began sopping up the curry and yogurt left on his plate.

Watching him eat, Tasman took a sip of wine. "Here is something I would have you know—Esmeralde and Indigo Rose have knit a crystal-dyed shawl patterned with a Fire and Ice motif designed to protect its wearer from the voices of the ancients. It is crafted to spare Sierra from Mae's affliction should she attempt to pass through the ancient city to the First Folk tombs uninvited."

"Don't the witches believe that Mamie Verde will guide them safely to the graveyard?" Kendrick asked.

The Dark Queen laughed harshly. "If that is their plan, they are sadly mistaken."

"I understood that Aubergine meant to catch us unaware by ensuring her group reaches the Lost Caves first." Kendrick said.

"As Guardian, Mamie must live by ancient rule, unable to honor any prior allegiance," Tasman explained. "Reborn, she may recall no one, not even her faithful servant Ratta. She is a mere sentinel of the dead, charged to protect and serve until Sierra takes her place. When your wife arrives, my hope is that Mamie will trap her there."

"'Tis lonely life." Kendrick ventured.

Tasman reached for him. "One Sierra shall taste soon," she promised.

As their fingers interlaced, the ancient embers fuming within Tasman caught and roared to life. Heat flushed her cheeks as flames of desire danced in her breast. Feeling the hot tendrils erupt from their union to leap up his arm was more than Kendrick could bear. With a look of alarm, he shook her hand off. "Enough!"

"For now," she conceded.

Kendrick watched with relief as hot blood began to drain from her face. One day he would give in to Tasman's keen lust for fire, for he would be unable to quell her burning need or curb his raging desire. He feared the inferno could kill them both, and he planned to postpone that terrible day until he was certain he would be the only survivor.

Tasman waited until the blaze inside her subsided to a manageable heap of glowing coals before she spoke. "Esmeralde's coin has shown me a few curious turns of events. Several of Little Teal's fossick boys have found their way to Potluck Yarn."

"That's odd." Kendrick frowned. "What would fossickers want with knitting witches, other than a few coppers for the dye crystals and odd shards they collect?"

"They seek ransom for our little fossick girl, a boy they know as Trader," Tasman purred, deciding to omit she had recognized his youngest son among the group.

"They would trade the lost stone?"

"Something else." Her green eyes sparkled. "They search for an ancient Skell Little Teal has knowledge of, supposedly."

"Which one? I thought we decided all the Skells were gone."

Tasman smiled. "Half of the true parchment of House Crystal Keep."

Kendrick was speechless. "Could it be?" he finally stammered out. "For twenty years we've chased rumors of mythic stones and Skells. Such stories were nothing more than tall tales of cracked crystal and ripped cards to me."

"Yarns of old are spun from the truth," Tasman said soberly. "Lest we forget, the ancient world froze to ice over the misuse of broken stones and tattered parchments."

"Fossickers crave finding odd bits." Kendrick nodded slowly. "This ragtag group could be hunting a Skell of old that still survives."

"My spying eyes have shown me the Skell is secreted within a deck of common playing cards in the same rooming house where our fatherless captive was born." Tasman pursed her lips. "The fossickers would trade it for Little Teal's freedom."

"Why not just take it?"

Tasman's eyes arched. "Unchallenged? I think not."

Her brother looked at her in earnest. "Is a broken Skell worth the trade?"

"Not in place of the stone, but fortune may bring us both." Tasman alerted the guard who waited just behind the inner drapes with a flick of her eyes, before turning to her brother. "I would have the card."

"What of the other half?" Kendrick asked.

"Don't trouble yourself with its twin," she said sharply.

His look was cynical. "Let me guess. It's safe."

Before she could reply, the tent flap opened and the curtain was thrust aside to reveal Trader held fast.

"Little Teal, how pleasant to enjoy your company once more," Tasman mocked. "Join us, we're just finishing dinner." One of the guards thrust the bedraggled girl forward to kneel with her hands bound behind her. It was then that Kendrick also noticed the fetters that joined her small booted feet. "I trust you have not eaten?" the Dark Queen asked with feigned politeness.

"I have had no food since yesterday," Trader said carefully with downcast eyes. "You know it as well as I do."

"Dear brother, untie the poor girl's hands so that she may sup," Tasman scolded Kendrick in feigned disgust. She picked the serving spoon from remains of lukewarm beef and potato curry that had cooled and congealed. "Let me fix you a small repast."

Watching her warily, Trader said nothing as Kendrick loosened the hemp bindings from her chafed wrists. She rubbed her reddened forearms carefully, her eyes trained on a round of pocket bread in the nearly empty basket. Kendrick nudged it closer.

"It seems your loyal fossickers are in Bordertown searching for a certain card I would possess." Tasman said pleasantly, heaping potatoes and beef onto a plate. "Part of one, anyway."

Trader gave her a blank stare.

"Where is the half Skell of House Crystal Keep?" Tasman held a ladle of yogurt over the cold food.

Afraid she would eat nothing, Trader snatched a round of bread from the basket and ripped it in half. Baked into the pocket were sweet onions. One piece she stuffed into her mouth. The other found its way into the top of her leather jerkin.

Tasman measured the girl with cold green eyes. "Who has the lost stone?"

"How would I know?" Trader chewed and swallowed.

"One of my spy coins depicted Aubergine and Winter Wheat picking at a stone lashed to a broken stick," Tasman told her.

"That was my hiking pole." Trader looked at the uncovered serving dishes with longing. Her eyes flashed. "You snapped it in half when I defied you, remember?"

Caught aback, Tasman dropped the ladle into its tureen and turned to her brother. "It couldn't be."

"What?" he asked.

She set the plate of food down slowly. "The girl's walking stick had a bit of stone decorating the pommel. I thought nothing of it."

Trader reached out until her foraging fingers found the rim of the plate and inched the curry closer. Neither Kendrick nor Tasman seemed to notice.

"How long had you possessed that pole?" Tasman demanded.

"Since I was a child," Trader answered truthfully. "It was my mother's unchallenged. When she disappeared, the witches gave it to me."

Without waiting for further invitation, she began dipping chunks of potatoes and beef into the yogurt sauce with her fingers and wolfing the cold curry down.

"The witches gave her a jewel?" Kendrick hissed at his sister.

The spicy foreign food watered Trader's eyes and stung her nose, but did not slow the speed of her consumption, though she had no water.

"The Teal you see here was born to Tracery's unwed sister, above an alehouse along the docks." Tasman gave the filthy girl eating with her hands a disparaging look. "She could not have possessed such a stone."

"But she may have . . . Broken shards!" Kendrick swore loudly. "Were you really that close? Did you risk the necklace only to return with this girl empty-handed?"

Tasman paused to consider Trader, whose face had grown so flushed from hot spice she was forced to stop chewing. The girl sucked deep cleansing breaths, unmindful of the tears that washed down her face, so grimy that the wet tracks looked clean.

No," she said finally. "The rounded rock I glimpsed on the table in the yarn shop resembled nothing but beach glass. I have seen many such stones washed up along the shores of the Crystal Lakes whose waters pool and repool, smoothing jagged crystal into purple pebbles. What Aubergine took from atop the stick was nothing but river rock."

"Are you certain?" Kendrick persisted. "If Tracery Teal recovered the lost stone when the necklace broke, could she have secreted it with her sister?"

"How?" Tasman wondered aloud. "Teal dissipated into green smoke. I destroyed her."

Trader licked her plate clean and laid it on the tablecloth. "You did not destroy my aunt completely," she said quietly.

"She was gone before you arrived on this earth." Tasman shot a glance toward the waiting guard and in seconds Trader's wrists were bound once more.

"Whose stone was it?" Kendrick asked.

Tasman gave him a puzzled look.

"Before it was lost," he explained. "You've told me time and again; the necklace was strung with twelve stones in order of each of your places around the dye pot. Whose stone was it that broke from its setting? Whose became lost?"

"Teal's," Tasman admitted.

"If the stone was hers unchallenged, any one of the witches could have offered it to Teal's next of kin, even a barmaid from a rooming house," Kendrick argued. "What better way to hide it and her daughter than to decorate the pommel of a child's walking stick with a stone others saw as beach glass and disguise the little girl as a fossick boy?"

Tasman grimaced in displeasure.

Kendrick held his hand to his sister's face, his thumb and forefinger barely spread. "You were that close to the lost stone—that close."

Trader flashed the Dark Queen a triumphant smile.

"You think that's funny?" Tasman sneered. "You won't find anything else to laugh about." She gave the girl a cold glance. "I'll have that stone tomorrow night."

"How so?" Kendrick asked, unconvinced.

"I'll just have to pay a little visit to the Cask and Barrel Tavern," she said simply. "I can inhabit one of the serving wenches, musicians, even one of the revelers if I choose. No one will know until it's too late." Her green eyes flashed at Trader. "If her bit of purple glass really is the lost stone, which I truly doubt, it shall turn up at some point in the company of her sorry coven of aging witches."

Tasman gave a slight nod and the same guardsman who had brought the girl into the pavilion pulled her to her feet.

"You're nothing but a pawn, but pawns make for good barter." Tasman smiled cruelly. "I understand they call you Trader, after all."

"Sometimes." The girl tried to sound brave. "Or Traitor. I have lots of names."

After the girl was gone, Kendrick turned to his sister. "We'll have to split up again if we want to locate both the stone and the Skell."

"Find that deck of cards in the rooming house in River Walk before the fossickers do," Tasman insisted. "Burn the place down with the fossick boys inside if need be."

"Let me find the Skell first," Kendrick cautioned. "You may recall that I set fire to several taverns along the river some time ago and discovered nothing."

"We were seeking stones then," Tasman reminded him. "Not Skells."

"Even so—" Kendrick began.

She cut him off. "I must have the lost stone. Not for myself mind you, but to keep it from the others." Shaking her head, she gave her brother a frustrated look. "Don't worry, I'll find it."

STONES AND SKELLS

"I'll have some, too!" Smokey shouted.

CHAPTER 7

River Walk Ruse

INDIGO KNIT INTO THE NIGHT, HER rosewood needles clicking and clacking until her fingers felt tied into knots. "I've not another stitch in me," she complained at last, reaching for her tobacco pouch on the night table between the two rumpled beds.

Esmeralde snatched the bag of cured leaves away. "Not around the yarn," she admonished. "And not in our room."

"Then you knit some." Indigo handed her the mostly finished lace shawl. "Decreasing in a pattern stitch with no discernable repeat is driving me mad."

Esmeralde held the triangular garment up to the light. "Indy, you're almost done!" she exclaimed. "I can see the Fire and Ice pattern. And it's coming to a point!"

"I'll give you a point," Indigo said, reaching for her bag once more. She began to roll a bit of dried glacier weed into a Smokie. "There are a couple points I've been trying to make ever since those fossick boys arrived."

"We love fossickers," Esmeralde interrupted. "They show up with treasures and trinkets, all sorts of oddities." Setting the lacework aside, she unearthed a flask of cordial from her Possibles Bag, and began to search around her bed stand. "I wish one would appear right now with wine cups."

"The glasses are outside in the hall." Indigo waved her hand toward the door. "Where we left them last night."

Their room was the same dormered cell they had shared as schoolgirls, except now the whitewashed walls were streaked with water stains and the knotty pine floor had dulled to gray. A scarred night table separated their two narrow beds that sagged terribly, worse than Indigo remembered.

Esmeralde rose from her cot and opened the door to retrieve the two sticky glasses. "Mayhap it was the maid's day off," she ventured, regarding the dregs at the bottoms of their cups.

"The maid was Tasman in disguise, and she disappeared with our fossick girl Trader. Don't you remember?" Indigo cracked their window, letting cold night air rush in. "Lily hasn't had a chance to look for new kitchen help yet."

"Mayhap she's afraid." Esmeralde's eyes narrowed as she watched Indigo drag a chair to the open window and light her smoke. Leaving the dirty wine glasses on the night table, she uncorked the Crystal Cordial. "No one is who they seem. Trader and Tasman were both masquerading as others."

As Esmeralde nipped from her flask, Indigo blew smoke rings into the night. "Yes, Trader was a girl garbed as a fossick boy, even I know that now," she conceded.

"And now the Potluck harbors two Middleland fossick boys for no apparent reason," Esmeralde declared. "Who are they trying to fool?'

"No reason?" Indigo held out her hand impatiently. Esmeralde took another swallow of cordial before surrendering the flask. "Heavenly hand knits," she swore softly. "There has to be a reason."

Esmeralde wiped her mouth on her nightshift sleeve. "Thus your various points."

"For the love of the Lost Caves, that's exactly what I'm trying to puzzle out!" Indigo sipped from the flask, lost in thought. "Garth said those boys would fare to the borough of River Walk in search of somewhat to free Trader."

"River Walk's just a warren of creaky docks and cheap rooming houses from what I glimpsed when we drove the wagon through the Southern Gate," Esmeralde said. "Flat beer, sour wine."

"Garth said the two fossickers seek a tattered Skell, an original parchment like what you see in the cards." Indigo let out a lazy trail of smoke. "Do you think that boy would lie to us? Is he actually someone else we don't know?"

"Not one of Sierra's own." Esmeralde wrinkled her nose as the spicy scent of burning glacier weed wafted her way. "Unless he himself does not know who he is."

"That could be." Indigo glanced at her friend. "You know, there's a lot of chatter about burning men and male magic floating around the Potluck lately."

"And boys," Esmeralde added. "When was the last time Lily let us have boys in our rooms?"

"Never." Indigo gave her a meaningful look. "She never did."

"Well there are boys here now," Esmeralde declared.

Indigo snorted. "More than there used to be."

Esmeralde waved away smoke. "Holey socks Indy, didn't you agree not to puff in here? You know I can't stand the smell. Would you rather room with Lavender Mae?"

Indigo stubbed out her smoke on the windowsill. "Not in this lifetime."

"Skells these days involve gambling," Esmeralde ruminated. "When Trader was a boy, she got herself into a lot of trouble with dice and cards."

"The card these boys seek is different, a First Folk Skell." Indigo shut the window. "It's all torn up. With age, or whatnot."

"Few ancient parchments survived the Age of Ice." Esmeralde up-ended her flask into a wine cup, sighing at the few drops that dribbled out. "Could it be valuable?"

"Valuable?" Indigo shrugged. "Powerful, mayhap."

"Powerful enough to help us rule the Potluck?" Esmeralde asked.

"Any one of us," Indigo's voice drifted off. "Tasman especially, I would think."

"Maybe we need to find that Skell first," Esmeralde said. "The fossickers may be up yet. Are you hungry?"

"It's past midnight," Indigo grumbled, going to the door. She peered into the empty hallway. "Surely Smokey Jo and the fossick boys have long since ransacked the kitchen for leftovers."

"Scarce," Esmeralde rose and threw a robe over her shift. Taking the candlestick from the bedside stand, she followed Indigo. "Skells and food this late in the evening can be very scarce."

"There was bread pudding," Indigo recalled, as they crept down the stairs, the candle casting long shadows before them. "With hard sauce."

"Surely there's some left," Esmeralde whispered as they bumbled along the dark hall.

A low lamp burned on the cookstove in the kitchen. The sink sat cluttered with sticky dessert plates. On the counter, the icing bowl was scraped clean.

"Boys!" Indigo swore. She ran her index finger around the rim of the bowl and touched her tongue. "Not a taste."

From the hallway a door clicked open and Smokey Jo emerged from Aubergine's private quarters. She yawned in the kitchen doorway, rubbing her eyes. "I thought I heard more folk out here."

"We're looking to snack." Esmeralde eyed the empty pudding tin and the sink of dirty dishes.

"The fossick boys have come and gone," Smokey admitted. "But they didn't get this." Opening the pie safe, she pulled out a browned apple crisp. She gave the other witches an anxious look. "Lily says no one's supposed to touch anything apple until tomorrow."

Without comment, Indigo went to the icebox for the pitcher of clotted cream while Esmeralde rummaged for clean dessert bowls.

"I'll have some, too!" Smokey shouted.

Indigo smiled. "We've heard your new fossick friends know of a boardinghouse where a certain ancient card may be hidden," she said to Jo, heaping their three small bowls with crisped apple sprinkled with brown sugar.

Esmeralde ladled out dollops of cream. "Half of a Skell, anyway." She handed a bowl to Smokey Jo. "How could that be?"

"It's no secret Trader was born to an unwed girl in River Walk," Smokey Jo tattled, sifting through the silverware drawer for clean spoons, "who most likely lived at a boardinghouse." They sat at the small round table. "And worked for barter."

Swallowing a bite of dessert, Indigo pointed her spoon at Esmeralde. "I am inclined to think there might be some truth to this talk of ancient Skells."

"There was likely something in it for Trader," Esmeralde suggested, licking cream from her fingers.

"The Skell is Trader's, but not unchallenged," Smokey volunteered, between bites of apple. "That is part of the whole problem, from what I've heard. Plus you need both halves of the card to make it work."

"Make it work how?" Indigo asked.

"That I don't know," the gnome said.

Esmeralde finished her crisp. "Indy, maybe there is something in it for us."

Indigo set aside her empty bowl. "I'm willing to stroll the river banks looking for any odd ancient bit, so long as it's useful."

"So long as the entire story is not a ruse," Esmeralde agreed with a belch. She rose. "Let's offer to escort the fossickers to River Walk and see what's about."

Her mouth full, Smokey looked from one witch to the other in alarm. She swallowed quickly. "Well you'd better hurry. Garth and them have quite a head start."

Indigo looked at the gnome in disbelief. "The boys are gone?"

"They ate and left." Smokey Jo clutched her bowl. "As I've already said."

Esmeralde shook her head at Indigo. "Once again, we've missed our chance for the power to rule."

"Perhaps it's not in the Skell cards, or any other." Indigo stifled a yawn. "There's naught to do now but finish the shawl."

After they had gone back upstairs, Smokey Jo surveyed the cluttered kitchen. "Lily is going to be so cross," she muttered. Standing on her toes, she placed her empty bowl atop the tippy pile of dirty dishes and scurried back to her room.

RIVER WALK RUSE

Trader veered toward the Copse
which promised both cover and aggravation.

CHAPTER 8

Cuts Like a Knife

THE LOWLAND GUARD RETURNED TRADER TO her makeshift jail behind the encampment. It was a stick-built stockade and she was shut inside along with two sheep and a goat the southern raiders had stolen to slaughter for food during for their march north. Because the soldiers didn't talk in words, it was hard to guess their intent. For the most part they ignored her, much as they did the animals.

No matter how much the hungry sheep baaed, no one fed them. They ate melting ice for water, pawed the ground in search of old grass beneath the snow, and nosed at the green branches that had been cut for the fence. The goat had even nibbled all the bark from the bottom of the slender posts, exposing raw wood that oozed sap the sheep favored. Whenever a drop appeared, one of them ate it before it could crystalize.

As she had last night, Trader sat on the ground with her hands bound behind and worked the hempen bonds until she could slip the ropes beneath her and slide her fettered feet through. With her hands now tied more comfortably in front, she snuggled up to one of the sheep who had already bedded down for the night. The old ewe was shaggy with her winter coat and plenty warm to sleep with.

With both hands, Trader reached into the top of her jerkin for the pocket bread she had stolen from the Dark Queen's dinner table. Too full from her feast of cold curry to eat it, she fed the bread stuffed with savory onions to the sheep, save for the butter knife she had hidden inside when she snatched the round of bread from the basket.

Holding the knife between her feet she worked the rope that joined her wrists against the dull blade for what seemed like an eternity until it finally severed. Dawn threatened as she cut the fetters from her boots.

As the camp began to stir, briefly Trader thought to cut and run. It was her usual plan whenever she was caught for petty thievery. Now that seemed selfish, for she had put her own fossick boys in danger. She had seen the Bad, Bad Man before—they all had. But only she knew that he was the Dark Queen's brother intent on stealing the Skell. She had to find a way warn her boys lest they encounter him in River Walk. As an armed guard circled the perimeter of the stockade, Trader re-strung the ropes loosely around her hands and feet and slid the knife inside her jerkin. She laid her head on the slumbering sheep's wooly side and fell asleep, exhausted.

In her dreams Trader was once again a little girl in River Walk, living over an alehouse along the waterfront. Her mother worked as a barmaid downstairs. Her name was Teal then and she wore smocked pinafores over simple shifts with matching ribbons in her hair. The few toys she had were homemade. Her favorite was a small green frog knit from wool yarn and stuffed with raw fleece. It had black button eyes and a mouth crafted from a scrap of red fabric. Teal spent a lot of time alone with the frog. She never left the Loose Goose without it.

When her mother wasn't tending bar, she entertained guests in their small room on the second floor. Teal knew better than to bang on the door when it was locked, for such noise made her mother's callers angry. Sometimes she and the frog would play in the hall until the visitors left. Other times they went outside to wander the riverfront.

Even as a young child, Trader had freedom to come and go as she pleased along the boardwalk so long as she could spot the carved wooden sign out front of the tavern, which displayed a huge white goose with flapping wings. The bold sigil was easy to see, even from the boat docks. Along the waterfront, Trader learned to shoot marbles and cast jacks, bet dice and wager Skells. She perfected sleight of hand tricks that drew laughter and sometimes a copper from the shipwrights and fishwives who plied their trade along the river.

Her skills sharpened as she grew older. No longer a cute maid in embroidered aprons, she roamed the piers in cast-off dresses too large for her slight frame, her eyes honed for forgotten items in the bars and taverns, whose candles burned long into the night. Sometimes she just scavenged things that seemed unattended. Branded as a petty thief among the docks, she plied her trade further from River Walk, into the affluent boroughs of Winter Watch and Artisan's Hand. She bartered her pilfers among the trading posts and pawnshops that riddled the alleys behind the Southern Gate. It was there she met her first fossickers. In her dream, the fossick boys worshipped her crafty ways and proclaimed her their queen, but in reality they scoffed at her because she was a girl, and a scrawny one at that.

One morning Trader returned to the Loose Goose from one of her nightly forays to find her mother missing. The barkeep claimed she had run off with a guest to avoid paying rent, but one of the serving girls murmured that her mother had met an unfortunate end. Trader took the stairs two at a time to find their room ransacked and most of her truck missing. When she crept downstairs, a tall woman with violet eyes waited at the bar with a curly-headed gnome. Asking no questions, she handed the tavern owner a few pieces of silver and took Trader home.

Trader did not care for the quiet life of Merchant's Pass, although she loved the handsome present of a carved ironwood walking stick with an amethyst pommel that the kind old witch gave her. It was hers unchallenged, Aubergine said, for the stone had belonged to an Aunt Teal, sister to her mother, a witch dead before Trader was born. Trader never in her life heard her mother mention such a relation, nor did she wholly believe in witches, but she loved the stick. If you tapped it on the ground twice, the amethyst orb lit from within, casting a beacon of light in the dark. Trader has seen such radiant stones of pink quartz and amethyst crystal at the Southern Gate Trading Post but never before harbored one, as they were expensive and rare.

Ward the crystal with your life, Aubergine had advised, *for there are those that would take it from you if they knew the gem's identity. This is Tracery Teal's one true stone that was lost and now you must misplace it further. Mislay yourself in the crowds of Bordertown, cast your nets to the Fisheries of the Far East, or lose your path along the far-flung trails of the Western Highlands with shepherd nomads, but never reveal that your name is Teal or let the lost stone from your sight.*

In Trader's dream, the walking stick gained her instant fame. She became the first female fossicker, the thieving Queen of River Walk, but in reality she had shorn her hair, traded her ill-fitting skirts for canvas breeches and left Bordertown through the Western Gate. It was easier to forget herself outside the city. With relief, she discovered her walking stick not only lent light but also warned against danger. Her childhood memories faded, and she mastered the art of self-reliance.

Eventually, she did fall in with some fossickers who profited from picking through bits of leather discarded by Woolen Woods tanneries. Tiring of them, she joined a ragtag band of boys who scavenged the Trickle for shards of crystal, swapping their finds for food and supplies at the Trading Post in Banebridge. Among fossickers, no one cared to ask her name or background or even her gender.

At the various outposts and flea markets where she bartered, she became known as Trader or Traitor, Little T or Trickle T, depending upon which group of fossickers she frequented. When finally she collected enough followers to set up fossick camp in a river valley east of Banebridge called the Dell, she found she favored the name Trader.

The sound of bleating animals woke her. With a start, she sat blinking in the sun. It was full day and the ravenous goat had finally eaten through the green branches of the stockade to push his way out toward supply and cook tents beyond. There was a clatter as a stack of soup tureens fell over and a sack of potatoes scattered. The old goat began to rip at the burlap bag. The sheep squeezed through the fence, and soon all three animals were chewing the starchy tubers with satisfaction. Hearing the ruckus, two Lowland guards circled the tents, but they were not well versed in the capture of herd animals and the wise old goat wandered further afield with the sheep as his captors approached.

Trader quickly made use of the distraction. Loosening her bonds, she squirmed through the fence unnoticed and crawled behind budding bushes set amongst river rock near the edge of the encampment, unsure of her next move. To her left, crimson tents ringed the Dark Queen's pavilion. Beyond, the narrow river valley offered little cover.

This late in the day, the Dark Queen must have already left for Bordertown if she truly meant to steal the lost stone from Aubergine before the witches could piece together the necklace. Trader desperately hoped that the old witch had taken the amethyst from her broken walking stick to secret it far away from Tasman's reach, no matter where the rest of their necklace lay.

Although she denied it during her cold curry supper in the Dark Queen's Pavilion, Trader had spoken to her band of fossickers more than once about the rumored Skell fragment and its whereabouts. It was a curious fossick too old and damaged to pass as a playing card, but an ancient relic nonetheless with almost certain value. The last time she saw it, her mother had inserted the etched triangle into an ordinary deck of Skells hidden in a secret hollow beneath the eaves in their room. Over the years, Trader had pondered whether that one bit of halved horn had anything to do with her mother's disappearance.

When she chose Clayton to lead the Dell fossick band in her stead, Trader took him, Micah, and small Ross aside, instructing them that should anything happen, they must seek a First Folk Skell scored on the diagonal from cards hidden within the walls of a second-floor room above a mead hall in River Walk. It could be used for bribe, barter, or ransom to buy freedom from those who would use her to get the stone.

Trader hoped that whoever had rifled her mother's belongings had not found the Skell, though in truth she never returned to look for the small triangle depicting a crystal. Growing up, she thought nothing of the scrap of etched horn except that it was an oddity. Of course that was before she had discovered its twin hidden in Aubergine's sewing basket, just after the old witch presented her with the walking stick unchallenged. The basket sat on a low shelf under the tambourine table in Aubergine's private chambers. Trader was tempted—so tempted—to snatch the relic, but the old witch had been so nice and, besides, the card reminded her of a life that even then she had resolved to forget.

Trader watched the Lowlanders corral the sheep and goat once more and herd them toward the stockade. Soon they would find her missing. Silently, she wormed away through the river rock, retreating from the narrow valley. With the encampment safely behind her, she rose to run toward the foothills, stopping at the first icy stream she encountered for a long cold drink. She scrubbed her hands and face with the icy water and tried to formulate a plan. Life on the run had led her to establish a network of secret hiding places complete with contingency plans to ward off unseen threats. Now might be a good time to implement one, she decided.

Certain that the Bad, Bad Man intended to burn down the rooming house where she had lived in River Walk, Trader's first thought was to flee north. How long it would take to reach Bordertown with soldiers swarming the tracks she was not certain, but she feared she was already too late to warn her fossickers. Their general strategy throughout the war was to stick together whenever possible. In an emergency, if they saw fire in Banebridge, they would go to the ice, meaning Bordertown. Just days ago Trader had watched from the stockade as clouds of wood smoke from the East billowed into the river valley. Possibly her boys had not been burned out of the Dell or the High Rocks, but the acrid haze that hovered on the horizon told Trader otherwise. Her fossickers had most likely gone to the ice days ago, and now they either had the Skell or they did not.

She tried to soothe herself with the knowledge that if all else failed and her gang was forced to split and scatter, their arrangement was to regroup at the Trading Post in Banebridge. This strategy had always worked well for Trader. When the Glacier Wars began again, Ozzie constructed a secret room over the shop, accessible through the large stone fireplace downstairs. If you ducked into the fireplace, to the side was another flue with a ladder fixed to the fieldstone. In the hidden room there were bedrolls and cider, Skell cards and snacks; and after the last patron left the bar, Ozzie's wife, Nellie, sent up leftovers for supper.

Those few fossickers Trader made privy to the sanctuary she held to a strict code of conduct called the Fossicker's Creed. This verbal contract lay between herself and the members of her assembly, known by other gangs of roving boys as Fossickers in the Dell. The Fossicker's Creed had never failed her. Youths she entrusted with knowledge of the safe house could not mention the refuge by name, even to each other. Any of her chosen who utilized the secret room paid Ozzie back in truck or trade. Boys who sought entry to the sanctuary foreswore an oath of secrecy and any breaking the vow suffered instant exile from the Dell Fossickers. Trader imposed the pledge on herself as well and it was this: Should disaster strike, disciples who fled to Ozzie must inhabit the refuge for three days hoping to find other survivors, no matter what peril. A boy who fled without waiting to regroup became an immediate outcast.

The Fossicker's Creed within Trader's hierarchy was also called the Three and Three, for her doctrine required three days and three specific words. Three days of waiting prepared for the group's survival and the choice of one of three codes to leave with Ozzie should any latecomers reach the refuge after the first fossickers were gone.

Although few, each utterance was fraught with import offering different meanings depending if fossickers left word or if previous boys left a word for them. The codes were simple spoken words: ONE, RUN, or DONE, but their weights increased dramatically as the list progressed, with different implications depending upon the situation and who initially arrived. The burden of determining the correct code fell upon the first fossicker to reach the safe house, which was why almost always nobody went there alone, unless he was sure Trader was already there.

Codes worked like this: If you left word ONE with Ozzie, that meant you had reached the sanctuary singly without company for three days. Alone, scared, perhaps injured, you possibly witnessed something happen to fossickers in your group and feared you alone remained. Trader had left word ONE with Ozzie many times over the years, when boys she traveled with were conscripted by the Guard, drowned in the Runne during the spring thaw, or had run home to mother.

Equally, if you reached the safe house alone and word ONE was left for you, it was typically good news, for it meant others in your group searched you out. Ozzie had diverse means of spreading information, and soon you would be reunited with your group. Time and again, Trader was so relieved after she left word ONE to circle the Dell, High Rocks, and the sandy apron beneath the trestle bridge that spanned the Runne outside Banebridge, collecting her fossick boys as she went.

 Word RUN meant literally just that. If after three days in the sanctuary, you left instructions to RUN, present danger remained and perhaps even the safe house itself was compromised. Not only were you on the RUN, but any fossicker who came to the Trading Post would be forced to flee without a backward glance. Instructions to RUN did not signify you would never encounter Dell Fossickers again, but you probably would not see some of them ever and not many soon. Trader knew firsthand that leaving a command to RUN was worse than getting one to RUN. Runners attracted attention and were easily caught.

Conversely, if you arrived at the Trading Post and Ozzie gave word to RUN, it wasn't wonderful news but it didn't have to be bad. Oftentimes RUN meant that the other fossickers had regrouped to circle their usual haunts until they found you again.

DONE was the worst word of all and Trader had never left nor listened to it. Breaking the Fossicker's Creed could cause any boy in the Dell to be DONE, due to misfortune such as betrayal, defection, desertion, and of course death. If Trader said a boy was DONE, his association with the Fossickers in the Dell ended permanently, the minute he got word, no explanation necessary.

Giving word the Dell Fossickers were DONE would be disastrous for Trader's group, but she feared getting DONE worse, for it could only mean somehow her group was disbanded without her knowledge. Her fossickers had met some unknown end, killed or betrayed by their own, and she might never know what had happened. DONE was final. DONE meant Ozzie had dismantled the refuge. DONE meant you would never see your own again.

Trader heaved a sign. She dreaded that her safest course of action would be to journey to Banebridge to see what word her fossickers had left for her at the Trading Post. She hoped that when she arrived she would find Clayton, Micah, and Ross safely waiting with the First Folk Skell. If they harbored the scrap, perhaps they could piece it together with the bit Aubergine had to somehow rid themselves of the Bad, Bad Man.

Rising, Trader moved silently through the underbrush, ignoring pangs of hunger coupled with the rancid smell of her filthy garb. She knew this area well. Soon she would arrive at the western end of the Middlemarch fairgrounds and from there hike the main track toward Banebridge, for she feared veering through the Copse without her walking stick. With luck, by nightfall she would pass through the Dell to gather a new set of clothes, whatever food was stashed in the packs, and truck for trade. She might even sleep at camp if it seemed undisturbed. Barring unforeseen delays like encountering the Northland Guard or Lowland soldiers, she might make it to Ozzie's by midday tomorrow. Since she was wanted by both North and South, it made sense to avoid anyone she might encounter. She needed to keep going. *Safe passage and food*, she kept telling herself. It became a mantra to keep her feet moving. *Safe passage and food.*

The temperature rose as morning became midday. Trader paused to gather some pine nuts and ate them in a sunny spot beneath the fragrant trees. Unnoticed on the bed of soft needles, she caught a glimpse of movement and crouched behind a log, her ears pricked and eyes trained on the figure passing by. Ahead of her, a tall traveler hiked with purpose through the forest. Could he be the Bad, Bad Man on his way to Bordertown, she wondered? If so, perhaps it wasn't too late to warn her fossickers. If she hurried, she might trail the Bad Man to River Walk and keep the boys safe. She rose to follow, but his strides were so long it was hard to keep pace. Breathing hard, she began to run. As she got closer, she recognized his gray uniform and realized he was only a scout from the Northland Guard, taller than most. Lightly armored, he moved swiftly and silently through the towering pines.

But not noiselessly enough. From behind a brush pile, two Lowland soldiers jumped him and wrestled the fair-haired boy to the ground. The lanky youth was no match for the southerners. After relieving him of his pack and tool belt, they bound him to a pine with his own climbing rope so they could go through his goods.

Trader was beginning to comprehend southern sign. Learning language had never been a problem for her along the docks and this tongue was another way of talking, just without words. She saw the Lowlanders meant to steal the fine braided rope and hunting knife from the guard's tool belt. With no use for the ice pick or wrought-metal crampons, they discarded them on the ground. As they went through his pack, finding rations and commissary chits, a few pieces of Northland silver, and a military road pass, she understood that they were undecided whether to take the scout hostage or kill him, for fear he had found their encampment in the narrow river valley.

As Trader backed away, thinking to put as much ground between herself and the Lowlanders as possible, she made the mistake meeting the eyes of the scout tied to the tree. He was watching her but not about to alert his captors, even though he faced the stockade or death. Although unusually tall, he was just a boy, no older than herself. His fair features and blond hair reminded her of Garth.

Trader could not make sense of what she did next, for this Northland boy was no one to her and her only weapon was a dull butter knife. She threw a few pinecones past the Lowlanders for distraction and then snatched up the ice pick. Her practiced hand inserted the tip of the hook through the smooth knotted rope and pulled the loop free.

"To me," she hissed, loosening the tall boy's bindings. "Don't look back."

From the pine ridge, Trader fled down toward the marshy bog along River Runne's edge, not waiting to see who followed. Across the shallows on the far side of the river lay Middlemarch, where she doubted Lowlanders would venture now that the Northland Guard occupied the fairgrounds.

Nearing the swamp, Trader beckoned to the scout before plunging in. Wading through the muck was treacherous unless you knew where to step. One slip and he could mire in the peat, although she doubted he was as heavy as the Lowland soldiers. Trader could hear them crashing through the bog, losing ground each time their feet broke through the shifting turf of matted grasses into the mud below. When she finally reached the riverbank above the Middlemarch bridge, Trader stopped for breath. She was alone.

Afternoon shadow crept across the fairgrounds, whose striped tents had been struck and stalls boarded when the fair ended. Beyond the empty livestock pens, the Northland Guard had set up camp. Even from here she could discern row upon row of gray tents in the distance, under the smoky haze in the dusky valley.

Behind her, the lanky guard broke from the bog to splash through the shallows, washing away the mud that had come up over the tops of his boots. The spring runoff had receded considerably since the Middlemarch Fair, the river just knee deep.

He clambered up the steep bank to join her. "Niles," he gasped. "Well met."

"Trader." She shook his huge hand before turning toward a nearby freshet that fed into the river.

"It isn't safe to drink that without treating it first, fossick boy." He handed her a water skin the Lowlanders hadn't bothered to take from him. "Don't you know that?"

"I wasn't aware." Trader tipped her head back to guzzle water.

Niles took in her filthy clothes and matted hair. "Can I ask where you've been?"

"Imprisoned." Trader shook the last drops of water into her mouth. "Stuck in a Lowland stockade with a goat and two sheep, nothing to eat. How about you?"

"I was fine until—well you saw," the tall Northland boy said.

Trader handed him the empty skin. "Your fate would have been mine or worse."

"I'm obliged for the rescue. Anything I can do . . ." Niles' voice trailed off as Trader frowned at his uniform, and shook her head. "I should get back to my unit," he murmured awkwardly. "I'm long overdue."

Trader gave him a curt nod. "And I've lived to fossick another day, I expect." She scanned the main track. "Let's pretend we've never met."

"Agreed." But as he turned toward the fairgrounds, something made him pause. "Say, fossick boy," he called after her retreating figure. "Just by chance, you haven't come across a deserter named Warren Blue, have you?"

Stopping in her tracks, Trader turned around slowly. "And his sister Skye and his brother Garth? Of course I have." She put her hands on her hips. "But Warren's no deserter, and I'm no boy."

Niles offered her an unblinking stare. "I would see them again one day, Warren and Skye."

Trader examined the Northland boy once more. Could this be the sledder Skye mentioned, who helped her elude capture at the World's Fair? It seemed unlikely but perhaps he was. The list of folk you could trust grew shorter during wartime while sometimes your circle of friends flung far wide, she reminded herself. "Are you the soldier who helped Skye escape the Guard?" She asked at last.

"We rode right across there, in plain sight on mountain ponies." Niles pointed to the high arched bridge spanning the river.

"I've been on those horses once or twice. Not fun," Trader said, remembering the gallop through the Copse to Indigo's cottage, the night she and her companions were chased by soldiers. She looked from Niles to the Middlemarch bridge, sandwiched between guardhouses, and cracked a smile. "I bet your feet dragged on the ground."

"Just about." He flashed a quick grin. Then a horn sounded and his face grew sober. They watched the sentries change in silence. He turned to go. "Send word from Niles of the North."

For once, Trader was sick of words. She had no desire to leave word, get word, or pass along word to Skye and Warren from a boy who might soon be dead.

"Bring word yourself, northern boy," she said angrily. "Warren and Skye are safe in Bordertown and that's where I'm going. Come along."

"My unit will arrest me for desertion," Niles muttered, as he began to accompany Trader toward the main track.

"You're long overdue, remember?" She gave him a hard look. "They will fear you were captured by Lowlanders, which you were. No one will look for you."

Niles let out a sigh. "They will hunt me down."

"We're all of us hunted." Looking up at him, Trader laughed. "It won't be so bad if we can find you different clothes."

Maybe it was the smoke growing denser as they hiked toward Banebridge, or perhaps just a feeling of dread that made Trader veer toward the Copse which promised both cover and aggravation. The main track lay deserted and that bothered her. At the edge of the tangled woods, she pulled out the ice pick and butter knife—all they had for protection against the roving branches. She wanted to give him the knife, but judging by his long wingspan, he might do better with the pick.

"Keep close in the Copse," she warned, afraid that Niles of the North would have no clue what she meant.

Once again, he surprised her. Reaching within his tunic, the scout retrieved a chunk of pink quartz which almost immediately lit from within. Taking the ice pick, he handed her the glowing rock.

"Lead the way," he said softly, his face rosy in the light.

Garth frowned, considering. "We're looking for a bird—a big white goose probably."

CHAPTER 9

In the Cards

SNEAKING AWAY FROM POTLUCK YARN BEFORE first light in search of an ancient Skell card had sounded like high adventure to Garth when Clayton and Ross brought it up last night. The parchment they described was rumored to be hidden in an unsavory district of Bordertown in rooms over an alehouse along the docks of River Walk. Restless in cots tucked under the slanted walls of the narrow attic where Tasman once slept, the boys decided to raid Lily's kitchen and think on it. Over dessert, their budding plans blossomed.

"Trader said there was southern folk chasing him," Ross insisted stubbornly as he dipped his spoon into the icing bowl. "And they was pure evil!"

SECRETS OF THE LOST CAVES

The three of them sat hunched over the small round table near the cookstove, dividing the last of the bread pudding and hard sauce Lily had served with supper that evening.

Clayton pushed his new gauntlets up over his skinny wrists. Meant to be worn under the sleeves of a military coat or chain-mail tunic, the finely knit wristlets were far too large and looked silly beneath the cuffs of his nightshirt. Yet they were knit from finely spun wool beaded with a motif that Lilac Lily said warded danger. She had given them to him yesterday after freeing the boys from the rolling cage, and he refused to remove them, even for bed. The beads were arranged into a pattern that looked like a lidded eye. Evil Eye Wristers, Clayton called them.

"Trader said when bad folk come with fire, you go to the ice." Clayton told Garth. "We thought he meant Bordertown, but mayhap it was the Northland Glacier."

"They did come with fire!" Ross cried. "Micah unsuppered and in his place was the Bad, Bad Man." He gave Garth a wild stare. "You never met him?"

When Garth shook his head, the small boy's voice quavered. "Fire shoots from his hands. He burned down our camp in the Dell. So then we went to the High Rocks!"

"It was the same there." Clayton polished off his pudding. "All burnt up."

"Whatever for?" Bewildered, Garth dropped a spoon into his empty bowl. "I just don't get why."

Ross squirmed in his chair. "He was lookin' for something. Maybe he thought them witches had it."

"When we went to the remedy witch's place to find somewhat to conjure Micah back, her cottage was burned flat, with cinders still smoking." Clayton told Garth.

"Does Esmeralde know what happened to her place?" He asked.

"Dunno." Ross shrugged, busily scraping the icing bowl clean.

IN THE CARDS

"We ain't saying nothing," Clayton added. "Trader says you never want to get her mad cuz of what spells she can cast on you from that bag of glass vials she carries."

Ross's eyes lit up. "Poxes and rashes, cold sweats and ague, stinging nettles and gnats . . ."

Garth held up his hand. "I get the sense of it. No more."

"Well its awful what she can do," the small boy whimpered.

"What do these southern folk want?" Garth asked.

"Trader says it's a sundered Skell card, First Folk fierce." Clayton's brows furrowed. "It's half to another and, together, when they're whole—well, we don't know."

"We was only s'posed to find it to use for ransom, if something ever happened to Trader." Ross pushed his bowl away. "Something's happened to him, ain't it?"

"More than you know," Garth grumbled, rising to stack their empty dishes in the sink. "I'll tell you the truth, just promise not to call me a liar." He turned to eye them both. "You might not want to sneak over to River Walk looking for a torn-up Skell card, to ransom somebody who maybe can't be saved."

"Trader's our leader still," Clayton argued.

"He wants us to save him, so's he can come back and lead us s'more," Ross added.

"Trader's no fossicker, risking freedom on a fool's errand," Garth said evenly, lifting his chin toward Clayton. "Like as not, you and me could get caught by daybreak if we sneak out of Merchant's Pass. What if we get locked a rolling cage again? There might not be any Lily with Northland silver to free us this time."

"What are we s'posed to do, leave?" Ross asked. "Whyn't you tell us what happened to Trader?"

Clayton looked at Garth suspiciously. "Yeah, how come no one wants to say what really turned out?"

117

"'Cause you won't like it," Garth said. "Trader's real name is Traces of Teal, after an aunt who was one of the Potluck Twelve. Trader's a witch, not a boy."

"There ain't no boy witches," Ross objected.

"You got that one right," Garth agreed. "Trader's a girl who's been hiding her whole life, until finally they caught her."

"Trader's a girl?" Ross screwed up his eyes. "Not likely!"

"I always wondered." Clayton shot Garth a knowing glance. "For sure?"

"Most definitely," he said. "Same as my sister."

"The Bad, Bad Man was lookin' for a girl," Ross remembered.

Clayton nodded slowly and turned to Garth. "Who's this *they* that stole Trader?"

"The Dark Queen," he replied. "She shape-shifted into a serving girl hiding in plain sight right here in this Potluck, and vanished with Trader while the witches were holding their simmer around the great pot."

"How could them witches let anyone kidnap Trader?" Ross asked in dismay.

"The Dark Queen used to be a witch herself, that's all I know," Garth said. "When the Twelve left the simmer, Trader was gone. Skye said so herself."

"Your sister's a witch?" Clayton asked. "I thought she was a girl. A pretty girl, mayhap."

"No, she's a witch," Garth confirmed. "It's a mother and daughter kind of thing."

"What happened to the other girl?" Ross asked in a querulous voice.

"Trader?" Garth frowned. "The Dark Queen kidnapped her, like I said."

"No, he means the kitchen wench," Clayton said.

IN THE CARDS

"I don't know." Garth shrugged. "She was there and then she wasn't."

"She unsuppeared!" Tears of fear stood out in Ross's eyes. He tugged on Clayton's sleeve. "The dark witch made her unsuppear, just like she did Micah."

"Don't matter who Trader is, boy or girl. We need to get'm back," Clayton insisted.

"Yes!" Ross bobbed his head. "Before the Dark Queen unsuppears us all!"

With what began as firm resolve, Garth led the boys through the twisting streets of Merchant's Pass and into Artisan's Hand before he gave up finding his way in the dark. Although he remembered riding into Bordertown through the Southern Gate below River Walk last week, he could not retrace the route from the Potluck to the docks. It had been full day when Indigo drove the wagon beneath the bridge that spanned the aqueduct to join the slowly moving traffic on the Common Road that wound along the waterfront. Now it was not yet light and the boys were traveling on foot.

In River Walk, a ragtag band of boys had spied Trader hunkered in the back of Indigo's vegetable cart from the bridge above, and raced after her. That was a chase Garth would never forget. He watched in disbelief as Trader leaped from the wagon bed while the cart was still moving, to flee across the uneven planks of the boat docks like a circus performer. Jumping from skiff to skiff, she eluded the boys and disappeared into a maze of side streets and alleys behind the row houses that faced the river. It was hours before they saw her again. That was before anyone but Skye knew Trader was a girl.

Garth glanced at Clayton and Ross, snoring softly on burlap sacks piled in an unlocked shed in Artisan's Hand's warehouse district. When the fossickers woke, he did not want to have to say they were hopelessly lost. Leaving them sleeping, he slipped into the alley where roosters had begun to crow the dawn of day. An old workhorse hitched to a milk wagon clopped by on the street and Garth ran out to meet the driver.

"Excuse me!" He hailed the deliveryman. "But do you know the way to River Walk? My mates and I are lost, and our barge leaves from the Southern Gate this day."

"You'd better get a move on lad," the milkman advised. Halting the covered wagon, he turned, pointing back the way he had come. "It's straight east. Take this lane until it vees into the Common Road and follow that down to the boatyards. But look sharp. There's them with rolling cages prowling the cobbles. You may not be of age, but you're close enough for them that would trade a boy for a sliver of Northland silver."

"How far are the docks?" Garth asked, squinting at the dawning sky.

"A fair piece." The man lit a smoke. Noticing Garth's forlorn face, he chuckled. "Get in, if you like. I'll end up at the milk depot in River Walk eventually. You'll just have to wait while I make my rounds. It takes some time to get rid of all this milk."

Garth's face brightened. "I'll get my mates. Stay right there, alright?"

Less than twenty minutes later, Clayton and Garth lay in the back of the covered wagon, their feet comfortably propped on crates of milk jugs. Though it was chilly, small Ross climbed up to sit beside the driver, who he learned was named Gideon.

"We're fossickers," he mentioned to the milkman, eagerly scanning the stone and timber dwellings that lined both sides of the cobbled street. Lanterns glowed in the windows as dawn became day. Dogs barked in back courtyards and occasional alley cats streaked across the street before the wagon. Smells of fresh bread and frying bacon filled the air, and Ross nodded with satisfaction. "Fossicking's an exciting life, though it looks like yours is just a good."

With a laugh, Gideon halted the draft horse and handed the reins to Ross, who held them proudly. He trudged to the back of the wagon, to collect two crates of milk.

"Get your boots off of there!" He swatted at the feet of the two older boys.

"Whoa, Bess," Ross soothed the old mare, when she chanced to flick her tail at a fly. "Easy, girl!"

Garth cracked a smile. "Sounds like she is one fractious creature."

"Twenty years ago mayhap," Clayton murmured.

Gideon returned with the empty crates, pulling a half-gallon jug from one on top.

"I can't sell this one because it's got a chip, just so," he explained, holding out the crock of fresh milk. "Either of you want it? Don't cut your lip."

Pushing up his gauntlets, Clayton ran his finger around the pottery's rim. "I don't feel any chip."

"I doubt there is one." Garth took a swig of milk and held the jug out to his friend. Then the delivery cart jolted to life once more.

It was late morning when the wagon returned to the stables in River Walk, among a warren of warehouses a few blocks from the waterfront. After the boys helped Gideon stack the crates of empty milk jugs at the depot, he pointed out the way to the boatyards.

"You go down through here, and keep bearing left." He indicated a well-trodden path between the horse barn and the lumberyard beyond. "This way's the city docks. You'll see the barges pulled up alongside just under the bridge at the Southern Gate."

"We need to find a rooming house first," Garth admitted.

"A rooming house?" Gideon looked the boys up and down. "What kind of rooming house?"

"One over an alehouse across from the docks," Clayton explained.

"That doesn't narrow it down much." Gideon took off his toque and scratched his head. "There's plenty of them."

"I think it's called the Goose," Ross piped up. "Or something on the loose."

Gideon smiled. "I think you mean the Loose Goose."

"Probably," Garth said.

"Well that's way north, up toward Winter Watch." The milkman pointed upriver. "Nowhere near the Southern Gate." He frowned at the boys. "Now the Goose is still around, but the upstairs is boarded up ever since some rooms burnt awhile back." He paused to straighten his hat. "What do you want with that place? Even if you was old enough to drink, none of the alehouses down here open until noon, Garrison's orders."

"We left some truck there," Clayton said casually.

"An' we aim to get it back," Ross insisted.

"Yeah, well," Gideon shrugged and began to unharness the old mare. "Just beware of the Guard. The docks upriver are swarming with soldiers."

The three boys thanked the milkman and slunk from the barnyard to skulk along a series of side alleys until they were able to slip behind the first row of shops and pubs along the waterfront. Ross crowed with delight when Clayton showed him his gauntlets, for it seemed every time they were about to cross paths with soldiers, the Evil Eye winked in warning. Or maybe it was just the way the sun bounced off the beads.

They started snaking behind the tall row houses, wending their way north past walled courtyards and fenced gardens, trying to keep the river in sight from passing glimpses between the buildings fronting the boardwalk. The riverfront dwellings were constructed of weathered wood whose thick stone foundations bore distinct watermarks sometimes higher than the boys' heads, evidence that the water had flooded the borough time and again over the years. Between the boardwalk and the river, the cobbled Common Road wound around the rocky shoreline, where docks tilted into the water, barges strained at their ropes, and skiffs bobbed among the pilings.

"That tavern has got to be right up here somewhere," Garth said finally, as the group paused to catch their breath near a cluster of cheap eateries upriver. A pile of empty beer barrels ripe with the scent of hops had been thrown outside a delivery door and the odor of frying fish wafted toward them from an open window. "Ross," he decided. "You go have a look."

"Look at what?" The little boy balked. "How come me?"

"See what the tavern sign says, what else?" Garth replied. "Clay and me can't venture street side to read it. Gideon said we'd likely get picked up by a rolling cage along the Common Road this close to Winter Watch."

"I don't know my letters yet." Ross gave Clayton an uncomfortable look. "You know that."

Clayton shrugged. "I never learned letters."

"Just go ask somebody about the sign out front." Garth gave Ross a little shove. "It's close enough to midday that the mead halls should be opening soon. The one we seek must be on this block or the next."

As Ross disappeared through the alley toward the sunny boardwalk, Clayton offered Garth a gloomy look. "If we keep on walking upriver we'll see the Garrison pretty soon."

"We have to get to Winter Watch first," Garth said. "But I know what you mean."

Racing into the alley, Ross skidded to a stop before his friends. "Nobody will talk to me," he panted. "But hanging over the tavern door is a big pink pig, looking mean out of one eye."

"In a Pig's Eye," Clayton guessed.

"It means *never happen*. So, that's not the one." Garth frowned, considering. "We're looking for a bird—a big white goose probably. It'll be a bar with the upstairs burnt up, so look for blackened windows."

Clayton gazed behind them. "We passed behind a place on the last block somewhat charred on the second floor."

The boys retraced their steps to a two-story timber frame building they neglected to notice earlier. Garth shaded his eyes to scan the second floor and attic above. The vacant windows were blackened with smut stains that looked like they leaked from the openings like tear tracks. Downstairs, the dwelling seemed solid.

"Go see the sign in front of this shop," Garth whispered, his hands on Ross's shoulders. Nodding eagerly, the small boy sprinted down the alley.

In a minute he was back. "It's a goose!" he crowed. "A big sooty bird. I guess it could of been white once."

It's our place." Garth craned his neck. "How do we get in?"

"Oh it's open," Ross announced. "There was people inside. Some soldiers, playing Skells."

"But they was soldiers," Clayton reminded him.

"Right." Garth crossed to a small pump house attached to the back of the tavern. "Let's roll a couple beer kegs over. I bet we can get in from the roof of this shed."

After stacking a few empty barrels against the water shed, the boys climbed to the rooftop and shimmied into a second-story window about the tavern.

"Be quiet," Clayton cautioned Ross. "There's them that could turn us into the Guard downstairs."

"They won't hear nothing, cuz they're making all kinds of noise. Eating and drinking and playing cards. Fish 'n' chips is what they're serving today." Ross gazed up at the older boys. "Can we get some'pin to eat pretty soon?"

"Later," Garth said. It didn't take them long to search the burnt-out rooms on the second floor because they were vacant save for scorched boards, sooty walls, and smoked-stained rafters surrounding a few charred bed frames.

"There's nothing here," Clayton said as they approached the attic stairs. Running a grimy hand through his hair, he peered into the dark opening. The blackened treads that remained looked too brittle to climb.

"I can make it," Ross said. But as soon as he took the first step, it crumbled to coal and he fell to the floor.

"Hey!" Someone yelled drunkenly from below. "Something's up there!"

"Probably rats!" A woman shrieked, drawing a few laughs.

"Awful heavy for rats," another voice bellowed.

Below, a door creaked and a heavy tread mounted the stairs. "Ain't no rats."

The boys stared at each other, frozen. Clayton held up both wrists and the gauntlets slid to his elbows. The Evil Eye blinked, but there was nowhere to hide.

A burly youth in a plain gray uniform appeared at the top of the stairs, chewing on a hunk of fried fish. The thick locks that escaped his army-issue watch cap, along with his mustache, beard, and even the fringe of hair that curled from the top of his unlaced jerkin, were the color of rust.

"Fossickers." He eyed the boys in the hall. "What're you guys looking for?"

"Nothin'." Clayton turned to run.

"Skells, actually," Ross said in a small voice.

"One, anyway," Garth said slowly, measuring the distance between themselves and the opening that led to the shed roof.

"If it's cards you want, join us at the back table. We got a lively game going on." The husky guard paused to wipe greasy fingers on the front of his jerkin before shaking hands. "I'm Hairy."

"Garth." Garth clasped his meaty fist. "Well met."

"My friends call me Hair Bear." Finishing his fish, the brawny youth turned. "Come on down, but watch my buddy, Raven. He cheats at Skells."

"Ain't you soldiers?" Ross asked, trailing the heavyset boy downstairs toward the sound of laughter and smell of food. "We're s'posed to steer clear of 'em."

Behind them, Clayton pulled up his gauntlets, to show Garth the eyes had gone dull.

"We thought we was soldiers," Hairy muttered. "Til we let a witch escape under our watch. Now the Guard won't let us off guard."

"Hairy!" someone yelled from below. "Your shake of the dice."

"Fire thrice!" Hairy shouted back.

"They let you out of their sight long enough for a hand of cards," Garth noticed.

"We are playing Skells," Hairy allowed. "But that's only until we don't show up at the Garrison with a load of rusty swords and rotten scabbards off one of them barges. Then they'll come find us."

"Hairy!" Someone called. "Shake or you forfeit."

Hairy stood at the bottom of the steps. "You want to play?"

Clayton shrugged. "I'm a fair dicer."

Garth nodded. "If we have to run, it's up the stairs and out the window."

Hairy tromped into the barroom, followed by the boys.

"You find your rats?" the barmaid asked. Cleaning a glass, she looked past Hairy to Ross. "I remember you, little boy."

"I found me and Raven a few more victims, long as they got coppers," Hairy announced, heading toward a dim table in the corner.

"Ahhh fossickers!" A slight soldier with lanky black hair sighed as they approached.

"This here's Raven," Hairy said.

Tapping the deck of cards on the table, the skinny soldier gave the three boys a wolfish grin. "A game of Skells anyone?"

"We'll finish our round first." Hairy sat and shook his dice cup. Reddish hair dusted even his knuckles, Ross saw. "Where'd we leave off?"

"Fire thrice," Raven said impatiently. From one thin wrist he pulled a fine leather thong and twisted it into his long dark hair.

"Tigris!" Hairy shouted, letting the carved cubes of bone scatter across the table. "Eye!"

Raven shook his head sadly. "No Eye, I'm afraid. Just a little more Fire and only one Ice." He peered up at his friend's reddened face. "You don't need any more Fire."

"Shards!" Hairy pushed two commissary chits he had matched against Raven's across the table.

"If food tokens were coin of the realm I could have bought my way out of the army twice over now." Raven waved the chits back. "Commissary coupons are useless to me. No matter what I eat, I don't gain an ounce."

His eyes strayed to Garth and Clayton. "Got any money?"

Garth scanned the few old men sitting at the bar before he and Clayton took seats opposite each other at the table. "We got somewhat to wager."

As his friends pulled a few coppers from their pockets, Ross crept over to Raven's side. "Are you a soldier, too?" he asked the skinny youth, whose nervous hand kept straying back to his long black ponytail.

"What gave me away?" Raven shuffled the cards. "My ill-fitting uniform? This drab watch cap? Or perhaps these awful nailed boots the Guard makes us wear?"

As his fidgety fingers split the deck again, Garth thought he saw something amiss. "Can I see those?" he asked casually.

Raven straightened the worn deck and handed it over. "My father owns a tannery in Woolen Woods," he explained to Ross, splaying his booted feet from under the table. "We would never put our name on leather goods as shoddy as these."

"You going to eat your fish 'n' chips?" Ross wanted to know.

"I can't stand fish." Raven pushed his untouched basket toward the little boy.

"Is that what you did before the war, leatherwork?" Garth asked, examining the tattered Skells one by one.

Raven nodded. "And Hairy here was a smith's apprentice in Coventry. Now look at us." He gestured to his uniform dramatically. "Lowland fodder."

"Not even that," Hairy muttered, as Ross helped himself to Raven's greasy fish and potatoes. "They won't let the likes of us march with our unit to the Out Crops, and that's where the fighting's going to happen. The Lowlanders will be massing there, and maybe even the Dark Queen herself. Only me and Raven are stuck here, sharpening rusty swords and oiling rotten leather to outfit the next set of conscripts coming in."

"Is this a full deck?" Garth asked, showing Clayton torn parchments he found amongst the cards.

"As far as we know," Hairy said. "It's the set we always use here."

Clayton examined the tiny corner of a frayed eye, over which twin rivers were ripped from each other, but cast it aside for there was a larger fragment, a half Skell shorn on the diagonal, the depiction of a crystal etched in horn. His eyes widened. "What's this?"

"They're house cards." Raven took back the deck to examine the damaged Skells. "Barkeep," he called. "Got another set?"

"We can play with these." Garth eyed Clayton. "Do you mind?"

"I guess not," Raven said with feigned disinterest.

"Well that's good, because it's all we got. Some of them came from upstairs after the fire," the barmaid apologized.

Grunting, Hairy pitched in two commissary chits and Raven pulled a dog-eared road pass from his pocket to match the seven coppers the fossickers laid on the table.

"Are we all in?" Raven asked.

Clayton examined the bone dice before dropping them into the wooden tumbler one by one. He swirled them one way and the other. He shook the dice onto the table, threw them into the cup, and dumped them out again.

"I've somewhat more to wager," he allowed. From a flap knit into the underside of one of his gauntlets, he pulled out a folded length of fabric. Inside was a hammered silver shawl clasp set with a ring of garnet crystals. He eyed Raven steadily. "Do you?"

Raven gave Hairy a questioning look.

The former smith's apprentice gave a low whistle. "It's nice. Real nice." Taking the delicate silver oval in his massive hand, Hairy turned it over. "Here's the maker's mark, from the oldest silversmith in Coventry." He gave Clayton a questioning look. "Where'd you get such a finely wrought piece?"

"Clay found it in the Trickle." Garth took back the brooch. "It is his unchallenged."

"We have nothing so fine to wager," Raven conceded.

"I'll put my antique brooch against that Skell deck," Clayton offered.

"They're house cards," Raven protested. "Not ours to bet."

Listening to their exchange, the barmaid slid from behind the counter. "Go on," she urged Raven, her eyes on the shawl pin. "I'll find us another set of cards."

"Mind you he cheats," Garth murmured. Clayton nodded at small Ross who stood next to Raven, eating potatoes from his basket. "So do we."

Their game was cut short by commotion at the door. "Soldiers!" A serving girl sang out from the front of the bar.

"Looking for the likes of us, most likely," Hairy grumbled, offering Raven a glum look. "We're busted again."

Ross's eyes strayed to Clayton's gauntlets, whose Evil Eyes glinted. Stuffing the last of Raven's food into his mouth, he scooped the coppers from the table and darted up the stairs.

"I'll barter," the barmaid told Clayton. He reached for the garnet shawl pin. She grabbed it first. "Straight trade, no wager." She pushed the Skell cards into his hands.

"Just the one," Garth said, picking out the sooty parchment as Clayton let the other cards fall to the floor.

"Now go!" The barmaid urged, glancing toward the stairway as the Guard burst through the door.

Garth and Clayton pounded upstairs and hurtled out the second-floor window to join small Ross on the water-shed roof. The three of them sat blinking in the afternoon sun, listening and waiting. They heard doors slam and the odd shout and finally some grumbling as the soldiers cleared the hall. Then the voices died away.

Clayton looked at his gauntlets. The eyes had grown dull. "Do you think we found the sundered Skell?"

"No doubt." Garth showed him the ancient relic. "It's not parchment but horn. Real animal horn like what they only had in First Folk days." He shook his head in admiration. "What better way to conceal an ancient card, than in a stacked deck."

"It's how them witches always hide things," Ross agreed.

Clayton's eyes flickered toward Garth. "You know what they call it."

"Hiding in plain sight." Garth peered into the courtyard. "What do we do now?"

"Take the card and rescue Trader," Ross said simply.

As the boys began to clamber from the shed roof, Clayton held back. "Someone's down there."

Garth scrutinized afternoon shadows casting themselves across the cobbles. Dead vines clung to the crumbling walls and a pile of leaves raked last fall had blown into the corner of the tiny courtyard. Below them, spring grass was beginning to show through blackened timbers thrown from windows during the fire. The scent of wood smoke wafted toward them. "I don't see anything."

After a few moments, the boys dropped over the low stone wall into the alley, where the harsh odor of burning wood was more pungent. Smoke choked the entrance to the boardwalk. Creeping along the edge of the stone foundation, they saw flames licking the front of the building. A smoldering breeze blew the acrid cloud toward them.

"Something's burning." Clayton sniffed. "I think it's the bar."

"Can't be!" Ross exclaimed. "The Goose already got cooked!"

Before their eyes, a large form took shape in the billowing smoke, becoming deeper, denser, darkening to gray. Finally the mass disengaged itself from the fog and came toward them.

"Someone's looking for the First Folk Skell," Garth guessed. "Same as us."

Clayton's eyes teared looking down at his gauntlets, but he could see nothing through the smoke. He began to cough. "Let's go."

When they turned back, the boys found that the fire had engulfed the alley and they could barely see each other.

"He's comin' with fire," Ross whimpered, lost in the gray haze. "Clay, the Bad Man's comin' with fire again!"

"Then we go to the ice," Clayton promised, his voice unsure and far away.

Groping in the dark, Garth's hands found Ross's shoulders. "Hush," he whispered, "I'm right here."

Clayton's gauntlets brushed his sleeve. "Hang on to the card!" the other boy warned. "Use it for Trader."

"That's our plan." Garth began to cough.

A gruff voice came through the fog. "Plans change."

Swirling gusts of wind cleared the smoke from the courtyard. Wiping the sting from his eyes, Garth tried to discover where the words had come from. In the tavern's back courtyard, the smoky figure materialized into someone who looked familiar.

"Hairy!" he cried with relief. "I thought you left with the soldiers. What happened to the Loose Goose?"

"I lit it on fire," the husky boy replied in the same dead voice. His mustache and beard were frizzled. Singed locks rimmed his smoking cap.

Garth's arms went slack and he felt sick to his stomach. "Lit on fire?"

Ross started to moan. "He ain't Hairy."

"Time to scramble," Clayton said softly. "It's the only way."

Garth began to panic. "I don't know how to do it!"

"Come on," Clayton urged as he melted into the shade. "I said: Scramble!"

"Softly, like eggs scramble," Garth answered, trying to remember what to say.

"He's here!" Ross cried as the youth who had been Hairy approached.

As he lumbered toward them, the air around the brawny soldier rippled, and his features started to shift. For the first time, Garth understood the meaning of unsuppear. He watched in horror as Hairy's skin split like rotten fruit, and dropped to the ground as an unneeded guise. He turned to shield Ross from the carnage, but the little boy was no longer tangible, for he had already begun to sink into the shadows.

"Scatter," Clayton warned, his voice drifting away.

"Like sap buckets in the spring," Garth whispered back.

"Look, Clay!" Ross shrieked, just a voice in the fog. "It's the Bad, Bad Man!"

Garth lunged after them, but his hands fell through air. It was no use. He did not know how to follow the fossickers. When the tall man became visible, he was as alone in the alley as he had been on the sandy apron under the Banebridge trestle the last time the fossickers had disappeared. Garth gazed into Kendrick's eyes.

"Father," he said.

"A spyglass!" Esmeralde exclaimed.

CHAPTER 10

Tavern Tales

AT THE CASK AND BARREL TAVERN, fermented wine commonly called Crystal Cordial and heady ale known as glacier beer flowed freely from the wooden taps like the lively conversation at the bar. Located on a side street dividing the wealthy storefronts of Merchant's Pass from the cottage industry of Artisan's Hand, the two-story stone and timber tavern catered to the boroughs' craftsmen and business class alike. The first-floor neighborhood pub was the kind of barroom where flutes of fancy spirits shared serving trays with mugs of home-brewed beer crowned with foam.

Behind the burnished-copper bar top, cellar stairs led to a store-room, where thick stone walls maintained ideal temperatures to stock fine spirits year round. The cellar was lined with wooden racks filled with casks of ale, flasks of fine varietals, and barrels of beer. On the main floor a sweeping staircase near the fieldstone fireplace led to a second-floor balcony which accessed private rooms and dining areas used for special occasion.

Within the shops that fronted the winding cobbles of Merchant's Pass, rumor had it that any information could be bought at the Cask and Barrel for newly minted Northland silver. Amongst the scarred oak tables before the crackling fireplace, talk was loud and ribald, the stories bold.

As she sized up the inviting glow of the lantern-lit alehouse from the street slicked with rain, Esmeralde reflected that the boisterous inn looked just like the kind of place she and Indigo Rose would seek out in a city as diverse as Bordertown. It was too bad that tonight's visit to the Cask and Barrel was Aubergine's and Sierra Blue's idea. For some unexplained reason, she and Indigo had them in tow.

Esmeralde couldn't understand it. When she and Indigo slipped out of the Potluck after dinner, retreating to the alley for a nip of cordial and a puff of glacier weed, Sierra and Aubergine were waiting outside the dye shed's secret entrance wearing dark mantles over their dresses. It seemed they knew the other witches' plans. Aubergine wore a felt bag belted around her waist and Sierra carried a lantern, its wick turned down low.

It was then that Esmeralde pulled out her flask and took a long swig, for she knew there was no possibility of escaping whatever Aubergine or Sierra had in store for them.

Indigo just shrugged and lit her smoke. "We've been ambushed," she said.

Because she now possessed all the necklace stones, Aubergine had been insistent upon encountering a certain silversmith from Artisan's Hand to discuss repairs, while Sierra claimed she had interest in researching her role as the newfound Keeper of the Tales. Both of these tasks could be accomplished at a tavern called the Cask and Barrel at the edge of Merchant's Pass, but neither witch wished to venture into the rougher parts of Bordertown unaccompanied.

"The jeweler's name is Periwinkle," Sierra explained, as the four of them made plans in the back alley. "We have it on authority that he is most skilled in the restoration of cracked crystal."

"Why not just meet him at his shop?" Indigo turned up her collar at the cold drizzle threatening rain. "Wouldn't it be safest to make repairs there?"

"And risk Tasman discovering we sought him out?" Aubergine asked. "Surely you realize that the Dark Queen's eyes watch everywhere you find her shadowy coin."

Esmeralde's breath caught. From her Possibles Bag, she produced the round of southern silver traced with Tasman's visage that she had picked up in Banebridge, what seemed like long ago.

"A piece such as this?" She asked, holding it to the lamplight.

Aubergine's eyes grew violet. "Where did you get that?"

Esmeralde's voice began to falter. "At the Trading Post in Banebridge. I bartered a pair of ground glass spectacles to the store keep for the Lowland coin."

Sierra shook her head, murmuring, "Ozzie is not one of Tasman's minions. He could not have known these coins are spies."

"Spies?" Indigo peered at the hazy sliver of silver. "Where's the eyes?"

Aubergine's mouth set in a grim line. "I find it unsettling that the Dark Queen's spy coin has turned up that far off the main track," she worried aloud. "Who knew she was searching for the lost stone that far south?"

Sierra took the curious coin from Esmeralde and examined both sides. "The magical haze hovers over Tasman's profile, nowhere else. How long have you had it?"

"Over a week." Esmeralde gave her an anxious look. "What can she do? Look through it? See everything?"

Sierra lifted her eyes to Aubergine. "It explains how she was waiting for Lily in the market, posing as an unemployed serving girl." She handed the Lowland silver to her mistress. "The Dark Queen saw us coming and knew Lily would be seeking kitchen help."

With a sigh, Esmeralde gazed at the coin. "Now I notice an aura of dark magic."

"As do I," Indigo nudged her friend. "We should have known!"

"What is it, a portal?" Sierra asked.

"Exactly." While the others watched, Aubergine laid the coin in the flat of her hand, that all could witness the dusky film that clouded the engraved silhouette. Gingerly she picked at the haze like an unwanted cobweb until it finally pulled away from the coin, revealing the eye.

"A spyglass!" Esmeralde exclaimed.

Aubergine crumpled the dark shadow into a ball that fell to ash through her fingers, then put her thumb to the eye and cracked the portal. "Now it's just money."

Sierra nodded with satisfaction. "We shall spend it at the Cask and Barrel. I cannot wait to hear the tales the traveling bards are performing these days."

"You won't like them," Indigo warned. "Currently the telling of tales is like a carnival act, full of lutes and flutes and motley clothes. None of the stories ring true."

Sierra and Aubergine would not be dissuaded. Shepherding the two proper witches past more than a dozen interesting watering holes and wine sinks in the warehouse district in search of a certain alehouse that promised an elusive silversmith and the odd tavern tale put Esmeralde in a foul mood.

"Remember," Aubergine reminded them as they stood outside the Cask and Barrel at last. "Take care to hold no one's gaze. We're to hide in plain sight."

Once inside the smoky mead hall, Esmeralde quickly got rid of her Lowland coin by ordering cups of cordial all around while Indigo sought a table.

"There's naught but a couple of three-legged stools in the back," she reported.

"Drag them over." Esmeralde gave a short nod toward some free space at the curve of the counter, near the entrance. She gathered their four drinks in her two hands and nodded to Indigo. "You and I, we'll stand."

Settling Aubergine and Sierra on stools around the edge of the bar, they leaned against the counter, ears and eyes observant. Here in the back of the room, Esmeralde found she could both watch the entrance, and have a clear view of the stage. The tavern door swung open at regular intervals, offering a breath of damp air promising spring as well as revelers from the busy thoroughfare.

Near the hearth down front, the stage consisted of a stool and a leather hassock on a woven mat. After awhile, a flute player took the stool and a man with a skin drum strapped to his waist sat deeply on the hassock.

"A tale, a tale," the local patrons began to chant, tapping their mugs on the tables and bar top in time to the flute and drum.

"Tell us a tale, give us story, we need a yarn," a boisterous barmaid with long chestnut hair announced merrily to all, as she scanned the crowded room.

The throng took up the shout. "A yarn, a yarn, we need a yarn!" They repeated.

Finally, the flute player broke off his melody and waited until the drumbeats slowed to a stop.

"Is there a witchy woman among us?" His bright eyes strayed to the four at the curve of the bar. He winked at Aubergine. "A teller of tales?" His gaze brushed over Sierra to rest upon Esmeralde, and finally Indigo Rose. "Some stories of old?"

"Don't look at me," she mumbled.

"Sierra Blue, that's your cue," Esmeralde joked.

Before Sierra could reply, a red-faced woman with chapped hands and cheeks pushed her way through the crowded tables along the side of the room to assume the vacant spot between the musicians.

The flutist blew a few high notes. "Are you a witch?" His companion beat two quick pats on his drum for emphasis. "You don't look like a witch."

"No witch," the woman declared. "Just a poor prison cook."

"A convict cook are ye?" the drummer asked, drawing sniggers from several folk in the crowd. The flute player began to trill softly.

"Not myself a convict," the large woman protested, smoothing her hands over her apron. "I cooked soup and such for the sorry wretches jailed in the Burnt Holes."

"No one ever escapes the Burnt Holes," the drummer quipped, with a thump of his palms on the drum skins.

"Oh but some do," the cook claimed with a vigorous nod.

"What is she doing here?" Sierra whispered to the other witches, her face half-hidden beneath the hood of her cloak.

"The Guard fired me for letting a witch escape," the cook announced. "She was one of the Twelve, who knew all of her yarns. The witch disappeared when I ran from the dragon."

"Would she recognize you?" Aubergine asked Sierra softly.

Sierra glanced at the cook from the corner of her eye. "Most definitely."

"Indy, come close," Esmeralde urged.

Taking up her cup Indigo Rose sidled over to shield Sierra from view.

"If she recognizes me, I may give us away." Leaving the lantern on the countertop, Sierra pushed back her stool. "Perhaps I should go."

Aubergine surveyed the tavern. The crowd had grown to a mob blocking the entrance five-folk deep. Attempting to leave might draw more attention than staying put.

"Certainly not alone, and not just yet," she decided.

"Too risky," Indigo glanced toward the doorway. "Besides your jeweler is yet to show."

More banter between the cook and musicians drew chuckles from the patrons close enough to hear them over the buzz of the crowd. Then the drummer began to beat a loud cadence that ended abruptly. The audience quieted.

"It seems as if our convict cook has stories to tell after all!" the flute player announced with a flourish. He took up an impromptu tune while the drummer kept time with soft thumps on his skins.

The old woman's head bobbed. "I know my yarns! I tell them proper!"

The flutist paused. "Might you ken any cycles of the Woolgathering Tales?"

"You mean how the Twelve became Twelve?" The cook gave him a suspicious glance. "Those I never took to heart, for they are bedtime stories fit for sleepy children." She wagged her head. "The yarns I have down pat are the legends of the First Folk suns and the glorious days of old in a fertile valley between rivers that twined together like snakes." Demonstrating, she interlocked her fingers. "Don't ask me how that happened."

"She would do well to heed the Woolgathering Tales," Sierra murmured.

"They all would," Aubergine said.

The cook wrung her hands and wiped them on her apron, declaring, "I do not recall the words to any children's fairy tales, for I was never one to indulge in story hour."

"That's quite a shame!" With a practiced move, the flutist slid his instrument into the waistband of his tunic and escorted the old woman away.

"Wait!" she cried.

"The Woolgathering Tales are the only ones I have the melody for," he apologized, loud enough for all to hear.

"I know the beat by heart!" The drummer put a hand over his breast dramatically.

"Well I never!" the cook protested.

The musicians hustled her into the crowd and left her there. Upstairs, a slight man in motley clothing appeared. He leaned over the balcony. "I know all the cycles to Woolgathering Tales," he addressed the crowd in a deep baritone.

"It's Miles!" The drummer shouted. He beat out a hearty welcoming rhythm, as the bard skipped down the stairs.

"From Nowhere," the flutist announced with a high trill. "At last!"

From the front of the room, the audience began to clap and cheer.

"I think they planned this," Indigo grumbled as the brightly dressed bard took the stage. She glanced toward the balcony. "I'll bet he was waiting up there all along!"

"Of course he was Indy," Esmeralde said, trying to attract attention from an alehouse wench busy pouring wine. A bar back changing out an empty wine cask saw her gesturing with her cup and came over to collect their empty glasses. Esmeralde turned to her friend. "His name was smack on the playbill posted outside."

"Right." Indigo stood aside as the bar back flipped up the hinged countertop and rolled out the spent cask.

After letting the bar top down again, the ale wench slid fresh cups of cordial across the burnished copper. The crowd quieted for the bard who took his place between the flutist and drummer. He doffed his felt hat, bowing deeply to the audience to the right and left. Finally he clicked his heels and bowed center stage toward the patrons sitting at the bar.

"I'm Miles from Nowhere, just returned from the World's Fair with a fresh cycle of tales," he announced. "I'll regale you for a mug of ale and a copper or two or three."

The barmaid brought him a frothing tankard and took his felted hat. "Pay up," she cried, weaving among the throng with the brim upturned. "Pay up!"

There was a grumbling as she passed through the tables with the hat. Coppers began to plink into the felted bowl. Huddled with the flutist and drummer, Miles raised his head.

"That sounds like mere sprinkling!" He put a hand to his ear as if he could hear the odd coin strike another in the collection hat. "There are three of us here!"

"Make it rain!" The drummer pounded his drum. "Make it rain!"

"Does everyone know the Woolgathering Tales?" Miles asked as the thumping subsided. "Called How the Twelve became Twelve?"

"No," the crowd murmured, as the flutist struck up a merry melody.

"Just us four I bet," Indigo muttered. The barmaid flipped up the countertop to slip out with the hat to collect coins from the patrons seated at the far end of the bar.

"It's all about witches!" Miles teased.

"This isn't tale telling, it's a side show," Aubergine said derisively.

"I'll bet none of it rings true." Sierra looked at her companions helplessly. "What have happened to our yarns?"

"We told you," Indigo snorted.

"This is the way the stories go these days," Esmeralde added. "They're supposed to be funny. It's not intended that you learn anything."

Indigo dug out her change purse as the barmaid approached. The bowl of the hat was covered with coppers and the odd piece of Middleland silver depicting rams and ewes, worn coins practically worthless this far north. Indigo tossed in a few coppers.

"This story is from the second cycle, which starts with the least of the Twelve, small Josephine," Miles explained, as the drummer thumped along. "Many knew her as Smokey Jo for she once caught herself on fire quite by accident, but that is a different story. I call this tale The Chosen Gnome."

Indigo gave Esmeralde an uneasy look.

"Hush," she said. "Let's hear the story."

Miles cleared his throat. "Chosen or not, the girls paid no heed to the small gypsy child called Smokey Jo, though they forged and broke alliances according to whim." The flute player began a bantering trill. "The chosen were forever changing roommates in their dormered cells where . . . ?" His voice trailed off and he tapped his chin, as if he had forgotten. "Above a yarn shop! This tale is a yarn, after all."

The audience hooted as he paused to quaff his beer.

"Their mistress was queen of all the enchanted yarns, for magic was yet not outlawed," Miles elaborated. "She wielded crystal shards with a practiced hand, her favorite a deep purple amethyst, the color of eggplant. She reigned over her yarn shop in a distracted way, more often than not leaving domestic matters to a flowery woman who filled the rooms with lilacs and lilies."

"Among the witches, the dye queen was known as Aubergine, the housemother Lilac Lily, and a madam well past her prime, spinning yarns from the green hills of Coventry was called Mamie Verde," Miles revealed, drawing mirth. "Various teachers and students walked the halls, but only few were chosen. These are their stories."

As the barmaid tilted the bowl of the hat toward Sierra, Aubergine untied the bag from her waist to retrieve her change purse. She fished out a few coppers.

The barmaid smiled and tossed her chestnut mane. "It'll be a piece of Northland silver each for the likes of you."

"Whatever for?" Sierra asked.

The barmaid nodded toward Miles. "Methinks you're them."

Without a second glance, Aubergine pushed Sierra's lantern aside to throw her coppers into the motley hat. "You're mistaken."

"First came Indigo Rose, slender as a sapling and so rooted," Miles pantomimed a young tree bending in the wind." She was farm fresh from the foothills of Banebridge where the Runne flowed placid in the broad river valley." He flung his arms wide. "There were too many children in her family—and too few sons—so her parents sent her north to apprentice." The flute and drum struck up a lively tune.

"No boys," a drunken man shouted. "I've all daughters myself. Not a single son!"

As he continued, Miles snuck a glance toward the bar. "Indigo took to the kitchen garden right away, finding an empty bed in a room occupied by quick-witted Esmeralde. They got on for a time until crafty Esmeralde tattled to Lilac Lily about Indigo's penchant for smoking glacier leaf on the dye-shed roof. The result was unsatisfactory: Indigo's herb stash was confiscated, her plants culled from amongst the dill weed in the kitchen garden." The audience groaned in mock dismay.

The barmaid's eyes gleamed beneath her chestnut bangs. Covering the hat's opening with one hand, she held out her palm to Aubergine. "I've need of somewhat not for the collection if you're two of the Twelve." She lifted her chin. "I've got one calling himself Periwinkle just come in through the cellar, so's not to be noticed."

Aubergine uncinched her change purse and found two pieces of silver. The barmaid looked around quickly before depositing the Northland coins into her apron pocket. She couldn't help but notice a purple gem within the felted purse, sparkling among the coin of the realm.

"Your jeweler cautions you to avoid the front entrance," she whispered. "There's Guard outside, patrolling the streets. The only way out is down the cellar stairs and through the storeroom." She inclined her head. "Watch for me at intermission. Folk come and go at the break. Few will notice you're missing."

Aubergine belted the felt bag around her waist once more, leaving her change purse lying within reach on the bar top. It lay slightly open and from her vantage point, Sierra saw the amethyst crystal winking in the light. Passersby might notice it, too, if it was what they sought.

"After a few days of cold silence, Indigo flounced across the hall to room with Lavender Mae, who snuck glacier weed a bit, herself." Miles skipped across the stage, and the audience chuckled once more. "Mae was infatuated with dye crystals and bright as a shooting star, but orphaned at birth, she grew up a bit eccentric. Even at a young age, she sung tuneless ditties to herself in the washroom."

"He is talking about us," Indigo complained.

"Of course he is," Esmeralde clapped her shoulder. "The tale is called How the Twelve Became Twelve. That would be us, after all."

As they squabbled, Aubergine nudged Sierra, for the fat prison cook had emerged from the crowded tables near the stage.

Sierra saw the old woman pull on a cardigan sweater. "Perhaps she's leaving."

"Hopefully." Aubergine looked away.

"Feeling contrite, Esmeralde invited Smokey Jo to sleep in the vacant bed in her room, but found she could not bear the lonely gnome more than a few moments at a time," Miles cried in mock dismay, causing several drunken hecklers to moan as well. "Smokey was so bereft of friendship that she almost always never left her queen's side except to light the hearths—for a little fire starter was she—making the others leery." The drummer thumped twice before the flutist trilled yet another melody and the crowd quieted slightly.

"In the end, Esmeralde filled her vacancy with a table for mixing tinctures and teas and soon could concoct simple remedies for all!" Miles exclaimed proudly. "She sold them for a few coppers lunchtimes and before bed until she earned enough coin to buy her first Possibles Bag. It took years to fill that medicinal pouch to her satisfaction."

"The bard knows too much," Indigo hissed angrily.

"He does tell tales out of turn," Esmeralde observed, trying to calm her down.

Sierra kept her eyes trained on the bar, where her lantern stood beside the cup of cordial she had barely touched.

Indigo stared at the bard with suspicion. "No one is supposed to know such trifles about me," she said crossly.

"Or any one of us," Aubergine agreed. "Indigo, what did I say about looking folk in the eye?"

"Broken shards!" Indigo swore, averting her gaze.

"Now we'll meet Studious Sierra and Tracery Teal," Miles revealed to the patrons in a hushed voice. "Too clever for her own good, Sierra roomed with temperamental Teal unless Teal was in one of her moooooooods." Drawing the word out, he paused for the flutist to pipe a few morose notes. The audience roared. "Sierra hailed from the frozen North and Teal came from the harsh coastal islands of the fisheries back east for her schooling. The girls were so different, yet they got along. Both possessed the inner strength to follow the yarn queen's footsteps but only Sierra had the serenity to see beyond her years."

Miles paused to telescope his fists around his eyes. "The girls called it her lion eyes." He peered into the throng. "Able to glimpse the future, she accepted her fate under the guise of complacency. Sierra was a young lioness lying at the edge of the Savannah, calmly watching her prey, enjoying the wait."

Suddenly the barmaid stood before Aubergine. "Another round whilst you wait?" Aubergine pushed away her empty cup. "Thank you, no."

Taking the wine glass, the barmaid eyed Aubergine's purse. "Are you sure?"

Sierra waved her away.

"As it turned out, neither girl could follow Aubergine's path because of the road taken by Tasman," Miles revealed mysteriously. "The Villain, Traitor of the South." The drummer pounded on the skins as Miles drained his beer.

"Teal crossed Tasman early in a churlish dispute over fixatives in the dye room, and although she thought little of such small slights, she discovered that Tasman forgot nothing."

The prison cook began to shamble through the crowd.

"I thought you said these minstrel stories never ring true," Sierra murmured.

"They don't usually," Esmeralde replied. "I'm beginning to wonder."

"Do you know this Miles?" Aubergine asked. The barmaid walked by, trailing her hand along the counter and the old witch pulled her purse closer.

Indigo stared into her wine cup. "I've never seen him before."

"Big and brash!" Miles swung his head from side to side. "Bold and rash, Teal acted ahead of her thoughts when it came to Tasman. One time Teal contracted a stinging rash from fire nettles thrown in her bed." The crowd gasped. "Another time she came down with a sudden ague so strong, it hurt her chest to cough." Holding his stomach, Miles hacked like a seasoned smoker. "Years later, after Teal disappeared, greenish traces of her remained like morning mist rising from the river, all recalled her as Traces of Teal."

"So the trap is set," Sierra muttered.

"It won't be long now." Aubergine sighed. "If we become separated, don't tarry for my sake."

"I cannot open your lidless box," Sierra protested.

Aubergine grasped her hand. "Don't worry over that now."

"Now for Tasman the Traitor," Miles said in a hushed voice. "She was a loner, who kept her own council in a darkened attic closet." The crowd drew a collective breath. "With no friends or family, she appeared at the yarn shop unbidden one day to stand on the stoop in the rain unyielding until Lilac Lily took pity and let her in."

"Even dripping, Tasman could not help but exude evil. The other girls shrank from the aura surrounding her like a cloud of gnats!" Miles jumped at an unseen swarm of flies overhead. "Gifted with no social graces, Tasman rarely spoke. Although few and far between, her remarks cut like a whetted knife." He clutched his bicep as if someone had stabbed him.

"Ooooh," the audience cried in pain.

"I can take no more mockery of the Twelve!" Indigo slammed down her wine cup and nudged Esmeralde. "Let's go drink someplace else."

"Wait," Sierra hissed furtively. She glanced from Indigo to Esmeralde. "Who knows the cycle of Woolgathering Tales better than I?"

"No one," Indigo declared.

"Who knows them at all?" Sierra questioned.

"Just we few." Dawning awareness crossed Esmeralde's face. "For the love of the Lost Caves! Indy, don't you see? The only way the bard could know the tales as we do—"

"He has to be one of us!" Indigo stared at the scrawny minstrel, as the prison cook came toward them.

"Is he she?" Esmeralde whispered. "There is a gypsy look about him."

Indigo adjusted her bandana. "I'll not be fooled again," she promised.

A sudden drumroll broke their conversation. "Intermission!" Miles shouted. "After the break, I'll continue with Tasman the Traitor!"

Aubergine and Sierra stood to search for the barmaid, who was nowhere in sight. Aubergine grasped Sierra's arm unsteadily as dozens of patrons streamed past them, upending their stools.

The serving wench appeared from the cellar stairs. "Not that way!" she called to the witches above the din. "The Guard waits without!"

But it was too late for Esmeralde and Indigo; the throng surged through the door like a wave carrying them into the night. Aubergine and Sierra held tight to the edge of the countertop as the crowd rippled past, threatening to pull them into its wake.

The barmaid opened the hinged countertop. "Over here!" she beckoned.

It was impossible for Aubergine or Sierra to make headway against the human tide pouring outside. When Sierra looked up, the prison cook stood before her.

"It's you!" the hulking woman bellowed. "The witch who was lost!"

"No more lost than you!" Sierra denied as the red-faced woman grabbed at her.

Twisting away, Sierra sensed something wrong. The air surrounding the old woman began to ripple and nearby patrons shrieked in earnest as they stampeded outside.

"Hurry!" the barmaid shrieked, ushering her through the opening in the bar top.

When Sierra looked back, her eyes met Aubergine's. Though flecks of gold stood out in her irises, her lion eyes could not discern what had hastened such a rush. The Potluck Queen stood her ground like a lone rock in a tidal bore, mustering what strength she could to keep her footing in a swirling sea of terror. Outside wind whipped tendrils of long gray hair about her face, registering shock.

Sierra turned her golden gaze back to see the cook confronting her already beginning to disintegrate before her eyes. The shapeless cardigan dropped to the floor, and became ground underfoot by the wave of receding customers.

The ale wenches squealed in horror as they fled or hid; even the musicians had disappeared up the stairs. The bard Miles was nowhere.

"I'll have the amethyst," the cook said in Tasman's cold voice, shoving Sierra aside like a child.

Losing balance, Sierra crashed to the wet floor. Among the upturned wine cups and barstools, her lantern lay on its side leaking oil. She righted it and crawled under the bar. The Dark Queen focused her ice-green eyes on Aubergine.

Having observed Tasman's transformation from kitchen cook to Dark Queen, Sierra now realized why the fossick boys claimed that the unfortunates she inhabited when she shape-shifted *unsuppeared*, for it was clear that Tasman discarded her hosts like costumes no longer needed when she was done using them as a guise. As her unforgettable features surfaced, the watery-blue eyes in the cook's chapped face decomposed just as quickly. In minutes, not one defining trait of the old woman remained. Looking at Tasman's stony face, Sierra understood that she had destroyed the prison cook as easily as she had done away with Tracery Teal when they were young. In vain, Sierra searched the barroom floor for some remnant to prove that the cook ever existed, but even the old woman's sweater and food-stained apron had vanished.

The Dark Queen and Potluck Queen faced each other across the scuffed oak floor. "I'll have the lost stone that was atop Little Teal's stick." Tasman's voice resonated in the nearly empty tavern. "Don't try to convince me it doesn't exist, for I saw it."

"Your spying coins will show you no more of our doings," Aubergine pledged.

"Where is the crystal?" Tasman demanded.

"Where is our Trader?" Aubergine returned.

"Waiting to be traded," Tasman mocked. She stretched out taloned fingers and the felted bag jerked from Aubergine's waist and upended on the bar. Toiletries and knitting notions rolled across the copper countertop to rain down around Sierra.

"It's here somewhere, I can feel it." Grimacing, Tasman shook the bag until nothing remained. A few more items clattered to the floor, but none of them was what she sought. Discarding the bag on the counter, Tasman strolled along the empty bar, searching for clues. "You were sitting here the entire time. It can't be far."

A serving wench hidden behind some overturned chairs rose to run and the Dark Queen sent a fire bolt from her fingertips that ripped through her body. Tasman bent to search the girl where she had fallen.

Feeling Aubergine's violet eyes upon her, Sierra nodded slightly in return. In silence she crawled across the sticky floor toward the opening in the bar where the barmaid crouched behind the hinged countertop, shielded by an empty cask. Her eyes strayed across Aubergine's change purse clutched in the girl's hand and the glimmer of amethyst within.

"Down the stairs!" the barmaid whispered, pointing the way with her free hand.

Sierra edged toward the wine cellar. Hugging the wall, she crept down the stairway, one step at a time.

"Of course!" she heard Tasman crow. "Hiding in plain sight as I thought!" Sierra flinched as the countertop slammed and her voice grew cruel. "You thieving wench!"

Strains of running and screaming began anew overhead. Sierra stumbled into the cool stone cellar lined with wine casks and beer barrels. The room smelled of aged oak and spiced wine. In the far corner, candles burned on a table commonly used for wine tasting. As Sierra approached, she saw a slight man she recognized. He sat at the table sipping cordial before a half-eaten plate of braised beef and cabbage. On a finely crafted chain around his neck swung a jeweler's monocle.

"I'm glad you came after all, Periwinkle," she said softly.

"And I you." He peered toward the ceiling with a frown. "That sounds like quite a disturbance. Should I be fearful?"

Sierra raised her eyes. "These days we all have cause for alarm, but don't panic just yet. Have you been waiting long?"

"I arrived before our appointed time by carriage, only to see soldiers in the streets," he answered. "I circled back on foot later and found a bar back loading empty casks in the alley who let me in through the cellar." He put his hands on the table. "Except for the noise from above, it's quite nice down here."

"It may be over now," Sierra said, straining to hear more voices.

He poured her a cup of cordial. "A serving girl brought me food and drink."

"She may be dead, I'm afraid." Sierra set her glass on the table.

He nodded without comment. "The necklace is safe?"

"I hope," Sierra replied as they heard booted feet overhead. She eyed the empty space at the foot of the stairs. "I expect we shall know any moment."

From above, a door slammed and a set of feet came quickly down the stone steps. Hair flying behind her, Aubergine emerged in the candlelight, out of breath.

"That went rather well, I thought," she said, crossing to the two at the table.

She held out her hand. "You must be our jeweler."

"At your service." Rising, Periwinkle bowed. "You must be the Potluck Queen."

"Call me Aubergine," she said.

"Well met." He poured her a cup of wine. "I am eager to see the stones with mine own eyes."

"Is Tasman gone?" Sierra asked.

With a nod the old witch sat and sipped some wine. "She stole our beach glass." She gazed up at the ceiling, but all remained silent. "On her way out, she killed a few folk."

"As is her wont," Sierra murmured.

"That barmaid would have been better off leaving my purse be. I saw her eye the amethyst with avarice." Aubergine shrugged. "What happened could not be helped."

Without comment, Sierra held up her lantern and carefully unscrewed the bottom.

"So much for hiding in plain sight." Aubergine raised her snowy brows as Sierra unearthed the tinderbox hidden within. "I'm afraid that ploy has seen its day."

"At least as far as Tasman is concerned," Sierra agreed.

"Is that silver box mine or yours?" Aubergine asked.

Sierra offered her the tin. "As I mentioned before, I cannot open yours." She watched Aubergine's practiced fingers find the invisible latch. "I believe mine still houses the cold-fire crystals I never threw into the sky."

"Answering fire." There was an audible click and then Aubergine removed the top of the box. "That seems so long ago."

As accustomed to rare jewels as he was, Periwinkle could not help but gasp as he gazed at the nest of dazzling gemstones. "I have never seen such a fine set of crystals," he uttered, his eyes sparkled in their blaze, his face luminous in their light.

"It has been half a lifetime since anyone has seen them together," Sierra said reverently. "There are twelve distinct stones, each representing one of us who had a place in a ring destroyed more than twenty years ago."

"The broken circle," Aubergine whispered to Periwinkle in earnest. "Make the necklace whole once more."

"Have you the skill to do it?" Sierra asked.

"It shall be my pleasure," the jeweler murmured putting the monocle to his eye. In the candlelight, he reached for the lost stone.

Carefully, he lifted Trader to his chest.

CHAPTER 11

Three and Three

WHEN TRADER AND NILES FINALLY BROKE through the tangled Copse above the Dell, Trader held up her hand for silence, for she already sensed something dead wrong. Both folk and animal had fled in fear through the verdant valley recently. She saw their wildly churned tracks everywhere, from booted feet to mule-deer hooves to small-game prints, all running one direction: from the Dell up the well-trod trail toward Banebridge.

In full dark the fresh scent of charred wood hung heavily in the air. Her crystal held high, Trader examined the blackened timbers. She touched a burnt tree trunk expecting to find warmth but the dead birch was stone cold.

"This happened days ago," Niles said softly, scanning the scorched ground all around them. "Was it a forest fire?"

"You would think," Trader murmured with a sinking feeling in her stomach. Her heart began to pound. "But no." With the orb of quartz blazing before her, she raced toward the Dell.

"Trader, wait up!" Niles called, loping behind.

But the fossick girl couldn't stop. Even though she already knew her worst fears would be confirmed, she had to see for herself. When she reached the site of her camp, the blackened hulk of the collapsed lean-to loomed before her. It was more than Trader could bear. She fell to her knees near the stream she and her band of followers had used for drinking and washing, now choked with cinders and bracken. All that remained of the tent and its contents were singed scraps of canvas amidst piles of blackened tins and broken crockery. The bedrolls and household supplies and packsacks of truck were burnt up, her fossickers gone. Trader dug her fingers into the wet earth, tears bright in her eyes.

Niles caught up and crouched down beside her. "What was here before?"

"A fossick camp." Trader swallowed hard. "Home to my band of boys. Everyone called us the Fossickers in the Dell. We built this place four years ago."

As she looked at him, tears of sorrow and disappointment spilled down her face. She did not even try to wipe them away.

Niles slung his arm around her heaving shoulders. "Who would do this?"

"Someone fossickers call the Bad, Bad Man." Trader glanced up. "Have you heard of him?"

The big boy shook his sandy head.

"He is the Dark Queen's brother," she said in a hollow voice. "He makes flames shoot from his fingers, and burns down anything he doesn't like." She began to rock on her knees, letting more tears streak down her face. When Niles tried to still her, she shrugged him off and wrapped her arms around her skinny frame.

"What would the Lowland Queen want with a gang of fossick boys?" he asked.

"Nothing," Trader said dully.

In the silence that followed, she avoided his gaze. Should she trust this northern sledder friend of Warren's? In truth it did not matter, she decided. Now she had nothing to lose. She lifted her glistening eyes to meet his, big and blue, just like Skye's.

"We're not all of us fossick boys," she whispered. "I'm not what I seem."

"Who are you then?" Niles asked.

"I think I'm a witch, but I'm not sure," Trader admitted. "And Skye is, too—her own mother is one of the Potluck Twelve." She nodded thoughtfully. "Your Warren and Garth, they are sons of witches."

"As must you be," Niles said evenly. "A son of a witch."

"I have no mother, and I'm not a fossick boy!" Trader said angrily. "I'm just hiding as one."

Niles frowned in disbelief. "Really? For how long?"

"What seems like my whole life! And I'm sick of it!" She shouted back, gripping the front of her filthy jerkin. "I'm a girl! Do you need to see?"

"Not at all." Niles shook his head.

"The Dark Queen hunts us down and to take everything away," Trader cried. "She killed my aunt and maybe my mother, for all I know. All over a stupid crystal and a ripped-up Skell. She made the Bad Man burn up my camp, scatter my fossickers . . ."

Niles put both arms around her. "I'm sorry."

"I said I was a girl, not some frail flower," she yelled, pushing him away. "I don't need your pity!" For emphasis, she punched him in the chest. "Get away from me."

He held up his hands. "Fine."

"I can't believe this," Trader sobbed, hugging her knees. "I can't believe this is happening. Especially now." She tipped back her head, taking in big gulps of cold air. "DONE," she said at last. "I believe I'm DONE."

"We'll find your fossickers," Niles said quietly. "And meet up with Warren and Skye again. You'll see."

"Doubtful. You know what I said to my boys?" She swiped at her face. "They never knew I was female, by the way. I told them if there was fire, go to the ice." She began to shiver from cold and exhaustion. "I bet they went up to Bordertown and the Bad Man killed them. I bet they're all dead because of me."

"You don't know that." Getting up, Niles brushed ashes from his pants. "Come on, let's go."

She gazed up at him, completely spent. "First Folk Skells. The lost stone. What does it matter when everyone's gone?"

"This place isn't good for you." Niles held out his hand. "Time to leave."

Trader shuddered. "I'm too tired. I just want to die."

"Stop it." He went to pull her up.

"I mean it." She pushed his hand away. "I spent the past few days locked in a livestock pen without food or water. I had to sleep out in the open with the sheep. Eat snow for water, pee on the ground." She gave him a derisive look. "I guess those Lowland guards found out I was a girl soon enough." Overcome with fatigue, she lay on the ground and closed her eyes. "I only saw the Dark Queen once and all she wanted was the stone that used to be on top of my walking stick and half of a Skell card."

THREE AND THREE

"What for?" Niles looked down at the small girl stretched out on the cold earth.

"She said it would buy my freedom," Trader answered sleepily.

Frantically Niles scanned the ruined campsite for a bit of blanket or canvas remnant; anything he could cover over Trader. She was fading fast and he wasn't about to leave her to freeze in a burnt fossick camp without a blanket or bedroll. As a sledder in the North, he'd seen soldiers on the trail much heartier collapse from hunger and fatigue. Sometimes they refused to rise. If Niles didn't load them on his sled to revive with hot food, warm blankets, and a blazing fire at base camp, they would die from exposure.

"Stones and Skells are magic," Trader began to drift away. "You'll see."

With nothing to warm her, Niles stripped off his Guard jacket and shrugged out of the knitted vest he always wore underneath. He'd had it so long he didn't know where it came from. It wasn't very clean, but it held his body heat so well that sometimes it made him sweat, even in the bitter cold of the Northlands. He wrapped it around the small girl lying on the ground. This time she didn't resist, for she was either asleep or unconscious.

Carefully, he lifted Trader to his chest. He had a hard time believing he ever thought she was a fossick boy. Wet lashes fell across translucent skin on her dirty face. He guessed her to be nearly his age, yet she weighed nothing. *How could someone so scrawny be so scrappy?* he asked himself. *How did she rule a gang of thieves, some of them twice her size?* It was then he realized he did not know what she wanted.

"Trader." He jiggled her shoulder. "Trader, wake up." When she didn't stir, he trickled a few drops of water from his canteen across her brow.

"Raining," she sputtered.

"Where are we going? To Bordertown?" he asked.

"No silly, the Banebridge Trading Post." She yawned. "To see if anybody left word."

"What if there's no word?"

She opened one eye. "Then we tell Ozzie Three and Three."

"Three and Three," Niles repeated with a smile as Trader nodded off once more. Cradling her in his arms, he held the pink quartz overhead until he found the well-trod footpath north. "It makes just about as much sense as anything else I've heard," he muttered to himself, moving swiftly up the track.

THREE AND THREE

Grabbing the ponies' headstalls, he led them out to the wagon and checked the alley again.

CHAPTER 12

Six of One

ALL WEEK, AS SHE EQUIPPED THE six for the journey to the glacier, Lily stacked their gear in the vestibule of the summer kitchen. When the witches were finally ready, no one could squeeze through the screen door past the bedrolls and packs, tents and foodstuffs, designed to last half a dozen travelers several weeks.

One problem Lily had was her inability to guess how long it would take the handpicked witches to find the Lost Caves or what they might encounter on their trek through the frozen wastes. On top of that, there was the matter of the extra pack.

Someone would be joining the six on their quest, but no one knew who. Lily felt for certain the unnamed traveler was no witch. Smokey Jo found the mystery exciting. Ratta thought it maddening. Wheat hoped the extra sojourner was her little sheep, Tracks. Indigo and Esmeralde were so happy to be chosen themselves, they did not care who tagged along. No one could speculate what Lavender Mae believed.

With Ratta's help, Lily checked through the bundles once more. Finally she straightened and put the heels of her hands to her aching back. "It's time to hitch the wagon," she told Warren, who waited in the kitchen in his Highland shepherd disguise.

Donning his hat, he brushed by Skye who tarried in the kitchen.

"What of mother?" She asked nervously twisting her hair. "She's not back yet."

"It can't be helped," Ratta said gruffly, wiping rough hands on her apron. "We dare not delay another day."

"But she's supposed to lead us." Skye frowned at Lily. "Isn't she?"

"Wheat kens how to get to the Burnt Holes, as does Mae," Lily said blithely.

"For all it matters, I bet even your brother could find his way back." Ratta eyed Lily. "I'll tell the others to gather their belongings."

After she left the kitchen, Lily took Skye's shoulders. "Let's sit for a minute."

When they had settled at the round table near the cookstove, Lily poured cinnamon tea from the kettle that simmered on the back burner throughout the day. She glanced at the girl's anxious face. "I'm not certain how to begin."

"It's about my mother, isn't it?" Skye guessed.

"It is." Lily stirred honey into their tea.

Skye took the cup of fragrant liquid Lily offered. "She's not going, is she?"

"No." Lily looked at the young girl who had so much more than she ever thought possible resting upon her shoulders. "Sierra is not destined to journey to Guardian's Watch before her time." She blew across her steaming cup. "Once she enters the ancient tombs, it is her destiny to assume the Guardianship and ward the First Folk until the next caretaker is chosen."

"I know that." Skye wrapped cold hands around her mug.

"What you may not realize is that once your mother sets eyes upon the ancient city, she must begin her watch," Lily said carefully. "During her tenure she is trapped within the glacier, unable to leave, as Mamie is now."

"Ever?" Skye's chin began to tremble.

"Sierra must serve her term until the next Guardian arrives," Lily explained. "Once relieved of her duty she will pass to the Land of Dreams, to safeguard us all."

"We will never see her again, outside the walls of ice?" Skye asked in disbelief.

"The Dark Queen is aware, as are Aubergine and I," Lily confirmed. "And now you. It would be Tasman's great pleasure to lure Sierra into the caves and imprison her prematurely."

Skye put her cup to her lips. "Does mother know her fate?"

"Far better than any of us," Lily replied.

"I heard Aubergine name her Keeper of the Tales." Skye gave Lily a troubled look. "And I knew that meant she would be the next Guardian someday, but I thought that was a long time off."

"Her term might start today or years from today." Lily set her cup down. "No one knows."

"Not even you?" Skye asked.

"Not even me. Sierra feigned interest in the quest, as a ruse to disguise the true intention of Aubergine's private counsel." She bent her head closer. "We can spare but six witches to undertake the journey, for the rest of us have much to do."

"You want me to go." Skye realized. "The bag you packed for my mother was mine."

"Yes," Lily said softly.

"Why?" Her eyes shone with tears. "I once sought adventure, but no more, for I've witnessed the price. I'd sooner stay to mind the yarn shop and look for Trader."

"The Teal you call Trader is already found by someone you know and trust," Lily revealed. "And of that I dare say no more. Your path lies elsewhere."

"Does it matter who goes or stays?" Skye argued, her face growing hot. "It's starting to sound like six of one, a half dozen of the other." Rising, she threw her napkin on the table. "Am I the seventh traveler everyone keeps speculating about? Six of you plus one such as me who is no true witch?"

"You are a true witch, you shall see," Lily soothed her. "Aubergine selected each of you carefully for the quest. Your small group is charged with finding Mamie Verde and convincing her to lead you to the Lost Caves before Tasman arrives with her minions. Only then have we a chance to protect the secrets of old."

"How were we chosen?" Skye asked, only slightly less angry. In the silence that followed, she kept her eyes on the housemother. "If I'm to go, I should know."

"Fair enough," Lily sighed. "As you may have discovered, I am gifted with a special understanding. I see the secrets of all I encounter to some extent, although Tasman has duped me time and again. I sense your hopes and dreams, your strengths and weaknesses. Possibly I know more than you are aware of yourself. Such talent is a heavy burden I have not borne well in the past. I advised Aubergine which of you should undertake the quest." She finished her tea. "She has concurred but for one."

"Who will join us?" Skye asked.

"I dare not tempt fate." Lily pushed herself up from the table. "But you'll find out soon. Your six of one will become six and one, and you will be the better for it."

"Seven of us?" Skye's eyes lit up. "Truly?"

"Not exactly," Lily answered.

"Could it be that Tracery Teal's ghost shall join us? Or Mamie Verde herself reborn? Or mother?" The girl's face grew somber. "Perhaps she has not returned because she is already imprisoned there, waiting for us."

"I can tell you this," Lily decided. "The six of you leaving today have been selected for specific abilities you possess. Ratta's necessity is twofold. Not only can she speak the language of the ancients, but she also may be the only one of us Mamie recognizes, now that she has transcended into a younger version of herself.

Winter Wheat kens the ways of all animals, and may possibly be able to gentle the whirling Dervish should you encounter him once more. Such familiars are sworn to protect First Folk crypts, and we hope that Wheat can gain passage through the tombs unharmed. The cabochon beetles tied to her staff have the ability to detect any danger.

Esmeralde has fully restocked her Possibles Bag with concoctions designed to hurt or heal, while Indigo Rose specializes in herbal remedies and restorative arts. Together they possess powers greater than the sum of their parts. And Mae," here Lily paused. "Well, she is Mae of course, but she alone has made the journey through ancient tombs to the Crystal Caves beyond."

"What of me?" Skye asked at last. "I have no talents. I am a spinner of yarns, but certainly no Keeper of Tales. I cannot conjure or heal or speak in silent tongues. What can I possibly add to the group?"

Lily reached across to take Skye's hands in her own. "That remains to be seen, for you my child symbolize the delicate balance of what we know as good and evil. The scales are skewed now. The natural world is dying. It will be up to you and your brethren to create equilibrium again."

"But how . . . ?" Skye's voice trailed off.

"That you shall discover when you assume your mantle," Lily assured her. "Which is the Fire and Ice shawl we witches created together. Wheat chose the fleece and Mae the crystals. Aubergine offered an incantation to infuse it with special powers while Esmeralde stirred the pot and the Teal you call Trader marked time. You spun the fleece Smokey Jo caught from Wheat's carding combs into fine yarn from which Aubergine patterned a shawl that Indigo knit into the night."

"The shawl was meant for my mother," Skye interrupted.

"No, always for you," Lily said gravely. "Sierra's charge is to tell the yarns, not to knit or transform them. Indigo Rose carries the finished garment enfolded in silk in her pack. When the time comes and she drapes it around your shoulders, you shall assume Sierra's legacy not as the witch she is now, but the one she was when young."

"I will be a proper witch at last?" Skye ventured.

"That and more." Lily rose to take their empty cups.

"Will I inherit her all-seeing stare?" Skye's eyes shone. "Will I know her fate as well as mine?"

"I can say no more, lest I speak out of turn," Lily said, her back to Skye as she rinsed out their cups. "In private counsel you were chosen for this quest, and neither Aubergine nor Sierra has returned to say different."

Skye frowned. "Why did you wait to tell me?"

"Don't forget, I know your thoughts." Turning, Lily wiped her hands on a towel. "Lately you've spent quite a bit of time outside these walls in idle conversation."

"I have been talking to the stable hand," Skye admitted, her face growing pink.

"And the fossick boys, and the groundsman," Lily added. "The Dark Queen has eyes and ears everywhere. In order to safeguard our plans they must be kept secret from all, at times even you."

Outside, Warren scanned the deserted alley before slipping into the stables to harness the ponies. It bothered him that there was still no sign of Garth and his fossick friends who had left on a lark two nights ago in search of a rumored card of old. It also troubled him that of the four witches who had gone barhopping on a fool's errand to find a jeweler able to remake Aubergine's necklace, only two had returned and neither of them had been his mother.

When questioned, Indigo and Esmeralde insisted they had been swept away by a throng leaving a large tavern bordering Artisan's Hand during a break in the nightly entertainment and had decided to seek libations elsewhere.

"We didn't care for the patrons or the performance," Indigo declared.

Esmeralde agreed. "There was a man banging a drum, another trilling on a flute, and between them a gypsy dressed like a dandy shouting out stories."

"To tell you the truth, his tales weren't even that good," Indigo added. "We left Aubergine and Sierra sitting at the bar and went to find another tavern less crowded."

"Or two or three," Esmeralde said. "We were just as surprised as you to find that they weren't in their beds come morning."

"Good for them!" Indigo winked at her friend. "I thought you and I were the only witches that stayed out all night anymore."

As he brushed Shep and Chuffer and threw on their harnesses, Warren's stomach filled with growing dread. Breakfast has passed with no word from Aubergine or his mother, but Lily was behaving as if everything was going as planned. Even more peculiar, he had learned that after he loaded their gear, Lily wanted him to drive the six witches to the trailhead, though the stable boy was perfectly capable. The rutted road ended just below a camping area called the Crossed Tracks and Wheat knew the trails well. They were the same routes that Highland shepherds used to migrate west for winter, and drive their flocks east come spring. From there the witches could find their way into the glacier through the Burnt Holes, or follow Mae south to her lair if they trusted her direction.

Wheat had insisted that Warren bring her little sheep, Tracks, to supplement his disguise as a shepherd, but he knew she had alternate plans. Yesterday, when Lily disclosed that another traveler would be joining them, the witches were abuzz with conjecture. Now that the Jacob's stone bruise had healed, Wheat was convinced that Lily was alluding to Tracks and would undoubtedly attempt to take the ram on the journey. Warren did not believe the others thought Tracks was their secret companion and wasn't looking forward to the argument he felt would ensue when they reached the trail. Six witches embarking together on an impossible quest was bad enough. Six witches and one sheep searching for the Crystal Caves was pure folly.

Grabbing the ponies' headstalls, he led them out to the wagon and checked the alley again. Nothing.

"Won," came a singsong voice behind him.

Warren jumped. He hated it when Lavender Mae snuck up on him like that.

"Won!" she chirped again, before breaking out into giggles.

With a shake of his head, Warren turned to regard the scrawny witch. The passage of time coupled with her physical distance from the Northland Glacier seemed to be holding the voices inside Mae's head at bay. However slowly, she was regaining some semblance of speech, and seemed to understand more than she uttered. Not everyone comprehended what she meant, for her words were few and her pronunciation odd. No matter what Warren told her, she called him Won.

"It's Warren," he reminded her for the twentieth time since yesterday. "War-ren."

"Won!" She denied with a shake of her wild mane.

At least Mae had finally permitted herself to be dressed properly, he noticed. Lily had coaxed her into wearing long dark dresses like the other witches and Sierra had altered a traveling cloak to fit Mae's slight form, the same mantle from her bundle of magical garments intended for the World's Fair.

The biggest reminder of the old Mae was the dark line around her neck where her precious pouch had hung for twenty years. After she had forfeited the broken necklace and destroyed the pouch, nothing replaced it. She held her head higher without the weight of the bag and scratched her neck absently from time to time. That was all.

Often, Warren thought of the question Wheat asked when Mae gave up the necklace, a query that to this day remained unanswered. How was it that Mae came to harbor the broken necklace, Wheat had conjectured, when all knew that Tasman had escaped with it some twenty years ago when she fled south?

If Lily knew the answer, she wasn't saying and his mother and Aubergine remained tight-lipped. Warren looked at Mae, shyly sneaking glances at him as she traced circles in the dirt with the toe of her boot. Maybe she would tell them all one day.

Turning to the mountain ponies, he hitched them to the wagon's front bar and center pole. The two horses had not been out since their arrival at Bordertown and they pricked their ears back and forth and stamped their tiny hooves excitedly.

Running the long lines through the loops in the leather harnesses, he placed the double set of reins on the bench seat and offered Mae his hand. "Time to get in."

He helped her to the bench seat, and then he climbed up beside her to take the reins. There was an ashy taste in his mouth he couldn't get rid of, no matter what Esmeralde gave him to drink. He'd had it for days. Warren glanced at the gray sky that every so often sprinkled the ground with soot instead of rain. *No wonder,* he thought.

"Team." Warren slapped the lines lightly and the ponies stepped out eagerly. Mae clung to his arm. Since they had arrived at Potluck Yarn last week, she guarded him with jealous zeal. She sat next to him at meals and accompanied him on errands in the city, even when he was safely disguised as a Highland Shepherd. Mae made such a fuss when he and Garth opted to sleep in the attic with the fossick boys, that he was forced to remain in the second-floor dormitory, in a narrow chamber across the hall from Mae. Nobody would room with her, not even Indigo Rose, who smoked more glacier weed than Mae in Warren's estimation.

It would be difficult to abandon Mae at the Crossed Tracks and Warren secretly hoped that when they reached the trailhead, she refused to leave the wagon. In his mind it seemed cruel that the witches insisted Mae return to the glacier. He feared she would lose what peace of mind she had recovered in the presence of ancient voices once more.

He drove the team through the alley between Potluck Yarn and the pottery next door and halted at the kitchen garden gate. "You can go get the others," he told Mae.

With a girlish smile she jumped down from the seat, threw open the gate and danced across the garden path. When the stable boy came to hold the horses, Warren followed her inside.

The witches were scattered through the summer kitchen, packing last-minute necessities. Trading jokes, Indigo and Esmeralde checked through packets of herbs and ground crystals, keen to begin their adventure. Wheat smiled with satisfaction as she hooded her staff and scooped up little Tracks. Even Ratta seemed excited about the prospect of reuniting with Mamie. Lily was everywhere at once, adjusting packs, securing straps, and stashing forgotten items into bags and bundles. Only his sister, Skye seemed pensive. Warren did not like the look of her faraway eyes, for it reminded him too much of their mother's all-seeing stare.

Throughout the disarray, Mae was just Mae, skipping around as she stuffed a pantry sack with random treasures that appeared to have nothing to do with a quest for a set of Lost Caves she had likely found before. It seemed in minutes everything was loaded, although it really took the better part of an hour. Smokey Jo wasn't one of the six chosen for the journey, but Warren would have thought she was, for all the extra truck she kept piling in the wagon.

"You'll need this!" She offered Warren the Snowflake Watch Cap that Mae had given him in the glacier. "And these!"

Standing on tiptoes, she handed up the nailed glacier boots he had traded for trekkers last week. The shapeless shepherd's shoes hurt his feet so badly that he had returned to the marketplace and bought his boots back with Aubergine's ill-gotten silver.

"Stop giving me gear," he told the gnome in annoyance, shoving the hat and boots under the bench seat. "I'm coming right back."

When everyone was settled in the wagon, Smokey and Lily went to the garden gate to see them off.

"Good-bye!" Smokey yelled, waving wildly. "Don't be gone long! Bring me back something!"

"Safe travels," Lily called, as the wagon disappeared from the alley.

Smokey Jo shut the gate. "Warren isn't really coming right back, is he?"

Lily bolted the door. "But that remains to be seen."

"I remembered the hat," Smokey grumbled, following her to the summer kitchen.

"Well then, you did all you could, didn't you?" Inside, Lily sighed at the open cupboards and ransacked pantry. Discarded shoes and boots, along with a few unwanted mufflers and the odd sock, littered the vestibule. "The rest depends on Mae."

"Don't forget Aubergine." Smokey closed some of the lower cabinets. "It bothers me she has tarried so."

"I try never to underestimate our mistress," Lily said, searching for a broom.

Smokey slid her stool across the floor and climbed up to check the fire in the cookstove. "Perhaps we should have waited."

Lily swept the muddy entry. "The six were well picked, but The One was not my choice."

"The Magic of Men begins with fire inside, that's what Aubergine says!" Popping dry sticks into the stove, Smokey waited for the glowing coals to rekindle before replacing the iron lid. She beamed at Lily. "I love a merry blaze!"

"I know you do," Lily gazed out the window thoughtfully. "I'm just afraid we sent the wrong boy."

SIX OF ONE

Kendrick shot a blazing bolt from his fingers.

CHAPTER 13

The Bad, Bad Man

WHEN GARTH REGAINED CONSCIOUSNESS, HE FOUND himself lying on the ground in a tiny courtyard ravaged by fire. His eyes watered terribly and he could barely breathe for the smoke that surrounded him. Coughing, he sat and rubbed at a wen on the back of his head. His hand came away with crusted blood.

His other hand was useless, he noticed, for he could see it had burnt somehow. The bubbled skin smelled like cooked meat. His seared palm and ravaged fingers had no sensation and didn't hurt like the lump on the back of his head. Try as he might, he could not remember what had happened. He guessed that something had struck him and he had fallen hard. How long had he had lain like the dead, he wondered?

Wiping soot from his eyes, Garth squinted at the sky through an acrid gray film, unsure if what he saw was day dawning or waning. The sun was a hovering orange disc obscured by haze. Was it going down or coming up? His head swam so, he couldn't really tell. As he scanned the smutty courtyard, his dazed eyes came to rest upon the remains of a few empty beer barrels burning to coals near a low pump house attached to a building scorched by fire. He recognized this place. It was the back of an alehouse in the district of River Walk. He could not recall its name.

The walled courtyard's gate was open to the dusky alley beyond. The last thing he recalled was two fossick boys telling him to scatter. Although he recited the magical ditty dutifully with all the right responses, Clayton and Ross melted into the shadows without him. Obviously he had not learned the fossicker's ways. Perhaps he never would.

As his memory began to return, he remembered the cards they had played with soldiers in the tavern and its abrupt ending. After he spied an ancient Skell hidden within the deck, Clayton traded an amethyst brooch to the barmaid for it just before the Guard raided the alehouse in search of deserters. Who had come away with the relic he wondered, himself or Clay? With his good hand, Garth patted his pockets. They were empty. Perhaps Clay had taken the card when the fossickers scattered. His mouth stretched into a hint of a smile. Maybe he and Ross were ransoming it to the Dark Queen even now for Trader's freedom. His smile faded as he recalled someone else: the Bad, Bad Man.

He shook his head to clear it as the remembrance of what had occurred—had it been yesterday?—returned to mind. The last time he had the half Skell was when the fossickers disappeared and the soldier named Hairy shape-shifted into someone else. His father. The burning man the fossickers feared more than the rolling cage and the fiery phantom that filled their nightmares was his father, Kendrick Blue.

If he had not borne witness, he wouldn't have believed what occurred. After someone had put the tavern to the torch, the burly soldier Hairy materialized in the courtyard with singed hair and smoking clothes. As the fossickers melted into the shadows, the big boy bore down on him like someone possessed, cornering him behind the burning building. Slowly Hairy's body ripped open. Beneath was his father, who shed the soldier's skin like fruit peel. Blinking in the haze, Garth searched the sooty ground. All signs of the heavyset boy were gone without a trace like he never lived, *unsuppeared* like small Ross said. Garth wondered: If in later years he ever found the skinny soldier that Hairy called Raven, would the emaciated guard be able to recall a smith's apprentice from Coventry, with whom he had served at the Bordertown Garrison when young?

"Father," Garth had mouthed at the Bad Man standing over the husk of Hairy's body.

For a moment, Kendrick's face registered shock. Then his look turned to anger. "This is no place for you, boy."

"I found your hat in the Rill." Garth backed away from his father, his mind racing. "I thought you were dead."

"Neither fire nor flood can harm me," Kendrick growled, the watery-blue eyes Garth so remembered gone steely and cold. "You should have drowned as nature intended."

"Nothing about that flood was nature's doing." Garth gave his father a baleful stare. "You left me at the farm, hoping the river would carry me away."

"I opened the sluice gates to spill the Teardrop myself." Kendrick nodded in satisfaction. "Soon I will no longer need assistance from such man-made artifice for I shall have the power to wield the elements of fire and ice as the First Folk did."

"What brings you here?" Garth searched the courtyard for a weapon, anything he could use to fend off this monster who was no longer his father. All he saw were rocks and rubble burnt to glowing coals. "Are you going to use the river to flood the city?"

Kendrick laughed. "No, I came for the same ancient relic that brought you."

Behind them, a window blew out of the tavern kitchen, raining glass and bits of burning wood all around them. Garth's fingertips touched the half Skell in his pocket and closed around the triangle of horn. "You're mistaken."

"Am I?" Kendrick held out his palm. "I'll have the card. Leave the game of stones and Skells to those who know how to play it."

Garth retrieved the relic and held it high. "The card is mine unchallenged."

"I challenge you." Kendrick eyed the scored ballot. "Spare your life and hand me the Skell."

Garth held the triangle over a bed of live coals. "I would destroy it first."

As Kendrick reached for it, Garth dropped the artifact into the fire where it hissed and sputtered, but refused to burn. Watching in disbelief, he lifted his eyes.

"First Folk Skells cannot be ruined by fire or ice," Kendrick said.

As Garth grabbed a stick to flick the card from the embers, Kendrick shot a blazing bolt from his fingers. Garth cried out in agony as the flames engulfed his hand.

"Don't ever think you can fight me fire with fire." Calmly Kendrick reached into the burning coals and rescued the card unharmed.

Garth clutched his arm, his eyes watering as the skin on the back of his hand reddened and bubbled. He gazed at Kendrick in pain and bewilderment. "Who are you?"

"I have many titles: Lord of the Lowlands, Northland's Bane." Kendrick smiled faintly. "The Dark Queen calls me her Kindred Spirit. That name I favor."

"Fossickers call you the Bad, Bad Man." Garth gritted his teeth.

The Lord of the Lowlands regarded the youth holding his injured hand against his breast as a bird would a broken wing. "I fathered you. Above all else I am your father."

"Yet you would maim or murder me," Garth accused with red-rimmed eyes. He had so many unanswered questions that he did not know where to begin. "Why?"

"The Magic of Men burns strongly within me," Kendrick declared with resolve. "Though unkindled, its ember smolders within your breast as well. I should kill you now before you choke on your own smoke. My sister bade me as much."

Garth shook his head unable to comprehend. "Why?" he asked again weakly.

"First Folk Fire passes from father to son, and the Lord of the Lowlands needs no heirs." Kendrick held up the Skell. "I spare your life for this fossick, boy. Leave and do not follow me. I will not hesitate to strike you dead should we ever meet again."

Fire shot from his fingertips once more and Garth collapsed to the ground. That was all he remembered. He would take Kendrick's advice, he decided, and leave this place. But he intended to tell all who would listen what happened, and that the Bad, Bad Man was his father and the Dark Queen's brother, Kindred Spirit and Northland's Bane.

With his good hand, Garth grasped the top of the plastered mud wall surrounding the courtyard to pull himself to his feet. His head began to pound and he felt so dizzy he thought he might faint. Leaning over the low enclosure, he coughed hard enough to retch a mouthful of sour bile. After that he felt slightly better.

Peering down the alley, he tried to recall the route he had taken with the fossick boys from the dairy barns to the waterfront. Looking the other way, his breath caught in his throat, for he thought he perceived a shadow in the fog. The ethereal form had slunk in from the boardwalk along the riverfront. The ghostly figure was tall and wore a shapeless cloak. Was it the Bad, Bad Man returning to kill him after all, he wondered? Was the shade Death itself? He had heard somewhere Death appeared as a spirit to escort you to the Land of Dreams, especially if you did not want to go.

Garth closed his eyes, hoping he was hallucinating, but upon opening them, he found the wraith was still there advancing silently. He began to panic, his heart pounding so violently he felt certain the ghost could hear it, while his good hand on the wall became so clammy, he feared he would lose his grip. His head hurt so badly he was not surprised when he started seeing double. The one apparition separated into two tall figures whose faces were hidden by hooded cloaks. Hanging on to the wall, he pushed though the broken gate and lurched into the alley.

If he could just find his way to the milk barns, he thought desperately, as he staggered away from the creatures. He could wait for the milkman Gideon, who would surely help him get back to Merchant's Pass safely. Squinting at the sky, he saw now that the sun was rising, not setting. It was midday. How had that happened? By now, Gideon would have returned from his milk route already, stacked his crates, and gone home. Behind him, a spectral shadow reached for his arm.

Garth screamed at its touch. Trying to run, he stumbled and fell. The cloaked being stood over him, splitting into double figures once more. Even when he rubbed his eyes, it remained two and would not shift back into one. Overcome with fear and exhaustion, he fainted.

The two tall women let down the hoods of their traveling cloaks to scrutinize the boy lying in the alley. Sierra looked at Aubergine. "That's not one of the fossickers, it's Garth."

"So it is." The other witch bent to examine the wounded boy. "Esmeralde's going to have to see to that hand. Sooner rather than later."

"His own father did this." Sierra touched Garth's seared fingers. "Kendrick scorched him with a fire bolt. So much for the Magic of Men."

"Your boy is brave, but truly this was a fool's errand," Aubergine murmured.

Sierra smoothed Garth's dirty hair from his eyes. "Had I known."

"Tasman would have done anything to possess the half Skell." Aubergine's eyes glowed violet. "And now the one she calls her Kindred Spirit harbors it."

"Kindred Spirit," Sierra spat in disgust. "Northland's Bane. Does my husband's precious false twin sister know we bear the other half of the Skell she so badly seeks?"

"Most certainly, although she will admit it to no one, least of all her brother." Aubergine stood.

"No more than she will confess that she left the broken necklace unattended at the Potluck." Sierra gazed at the amethyst necklace that circled Aubergine's throat, each stone in order for the first time in twenty years. "You alone guessed that Mae would switch the real string of stones for the replica hidden in her pouch."

"Mae spent twenty years piecing that second necklace together," Aubergine mused. "She thought it was the only way to make us whole."

"What of the false stone she lashed atop the walking stick? Such a smooth bit of river rock will never fit the broken setting. The second necklace can never be whole."

Aubergine shrugged. "I now think Tasman never believed in the power of crystals. Her only interest in the necklace was possessing it to thwart us."

"The Magic of Men." Sierra gave Garth a look of regret. "Does he have it?"

"Most certainly." Aubergine glanced over. "Trust your second sight, Sierra."

Flecks of gold stood out in Sierra's eyes. "Both of my sons harbor the ember."

"Your daughter, too, to a lesser extent," Aubergine replied.

Sierra's lion eyes sought Aubergine's. "I see the six setting out in my mind's eyes, Skye included. We'll not reach the Potluck in time."

"They can't leave!" Aubergine said in alarm. "We're not back yet. We have the necklace, half a Skell, this Glacier Born boy . . ."

Sierra's eyes glistened. "They took Warren," she whispered.

Putting a hand to her throat, Aubergine fingered the necklace. "I've made a terrible mistake."

"Lily knows, but she's afraid to stop them from leaving." Sierra swallowed hard.

"I believed Warren was The One, even though Lily counseled otherwise." Aubergine gazed at Garth. "She was right, he is not The One. This boy is."

Sierra gave Aubergine a frightened look. "I pray Warren has Mae's Snowflake Watch Cap nearby when he starts to choke."

"Don't tempt fate by trying to predict a future that is out of our hands," the other witch warned. "Come."

Sierra took Garth's Potluck Hat from her pocket. Gently she put it on his head, and pulled the brim down over his ears. Both witches paused to flip up the hoods of their traveling cloaks, before lifting Garth by his armpits. Hauling the boy between them, they passed unseen onto the boardwalk before the charred hulk of the smoking alehouse formerly known as the Loose Goose. Even the sigil of the big white bird had burnt from the remains of the blackened tavern sign that lay on the ground. They settled Garth's limp body onto a dray that waited around the corner.

Sierra took the mule's lead rope. "I'll have retribution."

"That is all well and good." Aubergine walked beside her. "However things will look bleaker before they get better."

"Revenge is sweet but best served cold," Sierra murmured as they disappeared down the alley.

With a quizzical look, the bespectacled man raised his candle, to examine the shivering soldier.

CHAPTER 14

IN THE SECRET ROOM ABOVE THE Banebridge Trading Post, Niles could not sleep. He lay awake in the dark, his head pillowed on his crossed arms. In the bedroll next to his, Trader snored softly. It had been a few days.

He arrived here two mornings ago with Trader barely breathing, slung over his shoulder like a sack of feed wrapped in his old sweater-vest inside his jacket. Dawn was breaking and the air was frosty. He shivered as sweat evaporated from his jerkin and looked at the dark windows of the Trading Post, trying to decide what to do. Should he wake the shopkeeper? The store would not open for hours. He sidled to the back of the building where he found a stoop that led in to the owner's apartment. He squatted under its roof and examined Trader.

Her body was still warm, but he had heard no sound nor sensed movement since leaving the Dell hours ago. He pulled out his quartz beacon and shone it on her. Her face had begun to gray. Dark shadows ringed her eyes and her lips were tinged blue. Unfortunately, he had seen that look before.

With all his might, Niles pounded on the shop keep's door. After just a minute, he heard a heavy tread on the stairs. An old man with spectacles unbolted the lock.

"I'm here to ask word for the fossicker you call Trader," Niles explained in the dim light of the old man's taper.

"There's nothing." The old man prepared to shut the door. "There's been no word for Trader in weeks."

"If you have no word, then I'm supposed to say, 'Thirty-Three' to Ozzie," Niles wedged his boot in the doorway. "Are you he?"

"I am." With a quizzical look, the bespectacled man raised his candle, to examine the shivering soldier. He was a tall Northlander who carried an injured boy in his coat. "And the code is Three and Three, but I know what you mean." He eyed the form wrapped in the army jacket. "I'm guessing that's one of our fossickers?"

Niles nodded and Ozzie ushered him into to the entry of a dimly lit kitchen.

"Trader's just here." Niles laid her still body on the butcher-block table.

The old man lit a lantern. "That's our Trader?"

"She said to come here," Niles explained. "And then ask for word, and tell you Three and Three."

"Trader's no girl." Ozzie gave Niles a suspicious glance. "Do you even know what Three and Three means?"

"I have no idea," Niles said in desperation. "Don't let her die."

DONE

Bringing his light closer, the old man peered at the sunken face of the fossick girl. "Whoa, Nellie," he said softly, his eyes flickering up to the tall Northland soldier. "We're going to need my wife for this one."

"I expect so," Niles agreed.

Ozzie turned to call down the hall. "Nellie!" he shouted. "Nellie, we got a fossicker hurt out here!"

A gray-haired woman appeared in her nightgown and robe. "It's Trader." Ozzie gestured toward the butcher block. "Brought in by this soldier boy, unconscious."

Nellie gazed at the girl's tattered clothes and lifeless body. "Ozzie get us some clean sheets and heat some water." After he left, she asked Niles, "What happened?"

"Trader just escaped from prison inside a Lowland camp when I met up with her yesterday." He watched Nellie select a few bottles of liquid from the pantry. "She had hardly eaten in a week and I know for a fact that she'd been drinking untreated water."

"Did you rescue her?" From a knife drawer, Nellie selected a pair of kitchen shears and began to cut the rotten breeches from Trader's body. The rancid leather was caked with mud and tore easily.

"No," Niles said carefully. "She saved me."

Nellie smiled. "That sounds like our Trader."

Ozzie returned with sheets and towels from the linen closet. As Niles lifted Trader from the table, Ozzie pulled the army jacket away and spread the bottom sheet beneath. Niles laid her back down.

"We hiked to her fossicker camp in the Dell hoping to find food and water, but the base camp was burnt and her fossickers were gone. Trader couldn't take anymore I guess. She lay on the ground and wouldn't get up. She thinks they're all dead and it's her fault." He paused. "She wanted to die herself."

"What's this *she* business?" Ozzie pushed his spectacles onto the bridge of his nose. "Trader's a fossick boy. I've known him for years."

"Trader's been a girl from day one," his wife admonished, as the musty breeches fell to the floor. "You don't need fancy glasses to see that!"

Even though Trader wore the boy shorts favored by fossickers beneath her pants, Ozzie could tell Nellie was right. "For the love of the Lost Caves," he said, quickly covering her with the top sheet. Red faced, he fetched his wife a basin of water.

Nellie examined Trader's legs for cuts and bruises. "Don't worry, she's just half-starved and dehydrated, but considerably more than usual." She added a few drops of witch hazel and a squirt of mint soap to the water meant to wash the girl. "We'll have to cut this jerkin off, too. She needs a hot bath to warm up. Then sips of broth every few hours and sleep in the safe room upstairs."

"I'll do it," Niles volunteered. "I'll do anything."

"You look like you could use a little tending to yourself," Ozzie suggested. "Leave Nellie to do her woman's work. You sit by the hearth with me. We'll have ourselves a mug of warm cider and a hot bowl of stew."

"I carried her all the way here," Niles said, reluctant to leave the kitchen. "I'd just as soon sit with her awhile."

"Let me doctor the girl," Nellie said firmly. "When she's ready for a visit, I'll come get you."

Ozzie stoked the fire. Niles had barely finished his cider and was only halfway through the hearty stew and bread Ozzie brought him before he fell asleep in his chair.

A few hours later, Ozzie shook his shoulder. "It's first light," he whispered. "Go wash up at the sink. Nellie found some clean clothes that she's hoping might fit and there's warm water and soap. Then I'll show you the way to our hidey-hole upstairs."

Niles followed him into the kitchen. The butcher-block table where Nellie treated Trader was barren. All signs of her gone.

A pang of fear struck Niles almost as if Trader had punched him again. "Where is she?" He gripped the counter. "What happened to Trader?"

"Don't you worry about Trader," Ozzie said gruffly.

"Your girl's asleep." Coming into the room, Nellie handed him faded overalls and a homespun shirt such as a Middleland farmer might wear. "Try these on."

"I need to see her," Niles insisted.

"You need to wash first," Nellie said firmly. "I've just cleaned her up. You're not going into my parlor all dirty."

As he scrubbed and changed, Niles overheard Ozzie and Nellie arguing.

"We'll be opening soon," Nellie reminded Ozzie. "You know as well as I do, she's not safe right here, where anyone could find her."

"She's just a girl," Ozzie protested.

"Trader is Trader," Nellie said. "How many boys have we let her bed down with upstairs?"

"That was when she was a boy," Ozzie argued. "Now she's a maid and he's a full grown man. It's not proper."

"Will you stop," Nellie told her husband. "I can't keep running back here all day to feed and doctor her and neither can you."

Wearing clean clothes Niles appeared in the doorway. Even with his wet hair slicked back, the top of his head brushed the doorframe. He had rolled back his shirtsleeves as they were too short for him anyway, but there was no disguising the bottom of his pants which didn't even meet the tops of his socks.

"I don't care what you think is proper," he told Ozzie. "Trader saved my life. I'll not put her in danger."

Hiding a smile, Nellie glanced at his thin hairy calves. "These are children made old before their time, caught in a senseless war," she scolded her husband.

"When Trader's better, we're going to Bordertown to look for her fossickers," Niles gave Ozzie a cool glance. "And our friends."

"Well you better wait at least three days, because that's the Fossicker's Creed," Ozzie grumbled. He put on his hat and picked up his keys. "I'll open up the shop."

"You do that," Nellie said.

With a kiss to his wife and a disapproving glance at Niles, Ozzie left.

"I would sit with her now," Niles said simply.

Nellie let him into the parlor where Trader slept. Even in a clean shift and pantaloons she looked ghostly and frail.

"See? She's got an infection here," Nellie explained, pulling away some gauze to show Niles an open wound on the bottom of one foot.

"I don't see how she could even walk on that," Niles said, remembering how he had been unable to keep up yesterday, when Trader sprinted through the bog and across the river. He shrank back from the smell of festered flesh. "What's it from?"

"Rusty spike." Nellie showed him a piece of the splintered metal. "It had been there so long, I doubt she felt it." She bandaged the foot back up. "It's draining. I know it smells bad but you need to douse the wound with this witch hazel bath I made up."

Niles eyed the bottle of clear liquid. "Does it hurt?"

"It stings," Trader said, propping herself on her elbows. Her shift fell away to reveal a fine lace camisole, such as a woman would wear. "It stings a lot."

Niles smiled at her transformation, although he doubted it would make her act ladylike. "You're awake."

"I heard you arguing." Cleaned up, she already looked better. Nellie had washed and brushed her straggly hair and color was beginning to come back into her face. Trader looked at Nellie and grinned. "Tell Ozzie not to worry. I can fend off the likes of him."

"You will never have to. In truth," Niles promised.

"Did you tell Ozzie Three and Three?" Trader asked.

"I did," he confirmed.

"What are we waiting for?" She struggled up from her bedding. "We've only got two days left to dice and play cards upstairs before we have to leave word. Take me up."

Niles carried her to the ladder inside the fireplace flue and Nellie helped her up to the secret room. But he had a hard time mounting the treads himself, so uncomfortable did he feel in the claustrophobic space.

"Get up here!" Trader's face appeared in the square hole at the top of the ladder. She shone the crystal down the dark enclosure. "You're just like Clayton, scared of cramped caves and close tunnels. Come on up, you big baby."

That was yesterday. There had been no dice or card playing, just lots of meat broth and hot teas, frequent trips to the privy behind a screened corner, and sleep. In fact, Niles slept so much he thought he could sleep no more. But that wasn't the case for Trader. When she wasn't eating, she was talking or sleeping. Lots of times she talked in her sleep.

Lost in fitful slumber, Trader burrowed closer, mouthing a few unintelligible words that sounded like swearing. With a sigh, Niles pulled an arm from behind his head to comfort the small girl wrapped in blankets. He held her near, hoping she would quiet and be able to sleep until morning.

In truth, he did not know why he liked her so much, but he did. She was not beautiful like Skye, nor was she gifted with social graces or particularly well-spoken. In fact she could be unreasonably mean and nasty. He bent and kissed her on the forehead.

"Get away from me," Trader growled in her sleep.

Niles smiled in the dark. He adored her.

Perhaps he was attracted to the fossick girl because she was so fierce for someone so small, or maybe because she saved his life. When Trader gave up hope the other night, she might have died in his care, and he was relieved beyond words that she chose to live. Most likely his fondness for the young witch—who had many names, his favorite was Little Teal—had grown these past few days because he had heard her entire story, and she had listened to his. How Trader survived against the odds she was forced to face in her short life, he did not know.

He fantasized about bringing her home to his proper Northland parents in Winterhaven, and tried to imagine the disturbance that would cause. Landlocked by snow and ice, Northlanders rarely wed beyond their borders. His family would have a difficult time accepting even a half-blood northern girl from the Middlelands like Skye Blue, let alone a gypsy mongrel such as Trader. Especially since his father was governor of the Five Provinces and his uncle commander of the Northland Army.

Northlanders were serious folk who chose lifelong partners when quite young. They valued physical prowess and the ability to produce strong and healthy offspring, characteristics needed to sustain life in the bitter north. During the Winter Games last year, Niles placed in the top five in every competition he entered, even board skiing, which was not his best sport. After the awards ceremony, tall fair-haired girls from all Five Provinces threw themselves at him, while his mother looked on proudly. Both of his older brothers had bedded Northland maids, and while Marshall was unlucky, the eldest, Mason, had fathered a sturdy infant son. After his parents approved the newborn, Mason took the baby's mother to wife and moved into the handsome Winterhaven lodge his father had offered as a prize to whomever gave him his first grandchild.

His parents urged Niles and Marshall to try again. Niles neglected to tell them he had never tried the first time. Big blond beauties bent on procreation did not appeal to him, something impossible to explain to his mother. She had birthed three sons by the age of twenty.

Thankfully his father understood. When the Bordertown Garrison requested a Northland sledding instructor to train conscripts, he sent Niles south. By the time he reached the Middlelands, a half-blood youth named Warren Blue had arrived by prison wagon, to prove an even better sledder than he. This unwilling solider had bested full-grown men in competition during the Winter Festival held every four years in Bordertown. Instead of a rival, Warren became a best friend, when Niles learned that the reason Warren Blue was the best sledder in all the lands was not due to a desire to win games. He was a conscript from Top Notch, a dangerous pass in the Middlelands where he had been forced to flee from Lowland raiders and Northland Guard alike his whole life. The battle between the North and the South had never been his war.

Niles gazed at Trader's elfin nose and short dark hair. All he knew was he didn't want to leave her ever. He was afraid she would tell him to go, perhaps as soon as tomorrow when their three days were spent and she came up with the right word to tell Ozzie. She kept saying DONE. He feared that for him it meant good-bye.

They inhabited a pair of ravens Kendrick found picking at the carcass of a butchered sheep.

CHAPTER 15

Picking Battles

THE LOWLAND LIEUTENANT STOOD BEFORE HIS queen bearing an intent look as he waited silently, his men at arms behind him. Of middle age, he wore a deep-scarlet jacket belted over his burnished-gold tunic, and his hand rested on the hilt of the short sword at his side. Tasman's green eyes searched the rock-strewn river valley once more, avoiding the question embedded in his gaze.

When the Dark Queen and her Kindred Spirit parted ways before the aqueduct at the Southern Gate of Bordertown mere days ago, they had agreed to regroup at the Lowland encampment. To ensure swift travel, they inhabited a pair of ravens Kendrick found picking at the carcass of a butchered sheep and winged their way to the city. Both knew that the journey back would take time, for shape-shifting allowed for no baggage. As she hoped to have a crystal and he a relic, each would be forced to return on foot. Assuming they recovered these treasures, they planned to break camp and catch up to the Lowland Army already marching north.

Initially Tasman was annoyed by her lord's delay, but unworried; for his tardiness meant that he likely possessed the Skell. As time wore on and still she sensed no movement in the greening foothills beyond the narrow valley, fear gnawed at her like hunger, more persistent the longer Kendrick tarried. Their hasty camp in the Middlelands defended only by her Queen's Guard was not safe. What had befallen her Kindred Spirit?

When Tasman returned from Bordertown under cover of night, she discovered her small stronghold in turmoil, and the fossick girl gone. A search party sent out to recapture the girl attracted archers. Although these Middleland youths flew the flag of the Coventry Forge, their allegiance was obvious, for they wore the gray and white of the Northland Guard, camped at the Middlemarch fairgrounds.

More alarming, scouts returned with reports of Northland spies watching their camp and the Dark Queen feared attack. Although casualties were few, her Queen's Guard numbered less than two hundred soldiers. It was time to rejoin the southern forces massing at the icy Out Crops, for some strange reason she did not fully grasp. Looking at her lieutenant, Tasman lowered her lashes, which was all he needed. He blinked at his sergeant and the Lowlander began to strike camp, noiselessly.

Sighing, Tasman slipped into her tent for her cloak and other necessities. How she tired of warfare. Fighting for natural resources had seemed a fine idea years ago, when she had been searching for a plausible cause to cloak her true intentions. Now that she was openly in quest of the Crystal Caverns and determined to prize their riches, battling for simple provisions like food and water seemed pointless.

Yet here she was: waging war. The hostilities instigated when she had melted the caves now called the Burnt Holes in search of passage into the glacier more than ten years ago erupted into a full-blown conflict when the North got involved.

Until then, her marauders plundered the bountiful Middlelands unchecked, returning heavily laden with supplies. Oftentimes they pilfered entire fall harvests from farms ransacked along the unprotected border. Ranging further north, her Lowland looters robbed winter stores from village root cellars and grain mills. They carted off casks from vineyards, wheels of cheese from creameries, and crocks of butter and curd from local dairies.

With Kendrick's aid, Tasman's raiders constructed narrow causeways into which they cast chunks of ice mined from the Blind Side of the glacier. As it melted, the water flowed south to slake the thirst of her parched lands. Felling forests, the invaders hauled back timber, killing any wild game they flushed into the open and rustled flocks from shepherds and goatherds returning from the Western Highlands each spring. The fertile Middlelands was the breadbasket of the frozen North, and finally the Glacierlands could ignore the thieving southerners no longer.

What marked the northern entry into the war was an unfortunate incident easily avoided. A group of miners chipping ice had surprised a party of Clansmen hunting alpine moose at the base of the glacier. In the skirmish, the southerners had been unlucky enough to kill the Hed Clansman and his Glacier Born son. Reports of the occurrence filled Tasman with dread. Whether or not Northern Watch gave credence to the legendary Magic of Men, the death of the boy would not go unnoticed. She knew all too well that Glacier Born youths were sacred and few, for she had witnessed her brother Kendrick fawned over as a child time and again.

When some of her pillagers failed to return and others suffered casualties, she was not surprised, for she learned that the Northland Guard had recommissioned the vacant Garrison at Bordertown. Housing the Great Northern Gate, the massive edifice of the military base marked the northern boundary of the Middlelands and undisputed entry to the Glacierlands. Its barricades ringed stone towers built into the city walls and the stronghold was served by its own borough, Winter Watch, making it nearly impregnable.

In times of unrest, the Garrison held nearly a thousand soldiers. Until recently, it housed barely a hundred men, mostly veterans from the Battle of the Burnt Holes. Now that had all changed, for strife in the Middlelands had woken the North as if from hibernation, and the Guard was hungry for battle. Hearing rumors, the Men of Ice who ruled the Five Provinces had dispatched a battalion of soldiers clad in gray and white from the Out Crops to Bordertown. They returned with disturbing reports of desecration made even more shocking by the telltale odor of glacier burn in the air.

Within weeks, the Northland Guard returned to arm the Garrison and recruit young men to swell its ranks. In response, Tasman had no choice but to assemble an army of her own, although she had little interest in war. Free passage through the Middlelands had ended. Since she had not found a way into the Crystal Caves, she was forced to fight off Guard and push them back north.

Then her men had a literal breakthrough. Robbers mining ice along the Blind Side chiseled into a hollow crevasse that wound into the glacier. The tunnel sparkled with undisturbed ice studded with rocks and earth that the glacier had scraped up on its slow journey these past thousand years. Although the discovery delighted Tasman, she was unsurprised, for glaciers possessed lives of their own, creating caves and passages as they shifted south. Each spring runoff enabled the mountainous ice to glide like a frozen snail, releasing fossicks along the rock-strewn riverbeds that formed in its wake. When ice flows froze once more in fall, winter packed them with fresh mantles of snow. In its infancy, the Northland Glacier had lain completely within the bounds of the North. Now more and more of its icy peaks could be seen in the South.

Tasman hoped to push the Guard back far enough behind their borders to prevent them from meddling in the Middlelands, and long enough that she could lay claim to the Crystal Caves. Most of the glacier still lay within the Northland and Glacier Born were fiercely protective of their ancient ice. Even if her new passage did lead to the lost caverns, Tasman did not know what to expect. How would she thwart the rest of the Twelve, especially if the other witches got there first?

Securing the satchel that held the amethyst she had taken from the barmaid in Bordertown, Tasman returned to the fire. There she caught sight of her brother striding into camp accompanied by armed guards who had apparently met him at the valley's perimeter. Kendrick was filthy in soot-stained clothing and she could tell that he had shape-shifted once again. His eyes had that reddened look.

"The Lord of the Lowlands!" Relieved she signaled for food and water. "Finally."

"Northland's Bane," he replied wearily.

The Dark Queen watched as Kendrick tore off his ruined tunic. No matter how often she saw him shirtless, the sight of his pale skin unkissed by southern sun shocked her. Although not as tall as a true Northlander, her brother towered over her Lowland guards and was well muscled for a man nearly forty. He seemed unharmed except for the singed hair on his chest.

Kendrick mopped his face and neck with the clean cloth her maid offered, but laid the fresh tunic aside. He sunk to a seat by the fire.

"What happened?" she asked.

His red-rimmed eyes met hers. "I almost choked to death in my own inferno. After I set fire to that tavern in River Walk, I assumed the guise of a soldier caught inside, not realizing he had already half suffocated."

"Shapes shifting is nothing we do unless we must," Tasman said gravely.

"Well I had little choice," her Kindred Spirit answered.

She measured him coolly. "Did you find the Skell?"

He reached grimy fingers into an almost undetectable pouch strung onto his belt and flipped her the triangle of horn. "There's the card." He gave her a sour look. "You didn't tell me I would have to fight my youngest son for it."

"I thought it unwise at the time," Tasman said. "He's dead?"

Kendrick shrugged. "I shot him with a fire bolt and left him lying behind a burning ale house." His eyes flicked to the ancient relic. "Is that worth his life?"

"Oh yes." Her green eyes glittered. "It is the true Skell of House Crystal Keep."

"Half of it anyway." Pocketing the bit of incised horn, Kendrick accepted a skewer of mutton roasted with wild onion and a flask of watered wine from a kitchen boy's serving tray. He slid a chunk of grilled meat off the end of the spike. Behind him, Tasman's pavilion went down with an audible whoosh. He turned to watch two foot soldiers roll up the silks and canvas. "Leaving without me, were you?"

"It couldn't be helped," his sister explained. "We've been discovered by the Guard in Middlemarch. It's time to move on."

Kendrick chewed his mutton and washed it down with wine. "How did you fare on your errand?"

"I have the stone." She untied the purse at her waist. "It's the same gem I saw in the portal. Which is fortunate now that our little fossick girl seems to have escaped."

"I'm not surprised." He watched her loosen the bag's drawstring. "Fossickers are famous for getting themselves in and out of tight spots, as well as thievery. Just be satisfied that she took nothing with her."

"She took a butter knife," Tasman said, presenting him the amethyst from the Cask and Barrel Tavern. "And I believe she has taken refuge at the Trading Post in Banebridge. I saw somewhat through one of the coins you scattered."

"I can burn it down my next time through." Kendrick examined the gem his sister had killed a cook and several barmaids to procure. "Should we seek her out once more?"

"Not if we have the lost amethyst," Tasman replied.

"I wonder." Kendrick turned the smooth purple stone over. "Is it the one?"

"I cannot truly say." Tasman sighed. "I never knew my crystals as Mae did. As a girl, I ground the few I possessed into dye powder."

She pulled the broken necklace he wanted to see from her satchel. Between two deep purple crystals set in silver lay a bent finding housing a bit of jagged stone. With the heavy silver clasp she joined the circle, laying the gem as smooth as beach glass next to the ragged shard that remained. None of the jewels gave off a hint of glimmer.

Kendrick compared the two amethysts. "There's no sparkle. They are not the same stone."

"They could be." She scowled. "Perhaps you don't see the two halves the way I do, my brother."

"I look at them as they are," he argued. "Pry the cracked crystal from its casing and try to fit it with the other. Without a doubt the two don't match."

Tasman fingered the ragged edge of the amethyst set in silver before glancing at the glassy pebble in his palm. "Think of them as almost twins like you and me. The one shard lay hidden for twenty years. The other has passed through many hands."

"My stone is timeworn?" Unconvinced, Kendrick watched her lacquered talons pick at the twisted silver that held the bit of cracked crystal. "That's the difference?"

She nodded. "My rock is hard and unyielding as the day it was set." She worried it free to compare to Kendrick's. "Something altered the other, softening its edges."

Kendrick's watery-blue gaze met his sister's, cold and green. "They don't go together anymore."

"They do, but differently than they once did," she purred. "Perhaps the gem you hold spent ten years tumbling through freshets, then the next ten decorating a fossicker's walking stick. Mayhap a jeweler's polish purposefully prettied it to escape our gaze."

"No matter, we harbor both bits now," he murmured.

Tasman smiled. "And the magic within."

"The two share no resemblance," Kendrick said. "Yet they are halves to a whole."

Her fingers closed over his holding the polished stone. "Just like us."

He shot her a warning glance. "Don't start unless you want the whole camp set on fire."

Instead, Tasman picked the loose amethyst from his palm and held it to the light. "This could be part of Teal's gem, reworked."

Kendrick downed his wine. "It will not fit the setting, no matter who reforges it."

"We don't need it to fit," she told him calmly.

"There is no power in the necklace unless it's a circle," he reminded her.

"Exactly. We don't want the necklace complete; only Aubergine does." Tasman dropped the string of gems into her satchel. "What we need to do is keep these crystals separated."

As a soldier doused their fire, Tasman glanced about. The camp was flat and the tents and food stores were loaded onto wagons. With a grunt, Kendrick dumped the dregs of his wine onto the ground and passed his flask and empty skewer to a kitchen boy.

"We'll take the stones to the Crystal Caves," she promised. "When we get there, I'll grind them to dust."

"Our forces mass at the Out Crops." Kendrick paused to pull on his clean tunic. "Shouldn't we join them?"

Tasman shook her head. "Our true purpose lies within the glacier."

"Yet our army is leagues north," he pointed out.

"I am sick of war." She stood. "It is time to pick our battles, my Kindred Spirit."

"Perhaps it's time to part ways." Kendrick accepted his belt and sword from the Lowland youth he had chosen as a squire. "I thought you quite enjoyed confrontation."

When he smiled, the boy averted his eyes. Even so, Kendrick saw that the youth was pleased he had noticed the freshly cleaned and oiled weaponry.

"We need to end this conflict, before it consumes us." Tasman watched the boy buckle Kendrick's scabbard. "War does nothing but divert us from our goal."

Kendrick nodded and the boy left. Though silent, Lowland language was not so difficult to master as he once thought. If he planned to hold sway over southerners apart from his sister, he would have to learn their sign quickly.

"Tell me again." He smiled in feigned disinterest. "Why do we mass north?"

"As a distraction." Almost imperceptibly, she shifted her eyes toward soldiers standing behind him. "I overheard Aubergine tell the Twelve that she offered the Northland a false vision of southern forces clashing with theirs at the frozen Out Crops."

"That was no deceit." His brow furrowed as her Queen's Guard gathered around, forming a protective ring. "For her prediction is about to come true."

"Perhaps it's a trap," she suggested. "Perhaps the Northland Guard believes I will be leading my Lowlanders, and be more easily killed or captured."

"But why would knitting witches become involved?" Kendrick asked. "It makes no sense. The Middlelands are a pawn in the war, not in charge of it."

"Aubergine seeks to push the battle lines north so her witches can journey to the glacier unhindered," Tasman realized.

"Even with the necklace whole, her witches can't possibly gain passage to the Lost Caves without the card of House Crystal Keep," Kendrick argued. "Otherwise, why would we go to such lengths to recover the half Skell from River Walk?"

"Because it is half," she said derisively. "Who do you think harbors the other?"

"Aubergine, unchallenged?" Kendrick eyed her in disbelief. "I thought you said the card was safe."

"It is." Tasman gave a small nod. "With her."

"The Skell is safe with her?" He echoed.

"At least we know where it is," Tasman said coldly. "When the so-called knitting witches set out to find the Crystal Caves it gets a little closer every day."

Kendrick glowered at her. "I almost lost my life back there for nothing, it seems."

Tasman shifted her gaze toward her commander. The circle around them tightened. "We all do what we must."

Kendrick flung his hands up. "That's all? Just when were you going to tell me Aubergine had the Skell we need to pass through the caves?"

She gazed at him with glittering eyes.

"You weren't" he said in the silence that followed. "Even though I warned you. I told you it was foolish to leave anything unattended at Potluck Yarn."

Tasman stepped back. It was then that Kendrick finally noticed the circle of soldiers clad in scarlet surrounding them, their hands held lightly on the pommels of their swords. The Dark Queen's smile was both innocent and wicked. Any one of her men would attack her brother if she blinked but an eye.

He glared at her. "What now?"

"I control the Southern Army," Tasman told him. "But beginning today, the chore of leading it befalls you. You'll command my forces and win this stupid war."

"And when it's done?" he asked evenly.

"I'll grant you the Lowlands and Middlelands, whatever else you desire. Except the North. The Glacierlands are mine, including the Lost Caves and whatever prizes they may hold. I shall be your sister, Kindred Spirit, but also your queen."

"You have always been my queen," Kendrick murmured.

Tasman blinked and her soldiers fell into formation. "We're two days march from the Blind Side." Her Queen's Guard marched before them with the foot soldiers behind. "Leave me with six of my own at the secret passage. Then round the frozen Out Crops to rejoin our army and finish the North." She held out her hand. "I'll take the Skell."

"Why?" He gave her a mild look. "The half is useless without the whole."

"The witches seeking the Crystal Caves will bear the other, perhaps crazy Mae or your precious Skye Blue. They desire our bit as badly as we do theirs."

"Then don't trouble yourself." He fingered the small pouch at his belt. "It's safe."

"It may be yours unchallenged, but only at the moment," Tasman warned.

"You worry about Aubergine." Kendrick smiled. "I'll win the war."

His sister would not get rid of him so easily, he decided. His first task would be to crush the portal coins she had undoubtedly secreted among her guard. Then he would finish learning their southern language, one without words. As for the Skell, she would not get it without a fight.

PICKING BATTLES

It would be a tight fit and Niles hated cramped spaces.

CHAPTER 16

The Fossicker's Creed

"THAT'S IT," TRADER MUTTERED IN THE shadows of the darkened attic. "Three days and we've seen nothing of my fossick boys."

Niles sat on his bedroll, his face lit by the glimmer cast by the crystal orb. "They're not coming, then?"

"No." In the half-light, her eyes began to smart. "So now I must leave word."

He peered at her ashen face. "And what would that be?"

She shook her head. "We're DONE."

"Done?" The big boy's heart sank as he watched Trader roll her blankets into a tight cylinder and lash it to her pack.

The small witch wasn't quite her old self yet, but three days of little but sleeping and eating in the sanctuary above the Banebridge Trading Post had allowed her to think she was. Obviously she felt strong enough to strike out on her own.

"Done," she repeated, less forceful this time.

"I've been thinking about that." He leveled his gaze at the small girl, hoping she would not make him beg to stay with her. "What if I don't want to be done?"

"That's not the way it works," Trader growled, stuffing a few odd comforts into her knapsack. She glanced at his ice pick and climbing rope, next to the glowing crystal that had lit their way through the forest. "Pack your truck. All of it. We're never coming back again."

He looked at her, dismayed. "Trader, there's no need to split up. Let's make our way to Bordertown together, to that Potluck place. I've got business in the North."

When she looked up, her eyes shone. "Of course, silly. When I said done, I didn't mean us."

"What are you talking about then?" Sighing with relief, he looped his climbing rope onto his belt and reached for his nailed glacier boots. "I thought as soon as you felt better you planned to abandon me. All I've heard all week is: Done."

"It's the Dell Fossickers I'm done with, my own band of boys." A tear spilled from her eye. "This place is not safe and neither are they if they're with me."

"There's no need to cry," he said.

"I'm trying not to." She swallowed hard. "I failed my fossickers."

He reached for her. "You didn't fail anyone, Little Teal."

"Oh yes I did." Trader wiped her eyes. "I'm done with them and they have to be done with me. It's the only way."

"That's ridiculous." He hugged her close. "You are the bravest person I know."

"Maybe so," she said, with a crooked grin. "Considering you."

Laughing, he let he go. She walked with exaggerated steps, trying to get used to the dress Nellie had given her. The frock was spun from deep-green wool flocked with velvet such as a Middleland maiden would wear. On Trader it was a strange sight, especially since whenever she strode forth, her leather breeches showed beneath the hem.

"There's no choice," she sniffled. "I have to disband my crowd. Have you ever heard of the Fossicker's Creed?"

"No." He hooked his ice pick onto his belt. "What is it, some book?"

"Not written down. But creed is law just the same. Each group sets its own rules. When I started the Dell Fossickers four years ago, we took the code of Three and Three."

"I keep hearing you talk in arcane numbers." Grunting, Niles tightened the laces of his boots. "Secret oaths."

"Fossickers live by creed because they must," Trader said softly. "We're all of us orphans or castoffs or runaways, so we band together for the safety of all."

"In truth, you're the first fossicker I've seen up close," he admitted. "I know nothing of your ways."

"We're family, with the same loyalties you would expect from kin." She paced the room. "We share truck and trade, skills and secrets, and protect each other from those that would force us to fight for the North."

"Those are my people," Niles reminded her.

"Lucky you," she retorted. "I'd rather fossick than fight."

"As would I." He watched her walk. "What does it take to belong to your crowd?"

"Allegiance to our code of conduct, the Three and Three," she said. "It's how we protect ourselves. Three days and three words."

"What words?" Niles interrupted. "I assume DONE is one of them."

"The worst one," she replied. "For Dell Fossickers, if anything goes awry—say, half of us are put into rolling cages by the Northland Guard, or Lowlanders catch us unaware—those that are left must scatter."

"Scatter?" Niles asked.

Trader nodded. "It's a thing we do, something I taught them. I never realized it was magic until I found out I was a witch. You melt into the shadows of wherever you are and disappear. Then you meet up here and wait three days."

Niles looked around the empty room. "It didn't seem that long."

"It never does." She sighed. "Time spent here is for figuring out what to do. If none of your mates show up, you choose one of the three code words to leave with Ozzie, in case anyone straggles in after you're gone."

"Is this the only place your band is safe? Seriously?" Niles asked.

"Dead serious." She turned. "You saw what happened to the Dell fossick camp? Any of my boys would check here first. We don't have many words: just ONE, RUN, and DONE. They mean somewhat different depending on if you leave word or get it."

"Which is better?" Niles secured his pack.

She shrugged. "It depends. The hardship of choosing code falls to the first fossicker who arrives, almost always me. Usually I leave word for the others, but I've gotten word, too. I've left word ONE and RUN before. I've never said DONE." She stopped pacing. "Once we're DONE, that's it. The Dell Fossicker's Creed is broken. None of them will seek me out again."

"Why can't you just leave word ONE?" he asked.

"Because there's two of us." Trader eyed him steadily. "Leaving word ONE means you're alone. You fear something has happened to the rest of your mates. Sometimes my boys forget to look sharp and they get caught stealing at the market, or are chased by soldiers. Once

I thought some of them went through the ice during the spring thaw. Those times I came here to leave word ONE."

"Were you right?" he asked her.

"Never." She smiled. "Every time I thought I was the last one left, I was wrong. I would leave word ONE and then start circling all my camps: the Dell, the High Rocks, and under the trestle outside Banebridge, collecting fossickers as I went."

"At least one camp is ruined now," Niles remembered.

"They probably all are," she said.

He looked at her. "So why not leave word to RUN?"

"Because we're not coming back," Trader said simply. "Leaving word RUN means you plan to regroup your fossickers. They know to flee without a backward glance and wait for you to find them another safe haven."

"They can't hide here?"

She shook her head. "RUN means we're all on the run. A safe house isn't safe if it's been breached. Which it has."

"Not," Niles declared.

She gazed at his army jacket lying on the floor. "Like it or not, you're no fossicker, soldier boy."

He glanced at her dress. "Neither are you, witch."

"There's no such thing as fossick girls." She pulled her tangled skirt from the tops of her boots. "I can't tell my boys to run. Who would they run to?"

Niles rose and shouldered his knapsack. "I guess we're done, then."

"We are." She went to the chimney hole. "I'll go first to see who's about."

Trader snuck down the ladder inside the flue and hopped lightly into the hearth, skirting the dead ashes that lay there. In minutes she was back, motioning for Niles to lower their packs. He tied the pair to his climbing rope and lowered them one by one. She cleared the fireplace and motioned him down. He took a deep breath. It would be a tight fit and he hated cramped spaces.

"It's a little close," he whispered.

"Toss me your crystal," she urged him. "I'll shine the light up so you can see."

Downstairs, it was evening and Ozzie was just closing up shop. Nellie had a supper of summer sausage and potatoes with pearl onions simmering on the stove.

"Don't you look pretty!" She smiled, admiring Trader's deep-green dress.

"What is that supposed to be, a compliment?" the girl asked. "I keep telling you, I don't need a costume."

Over her head, Niles grinned at Nellie. Trader took her plate and flounced into the dining room. Niles helped Nellie carry in the bread and butter, water, and wine. In the kitchen, Ozzie filled his plate at the stove before joining them at the square oak table.

Trader looked up as he sat down. "I guess we're DONE," she mumbled.

"I was afraid of that. No sign of your fossickers and we've had a lot of soldiers passing through here today." Ozzie took off his spectacles and laid them aside. "There's some in the tavern still."

"We had curious visitors in the shop this afternoon as well," Nellie added. "Bearing odd barter."

"Times grow hard," Ozzie helped himself to the breadbasket. "Folk will trade anything they must, which allows little margin for those who would fossick."

"Fossickers are a dying breed, whose days are numbered." Trader scratched at the neck of her dress. "Besides who would want to join a group of boys led by a girl?"

"Fossickers might do well to dress like girls," Nellie remarked. "Considering how many boys in breeches end up as Lowland fodder."

"I'll tell your boys DONE if you wish," Ozzie offered, cleaning his spectacles with a corner of his napkin. "But that means your life here is over. What will you do?"

Trader pushed aside her plate and glanced at Niles. "We make our way to Potluck Yarn. I'm a girl and a witch. If I'm done fossicking, then I'm done hiding, too."

"You wish to join the Circle of Twelve?" Nellie almost choked on her wine. "That's a good way to get killed."

"My aunt was a knitting witch." Trader toyed with her drink cup. "Named Tracery Teal. The Dark Queen killed her over an enchanted necklace long ago. Though we never met, Teal's legacy is mine. When the circle is remade, her place in it is mine."

"Witchery is against the law," Nellie cautioned, pointing with her butter knife. "It doesn't matter who you are."

"No harm will come her way." Pushing back his chair, Niles stood to get another plate of food. "The fighting is down here. We travel north."

"Ah, but it is rumored that the war is moving north," Ozzie revealed. "Forces from both sides are marching through the Middlelands, stealing whatever supplies they can. Just days ago, soldiers raided the Mill on the Rill at the bottom of the Notch, taking even sacks of unground groats."

"Soldiers look for a boy known as Trader," Nellie told the small girl. "If what you say is true, even the Dark Queen seeks you out. You need better disguise than a dress."

Trader ran her fingers through her straggly locks, pushing stray tendrils behind her ears. "I'll grow my hair out. And wear it back proper."

Nellie smiled. "You'll have to do more than that, I'm afraid."

"You mean act like a girl?" Trader gave her a panicked look. "I don't know how."

"It will come back to you." The older woman rose. "Let me find you a head scarf."

"You'd do best to change your name, too," Ozzie suggested.

Niles returned from the kitchen with a second helping of sausage. "One of her names I like is Little Teal, after her aunt."

"My real name is Traces of Teal. For when my aunt died, mere traces of her remained like wisps of green fog." Trader looked up at Niles. "Teal lurks above the dye pot at Potluck Yarn still, waiting for something. Aubergine doesn't know what."

Nellie returned with a fine lace scarf that matched Trader's dress and arranged it around the girl's head to conceal her short hair. "Little Teal, it fits you."

"Fine," she huffed. "But I'm wearing my leggings underneath this skirt, so I can shed it if I want to."

The others laughed. Ozzie donned his spectacles and eyed Niles over the tops of the lenses. "So what now? Does the army hunt you? As a deserter, perhaps?"

The boy shook his head. "When the Lowlanders captured me, no one came looking. I expect that by now, my company believes I'm dead." He bit his lip. "My path lies north, back to my people. Perhaps I'll bring you, Little Teal."

She gave him an amused look. "Perhaps you will." She turned to Ozzie. "What do you think will happen to you here?"

"Hard to tell." He shrugged. "For now, the soldiers keep to the tavern. As long as the ale flows to their liking, we're fine."

As Nellie rose to clear the plates, she heard scratching at the back door. She smiled and put a finger to her lips. The sound came again, more urgent. "That sounds like who we've been waiting for," she whispered.

THE FOSSICKER'S CREED

With the soldier and the witch close behind, Nellie hurried through the kitchen. She unlatched the back door to find a bedraggled boy blinking on the stoop.

"Nellie?" he asked in a small voice. "It's me, Ross. Is there word?"

"Yes," she whispered, holding her lantern high. "Are you alone?"

"No, Clayton's with me but he won't come out of the shrubbery," the little boy glanced back into the shadows. "We been chased by soldiers partway here and there's some in the tavern it looks like."

"It's safe in the house," Nellie beckoned. "Come."

Within a few seconds, a tall youth appeared from the bushes and she ushered both boys inside. Entering the well-lit kitchen, the boys spied Niles and shrank back.

"Soldiers!" Ross cried.

"Just the one," Nellie said, pulling him in by his shirt sleeve.

"Maybe so." Ross peered at the tall Northlander whose head almost brushed the timbered ceiling. "But he's an awfully big one."

A door slammed behind them. "I told you it was a trap," Clayton muttered to Ross. They turned to run, but a witch blocked the doorway.

"Trader!" Ross shrieked, louder than before. He stared at the green dress and gave Clayton a desperate look. "Garth was right, he did turn into a girl!"

"I was always a girl," Little Teal told him. "You just didn't see it."

"I thought I did once." Clayton turned to Ross. "We've been ambushed by a soldier and a witch. Could it get any worse?"

"Hush!" Little Teal said sternly. "We've been here three days, waiting on you."

"Yes ma'am!" Ross giggled.

"Don't start that," she warned, as both he and Clayton let out peals of laughter. "I'm not even used to this dress yet."

221

Ozzie stood in the parlor doorway with two plates of sausage. "You boys come get some dinner," he said.

After they were seated around the oak table, Little Teal wrinkled her nose at the fossickers. "You boys reek of smoke, among other things. What happened to you two? Where's Garth?"

"We think he's dead," Clayton mumbled, not looking up from his plate.

"Dead?" She echoed in disbelief.

Ross nodded between bites of sausage. "We tried to save him."

Clayton met Little Teal's snapping black eyes with a hard stare of his own. "He took us to that alehouse in River Walk, just like you told us to do if something happened to you, remember?"

"You said if we saw fire, go to the ice," Ross added.

"If you disappeared we were supposed to find an old Skell to use for ransom." Clayton reminded her. "So we did."

"There was fire, just like you said. Lots of it," Ross confirmed.

"I saw our old camp," Teal looked at them desperately. "I never meant for anyone to die!"

"What happened in River Walk?" Nellie asked the boys quietly.

"We rode to over there with a milkman named Gideon." Ross looked up. "I liked him. And his horse."

"Garth found the Skell you wanted hidden in a deck of cards at a tavern called the Loose Goose," Clayton told Little Teal. "But it was only half of a Skell."

She nodded. "I've seen its twin."

"I traded the barmaid a brooch and Garth took the Skell," Clayton went on. "Then some Northland soldiers came in looking for deserters and we ran."

"Next we knew the whole place was burning," Ross blurted out. "In truth, Trader. We jumped through a window into the courtyard and there was the Bad, Bad Man. We didn't think it was him at first, because he unsuppeared into one of the guards in the tavern called Hairy, the same one who played Skells with us. When he walked toward us, Hairy's body ripped apart and slid away, like how a snake sheds its skin." Demonstrating with his hands, Ross gave Little Teal a terrified look. "The Bad Man was coming for us."

"I told the boys to scatter," Clayton said. "But after we melted into the shadows I remembered about Garth."

"He was no fossicker," Little Teal said sadly. "He didn't know how to scatter."

Ross began to whimper. "After the fire died down and the Bad Man was gone, there Garth lay, all burnt up."

"And the Skell was missing, I checked." Clayton said.

"So the Bad Man has the Skell and Garth's dead," Little Teal said dully.

"We watched for anyone else to come around, like maybe some witches." Ross fought tears. "It got too hard to see through the smoke. So we came here to find word."

Little Teal lifted her eyes to Ozzie. "The word is DONE," the shop keep said.

"I figured that much when I saw her in a dress," Clayton said sourly.

"I don't care if she's a girl," Ross told Clayton. "She can still be our leader."

"Never again," Little Teal admonished. "For I am a witch. After this day, don't call me Trader. If you ever see me, act like we've never met."

"It would be safer," Nellie murmured.

Niles looked across the table at the two boys. "Her name is Little Teal now and forever. She is to join the Circle of Twelve."

"What will we do?" Ross asked Clayton anxiously. "Start our own crowd?"

"Too dangerous," he warned. "The Bad Man torched our camp and killed our boys. Any day now, I might get put into a rolling cage. Where would that leave you?"

"Perhaps Ross can have a place here," Nellie exchanged looks with Ozzie. "We've never had sons."

"I don't know, he's awfully scrawny." Ozzie pretended to assess the small boy over the tops of his lenses. "I'm not certain how much help he would be in the shop."

"I know my numbers," Ross piped up. "Just not my letters so good."

"That's an easy fix." Nellie smiled. "Stay here, at least until the war is decided."

"Can I?" Ross asked Clayton.

The older boy nodded. He rose from the table, his hat in his hand. "If we're truly DONE, I'll take my leave to join the World's Fair Fossickers."

"I despise them," Little Teal murmured. "I always have."

Clayton held out his hand. "Trader, I will not forget our friendship."

"Teal." She stood and gave him a hug. "If ever we meet again, it's Little Teal."

"Teal," he agreed, with a brief embrace. He glanced at Ozzie and Nellie. "Thanks for supper." He gazed at Niles. "Safe travels." Doffing his cap to them all, he left.

THE FOSSICKER'S CREED

"Is there a way to quench the smoldering ember inside him?" Skye asked the other witches.

CHAPTER 17

The Magic of Men

WARREN HALTED THE WAGON BENEATH GREENING willows along an icy freshet for the witches' midday meal. He had been feeling feverish since they left Potluck Yarn and thought splashing cold water on his face might help. Though the rivulet ran clear, Esmeralde insisted upon them all putting a pinch of charcoal grit in their drinking skins and tossed a porous lump of it into the pot Skye was boiling for tea.

The purifying powder made the water taste like ash, but that did not matter to Esmeralde. Back in Bordertown Warren had seen her load an entire crate of Crystal Cordial into the wagon bed. He wondered how she thought to lug all that wine along the trail until he glimpsed her market bag, which looked a lot like Lilac Lily's. Then he understood—no matter how many flasks she stuffed into that satchel, it would not become heavy.

Mae laid her mitered afghan across the new grass, chuckling as it grew into a picnic blanket large enough for everyone. Warren watered the ponies while Ratta unpacked the food basket Lily had prepared. It was a nicely browned pot roast crowned with caramelized onions alongside a loaf of still-warm bread. Warren spread his meat thick with ground mustard on top of a round of crusty sourdough.

He was surprised at how easily he had passed through the Western Gate at Butcher's Block with the witches and the wagon. Was that because most of the soldiers from the Garrison were at war in the Glacierlands or because the witches wore their traveling cloaks, he wondered? He had not recognized the guards at the checkpoint, two Middleland youths who looked no older than his brother Garth.

Warren sat next to his sister, who was eating a slice of buttered bread. When she turned to him, he saw her eyes still held the faraway gaze he had noticed at Potluck Yarn.

"Something's wrong," she warned in a soft voice. "I can feel it." She watched him scan the riverbank. "Not out there, but within."

"I sense it, too." Grimacing, he put a hand to his breastbone. "Burning inside."

She sipped from her tin cup and glanced around warily. "Is it just us?"

"No, all the witches are watchful." Setting his food aside, he gave his sister a careful look. "Your face holds the weight of the world."

"I'm worried about mother and Garth," she murmured.

Warren eyed her curiously. "Can you see aught in your mind?"

"You mean fate or destiny like she can?" Skye sighed. "I have no such gift."

"You must have a special talent." Heat rose in his face. "All the witches do."

"I haven't a clue." She shrank back from his blazing eyes. "Why are you looking at me like that? Lily doesn't even know."

"Lily just glances my way and she knows everything," Warren said.

"It makes me sick to think I'm taking Mother's place once more," Skye admitted.

"Maybe it's your place now." Warren frowned at his food. A few minutes ago he was ravenous, but now he had no appetite. "Have you thought of that?"

"All the time." They watched Mae trip from the wagon to the picnic basket carrying a crock of honey. "But it's wrong. I'm nothing like her."

"You look just like her." Warren tried to laugh, but the burning sensation began to spread through his chest, making him feel nauseous. "You act just like her, too."

"You know who Mother is," Skye said, irritably. "She's the Keeper of the Tales."

"Only now." Warren coughed, tasting ash at the back of his throat. "Think on it. Who was she before?"

"A spinner of yarns." Skye shrugged. "She left her life of witchery to marry our father."

"No, before that." Warren's eyes gleamed. "When the Twelve became Twelve and she was our age." A smile played along his lips. "Who was she then?"

Skye looked at him as if he were a complete idiot. "Aubergine's apprentice."

Her brother sucked a deep breath. "And all thought she would become Aubergine's successor one day. Mayhap that's your real place."

"I have no place," Skye complained. "Warren I never wanted any of this, for me or you or Garth."

He drank a swallow of water in an effort wash the soot from his mouth. "Nor I."

"I thought to dance the Maypole once more as a maid before marrying Averill, and moving to the Mill on the Rill to share a life together. I expected hard work grinding flour for bread with Katarina but jovial times, too, and children someday." She smiled with chagrin. "Now Averill's dead and the Mill is probably ransacked or destroyed."

"By either side," her brother agreed.

"At least you get to return to the city," Skye murmured as Wheat walked by, followed by Tracks, his bell tinkling. "I may never know what happened to my mother or brother or even my father."

Warren put his hand to his chest once more. "You know what became of father."

"Is he the Bad, Bad Man the fossick boys warn of?" she whispered. "Truly?"

He ran his hands over his flushed face. "I believe so."

"Do you think he's done something to Garth or Mother?"

"It's anybody's guess." As Warren's eyes began to tear from the fire he felt within, he swirled the liquid in his flask. "Something's wrong with this water. Does it taste smutty to you?"

"It is a bit brackish." She peered into her mug before setting it aside.

Just then Lavender Mae scurried over holding a heel of bread dripping with honey and wormed her way between them on the blanket, upsetting Skye's tea.

"Mae!" she scolded, picking up the overturned cup as she moved aside for the skinny crone. She glanced at her brother. "Why is she so pushy?"

He shrugged and emptied the rest of his water out on the ground as sweat beaded his forehead. "I couldn't tell you."

Skye rose. "I'll get us some tea."

Licking honey from her fingers, Mae smiled at Warren and held out her bread. "Won?" She offered.

"War-ren." He shook his head and wiped his face on his sleeve.

Mae was acting peculiar, too, he mused, even for Mae. All morning as he drove the wagon she had perched beside him on the bench, refusing to move even when Esmeralde said, "My turn," and Indigo Rose complained about her hogging the front seat.

"This is my wagon." Indigo patted the plank bench over which she had folded a knitted wrap for a seat cushion. "That's my spot."

Mae shook her head quickly, pointing to herself and Warren. "Mae, Won." She explained, pushing Indigo's hand away. "Won, Mae."

The rest of the drive, she clung to his side like a leech. There had been no prying her away until they halted for lunch, when for a few minutes, Mae preoccupied herself searching the back of the wagon for a pantry sack containing the honey pot.

As she smacked her lips loudly, a wave of nausea rolled over Warren. His face grew feverish and his eyes would not stop watering. He drew a few deep breaths and glanced around. No one else seemed affected by the foul water.

Finished with food, Indigo and Esmeralde were smoking and drinking at the edge of the stream. Wheat took Tracks for a short forage along a game trail that led away from the freshet while Ratta packed up their leftovers. Skye was at the fire, pouring tea from the kettle. As he heaved himself to his feet to bridle the ponies, Warren began to cough.

Mae looked up from eating. "Won?" she asked.

A smoky film filled his throat, making him cough more. He hunched over the afghan, hacking uncontrollably.

Skye looked across from the tea mugs. "Warren, are you alright?"

He shook his head and gasped. She hurried over and knelt before him.

He looked into her eyes. "I can't breathe," he croaked.

Upsetting the picnic basket, Ratta barreled past Skye and elbowed Mae aside to pound Warren on the back. "Is it something he ate?"

"He didn't eat." Skye watched her brother gulp for air, his eyes wide with terror. "He said the water tasted like ash."

Suddenly Tracks nosed at Warren's reddened face. Behind him hustled Wheat in her voluminous skirts, stumping across the ground with her staff.

"He's choking," the shepherdess declared. "Did something go down wrong?"

Without waiting for answers, she cast her crook aside. Squatting, she ran a finger around the inside of Warren's mouth before lumbering behind him. With a grunt, she wrapped her trunk-like arms under his armpits and lifted him to his feet, compressing his chest in a practiced maneuver Skye had never seen before. Coughing hard, Warren expelled the stream water he had imbibed. His drew a ragged breath.

Skye sighed with relief, but her brother's reprieve lasted only a moment. Unable to maintain balance, he crumpled to the grass, retching and gagging. Skye put a hand to his face and drew it back quickly, for the skin on his cheek seared her palm. Whatever afflicted him had not been caused by the water.

"He's on fire!" she screamed to Esmeralde who was at the wagon unearthing her Possibles Bag. "He's burning up!"

"Won," Mae screeched, throwing herself at Warren. "Won, won, won!"

"Indigo!" Skye whipped her head around toward the other witches. "Esmeralde!"

"Get out of the way," Wheat warned, pulling Mae off Skye's brother. "This is no time for your antics."

But the distraught witch would not be deterred. "Mae," she shouted fiercely. "Won! Mae Won Mae Won Mae Won!"

As she struggled back to Warren's side, Wheat barricaded Mae with her staff. "Leave him alone," she commanded. "They're trying to make him better."

Indigo had already spread out her packets of herbs, and was busily examining the feverish boy when Esmeralde heaved her heavy bag of clanking vials onto the mitered afghan. She loosened the flap and pulled out a few glass tubes of possible remedies.

"What is it, Indy?" She asked breathlessly.

"I believe we've got us a Glacier Born," Indigo said gruffly.

Wheat did not believe what she had heard. "Impossible! Not Sierra's own!"

"The same," Indigo said grimly.

"Glacier Born?" Skye asked fearfully. "I thought Men of Ice were make-believe."

"Like witches?" Ratta retorted. "Or magic? Now you sound as simple as one of those fossick boys. Use your head, girl."

As she watched Warren fight for breath, Esmeralde bit her lip. "Glacier Born die." She glanced across his heaving body at Indigo Rose. "They all do."

"He needs air!" Skye shrieked madly.

"He needs water," Ratta murmured, rising to fetch the ponies' pail.

"And not just any water," Esmeralde muttered, sifting through her stoppered vials. "Glacier Born need ancient ice."

Tears spilled down Skye's face as she watched her brother suffocate. She wanted to comfort him, hold his hand, cradle his head even, but any contact would burn. She reached out instinctively.

"Don't." Wheat stopped her arm with the curl of her shepherd's crook. "There's no telling what you might unleash."

To Skye's horror, tendrils of smoke rose from her brother's nostrils. "You can't save him?" She sobbed, beside herself with grief. "None of you can?"

"Won!" Mae howled like a dog. "Wonwonwonwonwon."

With a look of regret, Esmeralde glanced at her Possibles. "I'll conjure up somewhat in one of my vials to douse the fire for now."

"How long does he have?" Skye asked.

The witches looked at each other, unwilling to answer. Skye's gaze came to rest upon Ratta, returning with the water bucket.

She shook her head. "He won't last the night."

Indigo layered cheesecloth for a cold compress while Esmeralde searched her glass tubes and Warren struggled for breath.

"What is it, some horrible disease?" Skye asked as he wheezed.

"Worse," Wheat said. "He is afflicted with the Magic of Men. Within him smolders a vestige of ancient sorcery not yet Kindled, an ember from the First Folk on the verge of bursting to flame."

While they watched, Esmeralde unstoppered a vial of hissing rocks, upending what looked like obsidian into the water pail. The liquid swallowed the black glass and a chilly fog rose from its surface.

"What's that?" Skye whispered.

"Ancient ice," Esmeralde rasped, as the glacier runoff crusted the bucket. "I've never had the opportunity to use it before. The story goes that it's the only way to quell First Folk Fire."

"It's more like a fossick." With her fist, Ratta broke the skim ice that had already formed and Indigo dipped her folded bandage into the frosty water. "Wizened and dry."

Skye watched Indigo wrap the cold compress around Warren's forehead. "Dry ice? There's no such thing."

As it melted down his face, Warren's eyes rolled back and he convulsed. It was impossible to tell who wailed louder, Skye or Mae. Skye's lament was short-lived for her cries dissolved into silent tears. Mae could not be consoled, shrieking on and on. When Wheat tried to catch her, Mae groveled beneath the wagon beyond reach of her crook.

Ignoring Mae's tirade, Esmeralde broke a chunk of thickening ice from the pail with a ladle and put it to Warren's lips. Most of it thawed so quickly that it rolled down his chin, but a bit dissolved in his mouth.

His convulsing subsided as quickly as it had started. Encouraged, Skye took the ladle and smashed out more ice chips, handing them to Esmeralde and Indigo, working to cool the fire raging within her brother. The smoke rising from his nostrils dissipated into nothingness. After a few minutes he no longer made huge rasping noises as he struggled for air. Mae crawled from under the wagon, creeping as close to Warren as she dared.

Later, when Warren was able to sit and sip icy slush from the dipper unassisted, Wheat searched the horizon. The temperature was dropping as the sun waned in the hazy sky. The foothills where they wanted to camp lay in the shadow of the glacier, miles in the offing. If the witches still planned to make the Crossings before nightfall, they had to leave now. Without waiting, Indigo went to bridle the ponies.

Warren rose to help only to retch up a mouthful of black ash, wet and cold. Although his face was still red, Skye reached for him and no one tried to stop her. His forehead felt mildly feverish, no more. Somberly, the witches reloaded the wagon. No one objected when Indigo took the reins and Esmeralde mounted the bench seat beside her. The other witches settled themselves around Warren who lay in the wagon bed, Mae closest of all.

"What happened?" he asked, when they once again were rumbling along the rutted road that led toward the western foothills.

"You harbor the Magic of Men, unawakened," Wheat answered, hanging onto the sideboards. "Do you ken the stories of the Glacierlands?"

Skye nodded. "Our mother's people are northern. She used to tell us old yarns as we knit before the hearth at night. According to legend, Glacier Born carry within them ancient fire, First Folk flames." Her voice grew distant. "But that would mean we descend from the Hed Clansmen. Who are they?"

"Not Sierra's folk." Ratta raised her chin toward Warren. "First Folk Fire passes only from father to son." She glanced at Skye. "That's why you don't feel a flicker."

Skye put a hand to her breastbone. "I sense something."

"You might do. Tasman felt the spark, too, or so she said." She frowned at Warren. "But it's not going to kill you."

"I'm going to die?" Warren asked. "My father's seed contains some ancient ailment that slays his sons?"

"Living through the blaze makes you First Folk fierce," Wheat explained. "All the carefully banked coals in the world couldn't help the ancients. They died in ice."

"Father is First Folk fierce," Warren said, almost to himself.

"Is there a way to quench the smoldering ember inside him?" Skye asked the other witches. "Can we drown the fire that he might live?"

"It has never been done," Esmeralde replied from the bench. "In all my years as a remedy woman I have heard only of boys consumed from within until they are nothing but charred husks of themselves."

"Besides, if we deny his heritage we tempt fate," Indigo warned the others.

"Look what happened when I tried to prevent Mamie Verde from assuming the Guardianship of the Crystal Caves," Ratta brought up. "Because I feared living alone, Lowlanders ran rampant through unprotected passages in the glacier for years, and what did I gain? Nothing. Even after I wrapped Mamie in the Never Ending shawl to keep her from crossing into the Land of Dreams, she was dead to me though she clung to life."

"*You would have Warren die?*" Skye asked the other witches in disbelief.

"Of course not," Indigo declared. "But even if we did find a way to douse his fire and he could refute he was Glacier Born, the boy that would remain would not be the one you see before you now."

"Remember my magic shawl?" Ratta asked the girl. "Do you recall how it sparkled?" She waited for Skye to nod. "When I unwrapped Mamie's body, the tiny pinpricks of light winked out one by one and the shawl fell to the floor, leeched of magic. Now it's nothing but an ordinary afghan." She eyed Warren coolly. "You would be stripped of magic, a mere man."

"That's all I ever thought I was," Warren said simply.

"Even if we did agree to help you break the curse, I've no more ancient ice in my bag," Esmeralde said. "In fact there is no possible medicine I've ever heard of."

"Think on it," Indigo advised, slapping the reins once more.

Warren felt more feverish as the afternoon waned. Though Skye kept wetting the cheesecloth in the last of the ice water and put it to his forehead, he grew hotter still.

When they reached the clearing below the steep track to the Crossings, it was almost dark. Indigo unhitched the ponies in the deserted glade near the trailhead. Many a highland shepherd had passed through here herding flocks west in early fall or back east come spring. There was an empty livestock enclosure, a lean-to, and even a few discarded cartwheels and wagon parts stashed under some brush. A windmill hitched to a spring-fed pump provided plenty of running water that overflowed into a clear pond and Esmeralde pronounced it safe to drink.

Unhooding her staff, Wheat walked the perimeter of the clearing with her little ram, Tracks. His bell tinkled softly while the cabochons clicked and clacked. Satisfied, she returned to the wagon.

"It's safe to camp. Tracks noticed nothing and neither did my beetles." Wheat gazed into the wagon bed where the flushed boy shivered and moaned. "Even on our own, we'd not gain the Crossings before nightfall. Let's spend the night."

Indigo led the ponies to the pond for water, before closing them into the livestock pen while Wheat and Ratta set up camp. Soon a fire blazed before the lean-to and the witches' bedrolls carpeted the wooden floor of the three-sided enclosure. Ratta put a large pot of stew Lily had prepared over the coals and unpacked the remains of the meat and bread left from their lunch. Esmeralde sat on a log outside the lean-to, sifting through her Possibles by firelight. Skye and Mae kept vigil over Warren who lay semiconscious in the back of the wagon. Sitting beside him, Skye could feel heat rolling off his body like a farrier's forge.

"Don't touch his skin," Wheat warned as Ratta let down the tailgate of the wagon. Together, they carried Warren to the lean-to and laid him across the bedrolls inside. His face was bathed in sweat.

"Is there nothing we can do?" Skye paused by the fire to ask Esmeralde. "According to Lily, it was supposed to be the six of us plus one, not six minus one."

"What makes you sure he's the one?" Indigo asked mildly. "There's still we six."

"Tracks is the one Lily spoke of," Wheat said heartily. She pointed her staff. "Don't any of you try to deny it."

"Tracks is a sheep you treat like a lapdog." Ratta snorted. "He's one spoiled animal, and that is all. I believe Mamie is the one Lily meant."

"If Mamie was the one, we would have no need for extra truck," Indigo argued. "Why would Lily pack a sack for someone awaiting us within the glacier?"

"I thought my mother would be the one," Skye said in a small voice.

"The one might be someone we've never met," Indigo said, with a shrug. "A stranger who even now tarries for us at the Crossed Tracks."

"Don't give up on this one." Esmeralde rummaged in her Possibles Bag, before glancing at Warren's feverish face. "He's nowhere near dead yet."

As Skye wiped his forehead with a damp cloth once more, Warren's eyes flew open. "Douse the fire," he pleaded with cracked lips. "I don't want to be First Folk fierce. Douse the fire. Let me die."

"No, Won," Mae began to growl, shaking her head. "No!" Suddenly she pounced on Warren and crouched over him. "Won," she poked his chest again and again. "Won, won, won." It took both Wheat and Ratta to pry her off.

"One!" Mae quivered with rage. "War-ren!" She rose and fled to the wagon.

"Apparently Mae thinks Warren is the one." Indigo lit a Smokie.

"She's only been chanting it for days," Ratta replied in disgust, as they watched Mae clamber into the wagon bed. "Haven't you heard her? One, one, one?"

"I thought she was trying to say Warren," Skye admitted.

"No, she thinks he's The One who will awaken the Magic of Men." Indigo's eyes slid toward Mae, who was rooting through the supplies in the back of the wagon. Over her head she held a glowing crystal. "The One who will guide us. But she's wrong."

"Let him live," Skye murmured. "Let him be the first one."

"He'll be neither the first nor the last." Esmeralde narrowed her eyes at Indigo. "Do you remember what we witnessed Tasman doing that night in the attic?"

"That was long ago," her friend protested. "Perhaps we made it up."

"Your father was a Glacier Born who lived," Esmeralde told Skye, with a disapproving glance toward Indigo. "We saw the shared vision. I am certain of it."

"After that, Tasman was never the same," Indigo admitted, blowing smoke.

"So much power," Wheat mused. "She had so much power for just a young girl. More than any of us at the time."

"Mae!" Mae ranted as she delved through the wagon in the dark. "One." Anything in her way she threw onto the ground.

"If he wakes, your brother might reach for your hand," Indigo revealed, firelight flickering across their faces. "For him to become First Folk fierce, you must grasp it and let the fire burn freely."

"Otherwise Warren will perish?" Skye asked.

"We've never seen it happen, but most likely he will choke on his own smoke," Esmeralde said.

Finally, Mae discovered what she sought, beneath the wagon's bench seat. It was the Snowflake Watch Cap knit from odds and ends of animal fur she had found in the glacier. The hat was creamy white with big blue crystal-dyed snowflakes splotched around the brim, and not terribly well made. She had given the cap to Warren weeks ago, after he had tried to rescue her in the killing fields.

Esmeralde pulled out a scalpel. "Should I cut an air passage in his throat?" She asked, as smoke rose from Warren's nostrils once more.

"If you don't, I fear he may asphyxiate on the smolder," Indigo answered.

"Or maybe more air will make him burn to a crisp," Ratta countered.

Mae skulked back to the lean-to clutching the crumpled hat in one clawed hand. Wheat held her at bay with her shepherd's crook. "Stay off of him," she warned.

Warren's eyes opened once more and tears streaked his reddened cheeks. With one last gasp, he held out his hand to Skye. "Release the fire," he croaked.

"Nooooo!" Mae gnashed her teeth. Like a Dervish, she leapt over Wheat's staff and clamped her cap on Warren's head, just before his outstretched fingers brushed Skye's. As he collapsed onto the bedroll, Skye felt nothing at her brother's touch. She squeezed his hand in vain, watching the heat drain from his face.

"Won!" Mae cried, beside herself with grief. "No-whoa-whoa-whoa!"

Skye gazed dully at Warren's motionless body. "We can't save him."

"Won." Shaking her head in sorrow, Mae smoothed the cap over the boy's head, searching the other witches faces, trying to make them understand. "No one," she finally said.

With practiced fingers, Aubergine easily found the nearly invisible fault line in the jewel that had been repaired.

CHAPTER 18

Circle of Stones

THE THREE WITCHES HUDDLED AROUND THE tambourine table in Aubergine's private study, watching her personal hourglass sifting crystals before them beside the half Skell of House Crystal Keep. Behind them, the heavy door stood shut and bolted against Smokey Jo. Although the gnome had strict orders not to interrupt unless Garth woke, so far she had pestered them plenty, and at no time was it regarding Sierra's youngest son.

"You knew," Sierra murmured to Lily.

"I suspected," she admitted. "When the six set out yesterday, I thought to dissuade them, but no one asked the question." She glanced at the Potluck Queen. "Smokey Jo must have sensed something, too, for she bade Warren to take the Snowflake Watch Cap."

"Did the others speculate?" Aubergine asked.

"At great length." Lily put a hand to her forehead at the memory. "Six and One: Wheat presumed the extra presence was her sheep, Tracks. Ratta hoped it was Mamie reborn. Skye assumed the one would be you Sierra." She sighed and rubbed her temples. "Most fanciful of all, Indigo and Esmeralde believed the term referenced their desire to overtake the Potluck and rule as one. Only Mae guessed it was Warren."

"Even she was incorrect." Sierra eyed them with worry. "He wasn't The One."

"The fault is mine," her mistress confessed. "Your other son is a boy. I refused to believe it possible that he could rekindle the Magic of Men."

"It is no time for regrets." Lily put a hand on her sleeve. "You did all you could without the necklace whole."

"I'll make no such mistakes in judgment again," the old witch promised.

Lily turned to Sierra. "Warding Warren's fate is not your duty, either. He alone chooses to live or die."

"Cast your second sight wide," Aubergine urged her. "Can you glimpse his glow on the horizon?"

"I searched for his fire last night." Flecks of gold gleamed in Sierra's tawny eyes. "But saw not a fleeting flicker in the dark. This morning I knew: His ember burnt out."

"Could it be that Esmeralde concocted somewhat from her Possibles to quell the flames?" Lily ventured. "Or that Mae called upon the cold fire contained inside the odd cap she knit to douse the smolder?"

"Lavender Mae spun the yarn for that hat from wild fibers gleaned from crags within the caves and dyed with crystals of ancient ice." Aubergine gazed at Sierra, her violet eyes deep in thought. "Just as your sons carry the glowing coal of the Glacier Born, Mae's Snowflake Watch is Glacier Born, too."

"Its sole purpose was to watch for First Folk Fire and cap it with the snows of winter," Sierra said with dawning realization. "What possessed her to knit such a garment?"

"Mae is wiser than any of us credit." Lily bit her lip. "Of that I'll say no more."

"I hope she infused the cap with enough crystal to keep the blaze from smothering my son." Sierra whispered. "If his smolder is but cold ash, it is unlikely that he survived."

Aubergine watched the last shards of amethyst run through the hourglass. "If he lives, it is in a world bereft of magic."

"That is the world most folk live in." Lily looked at Sierra's careworn face. "There is naught you can do for Warren. Your younger son needs our attention."

Aubergine hefted the hourglass. "Sixty minutes more?"

"Without Smokey pestering? Gladly!" Lily answered.

Sierra waited for Aubergine to upend the timepiece. "Garth's coal has not yet Kindled," she went on as if there had been no interruption.

"I refer to his hand," Lily said. "Without Esmeralde we can do nothing for it."

Sierra thought of her son's blackened knuckles. His fist had tightened into a gnarled claw overnight, the burnt fingers clenched as in death. Curiously, from his forearm to his shoulder, the boy's limb looked normal. After cleaning it, Lily found no infection or need to summon a bone-saw specialist. She had simply wrapped his hand in gauze and fashioned a sling from a sheet.

None were surprised at Smokey Jo's fascination with the burnt fist, or that she did not even ask permission to touch Garth's clenched digits that smelled of soot. His forefinger curled tight as snail in its shell particularly interested her.

"The fingers look ruined, yet something lives within," she insisted to the others at the boy's bedside. "Don't let anyone take off his hand."

"We'll let him decide when he wakes," Sierra murmured, smoothing hair away from his face.

But the problem was Garth did not stir. He slept through the night undisturbed while Sierra kept vigil. Even now, whenever Smokey Jo banged on the door during one of their breaks to ask if she could run to the market after a cone of kettle corn or when Lily was fixing lunch, she reported him still sleeping.

Aubergine fingered the sparkling stones that circled her neck. "I'm not certain we are meant to restore the boy's hand."

"What cure could there be, providing he is The One?" Lily asked.

"What his father started we can no more stop than the shards of time," Sierra agreed, as the amethyst slivers in the glass between them caught and tumbled. "Treating a scorched limb will do naught to alleviate the inferno kindling within. Is that true, Lily?"

"Smokey believes so," the housemother replied. "And that witch knows more about playing with fire than the rest of us together."

"Save for the Dark Queen and her Kindred Spirit," Aubergine picked the broken Skell from the table, "who would inflict death by fire for this relic's twin." She examined the faded etching on the triangle of horn. "What makes possessing it so crucial?"

"It's not just the one, but both halves she craves," Sierra said quietly.

"Do you recall how the story goes?" Lily asked.

"House Crystal Keep was the most powerful First Folk family, according to the tales of old," Sierra said with a nod. "Over time the Clan grew large and unruly. Unable to solve their differences, dissenters from opposing sides parted ways. To finalize their rift, they scored their Skell and broke it in half, each faction believing it possessed the more influential fragment. In ancient council, the ruling class used cards to cast votes and partial ballots held no sway at all. Half a Skell was worthless, yet House Crystal Keep never reconciled. The minute they clove the card, their rule began to end and so with it, the Magic of Men."

"Fire and ice!" Aubergine swore. "Tasman would merge the halves to resurrect ancient magic. She seeks to bend nature to her will much like the First Folk did."

"Even with the stones, both halves of the Skell, and the entire Southern Army she cannot rekindle male magic," Lily warned. "She is a witch, not a man."

"She would sacrifice her brother for the Kindling." Sierra's face filled with horror. "Or his sons."

Aubergine's eyes flickered to the shards of crystal, precious slivers marking time, tumbling through the hourglass. "Let's look to the stones."

Sierra helped the old witch unhook the heavy sliver clasp at the nape of her neck and together they laid the necklace of raw crystals on the tambourine table. The jewels sparkled as if alive, each gem glowing with intensity unique to the witch it represented.

With practiced fingers, Aubergine easily found the nearly invisible fault line in the jewel that had been repaired.

"Teal's stone?" Lily asked. "It barely casts light."

"Teal is neither in this world nor gone from it." Aubergine sighed.

"Now that her crystal is restored, surely she can travel safely to the Land of Dreams," Sierra mused. "Yet she remains."

Lily's look was less than patient. "Ask the question. Please."

"Tell us." Aubergine gazed at her. "Why does Teal linger?"

"She tarries for her namesake Traces of Teal," Lily replied.

"She'll likely have a long delay," Aubergine said wryly. "Especially if the Dark Queen still holds our Little Teal captive."

Once again, they studied the ring of glittering stones that sent random pinpricks of light across the room. Not far below the repaired gem lay a teardrop-shaped crystal so completely dark it looked black. Even when Aubergine closed it in her fist, the warmth of her hand could not coax a glimmer.

"Tasman's," Sierra uttered.

"Stone cold." Aubergine heaved a sigh. "As lost to me now as the day she fled." She touched another gem barely winking. "Nor can I reach Mamie. It's as if she vanished into fog, like Teal."

"The circle of stones will never be as powerful as they once were," Lily observed.

"No," Aubergine agreed. "But the rest of you still hold your sparkle." Smiling, she nudged a stone halfway down the necklace. "Lily here you are, shining bright."

With a shallow gasp, Lily put a hand to her heart. "I felt that, just as I did when I was young."

Aubergine tapped a large glittering amethyst at the bottom of the necklace. "And you, Sierra."

"I sense it, too, but that's no longer my place." Frowning, Sierra pointed to the dull crystal that represented Mamie. "Now that I'm Keeper of the Tales, shouldn't this jewel be mine?"

"The stones are set in our original circle around the dye pot. We can repair one, but never reassign it nor reorder its position." With a sigh, Aubergine stroked the dark orb. "Mamie reborn cannot rejoin us. She is no witch."

"Perhaps we need a different necklace," Sierra suggested.

"One day." Aubergine lifted it from the table and Sierra helped clasp the string of stones around her neck.

"Perhaps we could contact the Guardian another way," Lily offered.

"Perhaps." Aubergine adjusted the heavy circlet. "Do you still ken her thoughts?"

Lily shook her head in regret. "Mamie's mind is as remote to me as the power of her stone is to you. The only way to reach her may be a summons."

"The glass we use to mark such time smashed to the floor during our simmer," Sierra reminded them both.

"We have this small one here." Lily's eyes rested upon the miniature timepiece sifting the last grains of amethyst through its neck.

"We no longer number twelve," Sierra cautioned.

"And shall never again, more or less." Aubergine heaved herself up from her rocker. "Perhaps we few can coax a small vision of Mamie from this glass with the help of the necklace. I've done such things with my Simmer Stole before." Without waiting for an answer, she went into her bedroom for the shawl.

"It wouldn't hurt to try," Lily told Sierra.

Aubergine returned, arranging the lattice lace mantle across her shoulders. Before she could sit, banging began at the door. Lily had no need to check the hourglass to see that time had run out.

"Smokey Jo," she sighed.

"Has the boy woken?" Aubergine demanded through the barred door.

"I can check," was Smokey's muffled reply.

"If you're hungry, make yourself a lunch in the kitchen," Lily said in an irritated voice.

"Take your food back to Garth's room and sit with him while you eat," Sierra called.

"I already did that!" Smokey shouted. "Twice! I'm not one bit hungry now." A huge sigh of exasperation was audible through the door. "I wouldn't bother you except we have visitors!"

"We're not expecting visitors," Aubergine grumbled. "Tell them we're occupied. Tell them to go away and come back later."

"I can't! One is a very big soldier and the other is a little witch," Smokey said merrily.

"Big soldier?" Sierra gave Aubergine a quizzical look.

"Little witch?" Lily echoed, equally puzzled as Aubergine unbolted the latch.

"Is that Trader?" Sierra asked in confusion as the heavy oak door swung open to reveal a small girl with snapping black eyes standing before a tall Northland soldier.

"I used to be!" With a laugh, the little witch bounded into the study, tripping over the hem of her dress. Aubergine caught the fossick girl up in her arms.

"Little Teal?" she whispered in wonder, embracing the girl before letting her go.

"This is my friend Niles of the North." Standing, Little Teal pulled her tangled skirts away from her boots. She flashed the soldier a grin. "And these are real witches."

"Niles of the North." Her eyes gleaming, Aubergine took the soldier's hand. "I believe I know your father."

Next to the tall witch, Niles's height almost appeared normal. "My uncle commands the army."

"Yet the Clansmen look to your father," Aubergine replied.

Ignoring their exchange, Smokey Jo studied the tambourine table, taking in the empty hourglass, the half Skell, and finally the lively stones that winked and sparked around Aubergine's neck. "What were you doing?"

"We were thinking of conjuring a vision," Aubergine answered.

"Without me?" she asked in dismay.

"We ran out of time," Lily tried to soothe her.

"And we didn't have many witches," Sierra added.

Aubergine's violet eyes sparkled in amusement. "We have just the three so far."

"There's number four!" Smokey shouted, pointing to Little Teal.

"I'm fairly new to witchery," she protested. "I don't yet know how to knit."

"And I make five!" Smokey raised her hand. "Let me in!"

Without waiting for reply, she hustled into the study under a cloud of curious green fog, and went over to Little Teal where she cupped a hand to the girl's ear. "I can't knit either," she whispered loudly, "though I've been at it thirty years."

"What's this?" Niles asked, his head swimming in the haze that had filtered into the room and now hugged the ceiling.

"She makes six, more or less." Aubergine smiled. "That's Tracery Teal."

"Six witches?" he asked.

"Plus one!" Lily's face broke into a smile. "Look who it is, Sierra!"

"My son!" She rose to embrace Garth, who stood in the doorway. With his one good hand, he rubbed sleep from his eyes.

"He looks much like his brother," Niles murmured to Little Teal.

"Well Warren's much bigger, but not like you," she joked.

"Who are you?" Garth yawned at the soldier.

"Niles." He bowed his head formally. "And you?"

"The One," Sierra took Garth's singed fist in both her hands. As Niles stared at Garth in shock, Sierra smiled through her tears at the others. "He is The One."

Aubergine lifted the hourglass. "Shall we?" she asked.

Almost a thousand years had passed since
the ancients died and the world awoke again.

CHAPTER 19

Ancient Unrest

THE GUARDIAN WOKE UNRESTED. AS BEFORE, she was aware of discontent in the caves. It was something more than the mutterings she recognized as murmuring First Folk turning over in their graves among the ruined tombs on the bluffs beyond the ancient city of Tigeria.

She sat, feeling a faint prickle in her mind as if someone sought her out. The pressure was odd and yet somehow familiar. In another consciousness, a time out of mind she could barely recall, she had been cognizant of such probing. She tried to remember what it signified, but as usual nothing surfaced. Shortly she gave up.

Rising from the furs spread across the low stone altar, the young woman reached into the niche beside her and drew out a quartz crystal, breathing life into the orb until it glowed. Ice had melted in the stone vessel near the crystal while she slept. Idly, she lifted the shallow bowl and gazed into its depths. Instinct or perhaps forgotten habit prompted her to put the rim to her lips for an indifferent sip of water. Storing the bowl in its alcove, she let her eyes adjust to the narrow chamber of seamless stone rimmed with frost. She knew she was alone. Yet why did she feel watched?

The Guardian had little sense of time, for its passage meant nothing within the walls of ice. She could conjure up no vestige of her previous life but she knew she was reborn and a custodian in a long line of protectors. She was destined to replace a predecessor charged to leave the First Folk in her care before passing to the Land of Dreams. Yet the Guardian's Watch had been empty when she appeared with no sentinel of the dead to greet her, for she had come far too late.

The night she arrived in the vacant chamber, she followed sounds of exploding crystals to ledges overlooking the domed city, where fireworks burst over the ancient stone walls, reverberating into the caves beyond in welcome. As the display died to stray hisses and pops, still she waited.

No one came. She returned to her quarters to begin her solitary watch unalarmed, for nothing seemed out of order. The comfortable chamber held a fire pit laid with cold-fire crystal, a stone bench, and a sleeping platform covered with animal skins. Her predecessors must have often wandered through the city she glimpsed from the cliff, for shelves of curious relics filled the niches lining the stone walls. Exhausted, she lay down among the furs and slept.

Now, as she did whenever she rose, the Guardian slipped on the heavy mantle she had found here. Holding the orb high, she crept along a narrow passage that led from her tiny cell, casting rosy light ahead of her. The twisting path ended on the high ledges she had discovered that first night, far above the echoing voices. Before her, lay vast caverns housing the ruins of the First Folk. Their tombs dotted the bluffs beyond.

Almost a thousand years had passed since the ancients died and the world awoke again. In that time, the Northland Glacier had transformed from a youthful mountain of shifting snow and gravel crowned with a fresh white mantle of softly falling flakes to hoary yellowed outcrops of ice windswept with age. Within its bowels, ice thawed and refroze so many times that crevasses hollowed into a succession of caves caused by waterways carving new tunnels through the ice.

Even now, the glacier rested on flows that fluctuated according to season. Near the ruins of Tigeria's old stone walls lay evidence of two river channels that had once snaked around the city. Within these canals, artifacts freed from the ice fell into the melt each spring as the dwindling glacier slid south. Such relics tumbled through water veins to leech into riverbeds and wash up on lakeshores in the Middlelands, to the delight of fossickers and rue of those who warded the whereabouts of the ancients and secrets of the Lost Caves.

Gazing upon the broken circle of old city walls crowned by toppled tombs that rimmed the bluffs, the Guardian noticed a glimmer on the northern horizon, radiance emanating from the sacred caves of magic crystals beyond. She shook her head in agitation, as once again, something akin to the touch of soft fingers leafed through her consciousness. Whatever probed her mind would find little. Much of it was an empty vessel, hungering for thoughts and memories and the rest of it was sealed shut. How she wished the previous caretaker of the First Folk would appear. She called out to him in the ancients' silent tongue, but only the restless dead within the tombs babbled back.

On the few occasions when she ventured into the valley to explore the Tigerian ruins, the mounting voices deterred her, warning of walls that seethed with beings both dead and alive. Hesitant to traverse the maze of twisted streets strewn with fallen stone, she walked the perimeter of the ancient civilization that had been scraped up and swallowed by walls of ice. Beneath her boots was the ever-present rush of water. Once again it was spring and the glacier was thawing, migrating at an imperceptible snail's pace between the valleys of the Western Highlands and the Middlelands, even now carving rock and reshaping the foothills as it progressed south.

Treks beyond the ruined city brought the Guardian to the First Folk cemetery. Here crypts had burst and tombs tumbled due to erosion, looters, and scavengers. Although physically alone, she had much company among the vaults. The graveyard was alive with incessant voices and warning cries of a Watcher who had escaped the ice. Like herself, the whirling Dervish was reborn. The ancients murmured loudly as she approached and the Dervish looked like he would turn on her at any moment. He lashed his tail angrily before the crypt of the First Folk family he guarded. If not for her status, he would have smitten her as she paraded past.

The Guardian understood the First Folk's distress, but not how to appease them. Once again, she retreated to Guardian's Watch to ruminate, for within her sanctuary, she could hear everything. From the bluffs beyond came the murmur of First Folk punctuated by piercing shrieks of the Dervish. In the ruins below, her ears caught the odd slither and growl of the carrion creatures that occupied the otherwise vacant buildings.

The water rushed beneath. Was there more? She stilled, listening. Above all the cacophony, a lone voice emanating from within the ruined temples in the city center called out *Guardian*. Perhaps it was her predecessor at last!

With excitement bordering upon dread, she grabbed her glowing orb and hurried from her cell toward the passage leading to the valley below. Since her arrival, she had explored the hollowed ice caves within her watch and now knew them well. She discovered tunnels with steps hewn into the ice by unknown predecessors, and a passage where rooms of relics lay concealed among fallen stalactites. She found caverns whose domes boasted natural skylights and crevasses so small she had to creep beneath shelves of ice to reach them. Lower caves held great pools of crystalline waters dyed ruby and violet, their depths rippling with unseen creatures. Above, a dwindling passage opened to a blackened tunnel of burnt cells. Abandoned, they appeared to have been part of a prison. Something about the scorched ice tickled her memory.

Venturing north, the less evidence she found of infiltrators, robbers, and squatters until she discovered hollows hidden in the harsh Out Crops where hunters sheltered. Freshly scraped moose skins stretched over bone frames near fire pits hung with smoked meat were signs that they had inhabited such caves for generations in the far outskirts of the glacier, forever retreating south.

Breathless, the Guardian reached the lower valley, approaching the walls of Tigeria as noises within mounted. The city was dead, but the crumbling buildings were not vacant. Packs of rats and wolverines had overrun the sunken alleys, surviving on fish and other creatures trapped in the causeways when the waters receded each summer.

Climbing through a break in the barricade, she found herself on frozen rubble heaped in an alley. Here, the First Folk called to her in conflicted tones. As they had in life, dead ancients agreed upon nothing.

Keep out out out, one chorus warned.
Lay to rest those within in in, a second conclave advised.
Slay all trespassers! a baritone boomed.
Watch for Walkers still more whispered. *Watchers, walkers, witches, wolverines!*

No voice was the one the Guardian had heard imploring her as she stood listening on the ledges. Raising her crystal, she shone it over the ruined stone wall, which had once interlocked into one seamless face. Although disrupted, the pavers underfoot were intricately decorated. Picking her way through the alley, she recognized the linked circles of the suns Re and Rah and the twined rivers Tigris and Eye from which Tigeria derived its name. Turning into a wider passage leading toward the city center, the Guardian clambered over remnants of roofless storehouses, whose walls held limestone lintels, windows to nowhere. The cobblestone walks broke to rivers of ice. Soon she had to go out of her way to avoid the flows.

From the shadows something snarled. It was a wolverine feeding on a fresh pike flipped up onto the cobbles. Slick and dark, the bristling creature reeked of rotted flesh, scowling over the fish it fiercely guarded. Skirting its territory, the Guardian let out her breath and moved on.

Everywhere in the residential area of the once thriving city lay evidence of abandonment and loss. Outdoor kitchens in courtyards behind the larger dwellings contained smashed pottery, overturned clay ovens, and fountains tipped aside. From one ruined well spring, clear water ran in a channel chiseled through bedrock and down a series of carefully set stones, splashing into pools decorated with curious symbols of interlocking circles of the suns encased by braided lines of the rivers. The completed carving resembled a lidded eye.

Quietly, the caretaker explored the urban center, listening to the patter and snarls of the fish eaters, the rushing water beneath, searching for the one who called to her. It had been a male voice, beseeching her from ruins of the temples that lined the square, surrounded by the great canals. These buildings had been First Folk places of worship and even now echoes of hushed sanctity remained. She recognized the symbols Earth, Air, Sun, and Water, one on each of the four stone edifices, for relics inscribed with these same elements filled the niches of her chamber at Guardian's Watch.

She passed through the doorway of the Temple of Waters, whose arched keystone was incised with intersecting lines representing the twined rivers surrounding the city. Inside, the rush of the underground rivers reverberated in the stone walls and its thrum resounded beneath her feet. Intricate depictions of the city's twin rivers decorated a large fountain, where water fell into a pool of icy water before disappearing into a channel that emptied into the great canals behind the square. Other than that, the temple was empty.

Back in the plaza, she faced the largest temple which looked unfinished, for its walls held not even a vestige of roof. Approaching its entry, she recognized the carved circles symbolizing the great suns Re and Rah, and realized that the mausoleum had been constructed open to the sky to bask in their rays. Within, the First Folk had built a giant sundial to make meaning of the light the solar twins provided. Such power had enabled them to create a calendar which could accurately predict the passage of time in a bright world of double equinoxes. She wondered if the ancients had been able to control the change of seasons or beginning of the year.

As she turned away from the sundial, she glimpsed a line of luminous figures emerging from the Temple of Earth across the dim square. They wore white robes and she could see through their bodies to the buildings beyond. Instinctively, she shielded her beacon and drew back, but one of the ghostly figures noticed her and turned his head across the plaza. He let out a silent cry.

She froze as the spirit's hoary eyes met hers. His plaintive wail was the plea she had recognized earlier. He hurried across the square aided by a walking stick. She found she could understand him perfectly for he spoke the tongue of the Ancients, one without words. It was the same language emanating from the tombs on the bluff beyond. She knew it well.

Guardian, he implored her with eyes of frosted ice. *Free me from these walls, for I am done wandering.*

Who are your folk, Wanderer? She watched the line of pale walkers across the square slowly disappear into the Temple of Air, before turning back to the slight figure who wore a belted tunic and sandals. *Are you my predecessor, the Guardian that was?*

He leaned on his staff. *We are Walkers and Wanderers who await you Guardian. I am Cyrus, finished my penance. Guide me to the tombs that I may rest in peace.*

She regarded the wraith, draped in opaque robes. Although she could see through his milky face, her gaze did not penetrate the pupils of his hoarfrost eyes. *I don't understand. Aren't you deceased?*

I wish to be, he pleaded. *I am one of the undead who froze alive after the suns fell to earth. No one remained who could lay me to rest.* He glanced toward the Temple of Air from which the procession of ghostly figures began to emerge. *Take me to my family.*

The Guardian nodded, perceiving this was part of her custodial job. *You wish me to lead you to the ancient graveyard?*

The house crypts, he whispered in relief. *Tombs on the hill beyond the city.*

I know the way. She glanced at the line of spirits now approaching them, progressing toward the Temple of the Sun. *What of the others?*

They are unready. He averted his eyes. *They wander still.*

Forever? she asked.

Until they repent or find a host. He took her arm. *The city center is unsafe. Walk this way.*

He led her down a side street far from the temples surrounding the plaza. Only one bridge spanned the canal; the others had fallen into the channel. The stone walkway was empty and they crossed the river swiftly. On the other side of the causeway were lesser dwellings of sun-baked clay, none of which had withstood the slow shift of the glacier. Only mounds of crumbled brick remained.

What was this place? the Guardian asked.

Where the groundlings dwelt, Cyrus replied. *Commoners. Not to worry. The Walkers won't follow us here.*

She glanced back. *Why not?*

There's nothing to prey on. Cyrus scuffed his sandal through some rubble. *Guide me to the tombs before they convince me otherwise. Do you know House Crystal Keep?*

I've seen the crypt, the Guardian replied. *It is the largest among the tombs.*

Cyrus stared at her with unblinking eyes. *We were the most powerful ruling family, for all the good it did us.*

Answer me this: Why are your dead so restless on the ridge? she asked.

They sense invaders approaching the city. Cyrus planted his staff and looked around. *Some breech from the Blind Side to the West, while others trespass through the southern caves. Clansmen who call themselves our descendants creep down from the North. All come to find the Lost Caves and discover the secrets of old.*

What would your folk have me do? she asked.

Make the world whole. The city died without twin suns. House Crystal Keep fell when the Skell sundered. Cyrus gestured with his cane. *The braided rivers of the Tigris and Eye lay dormant now. All halves must be whole.*

I've seen the symbol you speak of, the Guardian mused. *It resembles a lidded eye.*

Twin suns surrounded by twined rivers. Cyrus nodded. *Tiger Eye.*

She looked at him in confusion. *The gem?*

The city, he replied. *Bear witness to other Wanderers frozen in time and they will help you. Avoid the Walkers. Before, I was unready. Now I would have you free me from these walls.*

You will have to show me what to do, she consented.

With the aid of his staff, Cyrus clambered over a pile of rubble. *Those who are ready leave by the North Gate. This way.*

Although she saw no wall or gate, the Guardian followed the Wanderer.

Beware of the unready, he advised, as they traversed piles of broken brick. *Like your Dervish watching the tombs beyond, Walkers can be reborn with fire within the ice. A Wanderer would be laid to rest, but a Walker would prey upon lifeblood to live anew.*

The Guardian paused. *I am reborn.*

Sometimes Guardians are. He seemed unsurprised. *Not the last one, though.*

Did you tarry among the Walkers, Wanderer? the Guardian asked when finally she could see the remains of the stone walls that had once surrounded the city.

I walked for a time, he confirmed. *Walkers will not trouble you, for they cannot inhabit the reborn, nor leave the walls of Tigeria.*

What happened to the previous Guardian, the one who was to meet me here?

He was well past his prime. None have seen him since he set out for the Crystal Caves.

How long ago did he take his leave? she asked.

Cyrus shrugged. *What is time but dripping snowmelt, a ripple in the water, a cast of light shining down through the ice?*

They reached a wide opening in the city wall facing the bluff rimmed with tombs where already the First Folk were murmuring in excitement. The Guardian had seen the gaping hole before, but not known it was the Northern Gate. As the door had been timber, nothing remained. The wailing from the graveyard grew. Cyrus smiled at the fanfare.

Stay with me just inside the city walls, he said silently. *I have something to say before you lead me through.*

Are you prepared to pass? she asked.

I have never been more ready to die in my whole life. He faced the cemetery. *I have done my penance to the sun and earth, wind and water. From sun and earth we get fire, from wind and water we get ice. Fire and ice.* He turned to her, his eyes watering. Already he was beginning to thaw. *Take me to my people.*

Take my hand. Together, they stepped through the gate. Cyrus began to dissolve. As they climbed the hill, he melted away. When they reached the crypt of House Crystal Keep he was just another voice among the incessant babble.

Make the Skell whole, he kept whispering. *All must be whole.*

As his voice faded, something dislodged from the disrupted tomb and rolled to her feet. The Guardian bent to pick up the polished stone rich with luminous layers of gold. She recognized it right away, a Tiger Eye.

The Guardian smiled, for somehow she no longer felt alone. She wandered the tombs, among the Dervish encased in ice. She usually avoided the one that had escaped, but now she got close enough to peer at his face.

Dervish do you hear me? she asked.

In response, it blinked its unseeing eyes and lashed its tail.

As she turned to leave, once again she felt a prickle in her mind, each tiny stab a pinprick of awareness. She had lived among brethren before, she was certain now. Among them was one who understood animals much as she did ancient language. She wished that person was here now. She wished all of them would come.

There were so many questions, whose answers lay on the glow on the horizon.

From his fingertips, Garth sent a flaming arc
into the water, making it hiss.

CHAPTER 20

AS THE LAST SHARDS OF AMETHYST sifted through the hourglass, the woman wandering among the tombs faded from view.

In her private council room, Aubergine looked at the circle of earnest faces surrounding the tambourine table. "We've reached Mamie at last."

"She didn't look like Mamie," Smokey Jo grumbled from the footstool near Aubergine's rocker. "Not one bit. Mamie was older than old when I was a child. We saw someone who looked like a girl."

"She is no longer the Mamie Verde that was," Lily reminded her, as Aubergine wrapped the darkened hourglass in velvet.

"She is the Guardian of the Ancients now," Sierra agreed, watching her stow the timepiece in the cupboard and secure the doors. "Mamie reborn."

"Do you think she remembers you?" Little Teal asked.

"Not yet," Aubergine touched the amethyst in her necklace that represented Mamie in the circle. "But I have a feeling she will. Lily, could you read her thoughts?"

"I gleaned aught the few times we pricked her memory, but for the most part, no." The housemother shook her head. "Nor do I understand the language she speaks."

"She didn't talk." Garth frowned at the witches. With a stray needle culled from one of Smokey Jo's tangled knitting baskets, he scratched inside his sling at the dead skin that had begun to peel from his arm. "Not to the ghost, not even to that dragon."

"Ancient language is silent," Aubergine murmured, glancing at the Skell fragment left on the table between them. "One without words."

"Don't pick," Sierra scolded her son, taking away the needle.

"It itches!" he protested.

"When Mamie was a witch, she called First Folk tongue Mind Speak," Lily explained to the boys. "Only one among us understood it, her handmaiden, Ratta."

"Ratta's not here," Smokey said helplessly. "If she was, I bet she wouldn't tell us anything."

"The creature you call dragon is actually a whirling Dervish straight from the tales of old," Sierra told her son. "If I'm not mistaken, he is the Watcher Wheat freed from the Lowland invaders, and he, too, has been reborn."

"He looked mean," Garth said. "I hope he remembers Winter Wheat."

Sierra picked up the jagged Skell, turning the triangle of horn incised with half a crystal over in her hands. "According to legend, Dervish do not attack unless folk try to get between them and the tombs they protect."

Niles nodded in agreement. "It's the city Walkers your six witches need to heed."

Little Teal gave him a skeptical look. "Those carrion creatures in the rubble didn't look friendly."

"Wolverines are harmless," Niles replied. "Unless provoked."

Smokey Jo heaved her stubby hands into the air. "I don't understand what happened at all! Mamie, I mean the Guardian, came down off her cliff and broke into an old city, only to wander around with a ghost, leave him at a graveyard and anger a Dervish. What do we make of that?"

"The ghost's name was Cyrus and as Guardian she laid him to rest," Niles explained to the gnome. "In return he gifted her a Tiger Eye, symbol of ancient Tigeria."

Sierra's eyes lit up at the tall soldier. "You do know your yarns!"

Little Teal gave Niles a sidelong scowl. "More likely he's guessing."

Garth grinned. "I think he knows their secret language."

"Might our Northland boy have something to tell us?" Aubergine asked Lily, unable to hide a smile.

"You can't keep anything from Lily," Smokey tattled to Niles. "Believe me, I've tried. She just looks at you and she knows everything. It's her special talent."

Niles eyed Lilac Lily across the table. "You truly know what I'm thinking?"

"Yes I do, Niles of the North."

He raised his brows. "Then tell me."

"Remember you asked," Lily sighed. "You're thinking: No one knows how fond you are of Little Teal. You're thinking: You shall convince her to journey north to meet your parents."

As Niles's face reddened, the others laughed.

"You like her?" Garth asked, his eyes going from the little witch to the tall soldier. "I thought you liked my sister."

"Why wouldn't he like me?" Little Teal taunted. "You liked me well enough before."

"You will be going north to your father," Aubergine predicted, "but I'm afraid that I am the witch who shall accompany you. I have business in the provinces."

Sierra gave Niles a curious look. "Like our mistress, I, too, am from the North. Who are your family?"

Niles studied the table.

"Tell them," Lily urged him. "Unless you would rather I?"

Niles stood. "My father is Steadfast Lars, leader of the Northern Watch."

"Your father is king of the north?" Garth asked in disbelief. "Lately, everyone I encounter has a secret title. What are you, a prince?"

"Prince or not that's nothing you want to spread around down here," Smokey cautioned. "Middleland folk are not fond of the North."

"We have no kings," Niles said. "Or princes. The North rules by counsel, much as the First Folk did. My father governs the Men of Ice. Of the Five Provinces ours is called Wintergarten, the largest, encompassing tundra from the Glacierlands down to the Out Crops."

"Then you are allies of the Hed Clansmen," Sierra surmised.

"They fall under our protection, although we do not abide by Glacier Born belief." Niles eyed Lily sheepishly. "I did master their silent language as a boy. It is required, for many Clansmen keep the old ways."

"We are graced with a trueborn son of the Northern Watch," Aubergine's eyes sparkled at the soft-spoken boy. "Interesting."

"The youngest and a mere sled scout," Niles protested in embarrassment. "My oldest brother, Mason, would be more to your liking. As is customary, he bedded a girl after his triumph at the Winter Games and married her when she bore him a strong son. My father offered him our family's ancestral home, Winterhaven Lodge, as a wedding gift. Mason shall inherit my father's lands and title or if something befalls him, my next older brother, Marshall. I am fit for neither family nor lodge, for I do not abide the old ways."

"You are fit for us," Little Teal told him fiercely. "You are fit for me!"

"My uncle Honorable Devon commands the Northland Army." Niles's steely eyes met Aubergine's. "Perhaps it is he you seek."

"No, I would meet with your father and the Hed Clansmen of the Out Crops," she decided. "I think they will be spellbound by what we witches have gleaned."

"Little Teal is right," Lily beckoned Niles to the table. "You are fit for us. Sit."

"Why would anyone in their right mind want to live in the Out Crops?" Smokey grumbled, as Niles took his seat.

Garth shrugged. "Because that's where all the fighting is."

Little Teal peered up at Niles. "You champion folk who by choice make their homes in cold, dark caves of windswept ice?"

"Clansmen are outliers who have dwelt within a fortress of ice for ages," Sierra explained to the girl in the green dress. "They claim to be descended from the Ancients and believe they carry within themselves smoldering embers of First Folk Fire."

Niles put a hand to his chest. "Glacier Born vow they feel live coal right here."

"Fire inside?" Tentatively, Garth touched his breastbone. "What for?"

"To rekindle the Magic of Men!" Smokey Jo shouted merrily.

"Magic that has lain dormant these last thousand years," Aubergine agreed, regarding the others. "Magic mostly unawakened until now."

Lily gazed at Sierra. "It is time your remaining son should know."

"And tempt fate?" she queried in a low voice.

"Remaining son?" Garth asked.

"Examine the boy's burns and you will see his fate is already determined." Lily's cool glance fell on Smokey Jo, who quickly hid her head. "Of that I'll say no more."

Fearfully, Garth searched Sierra's face. "What happened to Warren?"

"We believe he succumbed to First Folk Fire," she said quietly. "Too late we learned you were destined to accompany our six to the Crystal Caves, not your brother. By the time we brought you back from River Walk, he was gone."

"Warren was a true Glacier Born? As is his brother?" Sierra looked away, fighting tears. Niles' eyes slid to Garth. "No boy survives the Kindle. Did Warren know he possessed the fire inside?"

"We barely knew ourselves," Aubergine said. "Kindling is not customary in the Middlelands."

"What's First Folk Fire?" Garth cried in dismay. "What's Kindling?"

"Your mother knows the stories," Lily said gently. "Let her explain."

"I never met him for he was killed on a hunt long ago, but your father's father was Maddig Hoar, Hed Clansman of the icy Out Crops." Sierra paused to wipe her eyes. "Like all Clansmen, Hed Maddig held to the Glacier Born belief that he was host to glowing coals of First Folk Fire. He hoped that one smoldering seed of ancient enchantment would spark within one of his sons one day to rekindle the Magic of Men. According to legend, the lore died with the First Folk when their world froze to ice."

"Yet as his boys matured, Hed Maddig watched those few who had fire inside perish. As the ember Kindled, it flamed into an inferno, consuming each youth from the inside out. As the blaze subsided to ember and then ash, his sons would suffocate, unable to release the fire to feed on the air it required to produce eternal flame." Sierra paused.

"We believe your father was Hed Maddig's only Glacier Born son to reach manhood."

"Impossible!" Niles spread his fingers flat on the table. "I don't doubt that his father lives, but not all Clansmen carry the spark and of those who do, none survive Kindling. I've heard the stories time and again. As boys burn inside, smoke pours from their nostrils and water from their eyes. They die."

"My father harbors fire inside," Garth assured the older boy. "I have seen him shoot it from his fingertips." He held up his burnt fist. "Who do you think did this?"

Little Teal elbowed Niles in the side. "His father is the Bad Man I told you about. Don't you remember? He set fire to my fossick camp and unsuppeared my boys?"

"Who witnessed his Kindling?" Niles asked the witches. "Who watched him live?"

"We don't know," Aubergine admitted. "Nor how he mastered the fire inside."

"Your father may be powerful," Niles told Garth. "He may know his way around magical things. But he cannot be Glacier Born. If so, he is the chosen Hed Clansmen have been awaiting for centuries. The One."

"He is not The One," Aubergine revealed. "He forsook that name for Northland's Bane."

"You accuse others of secret titles." Niles stared at Garth. "Yet your own father is Lord of the Lowlands?"

"A rule he shares with his sister, the Dark Queen," Lily confirmed.

"Call him what you like, for he has many names," Sierra said darkly. "However you know him, he carries the Magic of Men, Kindled anew."

Niles mulled it over. "How did he survive?"

"We can only guess." Flecks of gold stood out in Sierra's irises. "First Folk Fire passes from father to son, just as witchery inherits from mother to daughter. Not knowing what to expect, we delayed Warren's Kindling as long as we could with Mae's Snowflake Watch Cap, but in the end even that wasn't enough."

"His ember burst to flame yesterday and now he is absent from my mind's eye. Before he was lost, he reached out." Sierra's tawny eyes clouded. "But for what?"

"I heard the Dark Queen call the Bad Man her Kindred Spirit when I was captive," Little Teal offered. "She wanted to possess his fire. She tried to take his hand."

"The Dark Queen is our father's Kindred Spirit?" Garth asked Sierra. "Not you?"

"Tasman is Kendrick's sister," Sierra explained. "I never understood their bond. They were born on the same day to the same father, yet they are not twins."

Lily studied Little Teal. "Did the Dark Queen and her brother join hands?"

"No, he was worried they would burn down the Lowland encampment."

"Glacier Born die," Niles declared. "That is the reason Clansmen keep to their caves. Folk in the provinces consider Kindling disease."

"Then it looks like I catch it next," Garth said, hollow voiced.

"No," Sierra said fiercely. "You are The One. I've glimpsed your future, because you have one."

"Hush," Lily warned her.

"You shall avenge your brother," Sierra promised. "And save all Glacier Born."

"He is The One?" Niles asked. "But yet unkindled?"

"That is highly unlikely," Lily said, watching Smokey Jo. "Considering there is one among us who has a penchant for playing with fire."

"Of course he is The One," Aubergine proclaimed. "There was only ever the possibility of the three. Kendrick spurned his right when he allied himself with the Dark Queen. His oldest son Warren did not survive and Garth's fire has yet to ignite."

Garth nudged Smokey Jo. "You better tell them what happened."

"I'll get in trouble," she muttered. "Everyone dislikes it when I start conflagrations."

"We dislike it when you don't use the hearth or the stove to test your flames," Aubergine said tersely.

"Lily knows anyway," Garth whispered. "Everyone will when they see the burnt door to my room."

"Or the armoire," Smokey agreed.

Little Teal turned to the gnome cringing in her chair. "What happened?"

"You all thought Garth's hand was useless, like maybe the doctor should saw it off." Smokey let her voice drop to a confidential whisper. "But I knew better."

"We were afraid the burn might spread infection," Lily explained, exasperated.

"I assured you no." Smokey waggled a finger. "I thought there was something uncommon about the hand, something stirring in a certain sooty digit, perhaps."

"I do recall," Aubergine admitted.

"Well, I coaxed his finger to shoot fire." She sighed dramatically. "Someone has to repaint the walls."

"It's not her fault. Even while I was sleeping, I felt something burning, but not in my chest like you said," Garth told Niles. He pulled his sling over his head and held out his injured fist. "When I woke, it was in here."

Smokey bent her head over his stiff knuckles. "I had to straighten his fingers, especially this smutty one."

"Could his fire have Kindled?" Sierra wondered.

"Oh yes!" Smokey peered up at Niles. "Because smoke poured from his nose, just like you said. If you wait a minute, I'll show you!"

Huffing with effort, she began to work Garth's fingers free.

"You can't unfurl them on your own?" Little Teal asked.

Garth gritted his teeth in discomfort. "It takes the two of us."

"See? His hand is hot to the touch!" Smokey placed her small palm against Garth's. "Fire sizzles within." She gave Lily an anxious glance. "We practiced in his room. Please don't look!"

"Why didn't you notify us?" she asked. "You interrupted for every other reason."

"I thought you'd be mad," Smokey confessed. "Besides, there wasn't much time. Right after I straightened his fingers, the fire sparked out."

Garth grinned at the witches. "Want to see?"

Aubergine considered the velvet draperies and carpet, as well as the shelves crammed with rare parchments and leather-bound books. Placing her hands on the armrests of her chair, she heaved herself to her feet. "We'd best try this outside."

The six of them trooped into the dye shed and out the secret door trailed by the green fog of Teal. In the alley, Smokey clapped her hands. So many times as a child, she had played with fire here. Garth clamped his good hand over his singed wrist, holding it steady as once again, Smokey slowly straightened his blackened fingers.

"Aim for the puddle!" she commanded as the sparks began to sizzle.

From his fingertips, Garth sent a flaming arc into the water, making it hiss.

"The fence! The cobbles! The wall!" Smokey cried as he shot fire bolts toward the picket fence, the stone walkway, and even managed to light the carriage shed ablaze.

Niles doused the stable with a bucket of water meant for the ponies.

"That's enough," Aubergine decided.

Back inside, they gathered in the kitchen for a midday meal. Donning her apron, Lily set the stewpot to warm on the stove and brought a plate of biscuits to the table.

"Fire Kindled and a Glacier Born lived," Niles buttered a biscuit. "I never would have believed it."

"I'll bet Smokey Jo had more to do with it than she lets on," Little Teal guessed.

Perched on a stool next to the cookstove, Smokey stirred the stew, smiling broadly. "The others were locked away watching the hourglass, when he began to cough up smoke. That didn't deter me. As everyone knows, I am expert with fire."

"I thought Garth was too young," Sierra told Aubergine, her voice faltering. "Warren's fire failed to ignite until he was three winters older." She set out the napkins and silver. "I was hoping Garth's never would."

"Don't forget we spent much time trying to prevent Warren's Kindle." Aubergine took a seat at the table. "Mae, especially."

"Perhaps Kendrick hastened the Kindle." Lily carried a stack of bowls to the cookstove. "Perhaps the fire bolt that burned Garth's hand sparked the coal prematurely."

"What did you do that he might live?" Niles asked Smokey Jo in earnest.

"I do know how to charm a flame," she bragged, climbing down from her stool. "As the boy choked I uncurled his fingers, straightening the hot one. After fire shot from his hand, he stopped gasping. But as I mentioned before, we did scorch the walls quite a bit. When we left his room, the armoire was still smoking."

"Don't worry about the walls." Lily filled the bowls and passed them to Little Teal who set them on the table. "What exactly did you do?"

"She gripped his hand." Little Teal set a bowl brimming with savory stew before Aubergine. "Just as the Dark Queen threatened to do with the Lord of the Lowlands."

"Just as she must have done the first time," Aubergine said, deep in thought.

"That's how the boys live!" Sierra realized, rising as the teakettle whistled. "It's as simple as that. The boys reach out in supplication and you seize their hand, releasing the fire. Tasman must have joined hands with Kendrick long ago. He never reached out to me in that fashion."

"She and her Kindred Spirit rule as one," Aubergine mused. "Perhaps First Folk Fire is the source of her magic, not the amethyst necklace as we always thought."

"If so, she uses him as a pawn," Lily remarked.

Sierra had gravel in her voice. "They use each other."

"It's a pity there was no one to grasp Warren's hand," Smokey Jo ventured, checking the icebox for more butter.

"Skye was there," Garth said hopefully.

"And Mae," Lily added, ladling the last bowl of stew for herself.

"If they managed to save him, I would see his glow on the horizon." Sierra set the kettle before meeting Lily's gaze. "Don't tell me what I already know."

"Why wouldn't Skye let the fire out?" Garth grabbed his bowl and biscuits and went to eat at the counter.

"Maybe she didn't know." Little Teal joined him. "Maybe Mae wouldn't let her."

Niles leaned against the stove as he ate. "If there was a way to save one Glacier Born in ten, I would take my leave now to tell the Clansmen."

"We go north tomorrow, all of us." Aubergine promised. "We may be able to fight fire with fire, after all." Tapping the half Skell on the table, she offered it to Garth.

"Don't trust me with that," he implored her. "Its twin was taken from me, and that was when I had two hands."

"You'll get the card back," Sierra assured him. "Won't he Lily?"

"Yes, but not in any way you can imagine," she replied.

Green haze floating against the ceiling lowered and circled around them.

"It seems Teal is finally ready to take her leave of us," Aubergine said pleasantly.

"Before dessert?" Smokey complained.

"You can have pie after," Lily promised.

Aubergine's violet eyes sparkled at the girl in the green dress. "Little Teal are you ready to become a full-fledged witch?"

She washed down her last bit of biscuit. "It depends. What will I be able to do?"

"All that Tracery Teal could and more; for you inherit her mantle, in your case an old patchwork barn sweater," she promised. "Henceforth, your name shall truly be Teal."

"I love that knitted coat!" Smokey Jo protested. "Might I have it?"

"You, little one, have other talents." Aubergine smiled. "If you can rekindle the Magic of Men, your abilities are too gifted to waste on a cardigan that allows it's wearer to drift around Bordertown."

"I'll be able to fly?" Little Teal asked, her dark eyes dancing.

He sensed upturned eyes carefully scanning the ceiling
for the source of the fallen card.

CHAPTER 21

AFTER TWO DAYS' MARCH, KENDRICK LEFT Tasman and six hand picked Queen's Guard at the opening of the hidden crevasse her raiders had discovered along the Blind Side of the glacier. Then he moved on with the rest of their men. Finding no evidence of heavy foot traffic through the thawing tundra, he guessed that the main forces of the Lowland Army had not traversed the Blind Side as he had originally assumed. Instead, the ranks of foot soldiers had circled east, choosing the easier route south of the glacier. Along its eastern edge, the main track intersected three others at a seasonal encampment called the Crossed Tracks, before turning north past the Burnt Holes, eventually reaching the Out Crops.

Curious that, Kendrick thought. Casting a questioning glance from the unbroken trail to the lieutenant's unreadable face, he received only a noncommittal shrug in reply which could have meant anything. Kendrick did not care for this indecipherable man, who even now seemed more loyal to his absent sister than himself. He wondered why Tasman had not selected the seasoned commander to help her find the Lost Caves. He considered turning back. But when his Lowland scouts reported nothing amiss, he decided to forge ahead along the unused trail.

At dusk, they came upon a party of jubilant Clansmen back from the hunt with a fine alpine moose. Kendrick was unsurprised for the steady thump of skin drums had begun earlier in the day, before advance runners returned with sightings of hunters with a fresh kill around a bonfire. They were almost upon the site before Kendrick got a fragrant whiff of grilling meat. The camp was protected from wind by natural walls of granite and it was evident that Clansmen used the clearing often. They had lashed poles to dry strips of meat and rawhide stretchers for skins. Braided ropes dangled from the boulders above to hang game against the threat of predators. Sheltered by rocks, an old cook squatted at the fire pit, rotating the heart, liver, and tongue on spits. Behind him, a skinner deftly separated the precious white hide from the animal carcass while another man washed intestines in hollowed bowls of snowmelt for sausage skins.

Having grown up in a Clan, Kendrick knew that none of the moose would be wasted. Once cut from the head of the bull, the twin antlers would be honed for blades, scrapers, punch needles and pins. The cranium itself would be stuffed with freshly gathered herbs or ground seasonings, and wrapped in cheesecloth to marinate. As was tradition, the cook would later smoke this delicacy over green willow boughs to serve to the Hed Clansman himself as well as the hunter responsible for the kill.

Behind the rocks, Kendrick's raiding party watched as the moose was quartered and the meat butchered into manageable pieces for transport. Once again, Kendrick looked for advice from his lieutenant. This time, the dark man in scarlet raiment raised his brows, made a half circle in the air with one index finger and splayed both hands. Kendrick needed no translation to understand what the other man meant, for his southerners had not eaten fresh meat all week. While the lieutenant guarded their flank, Kendrick would pick ten scouts to circle the rim rocks. Once in position, he would signal his lieutenant and his raiders would move in to ransack the camp. Kendrick sniffed the rich aroma of the roasting organs and smiled. These were scents from his boyhood and he remembered them well. His soldiers would feast like Hed Clansmen tonight.

He held up his hands with fingers spread wide and chose stealthy soldiers with sharp blades, whom he considered masters of infiltration. He gestured to the others to fall back with weapons drawn, against hunters who might attempt to flee. Leading his scouts, Kendrick circled the boulders surrounding the camp carefully, searching for the easiest way to trap those within. The site was not set up as a fortress and the hunters could enter and exit the clearing by several paths through the rocks.

Slightly perturbed, Kendrick made a swirling motion with his hand and his ten assassins fanned out silently. Creeping closer, he saw that the hunting party was smaller than the ones he remembered from his boyhood. It contained no women, and hardly any youths, which he found odd. On his father's hunting trips, Hed Maddig almost always selected a new wife not yet with child to warm his bed. This was customary among Hed Clansmen yearning for sons, hoping to father one boy who might survive the Kindling. Among his sons he chose several for a hunt, usually ones closest in age to Kindle.

Screened by rocks splotched with lichen, Kendrick searched the camp, seeing nothing amiss. The North was at war, he reasoned. Perhaps custom among the Clans dictated that they confine women and children to their fortress within the icy Out Crops for safety, launching small hunting parties only as needed. Kendrick had not set eyes on the Clan's hidden stronghold since his own Kindling, more than twenty years ago.

He had never made sense of what occurred the night he Kindled. Fraught with fever he lay helplessly sweating in his sheets until one of his brothers found him in his bedchamber. Clansmen in traditional fur robes trimmed with crystal carried him on a stretcher to a cave coated in blue rime to lay him on an altar hewn from ancient ice. He had never seen the sacred caverns before, for none of his older brothers nor male cousins had Kindled. Of them all, only he carried the deadly ember.

His extended family filed in for the ceremony. Presiding over the altar, his father's shaman began to speak; at times he sang. Delirious, Kendrick fought for air within the cell reserved for Kindling, a chamber in which his Glacier Born ancestors had died. Slowly suffocating, he lost consciousness.

Then Tasman appeared in a lurid dream. He barely recalled her, for years ago his father had sent her south to practice lore among a coven of witches. She was not his favorite sister. Choking on his own smoke he cried out in agitation, no longer lucid, no longer coherent, and unable to care. Smolder rose from his nostrils, and he heard his father Maddig Hoar tell someone to take his sobbing mother from the candlelit room.

Kendrick's delusion transformed into nightmare. In his hallucination, Tasman offered to share his burden. She proposed to release the fire inside and spare his life if he would share the Kindled flames and become her Kindred Spirit. In his dream, she reached out in frightening reality. Though he could barely lift his hand, his sister needed no encouragement. She entwined their fingers, discharging the pent-up blaze burning out his core, taking fire to save him from certain death. His had no choice but to acquiesce to her after that.

Later, he woke to an empty room, the taste of ash in his mouth. The candles beside the altar had burned to nubs. Only rose-quartz crystals glowing from niches hollowed in the walls of blue ice lit the cave. He sat, his feet dangling over the edge of the altar with no idea where he was or how long he had been there. Beside him were offerings of scented water and dried fruit, victuals meant to ease his passage into the Land of Dreams. Kendrick drank the flask of water and ate a handful of figs, barely believing his family had left him for dead. He slid off the altar and grabbed a glowing crystal from one of the niches, vowing to prove them wrong until he felt the fire inside. He finally emerged from a labyrinth of caves to find himself at the Crossed Tracks in the Middlelands, where he joined a group of shepherds herding their flocks toward the stockyards in Bordertown.

Kendrick wondered what might have happened if he returned to the Out Crops to announce himself to the Clans as the one trueborn they had waited for generations. Since he vanished during his Kindling, his family believed he had burnt to cinders. Considering his pact with Tasman, it was better they did.

Ever watchful, she sank her talons deeply into him when he reached Bordertown. She lured him to Potluck Yarn to charm her classmate Sierra just before abandoning the Twelve to flee south. How could he refuse her? If not for her helping hand he would be cold ash, a horror he could never forget. His debt would be settled only when Tasman held the secrets of the Lost Caves and power to rule nature as the First Folk did.

Even from the Lowlands, Tasman controlled him. She convinced Kendrick to wed Sierra and distract her with farm and family that she might never be tempted to return to a life of witchery. Kendrick's role occupied all his time, so much so that Lavender Rill Farm seemed a prison without walls. As the years passed, he came to grudging terms with his double life. In the guise of husband and provider, he submitted to Sierra's desire for children, although as the one true Glacier Born, he desired no heirs. He bided his time, intending to slip away toward the Out Crops when Tasman wasn't watching him with her raven eyes. Unfortunately, she was always watching.

When the Glacier Wars began anew after the Battle of the Burnt Holes, folk in the Middlelands began calling Tasman the Dark Queen, as if they could sense her sinister intent. Quite by accident, a group of her southern raiders killed Hed Maddig, whose hunting party crossed their path. Although such unfortunate events occurred during war, Kendrick always wondered if Tasman had intended to deny him his family's safe haven, should he attempt to escape to the fortress of ice.

Kendrick scanned the rocks, noting that two of his men had already found good vantage, but unable to see others in the waning light. He was close to the campsite, but not as near as he would have liked. Clansmen were notoriously keen of hearing. It was rumored that Men of Ice harbored a sixth sense offering them an uncanny ability to detect danger, a quality much needed for dwelling in the harsh caves of the Out Crops. From between the boulders, Kendrick counted eight hunters in the flicker of the fire, plus the cook and two others he took to be servants. He had ten raiders rimming the granite plus more than seventy soldiers at his back. It almost seemed too easy.

The Clansmen finished carving the moose by firelight. The old cook wrapped the remaining entrails in stomach lining and rendered the steaming blood into a cauldron for pudding and sausage. After it cooled, the congealed mass would be packed onto toboggans along with the meat, hide, antlers, and bone for transport come morning. The cook signaled it was time to eat, and the hunters gathered around the fire to divide the grilled organs. A hint of a smile played along Kendrick's lips. It was time to kill these men and take their spoils. Raising his hand behind him, he signaled his assassins.

When after a few moments he sensed no movement among the rocks, he peered about in exasperation that sparked to anger. It was just like these Lowlanders to ignore his command, for the silent southern dogs still saw his sister as their leader and took orders from her loyal lieutenant. He would put a stop to that right now.

He crept among the massive stones, searching for his raiders but they had vanished. He wondered whether the cowards had crept back to those protecting their flank, or simply fled. Cursing his mistake for heeding the advice of Tasman's lieutenant, he descended from the overlook by the light of the rising moon. Almost immediately, he stumbled across the slumped form of one of his assassins who had fallen from the rocks above. Although the man's throat was cut, he still gripped a bloody dagger in his hand. Kendrick unsheathed his short sword, and searched the shadows cautiously. Seeing no one, he advanced noiselessly through the tundra toward the scrub where he had left his second in command with the bulk of his raiders.

The first body he found was a boy, pierced in the back by a Clansmen's spear. He turned the figure over with the toe of his boot to discover his squire, whose dulled eyes were frozen open in surprise. Other dead lay scattered among the scrub; few had escaped the Clansmen's ambush.

Kendrick felt his neck prickle as hunters materialized from the bushes. He was surrounded yet strangely calm, for these were his true people. His saw his raiders replaced by scores of Clansmen, their numbers the size of large hunting parties he recalled from his childhood. Their leader stepped forth, his hands on the shoulders of a youth, undoubtedly his son. The man was a young Hed about ten years Kendrick's junior, whose slate-gray eyes set into a lean face framed by a mane of blond hair held for him no flicker of recognition. The well-muscled huntsman held a spear whose hardened blade was wreathed in lynx tails. His crown was a skinned wolf's head whose eye sockets sparkled with cold-fire crystal and his robe an ornate mantle of alpine moose hide studded with amethyst shards. His boy's uncut hair was caught back in a leather sheath at the nape of his neck and clear blue eyes in his rounded face still held the innocence of youth. Kendrick guessed he might be Garth's age, were he still alive.

Beside father and son stood a stooped man in a similar cloak, the amulet of a healer strung around his neck. Kendrick's father had relied on such shamans who wore necklaces of tooth and ivory carved with flames and stalactites, believing that their lore contained forgotten knowledge of fire and ice that might spare Glacier Born from certain death. Kendrick had always viewed these advisors as sycophants bent on an easy life of coin and crystal within the Out Crops fortress of ice.

While he watched, two guards dragged Tasman's lieutenant from the scrub. The shaman pulled a thin dirk from the folds of his cape and pulled the Lowlander's head up by his curly hair, exposing his neck. Looking into his eyes, Kendrick was unable to decide whether or not his man had expected the ambush. He pressed his thumb and forefinger together, signaling that all would be well. This caused a ripple of derision among Clansmen who understood enough Lowlands sign to believe otherwise. Spears drawn, the hunters circled Kendrick, biding their time as they had all along.

How long had they lain in wait while their decoys lured his Lowlanders to their cook fire, he wondered? Who had devised this cunning trap? Although his soldiers were silent assassins, able to fight two and sometimes three on one with surprise on their side, they had been hoodwinked and slain. Kendrick recognized now that any attempt to reach the Out Crops by way of the Blind Side would have resulted in Clan attack. Was that why the Lowland Army had taken the longer route to the east, he asked himself? Had Tasman warned them? He searched the lieutenant's impassive face. Had this man known and if so, would he sacrifice his life?

As he had countless times before, Kendrick decided to save himself. To summon the ever-present fire smoldering within, he took a deep breath, willing the ember to burst to flame. When it caught, he coughed softly, swallowing the bitter aftertaste of ash. He flexed his fists, feeling heat spread from his chest, sending waves of warmth down his arms like pumping blood. He directed his fingers toward the sodden tundra, shooting fire that scorched a hissing line in the moss. As he burnt a protective circle around himself, the Clansman's boy let out a cry of alarm. The hunters retreated, and the shaman pulled the boy to the safety of the scrub. The only one to stand his ground was the Hed Clansman wearing the skinned wolf's face over his platinum mane. He seemed unimpressed by the black line in the wet earth.

Without warning, two hidden hunters sprang at Kendrick from the brush. In one swift movement he spun and with a flick of his fingers shot flames toward their chests and set fire to their spears before they had a chance to let them loose. Flesh seared as their burning shafts fell to the sodden ground.

Kendrick turned back toward the Hed Clansman, to see his lieutenant's stoic look of dread as the shaman cut his throat and threw him into the blackened circle. As the bleeding body fell at his feet, more Clansmen careened toward him with spears drawn. Flame burst from his fingers again and again. Although the remaining hunters shrank back as those in front went down screaming, Kendrick felt the fire within begin to ebb. He needed to refuel which meant food and sleep.

Straddling the body of his lieutenant as the smoke cleared, he scanned the remaining hunters wondering how much longer he could hold them at bay. Although it would have been impossible with his father, perhaps he could reason with this Clan. He sent a fire bolt into the night sky that burst into flame, showering them with cinders.

"I am The One," he shouted. "Kendrick Blue, son of Hed Maddig Hoar, trueborn survivor of First Folk Fire."

The Hed Clansman wearing the wolf's head gazed at him with steely eyes. "Hed Maddig died long ago. His Clan scattered. We do not know you."

"I am he who Kindled and lived," Kendrick insisted. "The One you await."

"We wait for him still," the shaman sneered, turning to his leader. "Lewellyn, this man is no one." He pointed at the body of Kendrick's lieutenant. "Nor was he. The one son of Maddig Hoar who Kindled in the Caves of Blue Ice burnt to ash. My master, Healer Horehound, himself performed the rites. Hed Maddig had many more sons, but none inherited the ember, and after Maddig was killed, they were left to wander."

"Perhaps you were one of those, as Healer Borac says." Lewellyn stared at Kendrick, a faint hint of recognition crossing his face. "Turned out and left to wander."

"You may not ken me." Kendrick smiled at the Hed. "Yet you know who I am."

Healer Borac held out his palms, but the ash had ceased to fall. Even the dark circle in the moss had lost its smolder. "Your Lowland fire play burns itself out," he observed. He eyed Lewellyn's huntsmen. "He is no one."

"No one." The Clansmen tamped their spear butts on the tundra.

Lewellyn held his hand up for silence. "This Northlander who leads southern invaders is likely someone, a man we would call traitor or spy." He gave Kendrick a look of hate. "Someone with a price on his head."

A knowing look lit the old healer's face. "Lord of the Lowlands? Could he be?"

The Hed Clansman stared at Kendrick grimly. "What say you, Northland's Bane?"

With a war cry, his Clansmen charged.

"Take him alive!" Lewellyn commanded. "He's no use to us dead."

Sending a blazing wall before him, Kendrick broke through the circle and sprinted along the edge of the glacier, turning every now and then to send fire bolts behind. His pursuers dropped out of range, but Kendrick was far outnumbered and knew he would not outrun these seasoned hunters. After awhile, his fire would die to coals once more and he would have to rest. But how? He had no defense with his men dead or scattered.

Kendrick scanned the scrub for a bear, beaver, bird—anything he could shape-shift into long enough to recharge and avoid detection. The tundra provided little sustenance for nocturnal creatures and the carrion birds he favored would not appear until first light. Running blind, he followed the contour of the ice, relieved beyond belief to discover a dry crevasse alive with bats. Although he was in full view of the men chasing him, he ducked inside the narrow cave, pleased with the small cries of protest he elicited from the bats he disturbed, clinging to the low ceiling near the entrance. The fecund smell of guano reminded him of rich earth. Whooping with victory, the Clansmen closed in, certain he was cornered. He had a few scant moments to do what he must.

Choosing one of the swooping mammals, he imagined first inhabiting its winged body and then occupying its nocturnal mind, a trick Tasman had taught him long ago. Closing his eyes, he began see him self as the blind creature he had selected, a large brown bat rhythmically arching its wings around the perimeter of the cave. As he shifted into its shape, he began to lose his humanity. Though he had transformed into another being countless times, it was always unsettling when his sense of self peeled away.

His shape-shift complete, he sensed rather than saw the hunters chasing him rush the opening of the cave and thunder to the end of the shallow enclosure, confused they could not find him. Kendrick would have laughed, except he was a shrieking bat.

Too late, he realized his folly. In haste he had forgotten to stash the half Skell he had been carrying in the tiny pouch belted to his tunic. Personal possessions were impossible to protect is such an altered state. Before he became a bat, he could have secreted the relic among the sleeping bats or hidden it within the guano itself. He had done nothing to safeguard his prize. Such recklessness he usually attributed to his sister.

For a few frantic moments, he tried clasping the bit of horn within his claws. When that failed, he attempted to enfold it in his leathery wings. His desperate flapping was useless. As he turned upside down to cling to the cave's ceiling, the card escaped his clutch. As the triangle tumbled to the frozen dirt, he detected a collective pause among the milling hunters and knew that one of them had picked up the Skell.

He sensed upturned eyes carefully scanning the ceiling for the source of the fallen card. Fearing discovery, he clung motionless to the underside of the low roof until the Clansmen vacated the cave. Outside there was a shout and a roar of recognition as the Hed Clansman took possession of the Skell. Kendrick was furious. He would steal the card back because he had to; otherwise he wouldn't dare show his face to Tasman. For now, he could do no more but remain unnoticed and bide his time until morning. Then he would fly to the ambush site and shed the guise of this bat for a proper bird, hopefully a raven or vulture lured by the scent of the fresh kill from the bodies scattered among the scrub. Flying high above the tundra he'd wing his way north until he saw his chance to snatch the Skell.

BLINDSIDED

Skye went to fetch the team of ponies
staked in some green grass at the edge of the stream.

CHAPTER 22

Waking to a World Without Magic

WHEN SKYE WOKE, SHE HEARD MAE grubbing in the wagon bed across the clearing, but was unable to see her through the morning mist. As usual Mae sang to herself, humming a familiar nursery rhyme into which she inserted her own random lyrics.

"Mae, Mae, Mae," She chirped. "Mae, Mae, Mae. Mae-yay-yayy-ay! Won and One, Mae, too!"

Last night, none of the witches had been able to pry her from Warren's body even after they laid his lifeless form in the back of the wagon and covered it with a blanket. Even though Warren had been her brother, Skye had no desire to lie with the dead and found Mae's clinginess morbid. There was much she did not understand about Mae.

This morning it was her sorry job to harness the ponies and drive the wagon back to Potluck Yarn in Bordertown with her brother's body. There she would await her mother's return, so that they might send Warren to the Land of Dreams. There was no choice, for the only other witch skilled in wagonry was Indigo Rose who was no kin. Esmeralde had given Skye a pretty funeral scarf knit in yarn shaded blues and purples to ease Warren's journey.

Skye's reddened eyes filled with tears anew as she blamed herself for Warren's death. Why had she argued with Lily when she learned she was one of the six witches chosen for the quest to the Lost Caves? It was ironic, for now that her wish to stay behind would be granted, she no longer yearned to retrace her steps to Bordertown. For the rest of her days, she would wonder if the cost of fulfilling her desire was her brother's life.

Wiping her eyes on the edge of her blanket, Skye rose to a sitting position in the lean-to. Although it was early, the other bedrolls were empty. After she finally cried herself to sleep last night she must have been so exhausted that she didn't hear anyone else stir this morning. Blinking, she looked across the chilly clearing, damp with fog. Wrapped in a wool shrug, Ratta sat with her broad back to the shelter, coaxing the cook fire that had burnt to ashes back to life. Draping a shawl around her shoulders, Skye silently joined her, watching the ruddy witch stir the coals and add dry sticks for kindling.

"Morning," Ratta grunted.

Trailed by Tracks, Winter Wheat trudged from the stream lugging a bucket of water to start tea, just as sun broke through the mist hanging over the mountains.

Tilting back her wide-brimmed hat, she squinted at the sky. "It's going to be a beautiful day for trekking."

Although everyone was making light of the situation, the mood was somber and the pleasantries forced. When Esmeralde and Indigo

Rose hiked into camp from a shallow pool downstream where they had gone to wash up, Indigo's swinging braids smelled strongly of the herb that calmed her and the scent of sweet wine surrounded Esmeralde. Crawling into the lean-to, Indigo sealed her packets of herbal remedies, while Esmeralde repacked her Possibles Bag with vials she had discarded in her effort to save Warren the night before.

The whistling kettle summoned the witches around the fire for morning tea. Indigo poured hot water into a mug to add special leaves from one of her herbal pouches before handing the cup to Skye.

"To ease your sorrow," she murmured.

"Thank you," Skye said gratefully.

Noticing everyone gathered for breakfast, Lavender Mae clambered from the wagon and tripped toward the group at the fire. She darted to the picnic basket to rummage within. Finding remnants of yesterday's sourdough loaf, she broke off two pieces of bread and dolloped the first one with honey from the crock.

Wheat stirred brown sugar into the oatmeal boiling for porridge, watching her. "One's enough, Mae." She cautioned. "Two will make you sick."

"One," Mae agreed cheerfully. "One and one! Two!" Quickly, she spread honey over the other piece of bread and scurried out of Wheat's reach.

Skye sipped the soothing tea as the others ate bowls of hot cereal. Finishing first, Wheat unhooded her staff and rose to scout the trail ahead while the others broke camp.

Indigo rinsed her empty bowl in the bucket. "I'll help you hitch the horses," she offered Skye.

Setting aside her cup, Skye went to fetch the team of ponies staked in some green grass at the edge of the stream. Not finding their lead ropes, she glanced at the wagon to see someone sitting in the bed, eating with Mae. For a moment she was unable to speak. Then she let out a piercing scream.

Ratta took her by the shoulders, preparing to shake her. "Get ahold of yourself, girl."

"He's alive!" Skye shrieked. "Look, look!" She sprinted toward the wagon.

Beneath her bandana, Indigo's eyes shifted to Esmeralde's. "This can't be good."

As they watched the commotion in disbelief, Wheat hustled into the campsite followed by Tracks and caught the glowing cabochons swinging from her staff up in her hand.

"We need to avoid the Crossed Tracks at all costs," she warned the witches breathlessly. "My beetles sensed danger ahead."

"There's no need to go looking for hazards," Ratta told Wheat sourly, her eyes trained on the wagon. "We've got plenty of trouble right here."

Skye caught sight of them and waved them over. "Warren's fine, come see!"

"I bet he's undead." Indigo bit her lip. "There's nothing fine about that."

"Or maybe reborn." Esmeralde took a deep breath and slung her Possibles Bag across her shoulders. "I wouldn't wish it on anybody."

Wheat cast her eyes across the clearing. "Might Warren's sudden liveliness have somewhat to do with that peculiar watch cap Mae knit?"

"The one she clamped on his head? Most likely!" Ratta shook her head in disgust. "Meddlesome Mae!"

Dumping the dregs of her tea on the ground, Ratta followed the other witches to the wagon. She thought about taking off her shrug but decided against it, even though the sun had burned through the haze making the morning warmer. She liked how she felt in the sleeved shawl: brash and decisive, with a crystal-may-care attitude. It suited her this day. In the wagon bed, Warren and Mae were just finishing the two hunks of honeyed bread Mae had pilfered from the picnic basket.

Skye grasped her brother's arm, all smiles. "We thought you were dead."

He gave her a wry grin. "I figured that when I woke up with a quilt over my face."

Scowling, Mae wadded the blanket the witches had used as a shroud and threw it over the buckboard. Wheat caught it deftly with the crook of her staff.

"Cut it out, Mae," she admonished. Pulling the quilt away, she aimed her crystals, creating a pinpoint of light on the crone's sleeve.

"Mae . . ." the scrawny witch uttered, scuttling back.

"We watched you die," Skye whispered to her brother. "All of us did."

In answer, he hoisted himself over the side of the buckboard, and gave her a hug. "Well I'm right here."

Ratta looked him up and down. "No one survives the Kindling."

"One!" From the wagon bed, Mae pointed an accusatory finger at each of the other witches. "One, one, one, and one!"

"How are you feeling?" Indigo asked, ignoring Mae's antics.

Warren frowned. "A little lightheaded, I guess."

"You had such a fever, it's no wonder!" Skye exclaimed. "Smoke was pouring from your face. Do you remember?"

"I recollect not being able to breathe." He glanced at Esmeralde. "You giving me ice." He shook his head. "Nothing after."

Esmeralde laid a practiced hand across Warren's forehead. "No burning here." She put a palm to his breast. "Or there." She turned to the others. "His Kindle has gone to cold ash."

"The ember is dead?" Wheat asked.

"If that misguided snowflake hat Mae knit quelled the fire, he'd be better off dead," Ratta said derisively.

"What does she mean?" Warren asked the witches.

"While you were dying last night, we all tried to save you, each in our own way," Wheat said. "Not surprisingly, Mae's was most peculiar."

"It was nothing short of ridiculous!" Ratta broke in.

Wheat tapped her on the shoulder with her staff. "Is something wrong with you? You're much more abrasive than usual."

"It's this shrug," Ratta grumbled. "Every time I want to be non-committal, it makes me decisive."

"Well take it off then," Wheat advised before turning to Warren. "You are Glacier Born," she explained. "All your life you have carried a smoldering spark of First Folk Fire. When it Kindles, you must release the fire or perish as it burns you from within."

"I felt the blaze," Warren thumped his chest and coughed. "I taste the ash still."

"Do you remember asking me to let you die? I reached for you," Skye said timidly. "But you did not want to take my hand."

"Instead Miss Crazy Mae clamped her mismade Snowflake Watch Cap on your head," Ratta muttered. "You shall never be the same."

"It sounds like she saved me," Warren said.

"Yes, Mae," the crone nodded vigorously.

"Yet part of you is dead forever," Wheat cautioned.

"I'm very much alive," Warren pinched his arm. "Look!"

"You woke to a world without magic. Do you know what that means?" Wheat asked.

"I wouldn't care to find out," Ratta shuddered.

"Truly not," Indigo chimed in.

"What are all of you talking about?" Skye asked, bewildered.

Esmeralde put her hand on Warren's chest. "He died last night, and the magic he held within perished, too."

Skye looked at her brother. "Yet Mae saved him when the rest of us could not."

"He is reborn, but not as himself," Indigo said grimly.

"He looks like himself," she retorted.

"He's not," Esmeralde said. "Until last night, Warren held inside him a live coal of First Folk Fire, what the Hed Clansmen call the Magic of Men. To survive, he had to release part of that power to another. When Mae doused the fire, it ended his chance."

"Does that mean if I hide in plain sight, he really will not notice me?" Skye asked.

"That and more," Wheat predicted. "Potluck Hats cannot affect him, nor will he be able to coax light from a crystal, make use of our bottomless bags, trust in magic, or understand our lore. Yet he lives."

"What am I then?" Warren asked.

"Common folk," Ratta snorted. "As most in the Middlelands are."

Warren gave them a hard look. "Well then, rather than serve as a hindrance to you all, I would take Mae and leave this place."

"Warren!" Skye cried.

"Well spoken," Ratta agreed. "Harboring no magic, you pose a burden to us all."

"I've had it with that shrug," Wheat muttered.

With Indigo's help, Esmeralde pulled the sleeved shawl from Ratta's back and tossed it into the wagon. Mae scurried over to try it on.

"You would have gladly abandoned your brethren to drive my body back to mother and Garth for a proper burial," Warren accused his sister.

"You would not take my hand!" she argued.

"While the rest of you forced Mae to guide you within the glacier, knowing full well the First Folk would invade her mind once more," he went on. "She is not crazy."

"Not!" the crone yelled, looking even smaller in the folds of Ratta's shrug. "Not Mae! Not!"

Helping her down from the wagon, Warren shouldered his pack. "Safe travels."

"Don't go," Skye pleaded. "We just got you back."

Warren glared at Ratta. "Without First Folk Fire I am obviously no use to you, and without her sanity neither is Mae. Find your way through the Burnt Holes alone."

"None of us will be going by way of the Burnt Holes." Wheat's amber beetles began to chitter and clack. "Lowlanders are close."

The witches and Warren left the clearing and climbed the steep slope above the trail to the Crossed Tracks in silence. Using her staff as a walk stick, Wheat paused periodically to consult the swirling crystals, which seemed to pulse with the cadence of many booted feet. Sheltered behind stunted pines growing in the ledges, she motioned to the others with her crook. One by one they clambered up the incline and crawled through the rocks to join her. Below them marched wave upon wave of Lowland soldiers in scarlet raiment.

"Where are they going?" Skye whispered.

"The Out Crops," Warren surmised, peering through evergreen branches.

"Aubergine's prediction was right!" Esmeralde mouthed in disbelief.

"But it started out as a ruse," Indigo cautioned, watching the Dark Queen's minions. "Just like that River Walk thing."

"This is no ruse," Warren assured them. "These are hundreds of soldiers."

Mae pulled on Warren's sleeve. "Mae's," she insisted in a guttural voice.

"What does she want now?" Ratta asked.

Mae rose and began to retreat down the hill. "Mae's," she said, stronger this time.

Warren gazed at her in disbelief. "You can't be serious?"

"Mae's, Mae's, and Mae's!" Scrambling up the rocky incline, she clutched his arm and tried to drag him back down.

"Quiet her," Wheat warned, as the rest of them crept away from the ledges.

"Mae thinks the only safe route to the glacier is south, past the killing fields," Warren explained, as they hiked back to the clearing.

South?" Wheat planted her staff in the ground. "I know of no trail south."

"You'd never find it unless you knew it was there," Warren told the witches. "She would offer you safe passage to her lair."

"Mae lives in a lair?" Indigo asked.

Esmeralde gave her a quizzical look. "She has a room at the Potluck like us."

"No, I meant before," Indigo said, glancing at the small witch in the large shrug.

"Yes, Mae's!" Mae said proudly, pointing to herself.

Skye looked around the campsite. "What about the ponies? We can't just leave them to forage."

Wheat's spotted ram nosed at her skirt. "Yes, I know." She looked at the other witches. "Tracksie would be happy to lead them to pasture."

"He's a sheep not a guide dog," Ratta snorted.

"He saved our flock from slaughter and led them to the lower valley." Wheat scratched the Jacob's head fondly. "He remembers the way."

"It's decided then." Warren pulled the halters from the ponies while the others shouldered their packs.

"Good-bye, old friend. Watch the flock and lead the horses to safety." Wheat held the small sheep close. "We'll meet again."

Skye hugged both ponies around the neck, and then Warren gave them a slap on the rump. "Go on, Shep," he urged. "Get along, Chuffer."

With a merry tinkle of his bell, Tracks began a brisk walk down a deer trail. He circled back around the reluctant horses one time and soon they were trotting along, too. In minutes they had disappeared from sight.

Stoic as ever, Wheat tried not to shed tears, although the others heard her honking her runny nose into a bit of cloth she used as a handkerchief now and again.

The witches stashed the wagon into the bushes and followed Mae to the Crossed Tracks. All that remained of the soldiers was their heavy tread along the muddy trail. Mae scrambled atop a rock and hunkered there on all fours. Stark still, she raised her nose to the air and sniffed in all directions.

"Ruff!" With a satisfied bark, she scurried down the southern track, beckoning Warren and the witches to follow.

WAKING TO A WORLD WITHOUT MAGIC

Peering through her scope, Tasman sought
the whereabouts of her other magic coins.

CHAPTER 23

The Restless City

WITH SMUDGE TORCHES HELD HIGH, TASMAN'S infiltrators approached the old city of Tigeria warily, the six of them moving as one toward the western wall. Hours ago, they had slipped unnoticed into the crevasse their raiding party had discovered on the Blind Side of the glacier weeks before. At first they had been forced to walk single file in cold dark silence. Gradually the narrow fissure widened into hollowed ice tunnels that grew brighter as they made their way toward the forgotten city. Even now, the Dark Queen sensed nothing but the dull thunder of water rushing underfoot as they emerged into the great cavern that housed the lost civilization of the First Folk. Above, dizzying snow domes pocked with natural skylights spiraled overhead above cliffs of graying rime, encasing the ruins within its hoary heights. Although not much more than heaps of shattered stone, the ancient walls looked much like Tasman imagined them, for she had paid rapt attention to the magical tales of Mamie Verde during her apprenticeship at Potluck Yarn. Even from this vantage, she recognized the remnants of the vaulted temples, one on each side of the plaza, monuments to the ancient's reverence for the four elements of nature, towering above all else in the city center, surrounded by the wrecked causeways of the twined rivers, Tigris and Eye.

The temples were dedicated to the natural world, specifically Earth, Air, Sun, and Water. How she hungered to control them all. Yet the legends mentioned a key to unlocking the secrets of old, and she did not understand what that meant. Was this key physical or a mere metaphor that referred to some sort of arcane magic, ancient lore she did not yet possess? Her past twenty years spent experimenting with the natural environment of the Lowlands had yielded nothing but an unbearably hot and arid land devoid of water and vegetation. Not a drop of rain fell, nor were the shifting desert sands able to sustain a blade of grass. It was not the southern landscape she had envisioned.

She nodded to her lead guard. He flicked his eyes and the other five soldiers fanned out across the base of the ruins, along what once must have been Tigeria's western defense. Everywhere the fortifications had tumbled, almost as if the city was under siege when the world had ended. But Tasman knew there had been no foreign invaders armed with battering rams or trebuchets attacking the outer walls, for the First Folk had waged war from within. According to the tales of old, the ancients had perished in a failed attempt to conquer the natural world more than a thousand years ago. Only the slow progress of ice melt as the glacier slid south coupled with erosion over time had toppled the walls of the dead city.

Tasman's men scaled the rubble beneath the ramparts while she waited with her guard below. Screened by a huge rectangle of carved stone that had dislodged from the wall, she bade the soldier to bring his torch close as she sought her spyglass from her satchel. She wished to peer through her remaining portal pieces. Her lacquered nails found the amethyst necklace first, joined by the heavy silver clasp, and then the odd stone that no longer fit its setting. She pushed them aside and reached for the telescope.

Shape-shifted within the body of a wealthy merchant, her brother had liberally strewn her magic coins about the Middlelands, paying for rooms he never slept in, treating people he did not know to rounds of ale, and tipping for entertainment he did not enjoy in order to place gold and silver coins engraved with the Dark Queen's profile into circulation. Few folk who possessed the tokens were gifted with the ability to recognize the haze of black magic hovering over Tasman's visage. To most, the spying eyes were merely newly minted southern money.

Thus far, only one coin was exposed as far as Tasman knew. Days ago, Aubergine had discovered the true purpose of a piece of silver stamped with the Dark Queen's image that Esmeralde harbored, and cracked its lens outside the Cask and Barrel Tavern. Unaware of the coin's intent, the remedy witch had carried it for almost a week after bartering a pair of spectacles for it at the Banebridge Trading Post. Tasman had gleaned much valuable information before the portal was discovered. It was time to check on her other spying eyes.

Peering through her scope, Tasman sought the whereabouts of her other magic coins. The first was a piece of gold hidden from her Kindred Spirit, sewn inside the cloak of her loyal lieutenant. Looking through it, she saw men moving north through the dark to the beat of Clansmen drums. Her brother and a handful of assassins crept ahead while her lieutenant and his detail protected their flank. Too late, her second in command noticed the huntsmen in ambush behind him. He was a faithful soldier and his sacrifice would sorrow her, but sending anyone other than her trusted man would have aroused Kendrick's suspicions. At present, she needed her brother occupied, out of her way.

She peered through the glass again, spying another portal laying among a tray of foreign coins behind the counter at the Banebridge Trading Post. Tasman watched as first Trader garbed in a green velvet dress and then a tall Northlander clad in farmer's homespun dropped from the chimney flue to the hearth. So there was a hidden room above, interesting. Tasman made a mental note to bid her Kindred Spirit to torch the Trading Post the next time he happened by. Through the tavern's swinging doors, she glimpsed a boisterous barroom of enlisted men attired in Northland gray, bent on drinking the night away before marching to the Out Crops.

A third spying eye Tasman found secreted in the vest pocket of a traveling bard known as Miles from Nowhere. She peered through this lens often when bored, merely for the measure of distraction his entertainment provided. This evening the storyteller regaled a throng of listeners from a street corner in Bordertown. Clad in a brightly hued vest beneath his overcoat and felt hat, he stood on a crate speechifying to the crowd. Strangely enough, he was finishing a yarn from the third cycle of Woolgathering Tales, called Tasman the Traitor. Smiling, the Dark Queen listened.

"Not as clever as Sierra or Tracery Teal but far more devious, Tasman did not become the Potluck Queen's protégée until the day she willed it so," Miles shouted over those gathered to hear. "Almost overnight, she proclaimed herself Aubergine's successor, little realizing that events would unravel like a half-knit sweater pulled from the needles."

Wasn't that the truth? Tasman thought. Often, she tried to reason how she failed to solidify her claim to Aubergine's legacy, once Kendrick was Kindled and successfully placed as a deterrent to Sierra's destiny. With her rival no longer in contention, it was obvious that Tasman stood to inherit Aubergine's magical lore. Or had it been? Now she sensed someone else had pushed her off course, diverting her life as she had distracted Sierra, but whom?

"Old Mamie Verde saw all but said nothing," Miles roared. "For even when the girls were children, she was so frail it seemed any day she might pass to the Land of Dreams. Barely speaking and confined to a wheeled chair, her care was entrusted to fiery-haired Ratta, a rough kitchen wench from her household in Coventry. The girls mistrusted the servant for certainly she was not chosen, as they were."

Miles crossed his arms akimbo in an exaggerated shrug. "But wasn't she? Even boisterous Teal feared to slight Ratta in the presence of Mamie, whom they all revered. Not merely a wise woman, but also Aubergine's lifelong friend, Mamie alone could spin the yarns of the First Folk whose world ended in ice, so that all might listen and learn."

He paused dramatically. "Mamie Verde bestowed the verbal history of the ancients upon Sierra, for until Tasman stole her place among the Twelve, all believed Second Sight Sierra would bear the weight of Aubergine's amethyst necklace someday."

Well that never happened, Tasman thought with a frown. With the necklace in disrepair tucked inside her satchel, it would prove near impossible. Yet the unresolved question still plagued her: Why hadn't Aubergine presented her with the amethyst necklace whole, along with the ceremonial Simmer Stole as she had planned? Had Mamie Verde silently warned her friend? Did Ratta know more than she let on? In truth, Tasman believed her naysayer was Tracery Teal until she learned Lilac Lily had used the young girl as a foil. So angry was Tasman that she conjured newly cultivated magic she had planned to cast over nature upon Teal instead, dissipating the acolyte into green mist that lingered still.

She watched Miles raise his hand for silence and the crowd quieted. "Sierra studied the stories of old until she could explain each tale, but when Mamie ceased to speak, no one thought for certain that all the legends were safe with Sierra."

Holding up a finger, Miles wagged his head. "Oh no! None but Ratta who lived as a scullery maid in chambers behind the kitchen separated from the other girls, knew there was one yarn yet untold. She had heard the tale time and again, while stirring the ashes in Mamie's hearth, close enough to heed the old woman's silent call."

Miles's voice became a conspiratorial whisper. "All believed Ratta was a mere servant, until that last terrible day at Potluck Yarn, when those witches who remained discovered this secret: Although she did not understand them, Ratta alone could recite all the yarns true as Mamie had revealed in a silent tongue called Mind Speak none but Ratta could hear."

Sighing, Tasman pulled the lens from her eye and slid the scope shut. All knew now that the untold story was the Guardian's Tale, the yarn Aubergine had bid Ratta recite when she summoned the Twelve to the last simmer. Unlike the others, this legend spoke of Lost Caves that could unlock the secrets of old. Once again, Tasman asked herself what that meant. Did unlocking signify there were unasked questions whose answers had yet to be revealed? If so, what crucial clues had she had somehow missed in the tangled yarns? Something having to do with the scrap of Skell Kendrick had kept from her, whose other half Aubergine possessed? Or did unlocking indicate an actual key that only the Guardian could locate, and if found would unbolt an enchanted gate or sealed chest? Unfortunately, the term *unlocking secrets* might be a First Folk turn of phrase implying nothing, its meaning lost in translation.

Sensing eyes upon her, Tasman raised her head. Satisfied the ancient ramparts posed no danger to their queen, her Lowland scouts were summoning her. Stowing the scope in her satchel, Tasman took her attendant's arm and picked her way through heaps of stones to the crest of the wall. She was dismayed to observe that the bridge once spanning the mighty Tigris River snaking into the city from the west had fallen into the water where it met the eastern river, Eye. Mere remnants of arched stone remained. Her men raised their torches to scan the distant river valley outside the city walls in search of another way across the Tigris, before giving her their eyes.

Tasman wasted no time in idle communication. Conferring via a series of tics and winks, she convinced her men that circumventing the river would unnecessarily prolong their journey. Undeniably, the most direct way north, and to the First Folk tombs visible on the bluff beyond, was through the streets of the old city. Hopefully unbroken footpaths remained across the aqueducts in the urban center.

She kept hidden her desire to search the temples that flanked the plaza for vestiges of ancient magic that might linger still. Although Tasman couldn't see from this vantage, it seemed unlikely that all the bridges would be collapsed across the canals surrounding the temples. What if there was no way across the water?

Her southerners for the most part were unfamiliar with river currents and unable to swim, loath to cross the jetties over the slabs of broken stone jutting through the canals. Yet they would not dare to defy her. Twenty years spent manipulating the landscape of the Lowlands had gained her both fear and respect. From here she saw a faint glow on the horizon past the ancient tombs, light she hoped emanated from the legendary Lost Caves. The shortest route to the tombs of the ancients visible on the bluffs and the valley beyond was through the city streets. What dangers did its ravaged walls hold, if any?

She gazed at the thoroughfares strewn with ruptured cobbles and fallen stone while her men waited. Standing water filled the alleys and there was no mistaking the slither and hiss of the cold-blooded creatures residing in their shallows, or the grunts and snarls of the territorial mammals dwelling within the broken hovels that preyed upon them for food.

Undoubtedly there were other voices, too, faint murmurings of the ancients that few but the Guardian could comprehend. The Dark Queen wondered if the dead were even now warning her away, or welcoming her within. Although she mastered the subtle sign language of the Lowlands years ago, she was never able to perceive, let alone translate, the inaudible tongue of the First Folk that Mamie and Ratta called Mind Speak.

In truth, Tasman was shocked when she learned that Lavender Mae had been plagued by ancient voices for years. How could it be that a crazy crone could perceive the First Folk, but try as she might, Tasman could not? Even worse, Ratta both heard and understood Mind Speak. As a child she had learned it from Mamie Verde, during the old woman's reign as Keeper of the Tales.

Sierra Blue held that hallowed title now Tasman reminded herself, straining her ears for the mutterings of the dead. She wondered whether Mind Speak was a gift now granted to Sierra as an authority on the yarns of old, or if only a witch who would one day assume Guardianship of the dead could hear and heed First Folk clamor. It would be interesting to see who succeeded Mamie, a lowborn kitchen wench such as Ratta or a Northland highbrow like Sierra. What of Mamie herself, now a Guardian and young woman reborn? If Tasman thought time would tell, it would not happen within these walls.

Time meant nothing in the glacier, a phenomenon Tasman witnessed firsthand during Aubergine's simmer. When Mamie transported to Guardian's Watch to begin custody of the First Folk, the last amethyst crystals passed through the heavy hourglass in the dye shed, and time stood still. If Little Teal had not upended the timepiece, the Twelve of them might yet be frozen around the dye pot. Tasman was more than pleased when she backed the frightened girl into the table and the enchanted glass shattered on the floor, its temporary hold over chronology destroyed forever.

On a ruined wall below, a wolverine scuttled from hiding to splash in the stone gutter that edged the alley. Sensing the Dark Queen and her soldiers on the rocks above, the creature bristled and scowled. Tasman glanced at her guard. Such carrion as slithered and hissed was no match for their daggers and throwing knives. With a wink, she motioned them into the city.

A pair of tall blond archers wearing Guard gray
entered the clearing with bows drawn.

CHAPTER 24

The Road More Traveled

"HOW WILL WE LEAVE THE CITY?" Smokey Jo asked anxiously as the seven gathered their packs in the summer kitchen. "Soldiers are everywhere, watching for witches."

Waiflike in her oversized traveling cloak, Little Teal spread her arms like wings. "I'll just put on the sweater my aunt Teal left to me and fly!"

"Lucky you." Garth gave her a sour look. "What of the rest of us?"

Aubergine secured her cloak with an amethyst shawl pin before straightening the hood. "We're walking straight through the Northern Gate, just like any other travelers journeying to the Glacierlands," she said brusquely.

"What if they arrest the lot of us?" Smokey persisted. "We're witches you know."

Little Teal's eyes widened at Niles. "And he's a deserter."

"We are witches." Aubergine offered a stern glance toward Smokey Jo and Little Teal. "Lest you forget, Niles is a true son of the Northern Watch, and we harbor a Glacier Born."

Sierra gave them a determined look. "None shall detain us unless we will it so."

Lily nodded. "Few would refuse passage to a group with Steadfast Lars's own."

Niles gave Garth's shoulder a rough squeeze. "Especially since we six have The One for protection."

Grinning, Garth raised his blackened fist.

"Keep that hand hidden," his mother warned. "You'd do well to play injured."

Aubergine raised her brows in agreement. "Let no one suspect the magic you hold within, before we are well within the protected borders of the Northlands."

"Six plus One," Smokey frowned. "They left days ago."

"That was a different set of six," Lily reminded her.

"And the wrong one," Sierra said sorrowfully.

"It seems the Dark Queen also has six companions," Aubergine mused. "I saw them in my hourglass this morning."

"Truly? Then perhaps Tasman believes she is The One," Little Teal conjectured.

"She is no one," Sierra said darkly.

"Well then." Lily sighed. "Let us hope our witches find the Crystal Caverns first."

"Let's hope to heavenly hand knits Lavender Mae remembers the way," Aubergine agreed.

Lily turned the shop's Open sign to Closed and locked the door. Shouldering their packs, the seven of them slipped out the secret passage through the dye shed to the alley. From Merchant's Pass, the most direct route to the Northern Gate was a hike through the perennial gardens surrounding the Citadel which had housed the government offices before the war. Now the city council met within the safety of the Garrison. As they passed through the abandoned park, Lily noted with sadness the weeds growing up along the walkways around the deserted Citadel. Homeless folk had pitched tents along the riverbanks, while roving children and stray dogs roamed the fallow gardens.

Past the Citadel, they crossed into the borough of Winter Watch which supplied the Northland Guard stronghold. When they reached the checkpoint before the fortress, the seven of them had little explaining to do. Aubergine nodded pleasantly to the foot soldiers in gray uniform, while Niles stepped into the guardhouse to identify himself and state their purpose and the others waited. Within minutes, he returned and the oaken doors were unbarred. The Great Northern Gate swung open as if by magic.

"What did you tell them?" Smokey Jo wanted to know as soon as the heavy gate clanged shut behind them.

"The truth," he explained. "I said I was Niles of the North, returning to Wintergarten with word for my father, Steadfast Lars, leader of the Northern Watch, and my uncle Honorable Devon commander of the Northland Guard."

"And they believed you?" Little Teal teased. "What did you really say?"

Grinning, Niles winked at Lily. "I said was in love with a pint-sized gypsy witch and that I was taking her back to my family's ancestral home of Winterhaven to present her to my parents in observance of the old ways."

As Niles bent to kiss her knuckles, the others chuckled. Little Teal's cheeks flamed red. "Get away from me," she scowled, withdrawing her hand to punch him in the leg.

Not long after they lost sight of Bordertown, the road from the gate met the Northland Track, and they found evidence of many booted feet. The muddy trail was churned to quagmire in places and the brush was beaten to the ground.

"Lowlanders," Niles said.

"How can you tell?" Garth asked.

"See the shape of their shoe?" The older boy indicated a square heel to toe impression in the cold mud. "Glacier boots have rounded toes, as do Highland trekkers. Lowlanders are accustomed to sand shoes, suitable for the desert."

Aubergine nodded. "There must be thousands marching to the Out Crops."

Little Teal pulled her patchwork sweater from her pack. "Can I go look?" she asked. "I can scout the trail ahead invisible. No one will be able to see me wearing this."

"You've barely mastered that cardigan," Smokey Jo scoffed. "What if you fall from the sky?" She gave Aubergine a pleading look. "Let me go—I won't be a minute!"

"No one needs to go anywhere." Sierra shot Aubergine a weary look. "I can see the Southern Army in my mind's eye, clearly."

"We hoped your second sight might have passed to Skye by now," Lily murmured.

"As did I," Sierra concurred with a slow nod. "It is hers by rights."

"Do you believe something befell the Fire and Ice shawl?" Aubergine asked Lily.

The other witch shook her head. "No, I think Indigo Rose has yet to unpack it."

"Why wait?" Sierra asked. "Esmeralde knows how to perform a simple ceremony such as the words we uttered when Little Teal assumed her legacy."

"When I counseled Skye, she seemed uncertain of her birthright," Lily said carefully. "Is it possible she refused your bequest, just as Warren could not accept his Kindle?"

"Warren may rather have died than inherit his father's First Folk Fire, but Skye denying my gift of second sight? I can barely believe it," Sierra said in despair.

"What are you talking about?" Little Teal asked. "Is Skye becoming a full-fledged witch like me? Will she be able to spin and knit and fly invisible as I can?"

"She could always spin and knit," Garth said.

"And you can just barely fly," Smokey added. "To say nothing of passing unseen while circling overhead."

"I can do more than you think." Teal gave her a meaningful glance. "And I'll be able to do most anything I desire as soon as I find time to hone my craft. You'll see."

"Of that we have no doubt." Aubergine offered her a tired smile, and then turned to Sierra. "So long as you possess your second sight, you might as well use it."

"We're scarcely a half day behind the Lowland Army," Sierra revealed as flecks of gold gleamed in her tawny eyes. "They divert west toward the Out Crops where the Northland Guard awaits them in battle."

"Does the Dark Queen lead the South?" Lily asked.

Sierra shook her head. "Nor does the one she calls Kindred Spirit."

"Curious." Aubergine shrugged. "Be that as it may, our path lies north."

Niles adjusted his pack and started up the side of the muddy track. "To Wintergarten!"

Even as he shouted the name of his home province, a flutter of anxiety crept into his chest. He had not laid eyes on his parents or two brothers in nearly a year. What would they make of his consort with witches?

Two mornings later, scouts from the Northern Watch found them camped in a grove of towering pines. Lily broke eggs into a pan over the cook fire while Aubergine enjoyed a cup of sweet birch tea with Sierra. None of the others had stirred. The top of Smokey Jo's curly head was barely visible from her blanket next to Garth's bedroll and Niles had chosen a secluded place further from the fire for himself and Little Teal.

A pair of tall blond archers wearing Guard gray entered the clearing with bows drawn, but unnotched their arrows as soon as they noticed the witches. From behind them stepped an older man, whose light hair had begun to whiten with age.

"Well met, Potluck Queen Aubergine," he greeted her with a stiff bow.

"And you, Deliberate Rye." A glint of recognition lit her eyes. "Although in truth I am queen of nothing but a yarn shop these days."

"And my aim is not as deliberate or true as it once was," he admitted with a hint of humility, "thus my young marksmen here, Jayden and Jeffryn."

"At your service," the bowmen said in unison and lowered their eyes respectfully.

Observing them, Lily wondered if they were identical twins.

"Second Sight Sierra." Deliberate Rye held out an arthritic hand. "It has been far too long."

"Truly," she replied, squeezing his palm.

"I'm Lilac Lily," Lily said, wiping her hands on her apron.

"Well met," the others replied.

"Are you hungry?" Without waiting for an answer, Lily beckoned the three Northlanders to vacant logs near the fire. "Sit with us and have some tea!"

The fragrant sizzle of bacon coupled with sounds of crackling wood stirred Smokey Jo from slumber. Sitting up in her blankets, she stared at the group engaged in quiet talk around the campfire.

"Twins!" she whispered hoarsely, shaking Garth's shoulder. "Look! Aubergine found a pair of twins. Large ones, and look-alikes, too!"

"I was still sleeping," Garth complained, blinking at the gnome. "Besides there's no such thing as look-alikes. You can always tell 'em apart, even when they're littermates like puppies or kittens."

"You cannot!" Smokey declared.

Without waiting for Garth to pull on his jacket or boots, she jumped up and scampered over to the two Northland archers. Even sitting side by side on a log eating breakfast, the youths were taller than she.

"Are you inseparable twins?" she demanded.

When they just stared at the gnome in wonder, she turned to Deliberate Rye. "I would know, as we don't have look-alikes in the Middlelands, at least not on purpose!"

"The term is identical twins," Lily said gently. "Don't be rude, Smokey Jo."

"I'm not trying to be," Smokey apologized, as Garth joined them at the fire. She glanced from one twin to the other. "Are they the same?"

"You can't tell them apart," Deliberate Rye said pleasantly. "They can barely tell themselves apart, but a finer pair of marksmen you'll never meet."

"See?" Smokey said to Garth.

"Who might you be?" one of the twins asked her shyly.

"What might you be?" the other added.

"I'm Smokey Jo!" She gazed upon at the two tall archers, her dark eyes shining. "I mean, Josephine, but nobody really calls me that."

"She's a gnome," Garth explained to the bewildered bowmen. "They're a kind of little folk like dwarves or sprites. Gypsies believe they bring good luck. Haven't you ever seen one before?"

"Never," the first boy replied.

"Nor dwarves, nor sprites," the other answered.

"I'm Garth, Sierra's son." Garth offered his good hand to the archers, before taking a plate of eggs and bacon from Lily.

"Jayden," the one replied.

"Jeffryn," the other shook his hand. "Well met."

"I shall call you J and J!" Smokey Jo announced merrily.

"Gnomes bring good luck?" Deliberate Rye regarded Smokey Jo, bemused. "Does she really?"

"What?" Garth asked, balancing his plate on his knees as he ate.

"Bring good luck?" Little Teal flounced into the clearing, wearing her patchwork sweater over her green velvet dress. "That remains to be seen."

"Who have we here?" Deliberate Rye eyed the small witch. "Not another gnome?"

"That's Little Teal." Garth talked between bites. "She was a fossicker named Trader until Niles fell in love with her. Then Aubergine turned her into a witch. I liked her better when she was a boy."

"Well met, everybody," Little Teal said informally, filling her tin cup with tea and honey. "I hear that's how you greet each other in these parts."

"Niles?" Deliberate Rye asked, peering past the small witch.

"Of the North," Garth explained. "Maybe you know him? He's big and blond like the lot of you." He gazed at the twins. "Though nothing as large as your look-alikes."

"Speak of the dead." Little Teal watched Niles stride into the clearing. "It's time you got up."

"Niles of the North, so it is!" the old man cried with pleasure, rising to clasp Niles's hand. He turned to his archers. "Trueborn son of the Northern Watch."

"Only one of them." Niles gave an embarrassed smile. "And a mere sledder at that."

The twins pushed their plates aside and stood quickly. "My lord," they murmured at once.

"Your Goodmother Gabriella will be delighted with your return!" Deliberate Rye beamed at Aubergine. "You failed to mention you harbored one of Steadfast Lars's own."

"In truth he leads us," Aubergine said.

Sierra glanced at Garth's sling. "We have business in the North."

"Your *return?*" Little Teal scowled at Niles. "I take it to mean you plan to stay?"

With her stubby hand on her hips, Smokey Jo sized up the twins. "You can sit right back down J and J!" she scolded. "It's first come, first served around here!" She watched Lily hand Niles a plate of scrambled eggs. "He's lucky Lily saved him pan scrapings, the laggard!"

Niles leaned against a tree, smiling at the bowmen as he ate. "Smokey Jo's right. We don't stand for ceremony. Sit, and well met."

After they finished breakfast, Deliberate Rye bade his archers to stand watch while the witches broke camp. Lily and Sierra began cleaning up while Niles and Teal rolled up the blankets and readied the packs. Able to coax Garth into fetching a bucket of water from a nearby pond, Smokey Jo doused the fire, bit by bit.

Rye took Aubergine on a short stroll to converse out of earshot. "May I ask what business you might have in the Glacierlands?"

"Sierra and I would meet with Steadfast Lars in private counsel," she told him. "We witches have a discovery that might very well please the North."

"An audience with Lars in the capital will prove nigh impossible," Deliberate Rye cautioned. "When last the Northern Watch met in council, the Five Provinces voted to prevail upon the Men of Ice to aid the North in battle against the Lowlands. As the ice fortress of the Hed Clansmen falls under the protection of Wintergarten, it is Lars's duty to convince the Glacier Born to swell the ranks of the Northland Guard. His brother Honorable Devon awaits him on the battlefield of the Northern Plains east of the Out Crops. Lars leaves the high council this day to return to Winterhaven Lodge, where he plans to ready himself to take leave of his family before joining his brother. I'm afraid your business with him may have to wait."

"It cannot," Aubergine said earnestly. "What business we have with Steadfast Lars concerns the Hed Clansmen and may directly affect the outcome of the war."

Deliberate Rye's brow furrowed. "How so?"

"Did you ever meet the Clansman Second Sight Sierra was married to, Kendrick Blue?" Aubergine questioned.

The old man paused before shaking his head. "I knew some Blues. Not one with that name, but there were many. Until the day he died, Hed Maddig Hoar lay convinced that if he fathered enough progeny, one of his Glacier Born would survive the Kindling."

"I am familiar with the Kindle," Aubergine replied. "Even now Hed Clansmen who hold the old ways believe that any male child they sire carries a vestige of First Folk Fire, what they call the Magic of Men."

"Exactly." Deliberate Rye raised snowy brows. "Whether that is true is not for me to decide, but the Northern Watch assumes that few Glacier Born ever possessed the legendary ember." He paused. "Hed

Maddig Hoar died in a hunting accident long ago, and the Blues fell from favor with the Men of Ice. If any of Hed Maddig's sons truly harbored cold fire, none survived the Kindling."

"Oh, but one did," Aubergine said in confidence. "This selfsame Kendrick Blue, who fathered Sierra's children and now calls himself the Lord of the Lowlands. He passed the ember to both of his sons—an older brother and this boy you see here." They watched Garth and Smokey Jo at the fire. "Sierra believes she has already lost the older son to the Kindle, for in her mind's eye she saw his fire burnt to cold ash." Aubergine turned her violet gaze to her friend. "The younger boy survived."

"He is The One?" Deliberate Rye asked in disbelief. "The legendary youth these Men of Ice have awaited for eons?"

"Most definitely," Aubergine answered. "Together, he and Smokey Jo did not merely rekindle the Magic of Men, they also discovered a method of releasing First Folk Fire that all who Kindle might live."

"Is that why the boy wears a sling?" Deliberate Rye asked. "As a result of the Kindle? So many young men return from war these days maimed, I assumed he was injured in battle."

"In battle with his father over a scrap of Skell etched with runes," Aubergine muttered in disgust. "As he wished to leave no heirs, Kendrick attempted to kill the boy with fire bolts."

"Where is this Lowland Lord now?" Deliberate Rye asked.

"It's anyone's guess," Aubergine admitted, as Sierra joined them. "In the Middlelands he is everywhere and nowhere, setting farms afire and devastating entire villages. Middlefolk call him the Bad, Bad Man. Here he is Northland's Bane. Southerners know him as the Dark Queen's Kindred Spirit—he has many names. Until today, we thought he might be at the Out Crops, leading the Lowland Army into battle, but Sierra did not see him in her mind's eye on the Northern Plains."

"He is brother to the Dark Queen?" Deliberate Rye guessed.

"Her name is Tasman," Sierra confirmed. "Often brother and sister shape-shift together as carrion creatures or birds of prey."

"And you believe they are here in the North? Look for them once more," Deliberate Rye urged Sierra.

"I fear I cannot." Sierra glanced at Aubergine. "I came to tell you just now. My second sight has vanished. In its place is dread."

"Does Lily know?" Aubergine asked and Sierra nodded. "Then we've no time to waste. Everyone," she called, "shoulder your packs. Niles, we make for Winterhaven Lodge. What's the fastest route there?"

"You would journey to my family's ancestral home?" Concern crept into his voice. "Aubergine, I was jesting when I mentioned presenting Little Teal to my family. There's no need to travel there. You will be just as well met in the capital city."

Teal snatched up his hand. "What do you mean, there is no need to introduce me?" The twins stared at her in alarm, while Deliberate Rye could only shake his head. Boldly the little witch brushed her lips over Niles's knuckles before he could disentangle his fingers. "Look who's embarrassed now!" she crooned.

In the silence that followed no one laughed, not even Garth or Smokey Jo.

"I understood that you wished to meet with the Northern Watch at the high counsel in Wintergarten," Niles addressed Aubergine stiffly. "My parents have fine apartments in the city center where you would be most welcome."

"Apparently there is no time for that," Aubergine apologized. "Your father is even now on his way to Winterhaven Lodge, to prepare for a parley with the Hed Clansmen. I must have an audience with him before he departs for the Out Crops."

"To Winterhaven, then," he said dully.

"Might you need direction?" Deliberate Rye asked. "Jayden and Jeffryn can guide you."

"I know the way," Niles gave him a level glance, "all too well, I'm afraid."

The twins offered him a short bow. "Then we take our leave, Niles of the North."

"As do I," Deliberate Rye agreed. "Until we meet again, Potluck witches, lucky gnome, The Chosen One," he said, bending to them each in turn. "Niles, a word."

As the others gathered their packs and left the clearing, Deliberate Rye detained Niles with a finger to his chest.

"Your brother Mason is wed to a fine Northland girl," he told the boy. "And your brother Marshall is betrothed. You would do well to do the same."

Niles looked toward Little Teal, who lingered at the edge of the clearing. "I can't," he told the old man helplessly. "I love her."

"A tiny mixed-blood wench such as that small witch can hardly offer you strong sons," the old man advised.

"I don't need a guarantee of strong sons," Niles said. "I need the witch."

Deliberate Rye shook his head. "You'll be hard-pressed convincing your father and Goodmother Gabriella that you are under her spell." He paused. "However, if she were to bear you a healthy babe first—"

"No," Niles cut him off. "She is a witch, not a milk cow. She has much to do before settling, if ever. I shall not entreat her to abide by the old ways."

"Then I wish you all the luck of the gypsies your Smokey gnome can offer." Deliberate Rye clapped him on the back. "For you shall need it at Winterhaven Lodge."

After he left, Niles walked over to where Little Teal waited.

"What were you arguing about?" she asked in a small voice. "He looked mad."

"Nothing." He shrugged. "Just my feelings for you."

"That's not nothing." She searched his face, focusing on the ever-present kindness in his clear gray eyes. "Your family isn't going to approve of me, are they?"

He shook his head. "I can't lie to you. No."

"Because I'm not tall and beautiful?" She blinked back tears. "Because I don't crave a life of home and hearth and a gaggle of children? Because I'm an orphan? A witch?"

He heaved a sigh. "For those reasons, and a thousand more neither one of us has thought of yet." He knelt until his head was level with hers. With his thumbs he wiped the tears that threatened to well from her eyes. "I don't want their life. We can make our own." His voice grew husky as he took both of her hands. "I love everything about you, Teal."

She looked back at him, her dark eyes shining. Then she wrapped her arms around his neck. "And I love you."

THE ROAD MORE TRAVELED

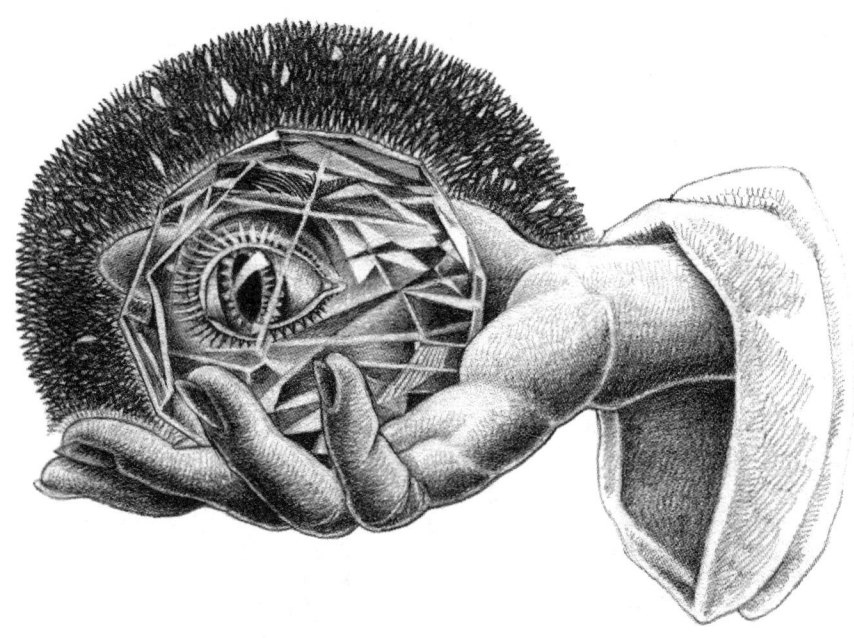

Awake now, the eye within the golden brown stone
raised its brow in question.

CHAPTER 25

The Guardian's Watch

Witches! THE ANCIENTS PROTESTED SILENTLY. *Walkers! Wanderers! Wolverines!*

Because their cries of unrest were more strident than usual, the warnings woke the Guardian abruptly. Throwing off her furs, she sat motionless on the stone altar, listening. Although she could discern no distant plea of *Guardian* among the rabble-rousers, she knew the dead would not cease their incessant mumblings until she walked among the tombs to quiet them once more.

Unwelcome Watchers! They whispered to her. *Watchers on the western walls.*

The Guardian knew that Watchers of any kind would not be welcome, for First Folk feared intruders above all else. For eons, fortune seekers and grave robbers had invaded the lost city, seeking spoils of raw crystal, polished gems, and carved statues from the sacred temples. Bolder raiders broke open the family tombs on the bluff overlooking the walled city, looting rare icons and hammered jewelry fashioned from precious metals, as well as funeral raiment woven with gold thread. According to Cyrus, few ventured as far as the Lost Caves and of them none had gained passage to the Crystal Caverns nor returned to divulge its secrets.

With resolve, the Guardian threw on her mantle and reached for her crystal, holding the pink quartz until it glowed with rosy light that woke the Tiger Eye, sleeping on a shelf above the altar. Almost as an afterthought, she checked the stone cup in the niche beside it. Once again, ice had melted to water within the vessel while she slept. She put the rim to her lips and swallowed, not as indifferently as before. Although the ritual still felt foreign, she understood that taking sustenance was not only expected but necessary upon waking, as were regular intervals of rest, voiding her bladder, and seeking warmth. Because time stood still inside the glacier, such realizations from her previous life revisited her in reveries, dreams she had during a period she remembered as night, when time had been marked in stretches called days and half each day was light.

The Guardian stored the cup in its cubby and slid her feet into the fur mukluks she had found. Such offerings appeared frequently on the low stone table before the altar and she needed for nothing. She favored the finely sewn boots which were waiting one time when she woke. It might have been morning, if the glacier had days. Despite that, she practiced a series of simple rituals whenever she stirred from slumber. After feeding from whatever sustenance she found at the table, she donned her mantle, kindled cold-fire crystal in the hearth, and listened for cries of Wanderers beseeching her within the city.

Sometimes she heard nothing; other times she perceived several voices pleading for help.

What happened next had little variation. After locating the wandering specters below from her solitary vigil on the cliff she now knew as Guardian's Watch, she trekked down to old Tigeria to escort those who were ready to pass through the city's ruined gates. One by one, she shepherded each restless spirit up the hill to the ancient tombs to rejoin its First Folk family.

The vast majority of the shades whom Cyrus called Walkers seemed distressed by her presence, turning their heads in avoidance if she offered to guide them to the ancient cemetery. Frozen while thriving, these unsavory spirits felt cheated by lives cut short prematurely and had no taste for death. Without living hosts, they remained trapped within the city. Wayfarers who trespassed within the perimeter of the city walls were fair game for ghostly Walkers craving a second chance at life. They preyed upon thrill-seeking adventurers and looters, deserted soldiers gone astray, the odd Clansman who had lost his way, any folk they could inhabit long enough to escape the invisible prison of Tigeria without involving the Guardian.

Once clear of the gates, such shades were loath to shed their new hosts. Avoiding the tombs that dotted the bluffs above, they focused their gaze northward, beginning their slow walk through the narrowing valley toward the red-orange radiance on the horizon. The Guardian hoped the ruddy bloom emanated from magical crystals within the Lost Caves but could not fathom what waited there. She would journey to the legendary caverns that lit the skyline and soon, for she already felt the lure of the fire. But whenever she consulted Cyrus, he dissuaded her from following the Walkers, claiming she had unfinished business left in the city.

Standing, the Guardian tossed a few crystals into the hearth to kindle a fire and seized the blinking Tiger Eye to slip into the secret passage leading to the cliffs overlooking the ruins of ancient Tigeria. Awake now, the eye within the golden brown stone raised its brow in question as she made her way through the twisting passage, holding the rose-quartz crystal in her other hand as a beacon. The Guardian smiled down at the Tiger Eye. She never went to Guardian's Watch without Cyrus. There the young woman stood sentry at the edge of the ice cliffs. Wind whipped her hair from her face as she scanned the stone city below.

There. She motioned to Cyrus, holding the polished rock before her so that he could cast his eye. *There are seven on the western wall.*

The eye widened as it recognized the figures. *Yes. Your work here is almost done.*

Finally. She breathed a sigh of relief. *Should I go to those below?*

Surely, the orb replied. *You must offer your services to all, even those who would avoid your touch.*

Who are they? she asked as the intruders descended the wall into the city.

The six are southern soldiers. His myopic eye blinked. *The one is a witch who craves the power of the crystals to rule nature as the First Folk did. You knew her as a girl in another life. Perhaps you recognize her?*

Not at all. She scrutinized the group picking their way slowly through the rubble blocking the city streets, who looked no larger than ants wresting grains of sand. *Do they require my services?*

Yes, though they will not ask, for what they call time grows short. Walkers may find the soldiers first.

She nodded. *What of the witch?*

She will not seek guidance, Cyrus predicted. *She would journey to the Lost Caves and learn its secrets. She pursues power greater than your own.*

That shall be her folly, the young Guardian predicted.

Perhaps, Cyrus said. *Perhaps not. You truly do not remember who she is?*

She gave him a quizzical look. *I remember but a vestige of my previous existence.*

As do I. There are other travelers approaching from the south who require your assistance. He blinked. *Witches as well, under the protection of a true Glacier Born. They would beseech you, but by another name.*

Aloud? she asked.

Soundly, he confirmed. *To aid them, search your memory and recollect how to listen. One of the witches is cursed by the First Folk. She cannot chase their voices from her head, nor does she understand their demands. Another enjoys the gift of second sight, an honor newly bestowed and not yet part of her lore. Two others practice remedial craft and believe they possess shards and talismans found in the caves unchallenged. They must ask the ancient's leave else suffer the fate of their crazed companion. And although the Glacier Born survived the Kindle, he will never hear nor heed you for his price is a world without magic. Of the six witches, only one understands you for she kens the language of old.*

How so? the Guardian asked.

You taught her another time in a previous life when she was but a child in your household. Then you were known as the Keeper of Tales.

Impossible, the Guardian said. *I never had children. Of that I am certain.*

Be certain of nothing, Cyrus advised. *This second group of seven needs you far more than the seven you see before you now. You could cure the witch plagued by voices, yet she may not let you.*

What of the mortal boy you call Glacier Born? the Guardian asked with interest. *Will the Walkers take him as well?*

He is no mortal, Cyrus blinked. *At his Kindling he succumbed to First Folk Fire as is the fate of Glacier Born since the world began again. But like yourself, and the Dervish that safeguards the tombs since fire and ice birthed him anew, the Walkers are unable to get under his skin.*

Both sets of travelers seek safe passage and guidance. Only one group cries out for help. Heed their call.

For the Guardian? she asked.

No, he answered. *Unlike Wanderers, witches have no need to be laid to rest. One witch will call aloud in her own tongue. She will call you by name.*

What name? the Guardian wondered, almost to herself.

You shall know when you hear it if you listen carefully.

I'll go to them then, she assured him with a nod.

Winking approval, Cyrus closed his eye. The Guardian retreated down the passage, pausing only to place the sleeping stone within its niche in the altar before hurrying down the ice caves descending to the city below.

THE GUARDIAN'S WATCH

Light snow fell as the travelers approached
the stockade before Winterhaven.

CHAPTER 26

Winterhaven

ONCE WITHIN THE PROVINCE OF WINTERGARTEN, the seven travelers bypassed the road into the capital and veered northwest along a narrower track toward the Winterhaven stronghold at the base of the Misty Mountains. By rights, the large compound was reserved for the leader of the Northern Watch and Niles's family had held the handsome lodge for generations.

Now his oldest brother, Mason, and his Goodwife Alyssa occupied the main house with their nearly two-year-old baby. As eldest son, it was Mason's duty to maintain the family's log dwellings, their lands, and holdings and host the boys' parents Steadfast Lars and Goodmother Gabriella whenever they journeyed north. The aging couple now spent most of their time in the capitol, where the high council maintained a well-appointed apartment for them within the safety of the city center.

Niles was surprised to hear from Deliberate Rye that his middle brother, Marshall, would soon wed as well. He wondered if the bride-to-be had presented Marshall with a healthy newborn, customary in the harsh climate of the frozen north, or if his father urged his brother to marry for reasons such as politics or war. He had been close to Marshall growing up for they were not even a year apart and shared a nursery as toddlers.

Light snow fell as the travelers approached the stockade before Winterhaven. The sturdy fence was constructed from whole logs twenty feet high pounded into permafrost side by side, chinked with a mixture of moss and clay. The top of each debarked log was sharpened to a point.

Smokey Jo blinked at pennants depicting a snowy glacier on a field of Northland gray fluttering on either side of the studded gate. Whether the stockade protected the lodge from wild animals or invaders she did not want to ask. Fat snowflakes drifted lazily as they approached the barrier, softening the greening landscape.

"Ohhhh!" she breathed. "Pretty!"

Garth lifted his face to the wet snow that immediately melted as it fell onto his cheeks and shoulders. He caught a few flakes in his mouth. "Poor man's manure."

Little Teal gave him a quizzical look. "What?"

"That's what they call spring snow in the North," Niles explained. "Farmer's Fertilizer, Peasant's Peat. It nourishes the fields and makes them green faster."

Sierra gazed serenely at the pleasant vista. "The growing season runs short this far north. You plant as soon as the ground thaws, harvest at first frost. Late snow quickens the earth."

"You do everything more swiftly around here it seems," Little Teal said.

Aubergine nodded. "Northlanders couple quickly and bear children young. It is custom, for only the hardy survive the frozen north."

"More folk die up here?" Teal asked.

Lily frowned. "Many of the Glacier Born do and you know why."

"But that's because of First Folk Fire. Plus it's just boys," she argued. "What happens to the girls?"

Niles shrugged. "My mother birthed three sons."

Teal gave Lily a pleading look. "Make him tell me."

Lily exchanged glances with Niles. "That may be all he knows. Truly."

At the guardhouse, torches flickered in preparation of Steadfast Lars's arrival.

"Niles of the North!" the old gatekeeper shouted jovially, throwing open the vestibule door. "In truth, we were expecting your father."

"Lars has not arrived?" Aubergine asked, as the watchman ushered them in.

"Not yet," he replied. "Goodmother Gabriella and her attendants travel with him by sleigh through the mountain pass which always takes longer." On the other side of the gate, he locked the heavy studded door. "Minister Mason waits in the great hall."

"Minister?" Niles laughed in disbelief. "Is that what you call my brother now?"

"It is who he is: our liege lord, minister to all." The old man shrugged. "Come."

He led them past an armory through a courtyard toward the lodge, a mammoth homestead built of weathered oak, whose ancient timbers arched three stories high. From the second floor, a covered balcony overlooked the cobbled square. On either side of the great hall, enclosed passageways connected newer wings to the main house. To Teal, the sprawling lodge resembled a falcon in flight. She stared up at the dizzying height.

"You grew up here?" she asked. Taking her hand, Niles nodded. "It's so beautiful, I would never want to leave," she whispered.

Along the edge of the courtyard stood a row of one-story outbuildings and workshops housing a stable and carriage shed, smithy, carpentry, and tannery. The far side had a granary, garden shed, smokehouse, and bread oven behind a covered well.

Scents of brewer's yeast and applewood mingling with cured hide and roasting meat smelled heavenly to Smokey Jo. She drew a deep breath. "You have everything! All for this one place?"

From the smithy came the ring of metal on metal. Next door, a cartwright rolled a wagon wheel into his repair shop. "Where do all the small folk live?" Garth asked.

"Some in the house," the guard pointed. "Some like me have cabins around back."

Approaching the great hall, Smokey Jo noticed the curls of smoke rising from the massive stone chimney. She could only imagine the fire blazing from the hearth within. The stockade gate creaked open behind them. As they turned, in flew a double-runner sleigh pulled by a team of four elk, silver bells jingling from their breastplates.

"This must be your parents," Lily said to Niles pleasantly.

"It is." Niles recognized the sleigh. He gazed down at Teal whose face had gone pale and determined.

"You North Folk have deer pull sleds?" Garth asked, marveling at the great bucks sporting huge racks of antlers. "What do you do with the horses, eat them?"

"Northlanders don't harbor horses," Sierra said with a smile. "These are elk, much more fit for harsh climate." Her eyes grew bright. "My grandsire had a team such as this."

"As did my father," Aubergine recalled. "And a bobsled, pulled by eight mountain dogs."

After the driver halted the sleigh, a footman on the bench beside him jumped down to fetch a set of wooden steps for the passengers. Aubergine's eyes sparkled, for tucked beneath furs behind the teamster were a stately couple that could only be Steadfast Lars and Gabriella. In the boot behind them sat a handmaid. Lars threw off the lap robes they had used to ward off the snow and dismounted. Although his forehead was creased with worry lines, his step was sure and his ruddy face healthy. His dark blond hair streaked with gray was cut shoulder length and brushed the ermine mantle thrown over his shoulders. Behind, the footman helped his wife and the maid gather their belongings, while the driver held the elks' heads.

"Niles!" Lars shouted. Even though his shoulders were starting to stoop, he towered over his youngest son. He clapped Niles on the back, before hugging him soundly. "What a pleasant surprise!" He turned to his wife. Though heavier set than Aubergine, she appeared just as tall. "Look, Goodmother. Your son is returned from his sledding adventures!"

Gabriella threw back the hood of her cloak to reveal graying braids twisted into a bun and secured with a fancy clasp of polished antler. Taking the footman's arm, she descended the few mounted steps pulled up to the sleigh bed.

Her face broke into a smile. "And he's brought company!" Handing the maid her satchel, she raised her arms to embrace her youngest son before turning to their guests. "Queen Aubergine, what a pleasure!"

The Potluck witch clasped her hands. "The pleasure is mine."

Gabriella's eyes gleamed. "Is that you, Second Sight Sierra?"

"Yes, Goodmother," Sierra murmured, barely recognizing the older woman for the weight she had gained. "It's been years."

"More than twenty." Gabriella grasped her arm. "How have you fared?"

"I've had difficult times," Sierra admitted. "And rewarding ones, too."

"It can be most trying when one's head and heart decide to part ways," Gabriella sighed.

"Thus I am here," Sierra said demurely. "Meet my youngest son, Garth."

Lars's eyes came to rest on the burnt arm protruding from the boy's sling. "One of Kendrick Blue's own?"

Nodding eagerly, Garth held out his good hand. "Well met."

"And you." The older man surveyed the rest of the group. "Who else do we have?"

"Potluck witches," Niles replied. "This is Lilac Lily, Smokey Jo, and Little Teal."

Lars's bushy brows peaked in surprise when he noticed the little witch gripping Niles's fingers. "Well then, very well met."

"And you," Teal said back with the others.

The door to the great hall burst open and a young man just slightly older than Niles but with all of his features strode forth wearing a fur cloak.

"Father, mother," he bowed before Lars and Gabriella.

"Mason," Lars acknowledged. "Potluck witches and Kendrick's own, this is my eldest son, Mason, Minister of Winterhaven."

"It feels more like administer most times," his son joked. "Well met!" he greeted them, with a nod. As his eyes lit upon Niles, his smile began to fade. "Brother, have you wearied of your southern exploits, and returned to assume your mantle at last?"

"Not at all, Minister," Niles said, feigning regret. "I bring you these Potluck witches and a true Glacier Born, who seek audience with father before hastening to the Out Crops."

"The Out Crops?" Mason frowned at the group of travelers. "You journey to the battlegrounds?"

Aubergine nodded. "Steadfast and Gabriella, Sierra and I would converse in private council concerning matters of the Hed Clansmen before we take our leave."

Lars put his hand to his brow. "It seems we all have concerns about the Clansmen and the Out Crops."

"Surely you'll stay the night?" Gabriella invited.

Niles offered his brother a stony look. "We would not overstay our Minister's welcome."

"This is still your home and you are most welcome," she insisted. "As is your Glacier Born boy and your witches." She turned to her oldest son. "Mason, let's stop standing out in the cold. Have someone show our guests to suitable chambers, and set the dinner table for seven more. Your father and I would take mulled cider in the council room with Queen Aubergine and Second Sight Sierra."

"Of course, Goodmother." Mason pushed the heavy oak doors to the great room open and ushered them in. "This way."

Once inside the great hall, the adult witches were shown to second-floor chambers near the council room that opened to the balcony overlooking the massive stone fireplace. Aubergine's room contained an adjacent sleeping alcove for Smokey Jo, and Lily and Sierra were settled into a handsome suite with a blazing hearth.

"Might I have a tour of your kitchen?" Lily asked Gabriella as Sierra and Aubergine were summoned to council.

"Certainly," Gabriella smiled. "Let me find Mason's Goodwife Alyssa."

Reluctant to abandon the lively flames roaring within the hearth below, Smokey Jo lingered in the great hall with the youths. After a few moments, she sidled over to Garth and began to worry at his sling, her eyes dancing in the firelight. Absently he pulled the knotted cloth over his head to let her work at his blackened wrist and curled lump of a fist.

Garth gazed at Niles and Teal. "What happens next? Do we three bunk together?"

"I'm not certain what is expected," Niles admitted, scanning the mostly deserted hall. At a table near the fire, a serving maid was setting out mugs around a kettle of hot cider mulled with butter and cinnamon. Near the back of the hall, a waiter lit braziers around the large dining table while a kitchen wench busied herself with crockery and place settings.

Niles ladled out two steaming mugs of cider and handed one to Little Teal. "Did you notice the guest houses to either side of the lodge as we walked in?"

"Like great wings," she recalled, wrapping her cold hands around the warm cup.

"Each is an entire house, connected to this great room by a timbered passage to ward the snow." Niles nodded to the bright hallway to their right. "I'm assuming this one has been given to Marshall as he's married now."

"The way is well lit," Smokey observed good-naturedly, breathing in the fragrant cider. She hustled over to help herself to a little bit.

Niles glanced toward the dark hall leading to the left wing. "So the apartments over here would be mine, I'm guessing."

"Have you ever stayed there?" Garth asked, peering down the unlit passage as he accepted a mug of spiced cider from Smokey Jo.

Niles shook his head. "I've never brought anyone home until now." He smiled down at Teal. "And they certainly weren't expecting you."

"Or any of us," she said simply.

Their ponderings were broken by a beautiful young blond woman, who swept into the room from the kitchen, a robust baby at her hip. The child's robes matched her dress of fine blue wool trimmed with rabbit fur. She gazed down at Teal as if from great heights. "I'm Goodwife Alyssa, wed to Minster Mason, and you might be?"

"Teal," the small girl stammered. "Little Teal."

"Traces of Teal," Niles announced formally. "My chosen." He gave her a reassuring smile. "My lady."

"She's really a Potluck witch," Garth grinned.

"As am I," Smokey Jo said proudly. Setting her cider mug on the table, she held out her hand. "Smokey Jo—I mean Josephine, at your service!"

Ignoring the gnome, Alyssa gave her brother-in-law a cool glance. The child in her arms began to struggle. Lest he start fussing, she let him down to toddle about the floor in his fur booties.

"I'm Garth. Well met," Garth said, with a short bow before the tall blond woman with blazing blue eyes. He smiled at the sturdy baby trying to pull himself onto a rush stool near the fire. "What's his name?"

"Ian," Alyssa said proudly. "Able Ian."

"Able Ian!" Smokey Jo exclaimed as the little boy overturned the stool and sat down hard on the stone floor. "Why, it seems everyone here has two first names!"

Alyssa took Niles by the sleeve and pulled him aside. "You've been gone all year and this is what you bring back?" she whispered loud enough for all to hear. "An injured youth and tiny little witches?"

"If that is how you prefer to see things, Goodwife," Niles chose his words carefully.

"How else can one view them?" She gave Teal a desultory glance. "I assume from your cow-eyed look and the way you clutch her hand, you would take the girl to wed. Your parents would never permit it."

Teal set her empty mug loudly on the table. "Permit what?" she asked innocently.

"Your match," Alyssa said lightly.

"I stopped requesting parental permission the day I left here," Niles assured her. "In case you've forgotten."

"His parents needn't trouble themselves to allow anything." Teal glared at the other girl, her dark eyes snapping. "Witches don't wed."

Alyssa rolled her eyes. "Mason is livid," she hissed at Niles. "As I believe is your father. Surely the Middlelands could have provided you someone more suitable."

"We are very well suited," Niles said calmly, watching her hurry toward the fireplace, where Ian had lost interest in the overturned stool in favor of throwing bits of kindling and pinecones into the flames. "I owe Teal my life."

"What is the debt?" Pulling her child away from the fire, Alyssa narrowed her eyes at the witch. "Name the cost to free him from your spell."

"There is no debt," she spat back as Ian began to fuss. "Nor spell. I owe Niles my life, too." She craned her neck up at him. "I guess we're even."

Alyssa gave the couple a confused look. Niles tried not to laugh. "If not for the witch, I would have died at the hands of Lowland soldiers," he confessed to his sister-in-law. "None of you would have known my fate."

Ian began to wail. "My sister still waits for you," she said abruptly, turning away. "More's the pity."

Teal stared at Niles. Before she had a chance to formulate the question that burned on her lips, another youth strode into the room, passing Alyssa in the hall. "Niles!" he shouted. "I heard you were back!"

"Marshall!" Niles cried.

As they embraced, Smokey Jo looked from one brother to the other. "I hope I don't get in trouble for asking," she mentioned at last. "But are you inseparable twins?"

Shaking his head, Niles laughed. "Nor what you call look-alikes, though we once behaved as if we were inseparable." When Marshall gave him a quizzical look, he attempted to clarify. "This is Smokey Jo; she is an inquisitive witch who must know such things."

"We're just brothers, one year apart," Marshall explained, his curious eyes taking in Smokey Jo's diminutive stature, nut-brown skin, and mop of unruly hair. "I must ask a question as well. Are you a woman grown?"

"I am a full-fledged knitting witch," Smokey Jo assured him with a firm nod. "Second of the Twelve." Shrugging, she returned to Garth's side to work on unfurling the fingers of his blackened hand.

"In truth she was born a gnome," Garth added, grimacing as she pried at his hand. "They're small when it comes to size, but big of heart."

"Plus we bring good luck," Smokey reminded, studiously working at his fingers.

"That, too," he agreed.

Marshall eyed the small girl in the green velvet dress. "And are you a witch as well?" he teased. "The enchantress the whole lodge speaks of? It is rumored you have our baby brother Niles under your spell."

Teal blushed as Niles pulled her close. "This is Teal," he introduced her. "Traces of Teal."

"Well met." A smile played along Marshall's lips. "So you've chosen a witch as your consort?"

Niles nodded in mock chagrin. "Apparently, as I just learned, witches don't wed."

"Rarely they do," Teal responded.

Niles chuckled. "Brother, I understand you will soon find favorable marriage, unlike myself."

"Favorable for the Glacierlands, perhaps." Marshall snorted. "It is not of my doing. Father decided a wedding might seal an alliance between the Northlands and the Out Crops."

Niles's eyes went wide. "You shall wed a Clanswoman?"

"The Hed Clansman's eldest daughter, no less." Marshall raised his brows. "A pugnacious wench named Gretchell, really quite a handful and not to my taste." He poured himself a cup of cider and sat down heavily in a leather-bound chair that glowed richly in the firelight. "She's big, brawny, and very, very blond."

Niles righted the rush stool for Little Teal before sitting in the chair opposite his brother. "I'll bet she shall make a wonderful sparring partner," he joked.

"Did this Clanswoman present you with a boy child?" Teal had to ask.

"She brought the baby for inspection, though in truth he is not mine," Marshall replied. "Our pairing is arranged to certain the Clansmen's support of the war, though according to our Uncle Honorable Devon, it has not happened as yet." He lowered his voice. "I travel with father to the Out Crops tomorrow."

"As do we," Niles revealed.

His brother stared at him. "Whatever for?"

"The witches discuss it with our parents as we speak." Niles glanced at the balcony, where the council room door remained closed. "Even if we had leave to explain, you would scarcely believe us."

"Perhaps you won't trust what I must tell you either." Marshall looked around the great room and leaned closer. "I am attending a Kindling, for the ceremony we believed was nothing but legend growing up is real! According to Gretchell, her youngest brother, Lorn, was born with a dormant ember, what Glacier Born call First Folk Fire inside his body. Some say this self-same spark can reawaken the Magic of Men."

Teal caught Niles's eye. "Wait." She beckoned Garth and Smokey Jo closer. "This concerns us all."

As they huddled around Marshall's chair, he looked at them in bewilderment. "You know of Kindling?"

"We know about the Magic of Men," Smokey Jo grunted, working to straighten Garth's stiff fingers. "Firsthand!" She gave Marshall a merry smile and the others laughed. "We're witches, you know!"

"And we don't speak out of turn," Teal cautioned as Garth opened his mouth.

"Tell them what happened to your wife's brother," Niles urged Marshall. "Perhaps they can help."

"Two nights ago, Lorn was taken abed with what he thought was dyspepsia, but it was really ancient fire igniting inside his chest," Marshall said softly. "The Clans call it the Kindle, a rare disorder that many believe no longer exists. According to Gretchell, it besets certain Glacier Born youths who come of age. Not many, just an unlucky few like Lorn." He gazed at the group solemnly. "There is no cure. They die."

Above them, the council room door clicked open and Aubergine and Sierra filed out, followed by Lars and Gabriella. Marshall gazed at the balcony before continuing.

"Yesterday, a dogsled arrived to ferry Gretchell and her babe back to the ice fortress. Lorn had been found in his chamber, awash in fever, and the Clan summoned her back to prepare his Kindling. It's a sacred ceremony, attended by family in a special cell rimed with blue ice deep within the glacier. According to legend, Lorn has mere days to live unless he is the mythic boy the Clansmen call The One: the first Glacier Born to survive the Kindle and reawaken the Magic of Men. Gretchell says it has never happened," Marshall said. "No amount of ice can quell the fire."

"Lorn does not have to die," Niles murmured to his brother.

"He has to find a way to let the fire out." Smokey Jo stole a look at Aubergine and Sierra conversing at the rail along the balcony. "We can maybe show you, in a minute."

"The Clan fears he's already marked for death," Marshall replied. "Years ago, one of Gretchell's cousins succumbed to the Kindle. From what she said, his end was a slow burn, terrifying to watch. Smoke poured from his nose and throat as fire consumed him until he could no longer draw breath."

"The Kindle is so horrible that the Hed Clansmen hold it in secret deep within the ice caves lest anyone hear the victim's cries. They hope someday a boy might live, but for generations they have watched Glacier Born die. " Marshall shook his head. "And Gretchell's babe? She assures all he's my son, willing to build truth upon lie hoping that his nurture at Winterhaven helps him to survive. None of our line has ever Kindled."

Smokey Jo gripped Garth's index finger and held it fast. "Show them."

Garth looked to the balcony. "Is it alright?"

"Explain to them first," Sierra said gently.

"I Kindled and would have died, except for Smokey Jo," Garth told the group. "The fire inside me burned and I smoked and choked. Everything, just like you said," he told Marshall. "Ash was pouring from my nose and mouth—"

"And ears!" Smokey Jo added.

"Somehow, I woke and everything was the same, except for this arm." He gazed at his damaged limb, held firmly in the hands of Smokey Jo. "I feel nothing."

"I heard the ember smolders in the chest until its time," Marshall said.

"It's supposed to," Garth agreed. "Unless you have a father like mine. He knew I was born with the spark inside, so he tried to kill me with a fire bolt."

"What kind of father does that?" Marshall asked in disbelief.

"The kind that doesn't want heirs," Niles told him grimly.

"Not knowing who he was, we called him the Bad, Bad Man," Teal murmured.

"Name him." In the silence that followed, Marshall looked up at the balcony.

"When I married, he was Kendrick Blue, son of Hed Maddig Hoar," Sierra said sorrowfully. "I don't know who he is now. He spurned the Clans long ago in favor of his sister, once a classmate of mine."

"Her name was Tasman." Aubergine gripped the rail, a storm brewing in her violet eyes. "Kendrick helped her betray us all to become the Dark Queen. Now you might know him by any number of names: Kindred Spirit, Northland's Bane."

Marshall gave Garth a hard stare. "Your father is Lord of the Lowlands? Who would kill us all in cold fire to uncover the secrets of the Lost Caves?"

"None of this is the boy's fault." Gabriella gazed at Sierra. "Yet this is what happens when your head follows the path your heart seeks to mislead you."

"Scarcely the point." Lars eyed his sons. "What you're missing here is: This boy is The One."

Marshall glanced at the disheveled Middleland youth. "You are the only Glacier Born to live, The One Clansmen have been seeking for generations?"

"Hardly," Garth said. "I believe my father was the first one."

"The Bad Man burnt down my fossick camp." Teal nodded to Garth. "We've seen him shoot fireballs from his fingertips. Why it happened we don't know, but he abandoned your Hed Clansmen to help his sister rule the South."

Garth glanced at Sierra. "My brother Warren Kindled, but with no one to help him, we fear he died somewhere inside the glacier. Now the burden falls to me."

"To rule?" Marshall asked.

"No, to save all Glacier Born, silly!" Teal snorted. "Unless someone releases the fire inside, Lorn will Kindle and die."

Smokey Jo couldn't contain herself. "The blaze comes out this finger. Want to see?"

"We would all witness such a feat," Steadfast Lars told Garth. "If you really are one of The Ones, shoot your flame into the fire."

"It takes us two," Smokey Jo warned. "He can't do it alone." Steadying his arm, she stretched his hand toward the fire pit. As Garth grimaced with concentration, she felt the heat spread from his chest and through his lifeless limb. "Here it comes!"

Sparks began to erupt from Garth's fingertips. There was a collective intake of breath as he sent the first bolt of flame into the hearth, then peals of delight as he shot fireballs up the chimney flue.

Marveling at the display, Steadfast Lars turned toward his wife. "We may have to stop the boy, lest he burns down the lodge."

"His fire's dwindling anyway," Smokey Jo allowed. Spent, Garth dropped into a leather chair. "It always ends like this." Grumbling, she went to fetch his sling.

"We burnt up my room at the Potluck by mistake," Garth admitted, as the adults descended the stairs to join them in the great room.

"It was an accident." Smokey Jo tucked his lifeless arm into the cream-colored muslin before tying it around his shoulder.

"I'm afraid I don't understand." Lars eyed Garth's hand which had once again begun to curl into a dead fist. "Certainly this lucky boy lived, yet how does that spare any other Glacier Born cursed with the ember?"

"Surviving the Kindle has naught to do with luck, nor can it occur alone," Aubergine said. "I believe that nowadays the ceremony lacks an ancient ritual perhaps once part of the process, something so simple it was omitted and then forgotten, as Kindling became more and more rare."

"If folk would just heed their yarns," Sierra sighed.

"What is this simple ritual?" Gabriella asked.

"Nothing but an act of kindness," Smokey Jo's eyes shone. "It's easy. You just take their hand."

"It's not as unassuming as it sounds," Sierra said. "From what I understand of the tales of old, you must be a Glacier Born maid."

"A witch does nicely," Smokey interjected.

"And then what?" Gabriella asked Sierra. "Do the maid and the youth rely upon one another for life?"

Smokey Jo considered Garth. "I would not say we're inseparable, like twins."

"What do you mean?" He laughed. "Since I got hurt, you never leave me alone. You're always fixing my sling and bringing me food and drink."

"You have just the one hand!" Smokey protested. "Plus you've been ill."

"I'm not saying I don't like it," Garth grinned.

From the dining area Lily appeared with an apron tied over her gown. "Dinner's ready!"

"I'm hoping we did not put you to work in the kitchen!" Gabriella cried.

"It was my pleasure!" Lily said, her face flushed from the heat of the bread oven. She turned to the others. "Come, you have a long day ahead of you if you're leaving for the Out Crops tomorrow."

"Aren't we all going?" Teal asked, as they took places around the dinner table.

"Not Mason." Marshall sat on the bench opposite. Unfolding his napkin, he glanced at his older brother at the head of the table, his mother and father to his left, Aubergine and Sierra to his right. "He can't leave, nor would he wish to," he murmured to Niles. "He ministers Winterhaven and all of its holdings in father's absence."

"A job I would abhor," Niles said under his breath, as a kitchen maid filled their wine goblets.

"I as well." Marshall gazed at his sister-in-law, seated next to their mother. "On top of that, Goodwife Alyssa is once again with child, thus her mood."

"Mason will never leave the lodge," Niles muttered, forking roasted venison from a passing platter.

"I don't expect so." Marshall speared a few pieces as well. He tore a hunk of bread and passed the rest of the loaf to his brother. "Our uncle Honorable Devon has set up camp at the Out Crops and drawn battle lines. After we meet with the Hed Clansmen, will you join us?"

Niles shook his head and reached for the crock of butter. "That's not our war."

"Of course it is," Marshall countered. "We've been fighting the South since they started raiding the Middlelands. Each year the Lowlanders come further and further north." He gestured with his knife. "If the army doesn't fend them off at the Out Crops, we'll be overrun."

"The real source of conflict lies within the glacier, secrets of which are hidden in a set of crystal caverns called the Lost Caves," Niles said, pausing to take a bite of bread.

"It's true," Teal agreed. "Only we witches can save you from the Dark Queen of the Lowlands." With a smile, she drank from her goblet. "You'll see."

"If you have discovered a way to save all Glacier Born, that is more than enough," Marshall told her. "It would seal the Northern alliance far better than marrying me off to a girl from the Clan."

"If this Lorn lives, the Hed Clansman will have an heir and be able to safeguard his grandson against the Kindle," Niles conjectured. "He'll have no need of you."

Teal shot Niles a mischievous look. "Perhaps Gretchell will take his hand."

"Just don't you take his hand," he joked.

"Not a chance." She gazed at Marshall. "Accompany us to the Lost Caves." She looked up at Niles sitting beside her. "I'd like him to come. I don't know why."

Marshall looked away, embarrassed. "Have you been offered rooms?" he asked his brother.

"No." Niles glanced toward his parents, laughing with Lilac Lily. "I suppose that means they want me to occupy the vacant house."

"Light the fire in that hearth just one time and they will expect you to assume your mantle," Marshall said grimly. "Save yourself both damage and retribution. Be my guests."

"Come with us to the Lost Caves," Teal implored him.

This time, Marshall was able to meet her eyes. "Depending upon how things fare tomorrow, I just might. Tonight the invitation is mine. Stay with me."

The creature reared and scowled
as Mae swatted at it with the broom.

CHAPTER 27

Witches and Warren

NEEDING NO GUIDANCE TO HER CLUSTER of ice caves within the southern tip of the glacier, Lavender Mae skipped ahead, gleefully humming to herself.

"It's just up here," Warren told the others softly, careful to keep his voice from echoing as they trailed Mae through the frozen tunnels by the light of the pink-quartz crystal he held in his hand.

Suddenly, Mae halted and her singing broke off abruptly. When the rest of them reached her, she stood motionless in the passageway staring down at the heavy stalactite that disguised the opening to her lair. Warren thought she was waiting for him to heave it away so that she could crawl into her chambers, until he noticed it was disturbed.

The scrawny witch gazed at the chunk of ice warily. "Maaae . . ." she warbled.

"What's going on?" Winter Wheat asked.

"Someone pushed aside the ice she guards her grotto with," Warren realized.

Ratta peered into the low opening. "She used to live in that rabbit hole?"

He nodded. "Someone's been in there since we left."

Climbing atop the stalactite, Mae sniffed the air around the cave entrance. "Ruff!" She growled.

"Is someone still there?" Skye wrapped her cloak more tightly around her shoulders as Mae yipped. "Or something . . . ?"

"Let's see what my crystals tell us," Wheat suggested.

Unhooding her staff, she nodded to Warren, who dragged the chunk of ice away from the dark hole. Crouching, Wheat approached the cave and thrust the amber beetles tied to her crook inside. She twirled the staff, but all she heard was the twin cabochons hitting and sparking. When she withdrew them, still clicking and clacking as they swirled on their sheep-gut tethers, the beetles encased in resin did not glow.

"If it was Lowlanders, they're gone." Wheat caught the crystals in her hand. Although chittering excitedly, the amber beetles were cool to the touch. Satisfied, she pulled the felt hood over her crook to calm them before turning to the others. "Whatever's holed up in there now is just some kind of ice-cave critter. It might pose a threat for most folk, but holds little danger for the likes of us witches."

Esmeralde rummaged in her Possibles Bag. "I've got the perfect powder to ward off pests."

"Is it a pox?" Indigo asked, her eyes alight with amusement.

"Oh yes!" Esmeralde pulled out a vial. "Of the finest pulverized crystal. And it works on any kind of pest: skunks, raccoons." She gave Mae a meaningful look. "Swarms of bees."

Ratta glanced at the stoppered bottle skeptically. "What kind of pox?"

"It's concocted of three types of ground quartz laced with shards of mineral," Esmeralde said cheerfully. "You'll see."

Ignoring their banter, Mae squatted on her haunches at the cave entrance, cocking her head this way and that. Crawling closer, she thrust her head into the darkness and almost immediately recoiled with a snort.

Skye turned to her brother. "Mae hears something within."

"She always hears things," he reminded her, tugging the brim of his Snowflake Watch Cap down over his ears.

"Come with us!" Indigo Rose announced, beckoning to the others.

Snatching the glowing beacon from Warren's grasp, she elbowed Mae aside and crawled into the cave, followed by Esmeralde with her Possibles. With a little growl, Mae skulked behind, with the rest of them trailing. They crept under the low overhang into an anteroom, which smelled of musty rushes, cold cinders, and animal musk. As they shed their packs, deep within the cave, something bumbled away.

"Did you hear that?" Wheat whispered. "There's a critter burrowing back there."

Blinking, Ratta surveyed the dim chamber. "Whatever it was, it made a mess."

When Warren lit a taper, Skye saw that Ratta wasn't exaggerating. Mae's bedroll was torn apart and the rack of glacier weed drying by the hearth disrupted. Even the yarn from her twig basket lay scattered across the rushes on the floor. Indigo cast the rosy glow of her quartz into the tunnel beyond. From its depths came a low snarl.

"Out!" Mae howled. Without warning, she grabbed the broom from the hearth and charged past everyone into the darkness. "Out of Mae's! Out!"

The others found her attempting to rout a wolverine that had taken up residence among the splintered chests and other spoils stored in hollows along the ice tunnel. The creature reared and scowled as she swatted at it with the broom, loath to leave the nest it had made from ruined tapestries. The hard-packed floor was strewn with fish bones.

"Ugh!" Skye covered her nose with her sleeve to ward off the smell.

Warren tried to pry the broom from Mae's grip, but she would not let go. Instead she kept thrusting the straw end at the animal, which refused to relinquish its bed of shredded drapery. Baring teeth, Mae and the creature hissed and spat at each other.

"Stand back," Indigo Rose warned with a wave of her hand.

Careful not to approach too closely, Esmeralde pulled the cork from her vial and tapped its contents around the edge of the wolverine's lair. A chalky film sprinkled from the glass tube to the tapestry. Satisfied, she stoppered the glass tube and nodded to Indigo. "That should do it."

"Do what?" Ratta peered at the wolverine guarding the mound of frozen cloth. "Nothing's happening."

"Give it a minute," Indigo said.

Little by little, foul fog infused the rear of the cave. All but Mae shrunk away from the sulfurous odor. Ratta began to cough. Wheat smiled in satisfaction.

"I ken critters," she told the red-haired witch. "He's not going to like this any more than you do."

As the wolverine's low snarls subsided to whimpers within the rising mist, Mae took her chance to sneak around and bat it on the rump from behind. The animal turned to bite at the broom halfheartedly, before abandoning its nest. Defeated, it slunk along the wall and fled.

The poxy cloud dissipated as quickly as it had appeared. Ratta picked up the broom Mae had abandoned and swept up the mess of fish bones coated with powder. As the haze cleared, Skye took the pink quartz Indigo had left atop a chest and cast its rosy glow down the length of the tunnel, revealing a haphazard hoard of cracked crystal, dented armor, rusty mining tools, and frozen funeral raiment piled at the back of the cave.

"What is all this?" she asked in wonder.

Esmeralde's eyes gleamed. "Everything I'd need to keep myself in business for a hundred years."

Indigo put her hands on her hips. "Is all of this truck yours, Mae?"

The crone gave Warren a defiant look. "Mae's!" she agreed.

"Well then, may I, Mae?" Esmeralde asked with a formal sweep of her hand.

Chuckling, Indigo touched a fat candle nub she found in a niche to the wick of Warren's taper. "Might I have a rummage, too?"

Gravely, Mae nodded her assent. Arranging the beeswax candle between them, Esmeralde and Indigo fell to their knees before the unique assortment of splintered trunks, lidless chests, and sprung casks that housed Mae's collection, in search of healing crystals, rare minerals, and other odd stones.

In the flickering light, Wheat noticed a pickaxe and pantry sacks tied with twine scattered between a wooden wheelbarrow and makeshift toboggan fashioned from old sleigh bobs. "Who'd have thought one small witch could have amassed such a hoard?"

Warren kicked at a dented helm. "It's mostly trash."

"It's treasure!" Esmeralde countered, holding up a ragged mesh purse with a broken clasp.

"They're relics," Ratta said, resting her hands on the broom handle. "Don't forget, we hadn't seen Mae in twenty years."

Unable to resist, Skye chose a raw stone the color of dried blood from a drawer and held it to the light. "Mother says garnets have healing powers," she murmured to Warren. "Aubergine wears a circlet of them knit into spun silk around each wrist."

"I've seen her wristlets." As Skye selected a second crystal, he stayed her hand. "Be careful."

"Just because you don't believe in magic anymore doesn't mean I can't," she complained.

"It's not a belief; it's a way of life." Warren pulled a small drawstring bag from his coat pocket. Loosening the cord, he emptied a handful of crystals into an open crate. "I took these from here to prove to the Potluck this place existed. They've been weighing on me ever since."

Ignoring everyone, Mae scurried back to the hearth where she gathered stray bits of cured glacier weed until she had enough to roll a smoke. Throwing a few shards of cold-fire crystal into the dead ash, she coaxed a small flame. Soon the sweetish scent of burning leaf preceded her down the length of the cave.

From a small chest, Indigo unearthed a sizeable sliver of obsidian. "Mae, you're rich!" she called down the passage.

Beaming, Mae skipped through the tunnel. As she cavorted past, Warren caught her around the waist. "Simmer down."

She blew a smoke ring into his face. "Ha!"

Coughing, he watched the witches pick through Mae's stockpile. "You don't understand," he said, as Mae struggled in his arms. "None of this truck is really hers."

His words fell on deaf ears. Even Ratta laid her broom aside to examine a curious icon depicting a lidded eye. No larger than a walnut, it appeared to be one solid piece of carved onyx.

She looked at Warren. "Some of these stones are eons old."

"And not taken unchallenged," he said pointedly. "They belong to the First Folk."

Skye picked through the blood-red garnets idly. "The ancients are dead."

"I could use some small bits to replenish my stock," Esmeralde murmured, her dark head bent in earnest as she sorted precious pebbles. "I don't think the First Folk would mind, would they, Mae?"

"Mind Mae!" The scrawny witch tried to pry Warren's arms away. She gave him a baleful stare. "Mind her!"

"Not right now," he said firmly.

"There are enough odd shards to mix gem elixirs." Surreptitiously Esmeralde scooped slivered stones into her satchel. "Infusions I have not seen the ingredients for in years."

"It's been ages since I've had the pleasure of a bracing infusion on a bitter cold night," Winter Wheat said wistfully. "But what would you use in place of brandy?"

Esmeralde eyed the shepherdess like she was crazy. "A drop of the cordial of course!"

"The crystals are not Mae's to offer," Warren warned, holding the small witch fast. "She wards them. That is all."

"I'd ward them, too, were it me. Just look at the tumbled stones!" Indigo exclaimed. "Star Sapphire, Tiger Eye, brindled Turquoise like bits of sky. Do you realize what fantastical flowers I could cultivate with these?"

"Out of season?" Warren asked. "Like the ancients did?"

"When you garden in a greenhouse, you can't help but force plants out of season," Indigo grumbled.

"That was the start of First Folk folly," he said softly. "Think on it."

"Are you saying this plunder is cursed?" Skye dropped all but one garnet back into the drawer.

"Tainted perhaps," Esmeralde admitted.

Ratta turned the carved onyx talisman over in her hands. "First Folk would call it stolen."

"Then it is fortunate that only you can hear their complaints," Wheat said, dropping choice bits of amber resin she had found into her felted knapsack.

"Mae hears the ancients, too." Warren loosened his hold on the small witch. "She just doesn't understand what they want of her."

"Perhaps all they desire is to punish her for her trespass," Skye said slowly.

"Mae," Mae cried plaintively, holding her head.

"Whether challenged or not, Mae pilfered these spoils from those who would steal them with no thought for herself," Warren explained.

"No profit?" Indigo loaded polished rocks into an empty pouch that looked like it had once held jacks or marbles. "What is the point?"

Mae quieted and Warren released her. "She harbors this stash to safeguard the First Folk."

"That's the Guardian's job," Skye said darkly.

"Mamie," the little witch admitted sadly. "Mae."

"Don't forget our Guardian arrived twenty years tardy," Wheat reminded them.

"I remember it always." Ratta met her hard gaze.

"Would you say everything here is spoils from Lowland raiders?" Skye fingered a few nuggets of Iron Pyrite. "Like what's this?"

"Worthless," Warren muttered.

"It's called Fool's Gold," Esmeralde said. "Foolish plunder."

"This hoard is most likely a mishmash Mae collected from the pickings of all," Ratta conjectured. "Robbers, prospectors, and fortune seekers alike. According to the ancients, many have sought to discover the Lost Caves and unlock the secrets of the crystals within throughout the ages. None ever returned."

"Mae and Mae," Her hands over her ears, Lavender Mae hunkered on the floor. "Mamie!"

"Something's amiss," Ratta whispered in agreement. "The First Folk cry out for the Guardian, warning of invaders approaching the walled city."

Frowning, Skye rubbed her temples. Esmeralde nudged Indigo, who looked up from sorting stones to glance at the girl. Swinging her head from side to side, Mae wrestled with herself on the hard-packed ground.

Warren eyed Ratta. "The dead speak to you? Truly?"

"They call out *Witches, Watchers,*" Ratta repeated in a far-off voice. *"Unwelcome on the western wall."*

"I doubt we'll be unwelcome when they find out why we came," Wheat grumbled. She unhooded her staff to check her cabochons once more.

"Do you think that is something I would make up?" Ratta asked Warren.

The amber beetles tied to Wheat's crook began to chitter softly. Skye put both hands to her head.

"What's wrong with you, child?" Esmeralde asked.

"I have an earache." She frowned. "Or headache."

"Mae!" Mae howled, rolling around on the icy floor.

"Now they warn of Walkers, Wanderers, and wolverines," Ratta reported. "The dead beseech the Guardian to defend the old city from intruders."

"What kind of intruders?" Wheat watched her cabochons hit and spark. "All we encountered so far was a carrion creature."

"Skye, do you decipher the ancients?" Esmeralde queried.

"No, but I hear them. Their voices rise like thunder." Skye's eyes grew bright with pain. "I can barely stand the din! None of you feel the pressure?"

"Not like you or Mae," Ratta replied. "Wheat wards herself with her beetles, Esmeralde and Indigo with Possibles and herbs. The First Folk can't invade my mind, for I understand them." She glanced at Warren. "Why do they have no effect on you?"

"I don't believe in voices inside my head," he said simply.

"Mae!" Mae yipped.

"I can't bear it!" Skye cried.

"Fetch the Fire and Ice shawl for the girl," Esmeralde urged Indigo. "Quickly!"

Her gray braids swinging beneath her bandana, Indigo hurried to the antechamber where her pack leaned against the wall. In moments she returned with the fine Suri Alpaca lace shawl, knit in an all-over candlelight pattern. Its bright-yellow and tangerine flames danced in the light.

Except for Mae, who lay moaning on the floor at Warren's feet, the witches gathered in a circle around Skye. Wheat tapped her staff on the floor to quiet her cabochons. Esmeralde adjusted her jaunty beret.

Indigo Rose cleared her throat. "Gather round." Then she began the incantation. "Skye Blue, today we six witches plus one bear witness as you inherit the mantle and legacy of your mother, Sierra."

When Indigo Rose paused to unfold the triangular shawl, Ratta and Warren hoisted Mae to her feet to join the group. As Warren shrunk back from the coven, Mae pulled him into the circle.

"One!" she insisted, spreading her fingers wide. "Six and One!"

Esmeralde nodded in assent. "This concerns us all."

"Just as the ember of First Folk Fire passes from father to son, so does Potluck lore pass from mother to daughter, aunt to niece, witch to ward!" Indigo proclaimed. "With this shawl infused with cold fire, we bestow upon you the gift of second sight, birthright of your mother, Sierra."

By the glow of the quartz crystal, Indigo settled the delicate knitted shawl around Skye's shoulders. The other witches began to chant: "Hone your craft, practice your lore, call upon your gift once more."

"Use your second sight wisely," Esmeralde advised. "Remember fate can be sidetracked for a moment, mayhap diverted for a good long while, but never changed. Somewhat you perceive on the horizon—just as what Lily sees in our hearts—is for you alone to bear witness, until such time as those among us would know our destiny."

Indigo overlapped the points of the shawl at Skye's waist, and stepped back. Wheat held the rose quartz high and the flames worked throughout the piece began to lick each other in the light. Skye drew a deep breath and her eyes darkened to sapphire as her view turned within. Pinpricks of violet stood out in her irises like stars in the night.

"What do you see in your mind's eye?" Warren couldn't help asking.

"Can I say?" Skye asked.

Indigo nodded. "What you will."

"I don't hear the First Folk. But I do see things, like visions on the edge of a landscape." She glanced at Ratta. "Are they still calling?"

"More so," Ratta replied. "*Witches, Wanderers, Walkers, and wolverines,*" she said softly. "*Watchers unwelcome on the western wall.*"

"Use your second sight cautiously," Wheat advised as the jeweled beetles encased in resin at the end of her staff began to glow. "Though my cabochons sense danger, we would know only what we need to this day."

"Casting your eye too far into the future could tempt fate," Indigo warned. "Your mother did and the Dark Queen led her astray. Lily did and Tracery Teal died. What you choose to tell us or not has the same affect."

"I saw a dawning horizon." Skye's eyes were troubled. "A brown bat flying over a frozen land. On the killing field below, the dead wore the orange of the Lowlands, and black ravens feasted on their innards.

When the bat landed, the ravens did not notice. The body of the bat split open revealing a man." She gave Warren a horrified look. "It was our father."

Esmeralde's eyes grew crafty. "The Lord of the Lowlands shape-shifts as well."

"He must have learned it from his sister," Indigo said.

Esmeralde hefted her Possibles Bag. "Perhaps we can find a fix for that."

"Is there more?" Warren asked Skye.

"Father inhabited the largest raven just as he had the bat and began winging north." Skye lifted her eyes to her brother. "He scans the ground seeking a man clothed in a jeweled cloak and a wolf's head crown who harbors an ancient relic he hungers for. He will kill for it. When last I looked, the bird had disappeared from view."

The scarab beetles tied to Wheat's staff hit and sparked so furiously she could ignore them no longer. She caught the hot crystals in her hand. "Time grows short. Danger looms all around us."

Ratta tucked the onyx eye into the recesses of her pack, as the others gathered their things. Taking the beeswax candle, Esmeralde and Indigo hurried into the depths of the cave for one last look among the crystals. Even Mae had a rummage, casting random objects from a tattered hide bag no one had noticed.

Warren glanced at Skye. "Carrion creatures may have occupied this cave, but no wolverine moved that piece of ice from the entrance."

"It would have taken a whole pack of them," she agreed. "You don't need all-seeing eyes to realize that."

"Who could it have been?" Wheat asked.

"Mamie!" Mae said determinedly.

"What were they looking for?" Warren wondered.

"Mae!" The crone thrust a broken fragment into Warren's hand. It was an ornate crystal key whose teeth had snapped in a lock long ago. All he held was the filigree head.

"What would I want with this?" he asked.

"Mind Mae," she warned.

"Do you think Mae means the Guardian came looking for us?" Skye asked.

"That's anyone's guess," Ratta said gruffly.

Skye held the blood garnet to the light before sliding it into a pocket sewn into her sleeve. "The Watchers on the Wall are Lowlanders," she blurted out. "I hope that's safe to say. I saw them there with the Dark Queen."

"Thus the ancient's alarm." For Ratta, it all made sense "We need to stop her."

"Look what we found," Esmeralde said, as she and Indigo approached the group.

Bathed in the rosy glow, Indigo Rose lifted several strands of amethyst crystals to the light. "These look like Aubergine's necklace."

"All of them?" Skye asked.

"Not!" Mae growled, grabbing for the strings of stones.

Wheat studied Mae. "When it was a broken circle, she ran off to find the necklace or piece together another just as powerful."

"It looks like she devised more than one." Indigo picked up a chain of five crystals and tossed it aside. "This attempt didn't quite work."

"Not!" Mae waved Indigo's discoveries away. With grimy fingers, she closed Warren's hand around the broken key he still held in his palm. "Mind Mae?" she asked.

With a sigh, he pocketed the crystal fragment.

"Could it be that Aubergine's necklace isn't the real one?" Skye ventured.

"It is has to be. Otherwise Teal would not have chased Mae disguised as a swarm of bees." Esmeralde gave the crone a knowing look. "I could have prevented that. There was no need for you to submerge yourself beneath the cold water of the dye pot."

"We thought Tasman had the necklace, save for the lost stone," Ratta reminded them. "She had eleven stones for twenty years."

"Mae?" Wheat asked. "Does Aubergine have the real necklace?"

"Yes!" the scrawny witch nodded. "Yes, Mae!" She pointed an accusing finger at each of the other broken necklaces. "Not, not, not!"

Warren shook his head. "There's no real way of knowing."

"But there is!" Esmeralde recalled. "Remember when we were girls? Aubergine had only to touch the stone that represented our place in the circle and it would glow." She placed her hand over her heart. "I would feel it right here."

"As would I," Indigo agreed.

"You forget," Ratta said. "We did not stay at the Potluck long enough to see if Aubergine and Sierra returned with the necklace whole."

"We can't waste time pondering that now." Indigo discarded the strings of linked amethysts into an open chest. "Our quest lies north to the ancient city."

In the anteroom, they shouldered their packs. "I've nothing in my Possibles that can guide us." Esmeralde looked at Wheat. "Do your jeweled insects ken the direction?"

"They sense danger ahead," Wheat answered. "That is all."

"What of the ancients?" Indigo asked Ratta. "Can you follow their voices?"

"As long as they're talking," she replied. "But their murmurings come and go."

Mae gave Warren a pleading look. "Mind Mae?" she asked in a small voice. "Mind her?"

"Yes." He turned to the others. "Mae will guide us. She knows the way."

The raven pulled Garth from the ground,
Smokey Jo still clinging to his arm.

CHAPTER 28

The Out Crops

GRUNTING WITH EFFORT, SMOKEY JO HEAVED open one of the great-room doors and stood blinking beneath bright sunlight in the courtyard. This frosty morning Winterhaven glistened with the promise of spring. The log buildings sparkled with a dusting of overnight snow already beginning to melt. As her eyes adjusted, she was astounded to behold not four but six elk harnessed to the double-runner sleigh, pulled around to the front of the lodge. The elk tossed their great antlers impatiently and steam rose from their nostrils. As usual, Smokey was tardy. The other travelers were mostly assembled and there was no place to sit.

Settled on the cushions behind the driver and footman were Lars and Aubergine, with Lily and Sierra squeezed into the boot. As Marshall had predicted, Mason elected to remain behind with his pregnant wife and baby. He and Alyssa stood off to one side. Not surprisingly, Gabriella was staying at Winterhaven as well to await Lars's return from the battlefields before going back to the city. It was a fine thing, too, Smokey ruminated, for the sleigh would hardly hold so many.

Then she gazed beyond the sleigh bed and understood the reason for the two extra elk. Tethered by forged chains to eyes mounted to either side of the rear runners was something that looked like a cross between a raft and toboggan, holding her comrades and all of their gear.

"Jo, come ride in the snow boat," Garth beckoned. "Sit with me."

"Snow boat?" Trotting behind the sleigh, Smokey glanced at Niles and Teal who were already seated in the wooden raft, their backs to the waxed runners. "Wouldn't you two rather turnabout so you can see?" She asked helpfully.

Niles shook his head. "You can catch a face full of snow that way."

"Riding backwards in a snow boat!" Smokey said under her breath. Stowing her pack, she hopped over the low railing to sit next to Garth. "Will wonders never cease!" She pulled her knitted cowl up over her ears and wound a long garter scarf around her neck as an extra precaution.

Teal glanced up when the great-room door opened to reveal Marshall in a fur robe identical to the one Mason was wearing when he welcomed them to Winterhaven.

"What's that cloak your brother has on?" she murmured to Niles as Marshall strode to the sleigh to have a word with their father.

"His mantle," Niles replied softly. "Signifying he is a son of the Northern Watch, sworn to protect the Glacierlands and serve the Guard."

"Do you own such a garment?" she asked, with a wary look.

"Yes." He put his arm around her. "Don't worry, I'll never see fit to wear it."

"I suppose this mantle is at the house you don't live in?" she ventured. "Collecting dust with the rest of your possessions?"

"That it is." Niles watched his brothers.

Teal shivered, recalling their scavenger hunt of the night before. By the glow of her quartz crystal, she and Niles had bumped around the cold unlit quarters he refused to occupy seeking extra blankets for Marshall's guest room. It troubled her to see the vacant cabin furnished down to details like a bookcase in the hall, filled with mementos from Niles's childhood. Clearly his family expected him there.

"I'll never understand your custom." She shrugged.

Niles looked away. "Nor will I."

"Good morning Brother, Witches, Glacier Born," Marshall called pleasantly, hauling his gear to the snow boat. "I trust you slept well."

"And you," the others answered, making room for him in the wooden bed.

When they were settled, Lars nodded to the driver, who slapped the reins and signaled the guard to open the gate. All waved farewell to Mason and Gabriella. Minutes later, the lodge disappeared from view. The travelers found themselves gliding down a snow-packed trail through stands of fir and pine sparkling in the morning light. The air grew warmer as they descended from the foothills below Misty Mountain toward the plains stretching before the inhospitable tip of the glacier known as the Out Crops.

"I love this snow boat!" Smokey Jo chortled, loosening her scarf so that the fringed tail flew behind.

Garth gripped the rail with the felted mitten on his good hand. "It's like a toboggan, only better, with sides!"

When the sleigh emerged from the woods, they glimpsed their first full view of the legendary Out Crops, an ice formation that marked the tip of the Northland Glacier. To Smokey Jo, the ancient walls of wind-swept ice resembled a hoary old man with bushy eyebrows and a frozen beard yellowed with age, looming larger as they got closer. When they reached the juncture of the mountain trail and the main track into Wintergarten, a company of Northland Guardsmen awaited them. The escort consisted of seasoned archers and swordsmen dressed in the familiar blue and gray of the Northland Guard, whose badges sewn to the breast of their belted jackets depicted snowy white cliffs on a field of gray. Their driver held the elk to a slow walk as swordsmen took position in front of the sleigh, while archers fell in behind.

Smokey Jo was delighted to discover Jayden and Jeffryn among those armed with quivers and bows behind the snow boat. When the driver halted to let Deliberate Rye on board to confer with Lars and Aubergine, she saw her chance to pester the twins.

"J and J!" she whispered loudly, with a furtive wave. "Get right over here!" She patted the backpacks piled in the back of the snow boat. "Come sit with us."

"Smokey they can't," Niles explained, watching Deliberate Rye converse in earnest with his father. "They're not allowed to break rank."

"I want them here," Smokey insisted. She tugged on Marshall's sleeve. "Right up between you and Garth."

Marshall hesitated. "For protection?"

Smokey considered the long bows the twins carried, and the quivers of brightly fletched arrows strapped across their backs. "Yes!"

"She's rarely wrong," Teal told Niles.

"Jayden, Jeffyn!" he directed. "To me!" The two boys loped through the ranks of archers to the back of the slowly moving sled.

"Look sharp," Marshall said softly, as the boys balanced themselves on the runners. "Eyes to the skies."

"Awatch," Jayden confirmed, reaching for an arrow.

"Aware," Jeffryn added, searching the horizon.

"Well met, J and J!" Smokey Jo beamed. "I feel safe now! Very well met!"

THE OUT CROPS

The news from Deliberate Rye was less than favorable. Lars's brother Honorable Devon, who led the Northland Army, was camped at the Out Crops, his men outside the safety of the Hed Clansmen's ice fortress, while he attempted to negotiate an alliance within. Unfortunately, no agreement had been reached, for the Clansmen were preoccupied with Hed Lewellyn's youngest son, Lorn, who was Kindling and lay close to death. Even now, family members prepared to accompany their shaman Borac to a ceremonial cave of blue ice deep within the glacier where the rites of the Kindle had been performed since ancient times. They would not return until the boy lived or died.

"The mood at the Out Crops is somber," Rye told the group. "There is little expectation that Lorn will survive and his passing will overshadow all else in the fortress for weeks to come."

"In the meantime, without the Hed Clansmen's cooperation, the Northlands could very well become overrun." Lars turned to gaze at Marshall. "My hope was that your union with Lewellyn's daughter Gretchell would allay this."

"That was before her brother Kindled." Marshall offered them all a helpless look. "Gretchell loves another. The babe is his son, not mine."

"I understand your plight," Lily let on. "More than you can imagine."

Marshall stared at her in surprise.

"It's Lily's special gift," Niles explained. "She perceives what is in your heart, but holds it in confidence unless prompted." He looked at his brother in chagrin. "For some reason, when it comes to my inner thoughts, she gets prompted more often than not."

The others chuckled but for once Smokey Jo wasn't amused. When the laughter died down, she stood in the back of the snow boat. "Take me to the ice caves!" she implored Deliberate Rye. "For I can save this boy you speak of!"

"It is said that gnomes bring luck to those around them," Rye acknowledged.

"This has naught to do with luck," she interrupted. She grabbed Garth's hand. "For the love of the Lost Caves, let us let the fire out! We know how!"

"I believe she can save the boy," Aubergine told the others.

"As do I," Sierra agreed. "Else my son here would not be with us right now."

"What you propose is easier said," Lars cautioned. "Dwellers of the Out Crops are called Clans for a reason, for they are insular folk ruled by family belief and ancient superstition. Outsiders find them aloof and unfriendly. Even if the Clan permitted you to attend the ceremony, they may not let you near the boy's body once he begins to burn."

"But Smokey has a way with fire. Tell them," Garth urged Lily.

"Our Josephine is skilled in the art of pyromania," Lily revealed. "Even as a child she forsook sleeping in her crib for naps in the coal bin behind the cookstove. Once she caught her hair on fire and the scent of singe followed her for weeks. Thus her nickname, Smokey Jo."

"She still smells sooty at times," Garth added.

"That may be so," Deliberate Rye allowed, "but another obstacle we face is reaching the Out Crops themselves. Although I am familiar with the route, what lies between this sleigh and the encampment is a boggy maze of streams and freshets shifting course daily as the ground thaws and runoff swells the waterways." He pointed to the left. "The Lowland Army lies to the East and scouting reports reveal that without the Hed Clansman's support our Guard is outnumbered. In the meantime, skirmishes between the North and the Lowlands rage throughout the moors. Much of the snow in the valley has melted to bare heath, churned to muddy slicks by many booted feet."

"Such muck will do nothing but foul the skis," Lars observed.

"Thus we make for the river," Deliberate Rye suggested. "It's the only way."

Before them, smudge-fire smoke spread across the plains, growing denser the closer they rode toward the glacier until the haze hid the sun altogether. The elk grew fractious; tossing their racks of antlers in a way that threatened to tangle their traces. The scent of death hung heavy in the air. Circling carrion birds cawed overhead; while on the sodden tundra below, vultures and wolverines feasted indiscriminately upon the dead. From the East came the muted ring of steel upon steel accompanied by shouts of surprise, disembodied warnings that knifed through the dirty air like ghostly cries.

The sleigh runners splashed through slush as the trail broke to icy rivulets, leaving muddy eddies in their wake. The elk began to founder in their harnesses as the metal skis caught on raw earth again and again. Finally the driver halted near a narrow creek bed swollen by spring runoff rushing south.

"End of the road," Deliberate Rye called, and they all piled out.

Little Teal went to retrieve her pack.

"Leave it," Niles told her as two soldiers bent to unhitch the snow boat.

"What for?" she asked.

Smokey's dark eyes danced from the raft to the river. "Let me guess! It really is a boat!"

"Of course it is," Marshall pulled out the two long poles stored beneath the gunnels. "As soon as we push it to the river we'll get back in."

Jayden and Jeffryn steadied the snow boat against the embankment while the others stepped into the raft, all except Smokey Jo. "We must have the look-alikes!" she beseeched Deliberate Rye. "We must!"

Unwilling to waste time deliberating, the old man nodded his assent. Minus the drag of the snow boat, the sleigh was more maneuverable and the driver was able to urge the elk forward and free the runners from the mire.

Rye mounted the bench seat and waved to the travelers. "We shall return in three days' time unless the Lowlands takes the plains. Safe travels!"

"And you!" they shouted back.

From the water, they watched their escort turn back toward Wintergarten, save for Jayden and Jeffryn, training their eyes on the sky as Miles and Marshall guided the snow boat down an icy tributary that fed into a placid pool before the mouth of the Out Crops.

Garth gazed across the silent water. On the far side of the lake was the icy face of the glacier and in its shadow the pitched tents of the Northland Guard, thousands strong.

"Is that the army?" Garth scanned the sea of blue and gray. "They're so many!"

Steadfast Lars fixed his eyes on the hazy smoke that obscured the eastern horizon. "According to my brother Devon, the South has twice our number."

Niles and Marshall poled the boat steadily through the shallows shaded jade from the crystal flour that had settled at the mouth of the Out Crops. From there, the current carried them toward a cluster of spindly docks. Soon they glimpsed the frozen fortress of the Hed Clansmen, visible within the opening of the ice caves. All the while ravens swooped and squawked overhead. As they neared the pier, a distinguished man clad in gray emerged from the encampment with several attendants. A mantle of alpine wolf was thrown over his uniform, the long tail fixed to his shoulder by a sapphire pin surrounded by raw crystal. Bareheaded, he wore his long white hair back in a sheath of braided rawhide in the custom of the Clansmen. He strode down to the landing to watch the boat dock.

"Well met, Brother," he greeted Lars from the shore.

"And you!" Lars called back.

"Uncle," Niles and Marshall murmured, ducking their heads politely toward the imposing man in uniform as they lashed the raft to some pilings.

Without waiting for them to gather their possessions, Lars stepped spryly from the snow boat to the dock and made his way down the gangplank to clasp Devon's hand.

"It's been too long," he apologized. "We have much to discuss."

"That we do. Let's walk ahead of the others." From under snowy brows Devon eyed the group disembarking the raft keenly. "Those must be your Potluck witches. Do I spy Queen Aubergine?"

"As well as Second Sight Sierra." Lars glanced back at Lily, Little Teal, and Smokey Jo. "The others I don't know. They possess somewhat more arcane and questionable magic and harbor a boy the gnome insists is a true Glacier Born."

Devon looked at his brother sharply. "The injured youth?"

"Sierra's youngest." Lars nodded. "Rumor has it that he was spawned by the Lord of the Lowlands."

Devon's eyes narrowed at Garth, his arm in a sling next to Smokey Jo. "The son of Northland's Bane? He who calls himself the Dark Queen's Kindred Spirit?"

"The same," Lars said wryly.

"Yet Sierra's son you say?" Devon frowned. "The boy looks more peasant than prince."

"The story only gets better." Putting a hand to Devon's shoulder as they ambled along, Lars lowered his voice. "Several of the witches allege that unbeknownst to his father, and quite by accident, this boy has rekindled the Magic of Men."

"They say he is The One?" Devon stared in disbelief. "Brother, do you know what that means?"

"Indeed. I myself claim nothing. However, the ember does burn inside him," Lars assured his brother. "With mine own eyes I watched the boy shoot fire from the blackened fist in his sling into my greatroom hearth. It was something to behold."

"Hed Clansman Lewellyn must know immediately." Devon glanced past the encampment toward mouth of the Out Crops. "If a true Glacier Born survives there may yet be hope for his son Lorn who even now lies burning with fever from fire inside."

"Marshall, Niles!" Lars called to his sons, unloading the raft on the docks below. "The Clansmen would meet with us. Gather the witches and Glacier Born. Leave the packs."

"There is aught else I would have you know," Devon murmured to Lars as they walked briskly up the cobbled path that led through the encampment to the ice fortress beyond. "Last week, Lewellyn took Lorn on a moose hunt, as is custom before the Kindle."

"I am unfamiliar with the premise," Lars said.

"It's a rite of passage," his brother explained. "The Clans feel a kill will enable the boy to assume the spirit of the alpine moose and thus elude death."

"Avoid death by killing?" Lars asked, bemused. "I'll never understand their ways."

"Nor I," Devon said. "According to Lewellyn's shaman—Healer Borac, as he is called—after the moose hunt, which was successful by the way, their party ambushed the Lord of the Lowland's own raiders north of the Blind Side. They held Northland's Bane himself captive for an hour or so."

"Did this so-called Kindred Spirit tell them his real name?" Lars asked.

"That's the part I find curious," Devon admitted. "Borac said he called himself The One, alleging he was Hed Maddig Hoar's sole son to Kindle and live."

"Hed Maddig had many wives," Lars said, as they climbed the steep embankment. "And many sons. But not one of them Kindled that I know of."

"The family would have kept it secret." Devon cleared his throat. "Clans will be clannish."

"I heard a rumor," Lars remarked. "Years ago, more than twenty I believe, of a boy who Kindled and disappeared. Stronger than most, he held out for days in the legendary Caves of Blue Ice. Finally, when it was clear he would succumb to the fire, the family left. After, when Hed Maddig's healer returned to collect the body, it had vanished. There was nothing left but cold ash."

"I remember." Devon paused to catch his breath at the top of the hill. Below them ravens swooped over the piers, squawking as they dove for food among the skiffs and fishing boats tied at the docks. "As I recall, Maddig Hoar didn't live much longer himself beyond that. Wasn't he the Clansman who perished in a hunting accident that renewed the war between the North and South?"

"I don't know." Lars heaved a sigh. "There were so many Clans it grows difficult to keep track." He gazed at Garth and Smokey Jo lagging behind the others. The gnome toiled slowly up the hill on stubby legs, flanked on either side by her protectors Jayden and Jeffryn. Ravens following their slow progress circled lazily overhead. When one of the blackbirds flew too near, Jayden notched an arrow and let it fly. Cawing loudly, the bird flapped away.

"What do you make of that?" Lars asked, as his two sons and the other witches crested the hill and joined.

Devon shrugged. "The carrion birds grow numerous and bold. They plunder the grain bins, strip corn from its stalks, scavenge the dead. They're a hazard." As he talked, the ravens returned to soar just out of arrow range. "Potluck Queen, well met!" he cried to Aubergine. "It seems your witches must harbor somewhat these blackbirds crave."

Her brow furrowed as she grasped his hand. "I certainly hope not. Well met."

"Lilac Lily and Little Teal is it?" Lars asked pleasantly and the witches nodded. "Meet my older brother, Honorable Devon, leader of the Northland Guard." He turned to his brother. "I trust you remember Sierra?"

"Second Sight Sierra," Devon acknowledged with a polite nod. He looked toward the fortress. "Hed Clansman Lewellyn and his daughter Gretchell expect us. Shall we go?"

Sierra glanced toward the noisy birds circling her son. "Let's wait for the others."

"Devon was just telling me about the Hed Clansmen's encounter with Lowland raiders north of the Blind Side last week," Lars remarked. "They were led by one whose whereabouts you seek."

"In truth?" Aubergine asked, with interest.

"The Clan believes he was Northland's Bane, but they are uncertain, for the man escaped before Lewellyn could question him," Devon replied. "It was quite dramatic from what I understand. Drawing a circle of fire in the ice, he struck the Clansmen down with thunderbolts that flew from his fingers like fireworks, before fleeing into a narrow fissure. Although it dead-ended, the huntsmen lost him among the bats roosting there."

"He disappeared?" Aubergine asked.

"Into air," Devon opened his palms. "All the Clansmen found was a broken bit of horn inscribed with some kind of ancient runes he dropped in his haste."

Little Teal watched Lily exchange glances with Aubergine and Sierra.

"It sounds as if you describe a Skell—a half Skell to be exact—the same fragment we seek," the Potluck Queen ruminated. "If it is what you found, then indeed your Clansmen did encounter the Lord of the

Lowlands, whom you know as Northland's Bane and the Dark Queen calls Kindred Spirit. He has many names."

"Skells? Are you referring to the game of cards and dice enlisted men employ to gamble away commissary chits in the mead halls?" Devon asked.

Aubergine smiled. "Not exactly. These are magic cards of the ancients, whose original purpose were ballots signifying voting powers of the sixteen houses of the First Folk ruling class. The game of chance we call Skells today is loosely based on such lore."

"How would the Lord of the Lowlands harbor such a rare relic?" Lars asked.

The other witches eyed Little Teal expectantly. "The half Skell of House Crystal Keep belonged to my mother," the small witch said. "She harbored it for years. Before she disappeared she hid it in an ordinary Skell deck in the rafters of the boardinghouse where we lived. I believe she died protecting the whereabouts of that bit of horn." Teal looked at Lily. "If you know, you should tell me."

"It is time," Aubergine said quietly.

"The Dark Queen's minions captured your mother," Lily told Teal. "When she was unable to convince them she had no knowledge of the Skell, they abandoned her in the desert. She died in the shifting sands of the Lowlands."

Teal bit the inside of her cheek to keep from crying. "Then it was no coincidence that the day my mother was taken, you arrived at the boardinghouse to rescue me." She raised her eyes to Aubergine. "Was there naught you could do?"

"Nothing but to safeguard your identity, as your aunt Tracery Teal wanted."

Teal looked up at Lars and Devon. "The Dark Queen did learn who I was and captured me at last. When the fossickers sought to find the Skell to buy my freedom, her Kindred Spirit burnt down the boardinghouse." She gazed at Garth. "The Bad, Bad Man stole the Skell and tried to kill his own son."

"As he would now," Sierra said softly.

"You had children with this man?" Lars asked in disbelief.

"We were married," Sierra said. "I knew him only as husband and father. With the Dark Queen's help, he hid his identity from me for twenty years. Not even my lion eyes could pierce her veil."

With a raucous caw, the largest bird of prey any of them had seen winged past the circling ravens to glide low over Smokey Jo and Garth, climbing the steepest part of the embankment below them. Its sleek body gleamed iridescent blue black in the half-light of midday, while its great-feathered head swiveled slowly from side to side.

"What in cracked crystal?" Lars asked, noticing the bird's enormous wingspan and leathery claws that ended in wickedly sharpened talons. Malice glittered in its beady eyes and the harsh warning that escaped its hooked beak was worthy of nightmares.

"That is no worldly creature," Aubergine warned. "I see an aura of dark magic."

"It's him! He's shape-shifted!" Little Teal shrieked as the raven swooped and dove. "Garth, it's the Bad, Bad Man!"

"Run!" Sierra screamed, as Miles and Marshall careened down the hill. "It's your father!"

Instead, Garth pulled his sling over his head. Waving the twin archers back, he held out his curled fist to Smokey Jo. "Help me with this."

She took his hand in both her own. A few seconds later the blackbird sunk its talons into the meat of his shoulders.

"Jayden! Jeffryn!" Marshall shouted as Garth screamed in pain.

Niles lunged for the boy but caught only air as the raven pulled Garth from the ground, Smokey Jo still clinging to his arm.

The twins let their arrows fly. Jayden's glanced off the bird's beak while Jeffryn's winged it, sending the bird spiraling, but without enough force to loosen Garth from its grasp. Grabbing the knife from the sheath in Garth's belt, Smokey Jo stabbed the great bird in the foot repeatedly, drawing more blood each time until it finally let go.

She and Garth plummeted to the wet earth in a disheveled heap, hitting the ground hard. Twin blossoms of blood seeped through the shoulders of Garth's tunic. He writhed in pain. As Niles ran to his aid, the bowmen moved swiftly, launching arrow after arrow toward the great bird. Righting its course, it circled just out of range. The raven made a lazy turn higher in the sky, preparing another dive.

Sierra spotted an oilskin tarpaulin draped across a row of canoes leaning against the embankment. "Over here!"

Lifting Garth by his feet and armpits, Niles and Marshall dragged him beneath the safety of the boats as the bird swooped again. Smokey Jo lay in the field with the wind knocked out of her, too dazed to move.

Pushing the oilcloth aside, Lily crawled underneath the row of canoes sheltering Garth. "Let's have a look."

Swiftly, she pulled a pair of kitchen shears from her apron pocket and cut the tunic from Garth's torso to reveal twin stab marks on both bloodied shoulders.

Niles shoved his head in the opening. "How is he?"

"The cuts aren't too deep," Sierra said with relief. "Although I do wish Esmeralde or Indigo were among us."

"I've a few kitchen remedies of my own." Lily handed her a small vial of alcohol to clean the wounds. "We'll need some cloth to bind his shoulders."

"There's a length of muslin in Aubergine's pack," Sierra recalled. "In the boat."

"I'll get it," Niles offered.

Hearing his urgency, Garth's eyes flew open. "Don't let the bird get Smokey Jo."

"The raven doesn't seek her." His mother tried to calm him. "It preys upon you."

"Jo has the other half of Aubergine's Skell," Garth croaked. "For safekeeping, as I was unable to ward the first one."

"I'll find Smokey Jo," Niles promised. "I'll keep her safe."

He backed out from under the tarp and rose to his feet, scanning the embankment for the rest of the witches. Aubergine had taken cover with his father and uncle in the encampment above. Below, Jayden and Jeffryn lobbed arrows into the sky to keep the raven at bay.

Niles put his hands to his mouth. "Smokey Jo!" When no one answered, he called to his brother. "We need to find the gnome."

Marshall spotted a small form facedown halfway up the hill, not far from where Niles was standing. He pointed. "In front of you!"

Niles sprinted to Smokey Jo, unmindful of the bird that hovered overhead. As he scooped the gnome from the sodden ground, the raven came at him feet first.

"Get down!" Marshall shouted.

Niles fell to the wet earth, protecting Smokey Jo's body with his own. A split second later, razor-sharp talons ripped through his jacket and raked across his back. His scream was drowned out by the sound of the entire embankment swarming with soldiers and Clansmen alike. Marshall knelt beside him.

"Are you hurt?" he asked, helping his brother to a sitting position.

Niles winced. "The bird dug into my back."

"What about her?" Marshall gazed down at the motionless gnome.

"Unconscious." Sucking a deep breath, Niles nodded toward the shelter of the canoes. "I don't think I can carry her. Can you take her to Lily and Sierra? I promised Garth." Marshall leaned over to gather up Smokey Jo, whose body flopped like a rag doll as he cradled it in one arm. He examined his brother's back. "You'd better come, too. Those claw marks look ugly."

Nodding absently, Niles took the hand his brother offered. As he stood, he realized something else was wrong, for he had missed Little Teal since the raven attacked Garth. Panicking, he scanned the landing below, trying to spot a green dress among the sea of blue and gray uniforms. "Have you seen Teal?"

"Not for a while." Marshall peered down the embankment. Then with Smokey Jo in his arms, he lifted his chin toward the docks. "Niles, there."

Niles squinted at the vessels tied to the pier. In the snow boat was Teal, pulling a patchwork sweater from her pack.

"Teal, no," he said in quiet dismay, knowing she would not hear him however loud he yelled. He watched her don the magical sweater to disappear into the sky.

Unable to contain the sudden cyclone, the temple's walls
vibrated with wind that howled and moaned.

CHAPTER 29

Walkers and Wolverines

TASMAN AND HER MEN WOUND THEIR way deep within the city center before encountering the ghostly Walkers. They had seen plenty of water snakes and wolverines and could even discern the long bony forms of arctic pike gliding through the river's icy depths below the causeways. The guards found the wolverines easy prey with the flick of a well-aimed dirk spinning through the air, the water snakes less so. The slithering creatures tended to seek deeper water and thrash about even when dead, so after losing a few throwing knives, the Lowlanders left them alone.

Picking their way through the cluttered alleys to a larger boulevard leading toward the city center looming with temples, Tasman felt they were followed. Once she spun around quickly, glimpsing a pale figure sliding among the buildings. She turned back slowly wondering if her mind played tricks upon her until her guard caught her eye. He had seen the specter, too, and motioned two men to drop back and protect their flank. The four soldiers ahead kept their daggers drawn, creeping through the streets in silence.

They halted at the city square, which was more of a rectangle. Four buildings flanked it, one on each side of the plaza, surrounded by aqueducts which met at the north and south ends of the quadrangle. Tasman was pleased. These were the great temples of worship the First Folk had erected to manipulate the four elements of nature: Earth, Air, Sun, and Water, just as she had imagined them. They promised clues, whether real or abstract, that might unlock ancient secrets. If even a remnant of old magic remained in any of the ruins, she would find it.

As they entered the square along a walkway of ruptured cobbles, a line of spectral figures emerged from a side street. Although they wore white robes, Tasman could see through their milky bodies to the buildings beyond. Her men surrounded her in a protective circle as the procession slowly crossed the plaza. After a moment, Tasman waved them aside, for the spirits gave them no notice. She could not tell if they were ignoring them or simply unaware of her party, so intent were they upon entering the largest temple, an unfinished edifice open to the sky.

When the ghosts failed to reappear, Tasman urged her men closer. A petroglyph depicting intersecting semicircles bordered by braided lines decorated the mausoleum's lintel. Taman recognized the symbol as the rivers Tigris and Eye surrounding the linked suns Re and Rah. The completed hieroglyph resembled the same lidded eye she had noticed painted over doorways or carved into fountains countless times as they maneuvered the streets.

Peering within, she noticed twin altars decorated with interlocking circles and guessed the sanctuary to be the legendary Temple of the

Suns. Before the altars, the spirits knelt in supplication, their mouths open in silent prayer. The great suns had fallen to earth long ago and not a vestige of ancient magic remained within the cold stone walls. Yet, how Tasman wished she understood what the ghosts were saying.

As her guards searched the urban center, luck was with them. The next largest temple was devoid of spirits. Entering the solid block edifice, Tasman recognized it as the Temple of Earth, for in the niches along the walls were small pyramids of rock, icons she remembered from childhood tales. Part of the roof had fallen in and she gazed up through the broken dome to the vaulted ceiling of the glacier. The walls quaked with the hum of old magic. Tasman smiled at the sensation.

Although she had a penchant for wielding water—nothing satisfied her more than creating flash floods like the one she conjured at the Teardrop, or sudden hailstorms she rained upon minions who displeased her—Tasman did enjoy manipulating earth to cause a decent mudslide or summon tremors now and again. Typically, her unnatural disasters lasted just long enough to disturb the landscape, serving as a physical reminder of the strength she possessed.

In the temple, Tasman approached the low stone altar incised with triangles; its flat surface mounded with samples of sand and clay, grit and gravel, peat and fine silt. Gripping the table with both hands, she leaned over the offerings and breathed deeply, invigorated to behold the heady variety of rich earth all in one place. Her soldiers hung back in worried anticipation as she recklessly raked her talons through the soil, exploring texture and color, sifting pebbles and dirt as a painter mixed pigment.

Disrupted, the shifting sands began to spill down over the altar as the grains sifted through her fingers again and again. Her lungs filled with the scent of loam, she exhaled a gust of wind, kicking up a dust devil that went spinning into the corner of the room. Another burst of air sent swirling ribbons of black powder, dun grit, and dried mud the color of ochre spiraling about her in a tornado. Within the whirlwind, her body became the eye of a storm.

Caught in the central vortex, Tasman raised her arms before the altar, to revolve ever faster, her dark hair whipping about her face, unmindful of the rivers of sand pooling over the shoes worn by her men. Trapped outside the twister, they watched in angst and awe as their queen harnessed what power the temple could surrender. Finally, the altar held not even one grain of sand.

Unable to contain the sudden cyclone, the temple's walls vibrated with wind that howled and moaned. As the small pyramids of stone toppled from their niches to the swirling sand, Tasman felt her feet leave the floor. Spinning as she soared, her body ascended through the broken dome, disappearing into the glacier's gloom. The Lowland guards left below were accustomed to cyclones both natural and born of their queen's artifice, and had sense enough to douse their torches and crawl through the sand that sucked at their boots toward the open doorway. Ceiling tiles rained down on them, as the whirlwind gathered centrifugal force, dislodging stones from the walls.

With a rumble that erupted into a roar, the temple imploded. Hovering above, Tasman quivered with delight as first the roof caved and then the walls buckled. When the building finally collapsed she released her breath slowly, riding the gust of wind to the plaza, where she leaned on the arm of her attendant, shuddering with each glorious wave of aftershock until the crumbled walls were silent. As the dust settled, her soldiers brushed grit from their uniforms and eyed her warily until she signaled them to move on.

On the other side of the square, Tasman was relieved when one of the footbridges over the causeway appeared intact. Beyond it was a wide thoroughfare and in the distance she saw the gaping hole of what had once been the city's Northern Gate. She raised her chin to her lead guard and he nodded. Her Lowlanders would be able to cross the river without wading through the murky water.

Behind them the ghostly procession left the Sun Temple, crossing the quad diagonally toward the Temple of Earth, oblivious to Tasman and her men. Reaching the ruins, the spirits stood before the heaped stones in confusion, for a dusty haze hung over the desecrated building and rubble blocked the doorway. Unable to enter their place of worship, they broke rank and milled about, beseeching one another with hollowed eyes and silent cries.

Tasman felt their eyes upon her. Glancing back across the square, she shuddered but no longer in pleasure. Wraiths at the rear of the procession finally noticed her group, and stood glaring with piercing blue eyes. While she watched, their mouths opened in silent howls of accusation and the figures froze. Without waiting to discover the consequences of her transgressions, Tasman urged her soldiers over the causeway.

They hurried toward the bridge. As they set foot on the overpass, more translucent figures emerged from a street across the channel. Unlike the ghosts in the square, these spirits did not move as one in a solemn procession. They gazed upon Tasman's guards with mouths agape in silent O's of protest beneath hungry blue eyes. As the wraiths poured across the footbridge, Tasman's soldiers fell back, taking expert aim at the milky figures. Their dirks ripped through the ghosts with no effect. The knives fell through air, glancing off the stone handrails into the water.

Arching her fingers, Tasman summoned what First Folk Fire she could muster to hurl flaming balls at the advancing spirits the way her brother had taught her, but this, too, produced little result. If the wraiths could not be stabbed or burned, could they be drowned? She hesitated. Sending tremors through the last remaining stone bridge would cause it to fall into the river, cutting her off from the Northern Gate.

The spirits kept advancing, close enough that Tasman could see the blaze of their crazed eyes. Frantically, she searched her mind for the yarn that would explain these angry creatures that seemed neither dead nor alive. None of the legends warned of such menacing Walkers, yet as she watched them cross the canal, she knew they were real. They meant to kill both her and her guards.

With no choice, she waved her men back, and cast a series of spasms toward the causeway. As the ground shook, the arched stones at the midpoint of the bridge fractured, sending first sand, mortar, and then the entire walkway plummeting. The blue-eyed ghost on the bridge disappeared into the water. Without waiting to see what the remaining spirits marooned across the river would do, Tasman beckoned to her soldiers. Keeping to the shadows, they retreated back toward the square, to find another way out of the city.

In the gloom cast by the opaque walls of the glacier, Tasman and her guard crept through rubble at the edge of the quadrangle, trying to remain unnoticed as they retraced their steps toward the western wall. The ghosts milling about the collapsed Temple of Earth had regrouped into a stately procession of worshippers, deliberately parading toward the Temple of Air. As the supplicants passed, Tasman's men crouched behind some broken pillars nearby, barely breathing. At the last moment, one blue-eyed Walker who had noticed them previously tarried behind.

While the other spirits marched toward the temple, the lone shade lingered, unable to see Tasman's group, but cognizant they were hiding. Tasman felt its eyes seeking her with the same kind of avarice she noticed on the faces of those crossing the canal. The line of ghosts gradually disappeared into the Temple of Air, and her guards rose from the screen of pillars unmindful of the spirit who lay in wait. As they sneaked through the shadows toward the boulevard leading back to the western wall, the lone ghost turned its blazing eyes upon them.

Although the transformation happened quickly, it seemed to Tasman to occur in slow motion. Stunned, she watched in both horror and fascination as the waiting wraith engulfed her attendant. It did not so much kill as seep into the man. *Was the specter shifting shape?* Tasman asked herself. *No, because the spirit did not become the soldier, so much as the soldier breathed life into the spirit.*

Lowlanders had few if any words, but her guard emitted an involuntary shriek of mortality as the ghost melded with his being. As the wraith fully possessed him, his features softened and his eyes began to dim. Tasman could only watch in confusion. *Why was this happening?* she asked herself. *What was the reason?*

The ghost gradually solidified into a man, and certainly no Lowlander. He wore burgundy robes and sturdy sandals. His weathered face and cropped beard looked First Folk fierce. *Was he an ancient reborn*, she wondered, *rejuvenated into the person he was when his world froze to ice?* Immediately, she knew she was wrong. In order to reincarnate, this man must have died once. She had a feeling he had frozen alive. There was something odd about him: his searing blue eyes.

When nothing of her soldier remained, the ancient man breathed deeply and flexed his fingers. Tasman felt the heat of his First Folk ember as it reignited, sending showers of sparks from his fingertips. Ignoring her men, he turned toward the river. Tasman followed his gaze to observe the spirits she had cast into the water rising over the stones of the ruined bridge. They clambered onto the causeway, their dreadful blue eyes blazing. Seeming satisfied, the First Folk man left the quad to walk unhurriedly toward the aqueduct at the north end of the plaza. Tasman turned to see her remaining men break formation, fleeing in terror toward the safety of the western wall.

As the wraith emerging from the river pursued her soldiers through the city streets, Tasman watched in a detached dream state, for a fragment of the tale she sought earlier was revisiting her at last. According to Mamie Verde's old yarns, these ghosts were sometimes called Wanderers and other times Walkers. They represented the ancient undead, hearty folk who braved the arctic after the suns fell to earth and the world froze to ice. She saw no children and few women among them, for the weak had perished to be buried in family tombs by those who remained. Then the ice age began. Succumbing to the cold at last, the few First Folk left had frozen alive. A thousand years later, when the world reawakened and the glacier slowly shifted south toward more temperate lands, these restless shades rose to roam the remnants of their ancient city. Neither dead nor alive, they remained in limbo, imprisoned within its ruined walls.

Those calling themselves Wanderers paid penance at the temples, seeking to be laid to rest with their First Folk families. Those known as Walkers with hungry blue eyes wished otherwise. Spurning the tombs, these undead hunted living hosts, sacrificing them to restore lives cut short by disaster so many eons ago. Repossessed, they could escape the city to march toward the glow on the northern horizon, lured to the Crystal Caves like moths to flame once more.

Tasman scanned the square. Pursued by the Walkers, her Lowlanders had vanished into the city streets. When a line of ghostly Wanderers appeared from the Temple of Air and advanced toward the Temple of Water, none so much as glanced her way. She wondered idly if her remaining soldiers would gain the safety of the western wall and await her there. She wondered why the spirits had spared her.

As she turned to leave, she felt eyes upon her again. While she lingered in the shadow of the pillars, one of the silent Walkers had discovered her, she realized with dismay. It was smaller than the others, the only female she had seen, its shape the outline of a hooded woman with long flowing hair. With blue eyes blazing, it offered her a terrible smile before gliding among the pillars. Backing away, Tasman fled into the dim labyrinth of shattered buildings beyond the square. The Walker followed unhurriedly, pursuing her no more quickly or slowly than before. The sounds of hiss and slither in the alleys were punctuated periodically by sharp screams ahead followed by silence. Tasman pursed her lips grimly, no longer questioning what had become of her soldiers.

Crouching in a courtyard to catch her breath, Tasman came upon another blue-eyed monster. As he turned to look at her she shuddered, for embedded in his First Folk face were the earnest features of her lead guard. He took a few tentative steps to test his new body and then breathed deeply to ignite the fire within before lumbering away toward the Northern Gate.

Tasman crept through the side streets, ever watchful for the woman Walker. Finally she reached the western wall. From the old stories she knew that once she gained the ramparts, the wraith could not follow her, for it would be unable to leave the city without inhabiting a host or receiving aid from the Guardian.

When only an alley remained between herself and the safety of the wall, Tasman rose from the shadows. Most of the passage lay submerged in icy waters running from a ruined fountain. A wolverine splashed through the shallows, searching for prey. Tasman went to the pond, unable to gauge its depth, but determined to cross it at any cost.

Suddenly the wraith engulfed her. She felt it envelop her like smoke from a wildfire gone out of control, invading her ears and eyes, nose and throat. As it infused itself within her, she screamed in agony. It felt as if the ghost was consuming her in a slow burn, feeding on vital organs from the inside. In what seemed like a futile attempt to live, Tasman did the only thing she could think of to do. She dove into the pond.

With steaming hiss, the wraith loosened its hold and rose to the surface, where it hovered like morning mist, patiently waiting for her to come up for breath. Her lungs bursting, the Dark Queen swam toward the wolverine fishing in the shallows. She reached out, her fingers touching wet fur, but it was too late. She needed air. Above, the milky-white wraith drifted over the pond as the last bubbles of life rose from her mouth and popped to the surface.

Just before she blacked out, she felt the shape-shift start to happen. Her body grew slick and musky. She was hungry for fresh meat. She was here to catch fish. She could breathe. From the shallows, her keen eyes glimpsed a shadow of something swimming lazily through the depths below and she lunged, stretching out a paw to snag it near. The shadow wasn't fish, she saw. It wasn't even alive. It was a bag of some sort, a satchel some other creature had discarded. From the recesses of her mind, Tasman recognized the purse.

Too late, she realized her folly. As the bag sunk, a long lens fell out of its open top along with a silver coin and a glowing crystal, followed by a heavy necklace held by a silver clasp. Without thinking, Tasman dove and pushed her furry head through its opening before rising to the surface. The wraith hovering over the pond searching for the witch it had relinquished, barely noticed the wolverine wading from the water. Unmolested, the animal shook and bristled before padding away, its neck adorned with a circlet of amethysts.

Back in the plaza, Tasman could see the wraith that had possessed her first soldier crossing the aqueduct above the city square. Five others followed him. With the necklace half hidden in the fur of her neck, she bounded along behind. Their pace was slow and she caught up with them easily as they carefully traversed the narrow aqueduct high above the plaza. The narrow wall had no rails and it was a long drop to the water below. Trailing along behind, Tasman was sure of herself, for the wolverine she inhabited had traveled this way many times before.

After descending from the aqueduct, the six Walkers turned onto a wide boulevard leading to the Northern Gate. Ahead a lone dark-haired woman stood in the alcove of what once was a postern door, conferring with some spirits. Tasman recognized her as the same woman she had seen in Aubergine's hourglass during the simmer, Mamie Verde reborn. Wearing a mantle of furs, the young Guardian turned expectantly. The wolverine gazed up at her with keen eyes, wondering if Mamie knew she was Tasman transformed. *Perhaps born-again Mamie didn't even remember her life as a knitting witch who once taught a student named Tasman*, the wolverine thought.

"*Mamie.*" When Tasman thought the name, it translated to a silent snarl. The young woman offered her an uncomprehending look. "Mamie Verde!" she growled aloud. "Guardian!"

If the Guardian understood, she did not say. She looked at Tasman with measuring gray eyes, before turning away to a group of ghosts trying to push through the gate to no avail, even though there was no door. Bounding about the rubble, Tasman found she could pass as she pleased through the postern doorway or one of many holes in the wall, though the ghosts could not. Only by taking the Guardian's hand could a spirit cross and be shepherded up the steep slope to the tombs above.

The blue-eyed First Folk did not have the same trouble. When the Guardian offered her hand, they shied away to walk six abreast through gaping hole of the ruined city gates, their eyes fixed on the glow of the horizon and what awaited them there. Excited, Tasman bounded behind, the amethyst necklace bouncing around her neck.

As its lifeblood pumped out, Teal reappeared
to slowly guide the great bird to earth.

CHAPTER 30

A Show of Hands

THE HUSHED GROUP STOOD IN STUNNED silence watching Little Teal astride the great black raven as it slowly spiraled to earth. She was still wearing the patchwork sweater her aunt Tracery Teal had bequeathed her, although it had slipped over one shoulder, making her visible to all. As she landed in the encampment, fresh blood beaded the raven's neck, and its beak worked in a silent cry, unable to squawk. Slowly the bird ceased struggling and its eyes glazed over. Only then did Teal loosen her grip on the dagger she had used to bring the raven down.

Unharmed, the small witch slid from the creature's broad, feathered back. Niles gathered her in a stiff embrace, for the waxed thread Lily had used to stitch up the rents in his back allowed little range of movement. Teal watched him blink back tears, his throat so choked with emotion he could not speak. She had caused him misery she realized, and she did not like how that made her feel. She eyed the others in the tight circle solemnly, knowing that the Northlanders and Clansmen alike would scarcely believe what they were about to witness.

As if they hadn't seen enough already. While she battled the great bird overhead, Teal's companions watched helplessly from the safety of the Northland Army's encampment. There, word spread quickly of the unseen witch attacking a giant raven that had injured three of her comrades, one who lay unconscious, perhaps near death. Among the enlisted men, wagers were taken over which fighter would fall from the sky and into the lake, witch or raven. Though they could not see her except when her sweater slipped from her shoulders, the Guard cheered her on.

The groundswell near the shoreline had attracted the attention of those enclosed within the fortress of ice, even the grieving Hed Clansmen. In response to the disturbance, the portcullis was raised and the drawbridge lowered on pulleys screeching with protest. Longhorns sounded and all made way as Hed Lewellyn and his attendants joined Honorable Devon and Steadfast Lars in the center of the clearing to witness the battle's outcome. The witches scarcely noticed the Clansmen, so intently were their eyes trained on the black bird tumbling through the sky, ridden by the witch that now and again appeared as a dark speck on the horizon, their own Little Teal.

Infuriated, the great raven struggled against its unknown attacker, twisting its head in futile attempts to bite behind its back, purring the air with its claws, cawing in protest again and again. The battle that seemed to take hours lasted just minutes more, for the invisible assailant was finally able to wedge a dagger into an artery that pulsed in the bird's feathered neck. As its lifeblood pumped out, Teal reappeared to slowly guide the great bird to earth.

Honorable Devon stood beside his brother Steadfast Lars staring at her in shocked disbelief, while Aubergine's violet eyes sparkled knowingly, appraising Little Teal with satisfaction. Nearby, armed Clansmen flanked Hed Lewellyn, king of the Out Crops, who eyed her warily. Lewellyn wore a wolf's head crown. The white-blond hair that flowed down his back framed a hollowed face whose steely eyes were dulled with despair, for his son lay dying in the fortress beyond the tents of the Northland Army. On the opposite side of the great bird's body, Garth lolled between Lily and Sierra, his shoulders heavily bandaged, barely able to stand. Twins Jayden and Jeffryn stood poised; their bows drawn against what they feared might lay waiting within the dying bird. Rounding out the circle were brothers Marshall and Niles, whose look of anguish was slowly replacing itself with relief. The only witch missing was Smokey Jo. Unconscious, the little gnome had been ferried to the ice fortress to share the infirmary with Lewellyn's son, Lorn.

As it stiffened with rigor mortis, the bird's body listed like a grounded ship and toppled to its side. After a few moments, the feathers on its blood-soaked neck began to ripple as if its heart pulsed within, though it was obvious that the raven had died. Teal backed away and let her dagger drop to the ground.

"It's starting," she warned as the twins took aim at the carcass. "Look sharp. If I am correct, you shall see what befell the fossicker we called Micah as well as the others who unsuppeared from my camp."

As she talked, the iridescent black feathers beneath the great raven's breast began to render and split, emitting the rancid odor of rendering flesh. Her eyes watering, Teal put her velvet sleeve to her nose and breathed through her mouth. The soft ripping sound reminded her of the rent of rotten carpet.

"I watched this happen to a soldier my mates and I played cards with at a mead hall," Garth remembered, as the bird's torso tore in a jagged line from beak to tail feather. "His name was Hairy. One minute we were laughing and dicing at Skells in River Walk. Then the tavern caught on fire, and poor Hairy unsuppered like he was never born. He walked out of the smoke and his skin dropped to the ground like a costume. Underneath was my father."

"Witches call it shape-shifting," Lily explained. "It is a forbidden form of something we commonly practice called hiding in plain sight. The same dark fate befell a kitchen wench I hired in Bordertown. We weren't aware the Dark Queen had hidden herself beneath the guise of the girl until it was too late."

"Not long ago, she possessed a prison cook who had been kind to me when I was imprisoned in the Burnt Holes," Sierra added, as what lay inside the bird began to emerge like a snake shedding skin.

"She inhabited the old woman to catch us unaware at a tavern called the Cask and Barrel." Aubergine put a hand to the heavy necklace that circled her neck. "She wished to steal the lost stone."

"Of those who are haunted, what is their fate?" Lars asked, as the bird's body began to peel back. "When such parasites discard them, are their spirits reborn?"

Aubergine shook her head. "When shape-shifters finish, they destroy their hosts to get out."

"Much like the Kindled ember kills," Lewellyn nodded grimly, his eyes trained on the bird on the ground. "Much like the fire inside."

"We have seen shape-shifters sacrifice those of whom we speak, yet there are untold others," Sierra murmured.

The raven shriveled to a husk, revealing a man sprawled on his side. His nose was crusted with dried blood where Jayden's arrow had struck the bird's beak and his upper arm was pierced where Jeffryn winged it. One of the man's ankles was twisted at an odd angle due to the way Smokey Jo had gouged the raven's leg, but most of the damage lay to the man's ribcage. Clinging to the bird's back, Teal had stabbed the raven time and again until she heard breastbones cracking.

Lewellyn nodded to one of his guards who turned the wounded body over with the tip of his spear to reveal the man's slashed throat.

"Look Garth," Little Teal said slowly. "It's the Bad, Bad Man."

Lars gazed at the form on the ground. "The Lord of the Lowlands, dead at last." "The Guard's sworn enemy, Northland's Bane," Devon spat.

"When I was captive, I heard the Dark Queen call him brother and Kindred Spirit, like they were inseparably linked somehow," said Little Teal.

"He told us he was The One: Kendrick, son of Hed Maddig Hoar." Lewellyn recalled. "The only Glacier Born who Kindled and lived."

"For twenty years I knew him as Kendrick Blue," Sierra said, barely able to contain her hate.

"My father," Garth sighed. "I just called him Father."

Aubergine turned to Lewellyn, the jewels of her heavy necklace winking in the light. "Hed Clansman, forgive me but what this man told you was untrue. He was not the one Glacier Born to Kindle and live. Kindling was never meant to work that way."

Carefully Sierra pulled back Garth's sling to reveal his blackened fist. "My son Kindled at the hands of his father who lies before you and would have died but for the touch of the gnome sharing your boy's sickroom, our witch Smokey Jo."

"The ember burns brightly inside?" Lewellyn examined Garth's forearm.

"It does." Garth nodded. "And I survive."

"Why didn't he wield the flames against the great raven who attacked him?" One of the Clansmen asked, looking from Garth to Niles. "The man-bird injured the small witch and his friend, this Northland prince."

"It takes two to summon the fire," Garth tried to clarify. "For me, anyway."

"Yet you are The One." Lewellyn bowed his head.

"There is no One," Garth insisted. "There are us all." Exasperated, he glanced at his mother. "Isn't there some old yarn you know that explains what I'm saying?"

"Several ancient legends suit." Sierra considered.

"This witch is Second Sight Sierra, Keeper of the Tales," Lars explained, as Devon motioned two of his soldiers to haul Kendrick's body and remains of the raven away. "You would do well to heed her tales of the First Folk."

Lewellyn dipped his wolf's head in Sierra's direction. "We would listen and learn."

"In the days of old, First Folk Fire Kindled within every boy who came of age," Sierra began. "Not one of them perished when the spark ignited within. Kindling marked a youth's passage to manhood, producing certain powers over natural elements warded by women, what the ancients called the Magic of Men."

"All sons lived?" Lewellyn asked. "Not just The One? Or as happens now, none?"

"Boys became men who learned how to use magic crystals found in nature," Sierra explained. "Tempered by the fire women sourced from within. Sixteen families ruled the walled city of ancient Tigeria so named for the rivers Tigris and Eye. The most powerful among them was House Crystal Keep, entrusted to ward the magic crystals. When the house sundered due to dissent and greed, the ability to utilize the crystals to balance nature was lost and the world fell to ice. The purpose of the Kindle died with the ancients. The rites Men of Ice hold today have little to do with First Folk intent."

"I have witnessed the ancient ritual once at the hands of Healer Horehound in the Caves of Blue Ice when I was a young, and again last year presided over by our Clan's shaman, Borac," Lewellyn disagreed. "It was the same each time. We prayed the ancients to spare our Glacier Born, but he choked on smoke from the fire within and died."

"Even if your healers do honor old ways, we witches feel there is something amiss," Aubergine ruminated. "According to our fire raiser Smokey Jo, a certain part of the ceremony is left out—forgotten perhaps—a ritual so small and seemingly inconsequential, it is no longer practiced: the laying of hands."

"Men of Ice perform the Kindle as it was done since the world woke up again." Stubbornness crept into Lewellyn's voice. "We lay our boy on the altar, surround him with Clan and call upon the ancients to release the fire trapped within. There is no laying of hands, just an offering of food and water to sustain the boy when he awakens reborn, or ease his passage into the Land of Dreams should he perish."

"I'll bet they all perish," Garth said under his breath.

"Someday one will survive," Lewellyn determined. "Another, such as you."

"So during your ceremony, no one offers the boy a hand?" Teal asked.

"No." The Hed Clansman regarded her as if she were crazed. "The fire burns so brightly that the Glacier Born's skin sears anyone inclined to touch it."

"That's your problem," Garth insisted. "Someone has to take his hand."

"And not just anybody," Teal agreed. "I think I know why. Lily, remember me asking you what happens to Glacier Born girls, and no one knew, not even Niles?"

"Nothing befalls our maids." Devon frowned. "They wed through favorable matches among families to become the Goodwives and Goodmothers nature intended."

"Nothing about matchmaking is natural," Teal argued, her dark eyes snapping. "Your ceremony fails for lack of free choice."

"No one chooses to suffocate," Lars countered.

"Suffocation takes many forms." Teal gave him a derisive look. "Matchmaking merely one of them."

"Smokey Jo knew all along," Garth realized. "She kept telling us, it takes two, a boy and a girl. One to harbor the fire and one to ward it."

"The girl protects a Glacier Born of her own choosing," Teal added. "Free will guides her to grasp his hand and release the fire. I am sure of it." She gazed at Garth. "We must find who it is that will take Lorn's hand at the Kindle, as Smokey Jo did for you."

Aubergine eyed Lily. "Could this be true?"

Pursing her lips, the housemother nodded slowly. "Most definitely. We have all noticed somewhat different about Smokey Jo, since Garth Kindled. She seems bound to him now, does she not? All because she performed a little act of kindness, a simple gesture that required no thought. She took Garth's hand."

"An act Tasman must have done with her brother before she placed him in my path, for he never reached for me in that manner."

"My young son will die this day," Lewellyn said without hope. "No sacred ceremony or act of kindness will change that."

"But it can!" Garth searched the witches' faces. "If we could just get Smokey Jo to wake up, she could save Lorn. She could show the Clans how."

An elderly man with thinning hair who wore flowing robes and the amulet of a healer strung around his neck made his way through the throng with his staff. His eyes sought the Hed Clansman's.

"Lewellyn, Lorn's Kindle draws near and the litter is prepared." He bowed his white head. "The Clan must assemble in the Caves of Blue Ice in hopes of welcoming The One we seek." His eyes flickered to Marshall. "Gretchell and the child await you."

Hesitating, Marshall turned to his father. "These men shall do nothing but send Lorn to the Land of Dreams. I'd rather not attend a ceremony to watch a boy die."

"It's their way," Lars said sternly.

"It's pointless," Marshall shot back.

"We need the alliance," Devon warned his nephew. "Do not disrespect."

The shaman nodded in satisfaction as Marshall joined him. He raised his brows. "Before we take our leave, is there one here known as Garth?"

Garth looked at him in surprise. "That's me."

"Your consort has awakened." The healer stumped away with his staff.

Garth's brow furrowed. "Do you mean Smokey Jo?"

"Mmm." The healer turned. "A small brown witch. She asks for you."

"Let us accompany you to the caves," Garth begged. "We can help."

"You're welcome to take my place," Marshall muttered.

"The ice caves are hallowed," the shaman said. "None are admitted save those of the Clan."

"But I am true Glacier Born," Garth argued.

"You are a boy of the Middlelands," the shaman disagreed.

"I have First Folk Fire inside," Garth told him. "And the ability to save your Lorn. Take me to my consort and I'll prove it."

The frozen fortress really was hewn from of ice, Garth noticed after he and Marshall followed the Clansmen over the drawbridge. Within, they passed crisscrossing tunnels studded with bedrock and shards of crystal, some of which seemed like trails meant for sledders, so steeply did they plunge into the glacier. Striding along the main passageway, Garth heard Smokey Jo's chatter long before they reached the sickroom. Her unmistakable voice filled with merriment echoed through the halls.

"You girls come close!" He overheard the gnome urge unseen others in a conspiratorial whisper. "Shh! There's no need to cry. He's not about to die, because I'm not about to let him!"

Garth grinned when he caught sight of the gnome in a ward of empty beds, presiding over a group of tearful young girls huddled around a litter. Propped with pillows, she sat comfortably cross-legged amidst the sheets of a rumpled cot, remnants of a honeyed bowl of porridge on a tray beside her. The only sign of anything amiss was the gauze bandage that circled her brow.

Hed Lewellyn and Healer Borac approached the gurney where Lorn laid not yet Kindled. The weeping girls parted ways. They were likely distant relatives paying their afflicted cousin one last visit before going to the ice caves. It was obvious why they were crying. The boy looked as if his flushed skin might erupt into flame any second.

Craning his neck toward the feverish youth, Garth relived the sensations: his face awash in sweat, too caustic to touch; the spark that threatened to erupt into flames down the length of his arm. He remembered the rush of hot breath as something akin to a blacksmith's forge roared to life within his ears and the taste of ash as he gasped for air, his glazed eyes focused only on the fire blazing within.

"Now listen up!" From her cot, Smokey Jo raised an index finger, oblivious to the girls' sorrow. "Is there a maid amongst you who cares for this boy Lorn more than the rest?"

The grief-stricken girls stared back like a herd of heifers, apparently speechless. Frustrated, Smokey Jo picked out a large blond girl holding a baby.

"You're his sister," she implored. "Tell me, who likes him best?"

"Gretchell," Marshall uttered from the doorway.

"Marshall." She gave her betrothed a neutral look as he embraced her. Not only was there no love in her eyes, Marshall was unsure she even liked him all that much.

"Gretchell," he repeated, this time to Smokey Jo. "Gretchell likes him best."

"Oh goodie!" Sighting Garth, Smokey clapped her hands in glee. "We have everyone we need." Hopping off the bed, she hustled over to lead Garth to the litter. "Look, you're just in time!"

"We must take him to the Caves of Blue Ice," Healer Borac urged, as Lorn began to moan.

"Not just yet," Garth reminded Lewellyn. "You promised."

Standing on her tiptoes, Smokey Jo gazed at the feverish boy fondly. "Pretty soon it will be time to let the fire out. It takes two you know." She beckoned to Gretchell. "Afterwards you have to ward him, forever. It's a big commitment." She glanced at the group of frightened girls. "That's why I asked you who likes Lorn best."

"It is I." Gretchell wiped her eyes. "Isn't he going to die?"

"He will if you don't get over here and help him!" Smokey scolded.

Garth cracked a smile. The way her head was bandaged reminded him of a story Lily had told him regarding Smokey Jo's adventures with fire when she was a baby. One time, Smokey accidently singed off her hair playing with flames in the brazier during breakfast one morning. According to Lily, the little girl had toddled around in a white headscarf with no eyebrows for weeks.

Gretchell passed the baby to a cousin and approached the litter where her brother lay. Standing on her tiptoes once more, Smokey Jo peered over the edge, satisfied that smoke had begun to curl from his Lorn's nostrils.

"It won't be much longer now!" she said, pleased. "When it's time, you need to take his hand, no matter how much it burns," she warned the girl. "Let's look for a good place to aim the flame, like somewhere not too combustible."

"For example, don't choose an armoire as we did." Garth hid a smile.

Gretchell stared at them without comprehension.

"I knew this would happen," Smokey Jo muttered, heaving a sigh. "Here, we'll show you." The huddled girls ceased crying to watch with interest as Smokey Jo painstakingly unfurled the fingers of Garth's blackened fist. Healer Borac motioned for two orderlies to lift the litter but Lewellyn raised his hand to hold them at bay.

"Must you do that on every occasion?" he asked Smokey Jo. "Align his hand?"

"His fire doesn't come out right since his father tried to kill him with it." Smokey gazed at Gretchell. "She shouldn't have that trouble with her brother, I don't think."

"There," Garth grunted, when his fingers finally straightened. "Ready?"

Smokey dipped her chin. Garth took a breath and coughed softly to start the Kindle. For some reason, he found it helped the ember ignite more easily.

Smokey held his arm steady. "The water bucket!"

Garth sent sparks hissing into the pail and one of the girl cousins screamed.

Smokey looked at her sternly. "Hush, or you'll ruin our concentration. The frozen floor!" she shouted.

Garth etched a figure eight pattern into the ice much like a skater might trace onto a frozen pond. "My, your surroundings suit nicely!" Smokey exclaimed to the Clan, her eyes shining at Garth's handiwork. "What else?"

"This sheet of ice?" He pointed to a partition between themselves and the hall.

"I should think so," she agreed.

But when Garth sent a fire bolt into it, the wall came crashing down around them.

"Oops, I guess that ice was not as thick as I thought!" Smokey said. "Or maybe it was fraught with fissures."

Garth looked at Lewellyn. "Sorry."

Smokey Jo clambered across the shattered ice to where Lorn lay smoking on the gurney. "Show's over," she grumbled to Gretchell. "No more fun and games."

"How will I know when it's time?" the girl asked, alarmed at the way smoke rose from her brother's nose and mouth, and even his ears.

"You shall think he is dying." Smokey Jo's eyes were alive with excitement. "And he will reach out for you. Then and only then do you take his hand."

"That is what our cousin did," Gretchell gazed at her father's grave face. "Do you remember? Just before he succumbed, he reached out blindly, but no one would touch him. His hand fell through air."

"No one wanted to die in fire, as this boy shall here." Borac gave Lewellyn an angry glare. "It's too late to take him to the Caves of Blue Ice."

"He would have perished anyway," Lewellyn murmured, "As they all do."

"Could we have saved my cousin?" Gretchell asked with a tearful look.

"I don't know." Garth shrugged. "But we can save your brother, here."

Just then Lorn's eyes flew open. His mouth worked in desperation, reminding Smokey Jo of a fish pulled from the water, gasping for air.

"Not yet, not yet," she crooned. Finally Lorn lifted his hand blindly. "Take his fingers," she commanded Gretchell. "Grasp his hand."

There was a hiss of smoke and sputter of sparks. Then something caught and fire filled the room.

Translucent hands and fingers appeared, stretching through cracks and fissures.

CHAPTER 31

Speaking Their Minds

"VOICES WARN OF WALKERS AND WOLVERINES," Ratta whispered, as the seven of them approached the southern wall of old Tigeria. Ahead, the road passed through a jagged maw rimmed with broken stone where the gate had once stood.

"What of the Watchers?" Indigo asked.

"Gone." From the opening, Ratta leaned against the wall to peer within. Before them lay a buckled thoroughfare fraught with frost heaves leading toward the city center. What part of the walk wasn't submerged under standing water was littered with rubble.

Winter Wheat glanced at the twirling beetles tethered to her staff. Agitated, the amber crystals hit and sparked at random. "It's not safe to enter the city," she said.

"Must we go around?" Esmeralde regarded Mae, who had wandered off so often since leaving her lair that Warren had leashed her with his climbing rope. "Surely she knows the way."

"Mae, can you see us through?" Warren asked, coaxing her toward the gate.

Cringing, Mae cringed and let out a shriek of protest that ended in yips.

"Not without consequences, it would seem," Indigo observed.

"Perhaps she is the witch the ancients warned of," Skye ventured.

"But not the only one, I'm afraid." Wheat caught the cabochons up in her hand to still them. "We would do better to clamber outside of the walls."

Warren scanned the eastern edge of the wrecked ramparts leading north to the aqueducts. "The bridges are down."

"That won't stop us." Planting her staff, Wheat stalked off. "I'll find a way."

Following, the others trudged along the outer edges of the city, keeping close to the crumbling walls. Through holes in the fortifications they glimpsed collapsed buildings of hard-fired clay in the alleys, and manses of seamed stone beyond. Rats scuttled along the sunken walkways past pools whose surfaces rippled with snakes, their triangular heads just visible cutting through the icy waters. The dead city echoed with an occasional cry of alarm followed by snarls of the creatures that resided there.

Although she was a seasoned shepherdess accustomed to distant treks, Winter Wheat could not hazard how long they walked. There was no sense of time underneath the gloomy dome of the glacier, and footing through the shifting rubble as they circumambulated the city was slow, especially when they were forced to ford a canal whose bridge had caved into the shallows. She found it helpful to focus forward. Beyond the Great Northern Gate, the legendary tombs of the ancients crowned a low bluff. The looming crypts were backlit by the flicker of fire in the sky that could only be coming from the Lost Caves, leagues beyond.

As they paused to drink from their water skins, Ratta broke out strips of beef jerky Lily had cured the week before and passed rations all around. Mae let hers drop to the frosty ground, content to wrest the smoked meat like a dog gnawing bone.

Skye tore off a bit of dried jerky and let it soften in her mouth. The ancients were muttering again, more urgently than before. She wrapped the Fire and Ice shawl snugly around her shoulders, to dull the distracting voices. The incessant noise was like the buzz of bees. Mae felt it, too, for her behavior was growing increasingly feral. Having gulped down her jerky, the crone snuffled the ground at Warren's feet for scraps. Then she bounded on all fours to a break in the wall, pausing to sniff the opening.

"Ruff!" she barked.

Warren patted his leg, and gave a gentle pull on the rope to entice her back. "We need to keep moving," he warned. "We have not gone unnoticed."

Sensing danger, Wheat's cabochons began to click and clack anew, the outlines of the twin scarab beetles casting a golden glow in the gloom.

"Up ahead," Esmeralde said softly, lifting her chin toward a milky arm reaching for them through a hole in the wall.

Other translucent hands and fingers appeared as well, stretching through cracks and fissures, trying to touch them as they neared the Northern Gate. Hurrying past, Skye saw that the luminous limbs belonged to ghostly figures watching them intently, with hoarfrost eyes blazing with blue ice.

Skye shrank from the specters. "What are they?"

"Wraiths," Ratta whispered. "The ancient undead. They call themselves Walkers and Wanderers."

Hiking ahead, Wheat gave the ghosts a wide berth. When a groping hand reached for her staff, she smacked it away and turned to Ratta in exasperation. "Since you hear everything these shades say, will they heed you? Can you keep them at bay?"

"No more than you can dissuade the animals whose thoughts you ken, or Lily can sway those whose minds she reads," Ratta replied. "Cloaking the power of suggestion in magic creates uncertain lore. We have all seen such enchantment backfire."

"Truly," Wheat agreed, setting their course further away from the wall.

"When I was young, Mamie taught me First Folk Mind Speak." Ratta gazed at the ghosts whose mouths gaped open in silent howls. "Even now the ancients are speaking their minds."

"They act as if they are imprisoned." Warren hauled Mae back as she sniffed at the fingers attached to one of the hands. "Yet I see nothing to keep them from leaving."

Indigo thrust her palm through an empty window opening. "The boy is right. There is nothing but air!"

"Indy, don't let them touch you," Esmeralde warned. "I've no Possibles for that."

"Perhaps these shades are First Folk who failed to die when the earth fell to ice," Skye said. "Frozen alive, neither living nor dead." Shuddering, she turned to Ratta. "Caught in limbo like Mamie was."

Wheat leaned heavily on her staff. "Some you name Walkers and others Wanderers."

"The Guardian helps them decide," Ratta explained, walking beside her. "The few called Wanderers seek to be laid to rest, but these grasping hordes are Walkers silently screaming for a different release from the city."

"Keep Mae away," Esmeralde warned Warren as the crone strained at her rope toward the groping hands once more. "What if these Walkers seek to invade her body as well as her mind?"

"Walkers would possess us as hermit crabs do shells to gain freedom to leave the dead city and enter the human world once more," Ratta said. The others stared at her in surprise. "Wanderers pass among the temples paying penance that they may die in peace, but Walkers seek mortal hosts."

"And the Guardian assists all?" Skye asked in disbelief.

"She hears all, but can free only the Wanderers who beseech her. She guides them to the tombs of their First Folk families, as Guardians have since the world began again. Look closely and you can see their mausoleums on the bluffs overlooking the city."

Snapping at grasping hands, Mae caught a mouthful of fingers, but was unable to worry at them for they dissolved into fog. As the cloud engulfed her face, she yelped and rolled to the ground.

"Get up!" Warren pulled her away from the dissipating mist. "No more antics!"

Groaning, Mae curled into a fetal ball. Warren could not tell if she was truly incapacitated or merely ignoring him.

"The ancients have finally completely invaded our poor little witch." Esmeralde looked at Indigo helplessly. "There's no earthly cure for that. No treatment, no remedy."

"Nothing," Indigo agreed, looking around the group. "Mae trespassed among the ancients time and again. There is no antidote for First Folk wrath."

"Mae meant no harm," Warren protested, looking at her motionless form.

"She stole from them," Ratta said harshly.

"All of us rummaged among the relics in Mae's warren," Wheat reminded her. "Even you."

"Perhaps the Guardian will have an answer for Mae," Skye ventured.

"Otherwise we may have to leave her here," Esmeralde agreed.

"We'll not abandon Mae!" Warren said fiercely.

"Then you shall have to carry her." Indigo considered the scrawny witch. "For she won't get up."

"Can we try summoning the Guardian for aid, as the First Folk do?" Skye asked.

"How would we call her without voices?" Indigo wondered.

"What do we call her?" Wheat asked. "Mamie Verde? Or just Guardian?"

"We call her by all the names we know, both silent and aloud," Ratta said determinedly. "We must speak our minds, as the ancients do."

"I don't suppose she remembers herself as she was," Esmeralde conjectured.

"No more than Mae does, I expect," Ratta concurred. "Nor am I certain she would heed the spoken word."

"I'll try anything." Warren bent to lift Mae from the ground. "Guardian!" he yelled into the sky. "Wherever you are! Guardian, we need your help!"

"Mamie!" Wheat bellowed, cupping her hands around her mouth. "Mamie Verde, Keeper of the Tales, Third of the Twelve! We entreat you!" She turned to Ratta. "That's all the names I know. Do you have others?"

The red-haired witch nodded and closed her eyes, focusing her speech inward, summoning the silent tongue of the First Folk. *Guardian!* she began, hoping to feel the half-forgotten prickle in her mind that meant her mistress was near. *It is your faithful servant, Ratta. (Do you remember?) We shared a life before.*

She paused, anticipating the pinpoint of recognition, followed by the soft flutter of Mamie's consciousness seeking her like fingers leafing through her mind. Detecting nothing, she scoured her memory for an association that might trigger Mamie's notice.

There was a farm in the hamlet of Coventry, in a place called the Middlelands. We lived in a wooded cabin. As you lay dying, I wrapped you in a Never Ending shawl knit from one unbroken strand of yarn. Do you recall a covered wagon, a pair of mules, a favorite rocker fashioned into a wheeled chair?

Ratta opened her eyes to silence. The others watched expectantly. "Nothing."

"The Guardian has to be listening," Warren insisted. "Or at least taking note."

In his arms, Lavender Mae's eyes fluttered feebly. "Mae!" she groaned. "Mamie!"

Mamie, Ratta repeated silently. *Hear us for we plead for guidance. One of our brethren has been invaded by First Folk voices and we would rid them from her mind.*

Dark clouds formed overhead. At what price? came the slow reply.

Ratta drew a deep breath. "At last I hear her."

"All I catch is distant thunder." Wheat scanned the frozen dome. "How can it rain inside of a glacier?"

"The Guardian is ahead, warding Wanderers from the Northern Gate to the tombs beyond," Ratta reported. "We must hasten to meet her before she takes her leave." She gave them a troubled look. "For some reason, she is convinced her work here is done."

The break in the wall that had once housed the Northern Gate swarmed with wraiths. Translucent hands reached out toward them in supplication, desperation, defiance. Another ghostly throng had crowded an alcove that had once held a postern door, Skye saw. Groping for her, they pleaded wordlessly, unable to escape the walls of their invisible prison without aid. She wondered what would happen if she let one take her hand. Then she spied a figure in a fur mantle and boots walking among tombs on the bluff beyond.

"That girl in the graveyard looks like the one we saw in the hourglass at the end of Aubergine's simmer," she said to Ratta. "Is she Mamie?"

Ratta's face lit in recognition. "As in the hourglass, now in the flesh."

Breaking free of the others, she hurried up the hill. *Guardian, it is your faithful companion, Ratta,* she called as she hiked the path. *Do you remember?*

The young woman turned in surprise. *Who speaks the silent language of the ancients? You witch, and these others?*

Only I am familiar with the First Folk's tongue. Ratta tried to hide her disappointment. The Guardian was just a girl, she realized, a young maid with an unlined face and hair that flowed down her back without a touch of gray. Her clear eyes held the innocence of youth. Ratta knelt in supplication. *Guardian, meet your humble servant.*

It is I who serves you, the girl replied. *For I must consider all who request my aid.* She watched the witches climb the hill to the cemetery, frowning at the scrawny crone groaning fitfully in Warren's arms, a rope secured around her waist.

Ratta followed her gaze. *This is the witch I spoke of, crazed by First Folk voices.*

The Guardian gave Mae a cool look. *She carries their curse. The ancients complain that this one trespassed among the tombs. They charge that she stole from their temples in the city, desecrating the altars, disturbing their rest. The sacred relics she pilfered from their places of worship and burial vaults she mistook as unchallenged.*

She meant to safeguard such treasures from raiders, invaders, Ratta protested.

The ancients take her for a robber, the Guardian said. *No better than other looters they seek to destroy. There is nothing left for her but to pay penance or pay the price.*

Then must we all, Ratta confessed with downcast eyes. *For we helped ourselves to the riches. Even I picked a carved stone from the plunder this witch hoards in the southern caves.*

What you took was a pittance. I have seen the spoils. The Guardian held out her hands. *Rise.* As their fingers met, a jolt of recognition sweep through the Guardian and shock registered in her eyes. *You!* she gasped.

"What is she saying?" Skye asked Ratta breathlessly, as the others joined her.

"You," Ratta repeated, afraid to break contact with the other woman. "She does not know what else to say."

Indigo scrutinized the Guardian with curiosity, wondering if Mamie had looked this way when young. Even in a fur mantle she was slight, with serious gray eyes and long tresses the color of bitterroot.

"Do you think she remembers us from twenty years past?" she asked Esmeralde. "Teaching us tales when we were girls as young as she appears now?"

"If she recalls anything about us, it would be our cleverness," Esmeralde replied. "How we excelled with crystals at the dye pot, herbs and spices in the kitchen garden, how we were always concocting new tinctures together."

Indigo nodded. "Even then we knew two heads were better than one!"

It is I, Ratta confirmed, as the Guardian dropped her hands. *We lived as one once when Mind Speak was our private language. Here, all know it.*

"You," she said again aloud. "Can you say it soundly, that my companions may hear and your First Folk may not?"

"You," the Guardian said solemnly.

Skye clasped her hands. "The Guardian speaks the tongue of the Middlelands." She bowed her head. "I am Skye Blue and this is my brother Warren, whom you did not know before."

The Guardian frowned. "There was an hourglass, filled with crystals before."

"In the Potluck dye shed but unfortunately it got smashed during the last simmer," Esmeralde explained. "We meant to send you to the Land of Dreams, but instead you are Guardian of the glacier, Mamie reborn."

"Mamie reborn," the young woman considered, tasting the words.

"Mamie Verde is your name," Indigo said. "Verde means green, forever young such as you."

"I am Mamie Reborn," the Guardian decided. "My work here is almost done. Cyrus told me."

"Cyrus?" Winter Wheat tamped her staff on the ground. "Aubergine spoke of a husband who disappeared before she came to rule the Potluck. Wasn't he Cyrus?" She eyed Mamie. "Guardian before to you?"

"Guardian's Watch stood empty when I arrived." Mamie shook her head. "The Cyrus I know is a Walker turned Wanderer I laid to rest among these plundered tombs."

She led them to the largest crypt in the cemetery. Like the others, the stone barricade was broken open and the burial chamber looted. Ratta peered inside. Nothing but scraps of frozen tapestry littered the stone floor beneath a cracked sarcophagus decorated with swirls of faded paint whose fantastical depictions of giant flowers and sun-swept waters were sad testament to what the ancients had squandered.

The Guardian rested her hand on the vault. "Cyrus belonged to this house, Crystal Keep, the most powerful ruling family of forgotten Tigeria, lying between the rivers Tigris and Eye. Cyrus counsels me as I keep watch from the overlook above, from a blinking orb he calls Tiger Eye."

"Is the gem alive?" Ratta asked, remembering the carved onyx she had found in Mae's lair. That, too, had held the shape of an eye.

"He sleeps in a niche over the stone altar in my chambers." Mamie nodded absently as she scanned the cliffs above. "None but the Guardian may enter the Watch."

"We seek neither your eye nor your watch," Wheat said gruffly. "For our path lies north. We would journey to the Crystal Caverns, pursuing passage to a certain set of caves all consider lost."

"I believe that is their glow on the horizon, though I've not ventured further than these tombs." Mamie lowered her voice. "Others came through the city, and I thought to guide them to the caves, believing my tasks were complete, but I was mistaken. Cyrus said to tarry, for one of you would call me by name." She gazed at Mae. "It was she."

"Her name is Mae," Warren said. "She's always saying Mae and Mae."

"What others?" Indigo asked sharply. "Was there a witch?"

"A witch with a captive girl who may have looked like a boy?" Esmeralde added.

"No." Mamie paused to think. "This witch scaled the western wall with soldiers in orange raiment. Men who spoke with their eyes. They did not ask for my help."

"Lowlanders," Wheat hissed. "Thus my beetles' alarm."

How long ago?" Indigo asked earnestly.

But Mamie Reborn only looked at her in confusion.

"We would know when they passed through here," Esmeralde elaborated. "How much earlier before?"

"We have no sun, moon, or stars to mark day from night," Mamie said. "There is no before."

"Time stands still in the glacier, because it has to," Skye realized with a slow nod. "Don't you see?" she implored the others. "Folk die while alive. Undead are reborn."

"Those imprisoned within the city are Walkers caught between worlds. There they remain until they consent to be laid to rest or find a living host." Mamie gazed at Mae. "Your witch must choose before we take leave for the caves. She must pay penance or pay the price of the reborn."

"What price?" Warren demanded. "You cannot cure her, nor chase the First Folk from her mind?"

"She carries an ancient curse," Mamie said calmly. "There is no earthly cure."

Indigo nudged Esmeralde. "What did I tell you?"

"Touched by a Walker, your witch is mostly dead," Mamie held out her arms. "I can lay her to rest that she never has to walk or wander."

With a grim nod, Warren bent to bestow her Mae's limp body. The crone opened one eye. "Mae?" she asked suspiciously.

Warren hesitated. Skye took his arm. "Lay her to rest," she counseled.

Gnashing her teeth, Mae began to struggle. "No Mamie!" Shouting belligerently, she glared at Warren. "No One!"

"I can't." Backing away, Warren settled Mae on a stone bench half toppled to the ground. "I just can't do it."

"Don't forget you are reborn," Ratta reminded him.

"Yes, into a world without magic," he pointed out. "I can't choose that for her."

"She chose it for you," Wheat said. "Just before she clamped that Snowflake Watch Cap on your head."

"I was dying," he argued.

"So is she," Esmeralde said. "There are no other Possibles for her."

Shaking, Mae rose from the bench. "Mae!" She pointed a condemning finger at the Guardian. "Mae and Mae!" She snatched the end of the rope from Warren's grasp.

"Don't let her slip away," Ratta urged Warren.

It was already too late. As if by magic, Mae summoned a final rush of energy and ran blindly from the cemetery. Soon she was scurrying down the hill toward the city.

"Let her enter the Northern Gate and she pays the price," Mamie warned.

"If the Walkers want her they will have to take me, too," Warren promised. Without another word, he was gone.

Skye watched in disbelief as her brother sprinted down the hill. "You were a witch once," she implored Mamie. "There has to be another way."

The Guardian shook her head in regret. As they watched Warren close the gap between him and Mae, Esmeralde and Indigo came over to console Skye.

"Warren may save her yet," Esmeralde encouraged, a hand on the girl's shoulder.

Indigo ducked her chin. "He's been able to bring her back so many times before."

At the city gate below, Mae snuffled the eager hands reaching out. Racing up behind her, Warren dove for his climbing rope trailing along the ground. Feeling the tug, Mae turned to him joyfully.

"One! Mind Mae!" She pulled the rope taut, jerking him through the gate. In seconds they disappeared into a sea of Walkers.

"Warren!" Skye screamed as Esmeralde and Indigo held her back. "Warren!" she cried out again, before collapsing into sobs.

Ratta gave Mamie a grim look. "Is he really dead this time?"

"Dead. And reborn." The Guardian's voice held no emotion. "My work here is done. Offer up what treasure you have taken and I shall guide you to the caves."

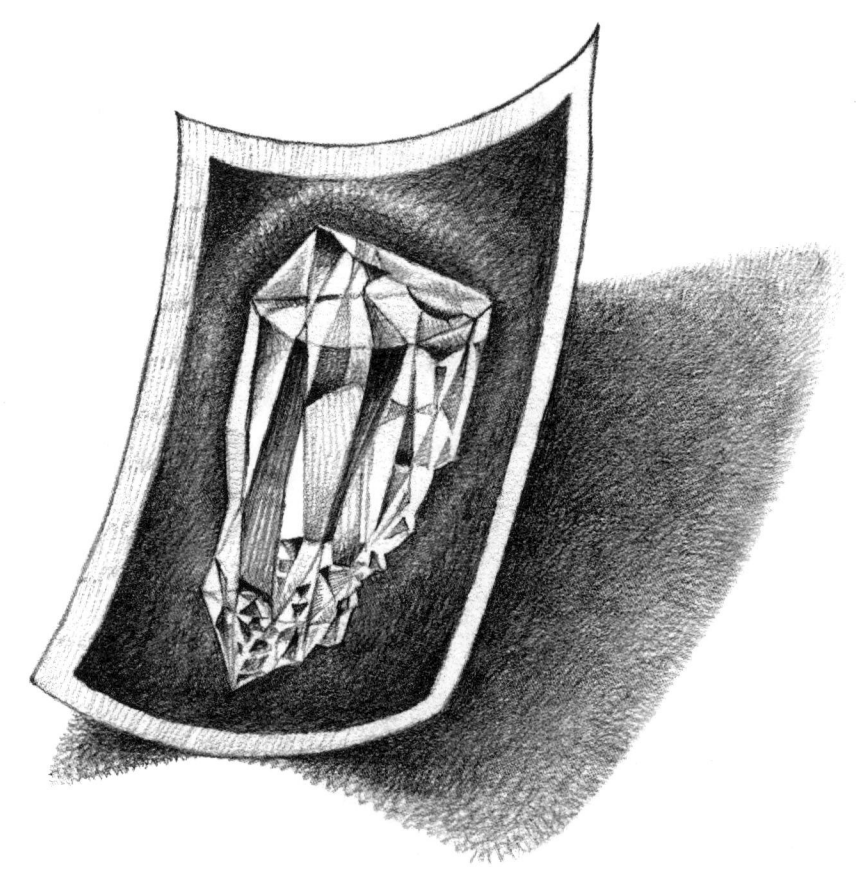

The image began to glow with cold fire.

CHAPTER 32

Consent of the Clan

SCONCES IN NICHES ALONG THE WALL flickered through the high narrow cavern of the Hed Clansmen's throne room. Mineral water dripped from its apex, as it had since the world began again forming stalactites that hugged the ceiling and stalagmites that spired from the floor. Even now, filmy liquid rich with crystal-rock flour plopped methodically into an iridescent pool near where the group gathered.

Rare animal skins carpeted the dais where old healer Borac stood. "For The One," he announced, holding forth the decorated gauntlet.

With what ceremony she could muster, Smokey Jo helped Garth pull the sling over his head. He handed his mother the length of knotted cloth and grinned.

"I guess I won't need this anymore."

"Act properly," Sierra cautioned, straightening his collar.

"Be polite," Aubergine murmured to Smokey Jo. "No more fireworks."

"Remember, I know what you're thinking," Lily warned in hushed tones.

"I wasn't really going to do much of that," Smokey Jo protested.

The youth and gnome mounted the platform spread with furs where the shaman waited with the shiny sleeve of embellished silver especially wrought for Garth. It reminded Smokey Jo of the plaster and horsehair casts bonesetters in Bordertown used for mending broken limbs.

Watching from the sidelines between Niles and Marshall, Little Teal could not help but notice the odd group assembled in the sparkling cave within the fortress of ice. Aubergine, Sierra, and Lily stood before the platform alongside the Northern Watch's leader, Steadfast Lars, and his brother Honorable Devon, commander of the Northland Guard. In a semicircle around them were Clansmen clad in traditional garb, their ceremonial spears studded with raw crystal.

Behind Healer Borac, a throne formed from stalagmites thrust from the floor of the fortress, its cylinders towering over the Clansmen. The wet pipes glistened with blue and rose minerals that over eons had leeched into the ice.

Upon the glittery seat sat Hed Clansman Lewellyn without his wolf's head crown. Instead, his blond hair was caught back in the traditional leather sheath favored by his folk. He wore a mantle of spotted saber cat, with one arm wrapped around the shoulder of his son Lorn propped on fur cushions beside him, while his daughter Gretchell lounged on a leather hassock with her babe at his feet. The blond boy looked peaked from his trial by First Folk Fire, for the ordeal had left him weak and lacking. In time he would regain all that he had lost, Teal realized, just as Garth had and more.

Teal and Niles had missed the Kindling, for they had remained behind in the Northland encampment with Lars and Devon to decide how to dispose of the raven she had killed and the Lord of the Lowlands. Only Garth and Marshall witnessed the miracle performed by Smokey Jo. The gnome had recited the tale so often since yesterday, Teal felt as though she watched the fire firsthand. According to Marshall, when finally Gretchell reached out to release the inferno trapped inside her brother, the sickroom erupted in hissing flames. The walls turned to water so suddenly they all were surprised the ceiling did not crash down around them.

When the smoke cleared, Lorn sat upright blinking in bewilderment in the litter meant to carry him to his death in the Caves of Blue Ice. Gretchell gripped his hand as firmly as she had when first charged with his care, for their mother had died when he was small. She waited for Smokey's signal before she let his fingers go.

Now upon the platform, Garth laid his injured forearm inside the gauntlet, and held his breath while Smokey Jo painstakingly wrapped the fingers of his burnt hand around the support covered with soft leather at the end. Neither of them could hide their excitement. The finely crafted sleeve was designed to hold his furled fist open while supporting his weakened arm. Smokey would not have to work so hard to straighten his stiffened fingers should Garth find yet another reason to release First Folk Fire.

"It fits perfectly!" she exclaimed, as Borac snapped the hollowed silver shut.

Wrought into the gauntlet's silverwork was a handsomely crafted metal locking device. Pulling the filigreed key from his pocket, the healer twisted the teeth in the lock until they heard the tumblers turn. Then he presented the key to Aubergine.

The Potluck Queen strung a finely knitted cable through the ornate end and put the necklace over Smoky Jo's curly head. Anxiously, the little gnome settled the cord around her neck, pushing the key beneath the collar of her dress.

"For safekeeping," she explained.

Then Sierra stepped forth to ease Garth's jacket sleeve over the silver gauntlet. Only the hand support showed from his cuff.

"It's barely noticeable," she said with surprise.

"All the better." Borac nodded in satisfaction. "It is not advisable to attract attention in the caves."

"How does it feel?" Little Teal couldn't help but ask.

"Fine," Garth waved his arm in the air. "The spun silver weighs nothing!"

Sierra bowed her head to Lewellyn. "We thank you for this most handsome and thoughtful gift."

"It is I who am filled with gratitude." The Hed Clansman regarded her with clear gray eyes. "Without your son I would not have mine."

"Don't disremember my part!" Smokey Jo raised her hand eagerly. "I helped most of all!"

"We can never forget your courage, small Smokey witch," Gretchell said gravely from her stool before the throne. She gazed at Aubergine. "Hereon I pledge to ward my brother wisely, ever in the fire gnome's debt."

Hed Lewellyn nodded toward Lars and Devon. "For your share, I shall grant your petition. The Out Crops will join you in war against the Lowlands. As allies, we pledge huntsmen from each Clan to defend the Glacierlands from the southern invaders. None shall pass through these caves without my knowledge."

"The Northern Watch will be pleased," Lars replied.

"We would ask twenty spearmen from each Clan to swell the Northland Army," Devon added.

"Done." Lewellyn beckoned to Borac. "There is one last matter."

The shaman crossed to the throne of ice and offered Lewellyn a finely stitched fur pouch. The Hed Clansman shook out a scrap of etched horn and held it up for all to see before presenting it to Aubergine.

"Potluck Queen, I would return the relic we recovered in the caves as a token of loyalty and friendship."

Aubergine accepted the fragment. "I thank you for the honor, but the ancient Skell is not mine." She rested her eyes on the small witch standing between the tall brothers. "It is Teal's unchallenged."

"Is that the same artifact?" Niles whispered to Teal as Aubergine approached.

"I think so," she murmured. "But it has been so long, how can I be certain?"

Healer Borac appraised Teal. "Raven Slayer, the horn is yours?"

"My mother had a card such as this." Teal looked at Aubergine. "I cannot keep it. Garth found the Skell thinking to save me and the price was his hand." She held the etched triangle out to Garth. "Take it unchallenged."

"Is that the relic your father stole from you in River Walk?" Sierra asked as Garth turned it over in his palm.

"The selfsame," her son muttered grimly. "Worth more than my life."

"And you found it in a cave?" Sierra asked Lewellyn.

"Of roosting bats," he confirmed. "Having seen your great bird, I have no doubt that the Lord of the Lowlands was hiding as one of those creatures."

"He could be anything," Garth said. "Bat, bird, bug. Except now he's dead."

"We hope." Aubergine cleared her throat. "There is one way to certain if the half Skell is real, for I have harbored its twin in a sewing basket in my study for more than twenty years. Smokey Jo, produce the other."

"Right here!" She pulled the piece of horn from a pocket sewn inside her sweater.

As one, gnome and Glacier Born fit the two halves of the First Folk Skell together along the diagonal score line and the triangles became an oblong square, no larger than a playing card. United, the etched lines depicted a large crystal. As they watched, the image began to glow with cold fire.

"Here is the true Skell of House Crystal Keep," Aubergine proclaimed. "Entire at last, as it has not been since the world fell to ice."

"Just as the legends foretold. Safeguard it well," Lily advised, "For it grants passage to the Crystal Caves only to the one who would possess it."

Smokey Jo tried pulling the card back apart. "It won't separate," she complained, huffing with the effort.

"The Skell was created uncut," Aubergine said. "Worthless unless whole."

"It is yours to protect now," Smokey Jo insisted to Garth. "As I keep the key."

"Are you sure you don't want it?" Garth asked Little Teal.

"I'm certain." She thrust the Skell into its fur pouch and stowed it in his pack. "You'll need it where you're going."

Devon caught Lars's eye. His brother nodded. "It is time we all take our leave, I'm afraid." He gave a short bow before the throne. "Men of Ice, we thank you."

Lewellyn stood. "And you." His gray eyes sought Sierra's golden gaze. "All of you."

"Must you stay?" Smokey Jo whined as the spearmen filed from the cave.

"Yes, little one," Aubergine replied. "To help Lars and Devon strengthen the alliance between the Clansmen and the North, I have much to do."

"We have never been apart," Smokey protested. "I'm not one for a glacier quest. You know I hate the cold!"

"Yet you must help Garth," the old witch said. "For you protect him now. You made that choice when you took his hand."

Glancing at Garth, Smokey Jo hung her head. "It's like we're inseparable twins, almost." She peeked at her mistress. "But Lily won't come, or Sierra?"

"Lily belongs at the Potluck, as do I when all this is over," Aubergine said. "For Sierra, the glacier quest comes too soon. Once within the caves it is her fate to assume the Guardian's Watch. Who knows if she'll ever return?"

"We'll be with you with our minds and hearts," Sierra promised.

"And thoughts," Lily added.

"That I won't miss!" Smokey grumbled. "You reading my mind almost before I know it myself!"

"I'll still know your thoughts from afar," Lily said pleasantly.

Sierra smoothed Garth's sandy hair away from his forehead. "We'll watch for you from Aubergine's glass."

"Will you be able to find us?" he asked.

She looked away. "When the time comes."

Near the throne, Teal and Niles were taking similar leave from a different set of people.

"Are you sure you won't join us?" Teal implored Marshall.

He shook his head. "I have assumed my mantle. My home is Winterhaven."

"That is a cloak I can never wear in a place I will never belong," Niles said.

With a sigh, Marshall gazed at Gretchell and Lorn on the dais. "My life is bound to her now, just as she wards her brother."

"You do not love the Clansman's daughter," Niles reminded him.

"Aught else ties us," Marshall said. "What does your lucky gnome say?"

"Taking a Glacier Born's hand charges you with his care forever," Teal said. "You become close, like twins."

"Your gypsy witch speaks true." Marshall watched Gretchell and Lorn. "They are closer than before. In time we will all be family." He gave his brother a keen look. "Now it's my turn to ask. Why do you leave, when you've barely returned?"

"Do not confuse visiting with homecoming, Brother." Niles joined hands with Teal. "Where she goes, I go. We're inseparable, too."

"Come home," Marshall urged. "Deliberate Rye is due back with father's sleigh. Don't fret about a mantle or empty house. Stay with me, both of you. Father will accept your small witch in time. This is not a mission for mortals."

"I need the witch." Niles shook his head in regret. "Thanks for the offer, but no."

"She has no need to present you with a babe," Marshall offered. "We'll find one. Gretchell knows folk."

"Teal and I have no need of mantles, or lodges, or babes." Niles squeezed Teal's hand. "Never can we heed the old ways. Offer our regards to Goodmother Gabriella, Goodwife Alyssa, and Minister Mason." He glanced at Marshall's betrothed. "When you wed at Winterhaven, what will her name be?"

"Lawful Sister," Marshall said with an ironic smile. "Sweet Sister Gretchell."

"And yours?" Niles asked.

"Warden," Marshall said, "of Winterhaven and the North."

Niles glanced at Lorn. "Warden of The One. That most of all."

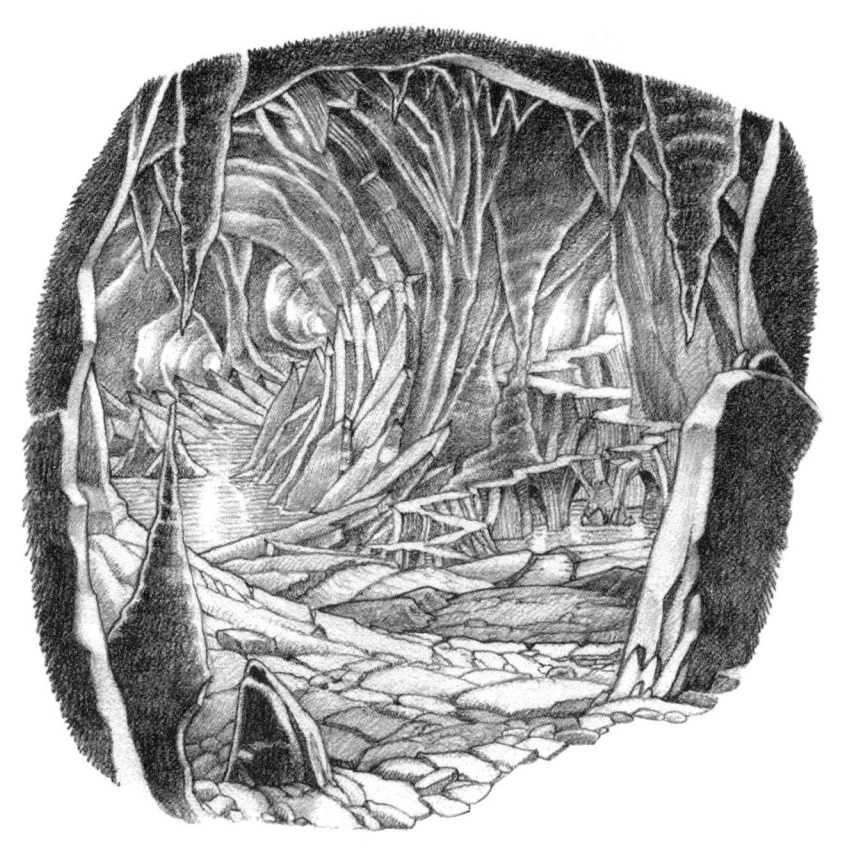

Skye glimpsed a gaping hole in the rock face
that could only be a cave entrance.

CHAPTER 33

Visions of the Lost Caves

THE TREK WAS ARDUOUS FROM TIGERIA to the foothills below the Lost Caves which glowed mirage-like on a horizon, never seeming to get much closer. Skye did not know how long or far they hiked so heartsick was she over the disappearance of her brother Warren, ever present in her mind. Her head down, she concentrated on putting one foot before the other as the five of them followed Mamie Reborn through the frozen valley.

Mamie was correct about the concept of time. It meant nothing within the walls of ice. The prevailing gloom was bone chilling, offering no distinction between day and night. The witches tossed cold-fire crystals into a ring of stones for warmth, slept when they were weary, woke when hungry, broke their fast and plodded on.

Although she had never journeyed to the Crystal Caverns, reborn Mamie found she knew the path, for the fire in the sky held a strange attraction. Lured by its ever-present glow, she guided the five witches without hesitation, circumventing the groups of Walkers marching north. Mostly, the rejuvenated dead avoided the witches, leery of the Guardian they had thwarted in the city. Blue-eyed Walkers in groups of two and three let out silent moans as the witches overtook them, especially if the trail was narrow and they strayed close. Preferring to keep their distance, the Walkers ambled at a steady but unhurried pace, drawn by the light of the Lost Caves.

Seeing Walkers disturbed Skye greatly, so fresh was she from the loss of Warren and Lavender Mae. Unlike the wraiths at the gates of Tigeria, translucent ghosts draped in robes and cloaks of the ancients, these hybrid beings shared solid bodies with their hosts. What horrified Skye most were their haunted faces. While all harbored the blazing blue stare of creatures possessed, some also carried distinctive features of the folk they had subsumed. Under the hazy forms she recognized the coppery skin of the Lowlands, the high cheekbones and long white manes favored by the northern Clansmen, and the cropped hair and shorn beards typical of Northland soldiers. She saw a few Walkers who carried the ruddy visage of the Western Highlands and one or two tiny dark men she mistook for gypsies, while others had traits she could not hazard to guess. She shuddered to think that somewhere behind them marched Walkers whose ghostly features were melded with that of a Middleland youth and a wispy-haired crone who were Warren and Mae.

Skye tried to imagine what might happen if these two hybrid beings overtook them while they slept, for Walkers seemed to need neither food nor rest. Casting their blazing blue eyes over the slumbering witches, would they pause or simply skirt their previous brethren as other Walkers did, walking no faster or slower than before? Watching the blue burn in the vacant eyes of the undead who stumbled ahead like sleepwalkers, Skye could not imagine that one of them was her brother.

There were hundreds of Walkers, thousands perhaps, she noticed as the witches crested a final barrier of rocky foothills. A steep trail zigzagged toward cliffs beyond where she glimpsed a gaping hole in the rock face that could only be a cave entrance. Walkers swarmed the switchbacks, teeming before the opening in the mountainside whose glowing depths cast a red radiance across the sky. Backlit by the sickly glimmer, a horde of Walkers crowded before the opening, shrieking in silence.

"We shall never get past," Skye murmured to Mamie. "Is there another way in?"

The Guardian shook her head slightly. "There is only one entrance, Cyrus said."

"Mayhap Cyrus doesn't know all," Ratta grumbled. "I speak the language. Let me talk to the Eye."

The Guardian secured the satchel at her side. "He's sleeping." She gazed at the witches like children. "Naught is to fear. Walkers are harmless if I am your guide."

"Even if we could push through—assuming we don't get attacked—the entrance still seems impenetrable," Wheat said gruffly. "Otherwise, the Walkers storm in like sheep flattening a snow fence."

Indigo scrutinized the cave entrance. "Could the opening be barred by some sort of spell, much as the walls of Tigeria imprisoned undead?"

"First the Walkers could not get out," Esmeralde mused, opening her Possibles Bag. "Now they cannot get in." She inspected a few vials by the light of her quartz crystal. "What a quandary!"

Indigo turned to Mamie. "You freed Wanderers from the city. Can you guide us into the caves?"

The Guardian was troubled. "I led Wanderers to the tombs because they requested my aid."

"As we do now," Esmeralde pointed out.

Ratta frowned. "Who enchanted the walls to contain the ghosts within the city?"

"According to the Eye, the first Guardians cast curses denying all undead egress from the city or access to the caves," Mamie explained. "They feared that if such shades ventured forth they might raid the caves and misuse the crystals, as they had before the world fell to ice."

"I'll bet the Guardians did not account for the Walkers," Wheat said grimly.

"No," Mamie said. "They thought only of those who would be laid to rest and pass to the Land of Dreams, as they had."

"Walkers or no, could the Guardians' curse be the same hex that afflicts the cave entrance and for the same reason?" Indigo asked. "To keep some in, others out?"

Esmeralde stopped fiddling with her vials long enough to cast a sidelong look at Mamie. "If so, I hazard she can gain us entry to the caves."

Indigo nodded several times in rapid succession. "I'm glad that's settled."

"As am I," Esmeralde huffed. "For I've no Possible ingredients to break an ancient curse." Bending to repack her bag, she shot Mamie a derisive look. "Well I did have, but they were in the few shards she bid me return to the ancients along with Skye's blood garnet, Wheat's amber insects, and Ratta's black eye, for the little good it does First Folk who have no access to my recipes."

The rest of her complaints were lost beneath the flap of a huge creature winging overhead. It swooped low over the witches before gliding to the cliffs beyond, alighting with its back to the cave entrance. The dark thing towered over the milky Walkers, who shrank back from its leathery wings stretched over a framework of bone tipped with talons. As the witches watched, the bat-like creature switched its great pronged tail, sweeping Walkers within reach over the edge of the cliff to crash down upon other undead crowding the switchbacks.

"What is that, a dragon?" Skye whispered in wonder.

"It's a whirling Dervish," Winter Wheat replied before Mamie could answer. "A First Folk creature ancient and rare."

"Ruling families of Tigeria kept Dervish to protect them in an imagined afterlife that did not exist." The Guardian regarded the shepherdess with curiosity. "This is the only one I've seen freed from the ice. He safeguards the tomb of House Crystal Keep."

"Its First Folk or treasure?" Skye asked, her eyes on the Dervish defending the cave.

"Both," Mamie answered. "For ancients foolishly believed they could carry possessions to the Land of Dreams as proof of stature they had attained in the world they destroyed." She eyed the witches. "Guardians care not for petty icons within richly painted coffins draped with raiment woven of gold thread. The Dervish froze with their masters, whose tombs were plundered anyway."

"If the ancients have no need of relics, why did we have to surrender our souvenirs?" Esmeralde asked irritably. "I looked forward to those bracing elixirs."

"I was fond of the eye," Ratta admitted.

"They are cursed." Mamie eyed Ratta. *And you do not need them, as you shall see,* she added in Mind Speak.

Wheat glanced toward the mouth of the cave, where the Dervish had begun to twirl in concentric circles, his tail sweeping the cliff clear of Walkers. "If I am not mistaken, he is the selfsame creature I freed from Lowlanders bent on stealing my flock. He was lashed to a sledge, chiseled from the glacier as they found him, encased in a hoary chunk of yellowed ice."

"Would he were yet so restrained." Mamie gazed at the winged creature. "The Dervish did nothing but flap in alarm among the ancient tombs in determent as I began my watch. Even as I laid his First Folk to rest, he disdained my approach. It was a relief when he abandoned the crypts, though I was unaware of his residence here. He may pose a problem, for like the shades of Tigeria, he froze while alive."

"He stirred as he thawed," Wheat explained. "I never meant him as a menace. Fearing that the Lowlanders intended to gift him to their queen, I melted the ice with ancient fire sparked from my amber beetles." She smiled in remembrance. "It was a glorious sight! He rose from his prison of ice like the legendary bird of old reborn from cold ash to return to his First Folk family."

"The Dervish never harmed me," Mamie assured her. "I spoke to him in the silent language of the ancients, never certain that he understood what I said."

"Whether he heeds silent tongue or spoken word matters not." Wheat watched the whirling Dervish. "For he kens me and I him. He shall not hesitate to let us pass."

Skye's turquoise eyes deepened to sapphire. Her breath grew shallow and pinpricks of violet stood out in her irises like motes. "You are mistaken."

"Absolutely not!" Turning to confront her, Wheat caught the girl's faraway look.

"Hush!" Ratta warned. "Lest the fleeting legacy of Sierra's second sight refuses to visit her daughter once more."

"Let our new witch unveil what visions she will," Indigo agreed in a hoarse whisper.

"Listen and learn," Esmeralde agreed.

"My mother's second sight fails me in my constant quest to seek the whereabouts of Warren and Lavender Mae," Skye confessed, fixing her eyes upon Winter Wheat. "But my pursuit does turn up a recurring image of your encounter with yon Dervish, an unexpected vision you will not care for, I'm afraid."

"Tell it true," Ratta encouraged.

Skye swallowed hard. "In my mind's eye, I search the horizon for my older brother, Warren, but see my younger brother, Garth." Her eyes flickered toward Wheat. "You shall gain passage from the Dervish only when Garth stands with you at the entrance to the caves that blaze with eternal light."

"Broken shards!" Wheat swore angrily. "Watch your mouth girl, for we will not be deceived by false prophecy from a maid who does not yet ken her lore! All know your brother's idea of adventure is a carefree night of dice and Skells along the docks of River Walk, as proven by the fossick boys he disappeared with. They cared so little for the gravity of our quest that they failed to return from their lark to see us on our journey."

"Craven fossickers!" Ratta agreed. "Devouring our food, pounding up and down the stairs, littering the entry with muddy boot and grubby packs."

"I saw Garth wearing a silver gauntlet beneath his sleeve to guard a blackened arm injured by the burn of First Folk Fire," Skye continued, the motes around her pupils disappearing as her vision waned. "The Clansmen of the Out Crops call him Glacier Born, The One."

"Is that where he tarries now, in the Out Crops?" Mamie asked. "For they are north of here, much further than these caves."

Skye nodded. "Trader is with him, only she dresses in green velvet now and goes by the name of Teal."

"Teal?" Indigo queried. "Then where is our Teal?"

"There is Smokey Jo and another boy, a friend of Warren's who helped us escape from the World's Fair on the ponies so long ago," Skye rushed on. "Niles of the North."

"Has aught befallen Aubergine?" Esmeralde and Indigo Rose exchanged glances. "Smokey Jo would venture nowhere beyond the Bordertown walls without her."

"Jo hates the cold," Indigo reminded them all.

"The four I saw left Aubergine, Lilac Lily, and my mother, Sierra, at an ice fortress near a battlefield," Skye said, unable to fathom why the witches did not believe her.

"Aubergine's disgust of combat rivals her dislike for stairs," Esmeralde grumbled. "It is impossible she favors war."

"That skirmish was a ploy to entice the Northland Guard to discredit us that we could ply our lore unseen," Indigo insisted. "Just like that ruse at River Walk."

"We must wait for Garth," Skye said quietly.

"Whatever for?" Wheat asked. "What prize does he harbor? Some kind of key to gain entry to the Lost Caves?"

"He does," Skye could not help but say. "In the shape of a card we call Skells."

"Skells?" Wheat shook her head in disgust. "Like the card game? Now I really don't believe a word you say."

"Then to you I'll say no more," Skye said bitterly.

"Your seer speaks of the Skells of old," Mamie told the others. "Ancient houses held such cards."

Skye gave Wheat a hard look. "Not playing cards."

"Voting ballots," Mamie said. "Every one of them thin shaved horn painstakingly etched. All are lost, some stolen by looters, others leeched from ice flows beneath the tombs to become buried beneath the silts of the Crystal Lakes, others destroyed."

"My brother found a broken thing, scored on the diagonal, cracked in half." Skye gave Mamie a bewildered look. "Mayhap destroyed. Even now he and his companions make their way past the Caves of

VISIONS OF THE LOST CAVES

Blue Ice." She cast her eyes downward, barely mouthing words. "We must wait."

"And so we shall," the Guardian decided.

As Skye retired to the hearth for a cup of tea, Esmeralde nudged Indigo. "I bet the girl saw more than she lets on."

"Like mother, like daughter," her friend agreed. "Not once do I think Sierra Blue ever told us all she saw in her mind."

"Well, it's not like she's Lily," Esmeralde admitted. "We can ask any question we want but she needn't answer unless she's inclined."

"Perhaps we shall see later," Indigo suggested. "If she is inclined."

After the others ate and bedded down, Indigo beckoned to Esmeralde from her bedroll. Quietly, they crept to where Skye still sat, brooding before the fire.

Esmeralde put the lukewarm pot of water back on the coals. Indigo got out the mostly empty crock of honey. Now that Lavender Mae was gone, the little dab left had lasted them several meals.

"We are wondering," Esmeralde stirred the pot. "For we believe everything you say you saw."

"Hallucinations, daydreams, visions, no matter." Indigo gave a jovial shrug. "All we would like to know is: Did you see more in your vision than you told us?"

"Nothing I want to say, or can even understand," the girl said dully.

"It's alright child," Esmeralde soothed. "Indy and I already fully comprehend that we shall rule the Potluck one day, two as one. It is something you need not articulate. What we would appreciate is any tidbit of knowledge that might help us on our way."

"I know nothing of your upcoming rule." Skye bit her lip. "Nor does Aubergine."

"Nothing?" As the pot boiled, Esmeralde took Skye's cup, thinking to slip truth powder into the girl's tea. She pulled a vial from her sleeve. "At all, you say?"

451

Joining them, Ratta stayed Esmeralde's hand. "She says she knows nothing."

Wheat appeared beside Indigo. "Whether we believe what she says or not, Skye is not obligated to tell us more," she reminded them both.

"Just being friendly." Esmeralde handed Skye a cup of unaltered tea.

"Social even," Indigo added. "We do not know how long we'll be together."

"There is no time within these walls of ice." Mamie stood behind them. "She does not have to say."

Grumbling, Esmeralde and Indigo rose from the fire to return to their bedrolls.

Skye got up, too. "I guess I'll turn in." She gave Winter Wheat a pleading look. "What I said wasn't a lie."

Wheat heaved a sigh. "I know that, and I beg your pardon. My hope was to get this ordeal over sooner rather than later." She risked an apologetic look to the Guardian. "I long for my little Tracks. I yearn for my bucolic life prior."

"We all miss our old existence." Ratta gazed at Mamie Reborn. "But it will be a long time if ever we return to our previous ways of life."

Although exhausted, when she finally closed her eyes, sleep would not find Skye for she kept reliving the end of the vision she'd had of Wheat, Garth, and the Dervish. As she drifted off, the imagery became a dream:

From the end of Winter Wheat's staff, the cabochons twirled on their tethers hitting and sparking, mesmerizing the Dervish. Wheat touched her crook to the nose of the creature that defended the mouth of the cave against the Walkers and he quieted. She turned to Garth, who held the Skell of House Crystal Keep loosely in his hand.

"He remembers me." She turned to the others, her eyes sparkling in the light. "He's going to let us pass!"

In her dream, Skye watched the witches, herself among them, gather their things along with Garth, Mamie, Teal, and Niles. They weren't alone. A wolverine with a curious string of amethyst stones strung around its neck watched from the shadows.

Secrets of the Lost Caves

DISCUSSION PROMPTS

 CRITICAL READING   ANALYTICAL REASONING   DISCUSSION PROMPT   VOCABULARY

CHERYL POTTER

SECRETS OF THE LOST CAVES
Discussion Prompts

Chapter 1
Why do we sometimes hide the truth about ourselves from others?

Chapter 2
What are signs that it is not safe to go somewhere by yourself?

Chapter 3
What kinds of sacrifices should we make for those we care about?

Chapter 4
What are some of the things you do for your friends that you would not do for anyone else?

Chapter 5
What can we learn from our mistakes?

Chapter 6
How can having lots of power be both a gift and a curse?

Chapter 7
What are some great ways to prepare for something new?

Chapter 8
How do you know if you are making good choices?

Chapter 9
Why do people sometimes pretend to be different then who they really are?

Chapter 10
How do you decide whether or not to take a big risk?

Chapter 11
What are some healthy ways to cope with a bad event?

Chapter 12
What are some ways to deal with missing family and friends?

Chapter 13
What does it mean to be betrayed?

Chapter 14
What type of person can you rely on?

Chapter 15
How do you make an agreement with someone you can't trust?

Chapter 16
What are important rule to live by?

Chapter 17
Name some ancient rituals we find in today's world.

Chapter 18
How do we use past experiences to guide future decisions?

Chapter 19
What is the difference between being a leader and a follower?

Chapter 20
What rites of passage do we use today?

Chapter 21
What are examples of using your inner strength?

Chapter 22
What does it mean to live with purpose?

Chapter 23
When is acceptable to keep secrets from others?

Chapter 24
What are some cultural differences we can appreciate in others?

Chapter 25
How do you know when someone needs help?

Chapter 26
What are some healthy ways to refuse to do things you don't want to do?

Chapter 27
Is something truly a gift if there are strings attached?

Chapter 28
What does it mean to be a good friend?

Chapter 29
What does it mean to lose your sense of self?

Chapter 30
How do we find courage?

Chapter 31
What does it mean to be at a crossroads in life and what are some examples?

Chapter 32
When should we and when should we not compromise?

Chapter 33
How can we anticipate what's going to happen?

WHERE TO BUY

Please go to our website www.potluckyarn.com to order the Student Workbook.

THE ENTHRALLING SAGA OF POTLUCK YARN CONCLUDES

Turn the page for the prologue and first chapter of Cheryl Potter's *Book Three: Crystal Keep*

Coming soon from Potter Press.

Sign up to get updates on new books from Cheryl Potter.

Visit www.potluckyarn.com

PROLOGUE

House of Cards

THE OLD MAN MADE HIS WAY ALONG the dusky streets of Bordertown in a hooded cloak, though many around him rushed past with heads bare. Waning spring had given way to flooding worsened by heat from wildfires that even now burned at the base of the Northland Glacier. The acrid air hung wet and humid, unusual this far north at summer's approach. Although he was uncomfortable beneath the hood, the unknown traveler preferred to sweat rather than risk notice. Like all true men of the Northern Watch he stood well over six feet tall, usually an anomaly in the Middlelands, except that these days folk from the Glacierlands were common both within and without the Great Northern Gate. Many families from the Northland's Five Provinces had sons stationed at the Garrison in Bordertown.

As night fell, the man lost himself among the throngs of day laborers pushing their way through the crowded streets toward the working class borough of Close Quarters, the smallest district in the walled city, a mere sliver in the seven pieces of pie that comprised Bordertown. The Quarters was a rough, crowded maze of tenements and hovels adjoining the stockyards of Butcher's Block, and the stench from the rendering sheds just beyond the stockade at times made the rank air difficult to suffer. The old man had chosen the Quarters for the warren of gambling dens clustered beneath the shadow of the wall. They seemed perfect places to hide in plain sight.

Once within Close Quarters, he found a crowded Skell hall whose scarred sign hung at an angle on one hook above the entrance, for the other had pulled from the rotted wood long ago. House of Cards, it read. Certain this was the place he sought, he bent his head beneath the low doorframe and went in.

The pub smelled of kicked kegs and old grease. Ordering a mug of hard cider from the barmaid, he took a seat at a tiny card table in the gloomy back room.

"I hate pubs, anything to do with rancid ale and sticky countertops really," the woman sitting across from him said.

"It could not be helped, Potluck Queen." Deliberate Rye let down his hood. His eyes were clear and gray. "I was followed. Your yarn shop is being watched."

Aubergine gazed back at him with violet eyes. "By whom? The Dark One is imprisoned within the city of Old Tigeria and her Kindred Spirit is dead."

"Would it were so," her companion lamented. His eyes scanned a pair of day laborers rattling dice in a wooden cup nearby and a loud group of card players clustered around a rickety table beyond to certain no one was listening. "Queen Aubergine, the body of Northland's Bane is missing. All that remains is the feathers and skin of the raven whose body he shape shifted into. Honorable Devon sent word from the Out Crops. He has seen with his own eyes. The Lord of the Lowlands is gone."

"How could that be?" Aubergine asked, alarmed. "Did the Dark Queen transport him lifeless somehow, just as we sent our Mamie Verde to Guardian's Watch to be reborn?"

"Perhaps," Deliberate Rye ruminated. "If Tasman is truly his twin as you suggest, joined in hand by the power of the Kindle just as your Glacier Born boy and Smokey witch are, they may nigh be inseparable. If Kendrick's living ember burned to cold ash, who knows how it affected his sister?"

"How could Tasman possibly have escaped the enchanted walls of the cursed city?" Aubergine wondered. "When last we looked into the hourglass in private counsel, Sierra and Lily and I witnessed the Queen of the Lowlands surrounded by wraiths."

"Some ancient spirits do seek to inhabit mortal flesh once more," Rye agreed with a sigh. "But I expect even undead Walkers would be no match for your Dark Queen."

"Assuming Tasman eluded the ghosts and somehow escaped the walled city, she still had to find a way to remove her brother's body," Aubergine mused.

"As well as a manner of rejuvenating the dead," Rye added.

"Dark magic mayhap, of no knowledge to me," Aubergine said grimly. "What safe haven could she possibly have at her disposal? Where other than a Simmer around my dye pot could any witch conjure up such power as needed to raise the dead?"

"The Caves of Blue Ice where Kendall Kindled and was reborn," Rye guessed. "The Crystal Caverns themselves perhaps."

Aubergine shook her head. "From what I've seen in my hourglass, none may enter the Lost Caves without an original Skell. The two halves of the ballot belonging to House Crystal Keep were made whole at the Out Crops to safeguard the passage of our Glacier Born, Sierra's own. Tasman the Traitor possesses no such token that assures safe travels."

"She may not need a ticket. The Lord of the Lowlands was also Glacier Born," Rye raised his snowy brows. "And there were sixteen original Skell cards, not just the one."

"Few ever surfaced," Aubergine reminded him. "Rumor has it that the Northland confiscated those that did and destroyed them long ago."

Rye sipped his cider and eyed her steadily. "You know that is untrue."

"The fragment of House Crystal Keep I found in a fish belly at the Crystal Lakes when Cyrus and I were young," Aubergine argued. "It lay hidden among balls of yarn in my sewing basket for more than twenty years until just recently."

Rye stared at the old witch in silence.

Unable to meet his gaze, she looked away. "The half Skell shared the basket with a whole card that came into my possession years later, a lesser ballot. I bought it unchallenged from a fossicker who unearthed it from The Trickle during the thaw one spring." Making certain no one was watching, she produced a rectangle of horn smaller than a playing card from her sleeve and met his eyes. "I believe it to be the card of House Rising Sun."

"So there are two." Rye nodded in satisfaction. "This lesser Skell and the one you made whole. That is enough for our purposes." Quaffing his cider, he set his empty mug on the table. "My Queen, the time has come."

"We are not prepared," Aubergine protested, secreting the card once more. "I need days to put things in order."

"Enter the glacier through the Burnt Holes and do not tarry," Deliberate Rye advised. "As the fighting is now in the North, no one will follow you through the old prison caves."

"You do understand that Sierra can never return?" Aubergine asked.

He nodded. "The cost of her second sight. All of us will have to pay a price, sooner rather than later." Deliberate Rye rose and clasped her hand. "Farewell, old friend."

"And you." Aubergine murmured.

"It may be a long time if ever we meet again," he said, before turning away.

Staring into her mead cup, Aubergine did not answer. When she was sure he was gone, she put up the hood of her traveling cloak.

As she crossed the muddy track outside the card house, Aubergine noticed a bard in a brightly colored vest and high felt hat eyeing the entrance from the corner and sensed something amiss. She recognized the man, she realized. He was the same arrogant songster who had plied patrons with doggerel about potluck witches at a certain tavern in Artisan's Hand, the very night she and Sierra met with a jeweler in the wine cellar hoping to repair the broken necklace. Aubergine touched the circle of amethysts around her neck reflexively before giving the well-heeled versifier, conspicuous in his motley dress, a suspicious glance. Certainly no one would throw coppers into his hat for forgotten yarns in this poor borough of the city. What was the tale teller doing in such a wretched part of town?

Certain she had passed him unseen, Aubergine turned and disappeared into the shadows.

CHAPTER 1

A Game of Skells

"YOU PLAY THE GAME JUST SO," Little Teal explained, sitting cross legged on her bedroll. Straightening the dog eared deck of cards, she shuffled it once more.

"Skells were oft wagered in the Garrison among enlisted men after hours." Niles glanced at the hand lettered pieces of parchment and curious bone dice. "I've never gambled with them myself."

"The cards are a Middleland pastime, ruled by luck of the draw. I'm fair at the dicing part." Scooping them up, Garth turned the two triangular pieces over in his good hand. Carved into the facets of each pyramid shape were numbers from 1 to 5.

Teal dealt them each four cards face down in turn. "Hidden within are sixteen cards, representing the houses of the Ancients. If you get one, keep it," she advised. "These are wild cards needed to play out your hand."

Smokey Jo pushed the pieces of parchment piled before her away without a glance. "Witches have no need of idle games that rely upon chance," she grumbled.

"There is no chance of a chance the way I play cards, even when I diced in the alleys to win a hand of Skells when I was masquerading as the fossick boy known as Trader." Teal's eyes shown at Garth. "I bested Warren from a week's worth of commissary chits and a road pass before I knew he was your brother."

"You cheated," Garth said flatly.

"Of course I did. There's no witchery in that." Teal looked at the boys expectantly. "Pick up your hands. Who wants to dice first?"

Garth grinned. "I'll take a tumble."

With a grunt, Smokey Jo rose and stalked off toward their packs. She did not care for idle gamblings, or the persistent cold within the glacier walls, although she was curious about the caves ahead, luminous and blue in the gloom of the ice. It had only been this morning that she and the others set out from the Clansmen's ice fortress within the mouth of the Out Crops. Already she missed Aubergine and Sierra. Soon, she supposed, she would even long for Lily.

On top of that, Smokey found herself constantly hungry. Her mouth watered for a paper cone of hot buttered kettle corn, soft molasses cookies sprinkled with brown sugar and a cup of honeyed lemon tea. In truth, she would prefer almost anything to the pounded rounds of Peasant Meal laden with lard or the salted moose jerky stowed in her rucksack.

Rummaging for the rose quartz crystal she used as a beacon, her stubby hand closed around a shard of rock candy. She thought she had eaten the whole stick of crystalized sugar at Winterhaven, but apparently a fragment had broken away and fallen among her provisions.

What a pleasant surprise! Smokey popped the sugar candy into her mouth to savor its sweetness, promising herself not to chew it up. She rubbed the rose quartz until it glowed. Things were looking better already, she mused. With renewed energy, she decided to explore the caves shining blue in the distance. They weren't that far. She glanced back at the circle of Garth, Teal and Niles casting cards between them. None of them would notice her scouting ahead.

Holding her rosy orb high, she hiked along the broad passage, lured by the luminous glow. When she got to the caves, what she found in the largest opening surprised her. Like the lesser alcoves, the ice that rimmed the walls sparkled indigo and navy from minerals that had leeched into the crusted walls over the ages. Except in this cavern, she discovered beeswax candles burnt to nubs secreted into chiseled niches behind a tall wrought table laden with ceremonial offerings, choice bits of dried fruit, salted nuts and watered wine at each end of its stone surface.

She sniffed the air and discerned her favorite fragrance: smoke. Folk had visited here recently. Perhaps they lingered still. She peered all around, even beneath the lip of the decorated table top, but the cave lay vacant save for a carrion creature that scuttled along the walls. Upon closer inspection, she saw that it was a large dark wolverine lured by the scent of food perhaps, a thirst for water or the open carafe of wine.

Bristling, it scowled but retreated as she approached the altar, too high to peer over. She climbed the low stone bench before it, huffing with effort and sat on the table top, letting her stubby legs dangle over the richly carved border, and looked around the sparkling room, sensing sanctity.

This must be the exact place everyone at the Out Crops could not stop talking about, she mused. The legendary blue caves where the clans brought their few sons cursed with the kindled ember of the

Glacier Born to die. It was good she and Garth had singlehandedly put a stop to such nonsense, Smokey Jo told herself proudly. This slab of stone would have been lost Lorn's funeral bench and others like her own dear boy might have perished here too—if anyone in the Middlelands even knew such a place existed—if not for her unique mastery of firecraft. Just walking into this cold dark cave was like visiting a tomb.

Shivering at the thought, Smokey felt sudden warmth around her neck. She pulled the silver chain from under the collar of her dress and held the small key to the gauntlet that enclosed Garth's burned arm to the light. It was hot to the touch. Not only that, but now she noticed there was light glowing from inside her pocket as well. A glimmer other than that of the rose quartz she had set on the bench or the gloomy blue gleam of the caves.

"Smokey, what are you doing?" Garth asked from the doorway.

Startled, Jo dropped the key. "Nothing." She glanced at her comrades who stood in the cave entrance before toying with the plate of dried fruit and nuts on the altar. "Athough in truth, I was thinking about trying a few of these dates."

"That's ceremonial food, fit for the dead to ward safe passage to the Land of Dreams," Niles warned.

"You're not meant to eat anything?" Smokey asked doubtfully.

Niles shook his head. "It just eases your journey."

"What good is food if you're not supposed to eat it?" Smokey asked.

"Smokey don't touch anything," Garth cried. "Just get down from there!"

As Smokey slid from the table to the bench, Little Teal pulled Niles into the room and twirled before the altar. Her face sparkled blue in the light. "What is this place?"

"The Caves of Blue Ice," he said solemnly. "Where the Clansmen have brought their kindled Glacier Born since the world began again."

Teal glanced around the cave. "It scares me to think about how many boys have died in this room."

Garth nodded slowly. "I wonder, did any of them live other than my father?"

Thoughts of the Bad Man gave Smokey the urge to hide the silver key dangling at her throat. Catching the bit of silver up in her hand, she dropped it quickly.

"What are you doing?" Garth asked again.

"It's burning," Smokey complained. "It's been too hot to touch since you walked in."

Kneeling on the bench, Niles ran his hand along the carved edge of the altar. "What do you make of this?" he asked the others. Before him were a series of oblong impressions, each wrought with a different symbol.

"They look like Skells," Teal observed.

"The card game you just taught us?" Garth asked.

"No, these are the real ones—this must be all of the houses." Teal paused to count before nodding to Niles. "Sixteen."

Garth stared at Smokey Jo. "It's not only the key that burns. There's something else alight." He pointed. "There in your pocket."

"Oh that." Smokey Jo pulled out the Skell the two of them had made whole to show him. "It was glowing before."

"Glowing before when?" Teal demanded. "How did that happen?"

"I was sitting up there on the table, thinking about snacking," Jo ventured. She glanced at Garth's stricken face. "I didn't eat anything," she assured him. "Just some old rock candy I found in my pack."

"What does it mean?" Garth asked Teal fearfully.

"Jo, bring it here," the little witch said. Taking the card from the gnome, she approached the altar where Niles knelt and climbed the low stone bench to stand beside him.

"It's this one," he said softly, glancing between her hand holding the etched horn and its carved likeness. "See the outline of the crystal?"

"House Crystal Keep." She touched her hand to the indentation. "And it's twin."

He stayed her hand as she went to fit it in. "I wouldn't."

"It may be the only way to find out," she protested.

"Find out what?" Garth stammered. He looked at them desperately. "What?"

"What's in the cards," Teal said simply.

Niles turned to her. "For us?"

She glanced at her comrades. "For everybody."

Snatching the Skell from Teal, Smokey Jo hopped up onto the bench and fit it into the carved niche. "Witches have no need of idle cards," she muttered.

Garth stared at her in horror, hoping nothing would happen. To his dismay, the altar began to tremble.

Teal glanced up at Niles. "There must be some mechanism in the pedestal."

Rising, Niles put his hands on the stone surface. "The top is locked." As the tremors subsided, he pushed with his palms. "It won't give way."

"Perhaps you need to hold all the cards?" Garth asked in the silence that followed. "The old ones, I mean."

"We have just the one." Smokey pried the spent bit of horn, no longer glowing, from its niche. "It's a broken relic at that."

"Skells aren't cards after all, because they're keys," Teal realized, her dark eyes dancing.

"Keys to where?" Garth asked.

"Or what?" Smokey mused, peering at the etched horn once more before hiding it in her pocket.

Teal lifted her eyes to Niles. "Did your Clansman know the nature of the cards?"

"No," the large youth shook his head. "Otherwise they would have used them to unlock the secrets of old long ago."

Tucking her necklace beneath the collar of her dress, Smokey laughed. "The First Folk must have been out of their minds! Serving food you can't eat! Using cards like they're keys! How in all the Lands could anyone come up with that?"

ABOUT THE AUTHOR

Cheryl Potter is a fiber artist and author, but is best known as the founder of Cherry Tree Hill Yarn. She has a BA from Middlebury College and an MFA from the University of Arizona. *Secrets of the Lost Caves* is her eighth book and second novel.

ABOUT THE TYPEFACE

An Old-Style serif typeface, Janson was cut by Hungarian Miklós Kis in the late 1600s. The version used in this book was produced by Hermann Zapf in the 1950s, based on Kis' original matrices. Janson's strong stroke contrast, sharpness, and legibility are just three reasons why this Humanist typeface is popular in book text.